The Graywolf Silver Anthology

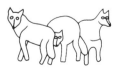

Graywolf Press would like to thank staff and board, our sales force and Consortium Book Sales and Distribution, our authors, our designers and freelancers, the folks at Stanton Publication Services, our readers, and our donors, for twenty-five years of loyalty and success.

Special support for this anthology was made possible by the wonderful generosity of the following individuals, to whom we are deeply grateful.

Marilynn and James Alcott
Ann Bitter
Richard Bliss
Page and Jay Cowles
Diane Herman
Kevin Martin
Katherine Murphy
ReBecca Roloff
Kay Sexton
Celine Sullivan
John Patrick Wheelihan
Margaret and Angus Wurtele

The Graywolf Silver Anthology

A RARE BREED
OF PUBLISHER
FOR 25 YEARS

Saint Paul, Minnesota

Publication of this volume is made possible in part by a grant provided by
the Minnesota State Arts Board through an appropriation by the Minnesota
State Legislature, and by a grant from the National Endowment for the Arts.
Significant support has also been provided by Dayton's, Mervyn's, and Target
stores through the Dayton Hudson Foundation, the Bush Foundation, the
McKnight Foundation, the General Mills Foundation, the St. Paul Companies,
and other generous contributions from foundations, corporations, and individu-
als. To these organizations and individuals we offer our heartfelt thanks.

Published by Graywolf Press
2402 University Avenue, Suite 203
Saint Paul, Minnesota 55114
All rights reserved.

www.graywolfpress.org

Published in the United States of America

ISBN 1-55597-289-6

2 4 6 8 9 7 5 3 1
First Graywolf Printing, 1999

Library of Congress Catalog Card Number: 98-88487

Cover design: A N D

Contents

Introduction to Graywolf Silver Anthology, 1999

FIONA MCCRAE

An anniversary, a birthday, a time to celebrate. It's a wonderful honor to be the director of the Press at such an auspicious time. I have recently completed my fourth year at Graywolf Press and remember vividly my first day here when I went into the warehouse at the back of the offices. There, proudly displayed on floor-to-ceiling bookshelves, were copies of our entire backlist. I was in awe of what I considered to be my literary inheritance, and echoes of that feeling return each time I enter that back room.

And what a time we've had in the last four years adding new books to those shelves. Poetry, fiction, and nonfiction by new and familiar Graywolf authors continue to reach audiences across the country, to garner significant review attention, and to win important literary prizes.

This anthology offers a generous sampling of the contents of some of those books. It was edited by three of us here: Anne Czarniecki selected the fiction, Jeffrey Shotts the poetry, and I made the nonfiction selections. Of course, we lobbied one another for our favorite picks, and had suggestions from other staff members, too. And all three of us had certain criteria we had agreed to follow: that the book be currently in print, that we would not include material from anthologies, that we would favor those writers who had published more than one book with us. In fiction, short stories are more natural candidates for inclusion than novels; essays make more agreeable selections for nonfiction; and the volume of extraordinary poets on the Graywolf list makes it a daunting task to narrow down to the few we could include between these covers. So if a favorite book of yours does not appear in the *Silver Anthology*, the chances are we regret its absence as well.

Everyone who works at Graywolf is driven by the belief that contemporary creative writing needs to be nurtured and published proudly. This belief was shared by our predecessors at the Press. We are particularly grateful, therefore, to our founder Scott Walker who has contributed a wonderful essay to this anthology about the early days of Graywolf Press.

Graywolf is and always will be about the books we publish, and I invite you to savor these gems from twenty-five years of independent publishing. I hope that you will agree with me after reading this collection of literary delights that there is no such thing as a simple definition of the Graywolf author. For above all, we delight in the range of voices we have published over the years. Indeed, it is in providing variety on the bookstore and library shelves that the work of Graywolf and other independent presses makes its greatest contribution to American literary culture.

The Beginning

SCOTT WALKER

Graywolf Press had quite a few lives previous to its current incarnation as a leading independent literary publisher.

The press was founded by Kathleen Foster and me, in the teensy (gas station/store) unincorporated town of Irondale, on Washington's Olympic Peninsula, among loggers and fisherfolk and tourists who came to watch loggers and fisherfolk. We built a shed that our authors called "the print shack," back by the raspberries. For Kathleen, Graywolf was one of her many sequential pursuits—falling between bartender and Rajneeshi, and a bit before real estate; she left after three years of outstanding design and printing. For me, it was an endeavor lived and breathed for twenty years.

The press got its name from our love for the Graywolf Ridge and Graywolf River in the Olympic National Park in Washington, a place we loved to hike. We also had a love and affinity for gray wolves—their independence, the fact that their survival as a species was threatened, and their intricate social lives.

The spirit of the times had a lot to do with the founding of Graywolf. Small was beautiful; a livelihood needed to be a "right livelihood"—beneficial personally and to society; power was to the people; aid was mutual; and economically low-scale living got points for style. The '60s and '70s mimeograph revolution became a revival of the arts and crafts movement, which became a flourishing movement of small presses and literary magazines in the U.S. and abroad.

Graywolf Press began as a small letterpress shop, printing a literary magazine and poetry chapbooks, at first none too well. We were a printing operation because it was cheaper to do the work ourselves than to pay for it being done elsewhere. The turn-of-the-century press we found cost just $160, and was powered by treadle—it was like riding a bicycle one-legged. The type we printed from was hand-set, letter by letter and space by space—which is, we found, a marvelous way to appreciate and absorb good writing. The pages, once printed, were folded one by one and gathered into booklets, which were sewn together into books; on quite a few of those little books the buyer would find the blood of the binder smeared in the center seam.

As we became proficient at design and printing, our books received more recognition and we began to attract not only better-known authors but book collectors too. The collectors valued our combining good emerging and established authors with nicely crafted and beautiful books. They must also have loved our foolish idealism: Because we felt urgently that our books ought to be read rather than simply collected, we never really priced them according to the effort it took to make them essentially by hand. They were priced instead at what book lovers like us could afford, which wasn't much! We'd put months of umpteen-hour days into making 300 copies of a book, beautifully, and sell the books retail for $4.00 (we'd get $2.40 each), so that people who bought them for the poetry alone would receive a beautiful book as kind of a bonus. The math is not pretty but our lives were fine.

Demand for the books inspired the next phase of Graywolf's development. Despite their appreciation for our bookmaking, those book collectors made us uncomfortable. We found out about one of them who never even took our books out of the wrappings they were mailed in, but rather put them in storage for five years before selling them, pristine, for more than *we* could afford. We wanted to create books for readers and not collectors, so we turned increasingly toward trade publishing—making books destined for retail bookstores, to be sold to readers.

Tess Gallagher's first book of poetry was a great success for her and for Graywolf. We met Tess in a bookstore and she took a shine to us and sent us the manuscript of her remarkable and resonant collection, *Instructions to the Double*. We spent over nine months treadling out 1,500 copies of her book; we took so much time that she was able to add a whole new section to it before we finished. We thought making 1,500 copies was wildly optimistic, but were going through such an effort to get them made that we never wanted to run out of them. However, in Tess we met more than a match for our own work ethic. On publication, Tess launched herself onto the road, gave readings and seminars, and sold the heck out of her book. We ran out completely in three months. At that moment we more or less gave up on running our entire operation as hand-crafted books, although we kept at it to some extent for several more years. We started having our books "manufactured" rather than crafted. (Last I heard, that first Tess Gallagher book is still selling, and has sold more than 12,000 copies—which is outstanding for poetry.)

As Graywolf matured as a trade publisher, publishing more fiction and nonfiction in addition to poetry, the more difficult economics of publishing became apparent. We found out firsthand why most of the larger publishers weren't taking as many risks—selling few copies of books just wouldn't work commercially. So we began to rethink ourselves economically and applied for nonprofit, tax-exempt status. A group of presses pursued this new concept of a literary publisher being similar to a symphony or theater or other established nonprofit organization. That argument carried the day with the IRS and Graywolf was among a group of presses who pursued that model, supported by individuals, corporations, and foundations that made tax-deductible donations to the work.

It took about twelve years from the founding of the press before we had confidence that it would last through the current month. Until then, every day was a wild, pressure-filled, anxiety-producing adventure. That's a long time to hang by the fingernails, but it's not so bad when you're hanging there in good company.

Graywolf achieved some recognition for its books. The Elliston Award, one of the more prominent awards of its time, assessing 360 books submitted by 250 publishers, named one Graywolf book (Tess Gallagher's *Instructions to the Double*) the best of the lot. Another book (Denis Johnson's *Inner Weather*) was one of two runners-up. That was encouraging! So was the ongoing correspondence with booksellers who seemed genuinely to love our books and the way we published them. One of the greatest pleasures of the work was the bottom-of-the-invoice correspondence with booksellers.

For me, though, our real success and our contribution to the field of publishing was—in addition to publishing some very fine books and remarkable authors—how Graywolf more or less hit on all cylinders of the publishing process. We selected good authors, established good relationships with booksellers, got books reviewed and noticed . . . the usual stuff. But we also took care of the invisible things: finding out-of-the-box places to sell books, developing a sound and well-run company, hiring great smart people, treating customers well and personally, earning some grants. The

Graywolf Way was and is to take the extra step in every aspect of what we do.

Guiding Spirits

Too many people contributed to Graywolf Press to thank them all, and it would perhaps be wisest not to name any of them for fear of bothering the unnamed, but the following people were fundamental to Graywolf's growth and development and should be cheered and acknowledged and thanked for their efforts:

- Kathleen Foster, cofounder.
- Sam Hamill and Tree Swenson, whose companionship and assistance were invaluable.
- Chris Faatz, whose enormous and compelling love for good ideas kept us cranking.
- Joseph Wheeler of the Centrum Foundation, mentor.
- Ray Carver, whose spirit continues to guide.
- Jim Sitter, who dragged us off to Minnesota! Bless his heart. And John Taylor, then of the Northwest Area Foundation, who welcomed us to town so warmly.
- Rick Simonson, bookseller extraordinaire.
- Authors, booksellers, board members, contributors, volunteers . . .

The Graywolf Silver Anthology

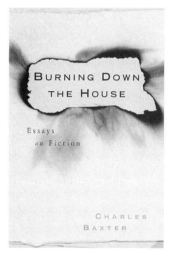

CHARLES BAXTER

Burning Down
the House

Essays on Fiction

Dysfunctional Narratives, or: "Mistakes Were Made"

Here are some sentences of distinctive American prose from our era:

> From a combination of hypersensitivity and a desire not to know
> the truth in case it turned out to be unpleasant, I had spent the last
> ten months putting off a confrontation with John Mitchell. . . .
> I listened to more tapes. . . . I heard Haldeman tell me that Dean
> and Mitchell had come up with a plan to handle the problem of the
> investigation's going into areas we didn't want it to go. The plan
> was to call in Helms and Walters of the CIA and have them restrain
> the FBI. . . . Haldeman and I discussed [on the "smoking gun"
> tape] having the CIA limit the FBI investigation for political rather
> than the national security reasons I had given in my public state-
> ments. . . . On June 13, while I was in Egypt, Fred Buzhardt had
> suffered a heart attack. Once I was assured that he was going to pull
> through, I tried to assess the impact his illness would have on our
> legal situation.

These sentences are almost enough to make one nostalgic for an adversary
with a claim upon our attention. There he is, the lawyer-president setting

forth the brief for the defense, practicing the dogged art of the disclaimer in *RN: The Memoirs of Richard Nixon*. I've done some cut-and-pasting, but the sentences I've quoted are the sentences he wrote. And what sentences! Leaden and dulling, juridical-minded to the last, impersonal but not without savor—the hapless Buzhardt and his heart attack factored into the "legal situation," and that wonderful "hypersensitivity" combined with a desire "not to know the truth" that makes one think of Henry James's Lambert Strether or an epicene character in Huysmans—they present the reader with camouflage masked as objective thought.

The author of the memoir does not admit that he lied, exactly, or that he betrayed his oath of office. In his "public statements," he did a bit of false accounting, that was all. One should expect this, he suggests, from heads of state.

Indeed, the only surprise this reader had, trudging gamely through *RN* looking for clues to a badly defined mystery, was the author's report of a sentence uttered by Jacqueline Kennedy. Touring the White House after *RN*'s election, she said, "I always live in a dream world." Funny that she would say so; funny that he would notice, and remember.

Lately I've been possessed of a singularly unhappy idea: The greatest influence on American fiction for the last twenty years may have been the author of *RN*, not in the writing but in the public character. He is the inventor, for our purposes and for our time, of the concept of *deniability*. Deniability is the almost complete disavowal of intention in relation to bad consequences. A made-up word, it reeks of the landfill-scented landscape of lawyers and litigation and high school. Following Richard Nixon in influence on recent fiction would be two runners-up, Ronald Reagan and George Bush. Their administrations put the passive voice, politically, on the rhetorical map. In their efforts to attain deniability on the arms-for-hostages deal with Iran, their administrations managed to achieve considerable notoriety for self-righteousness, public befuddlement about facts, forgetfulness under oath, and constant disavowals of political error and criminality, culminating in the quasi-confessional passive-voice-mode sentence, "Mistakes were made."

Contrast this with Robert E. Lee's statement the third day after the battle of Gettysburg and the calamity of Pickett's Charge: "All this has been my fault," Lee said. "I asked more of men than should have been asked of them."

Lee's sentences have a slightly antique ring. People just don't say such things anymore.

What difference does it make to writers of stories if public figures are denying their responsibility for their own actions? So what if they are, in effect, refusing to tell their own stories accurately? So what if the President of the United States is making himself out to be, of all things, a *victim*? Well, to make an obvious point, they create a climate in which social narratives are designed to be deliberately incoherent and misleading. Such narratives humiliate the act of storytelling. You can argue that only a coherent narrative can manage to explain public events, and you can reconstruct a story if someone says, "I made a mistake," or "We did that." You can't reconstruct a story—you can't even know what the story is—if everyone is saying, "Mistakes were made." Who made them? Everybody made them and no one did, and it's history anyway, so let's forget about it. Every story is a history, however, and when there is no comprehensible story, there is no history. The past, under these circumstances, becomes an unreadable mess. When we hear words like "deniability," we are in the presence of narrative dysfunction, a phrase employed by the poet C. K. Williams to describe the process by which we lose track of the story of ourselves, the story that tells us who we are supposed to be and how we are supposed to act.

The spiritual godfather of the contemporary disavowal movement, the author of *RN*, set the tenor for the times and reflected the times as well in his lifelong denial of responsibility for the Watergate break-in and cover-up. He has claimed that misjudgments were made, although not necessarily by him. Mistakes were made, although they were by no means his own, and the crimes that were committed were only crimes if you define "crime" in a certain way, in the way, for example, that his enemies like to define the word, in a manner that would be unfavorable to him, that would give him, to use a word derived from the Latin, some culpability. It wasn't the law, he claimed. It was all just politics.

A curious parallel: The Kennedy assassination may be *the* narratively dysfunctional event of our era. No one really knows who's responsible for it.

One of the signs of a dysfunctional narrative is that we cannot leave it behind, and we cannot put it to rest, because it does not, finally, give us the explanation we need to enclose it. We don't know who the agent of the action is. We don't even know why it was done. Instead of achieving closure, the story spreads over the landscape like a stain as we struggle to find a source of responsibility. In our time, responsibility without narratives has been consistently displaced by its enigmatic counterpart, conspiracy. Conspiracy works in tandem with narrative repression, the repression of who-has-done-what. We go back over the Kennedy assassination second by second, frame by frame, but there is a truth to it that we cannot get at because we can't be sure who really did it or what the motivations were. Everyone who claims to have closed the case simply establishes that the case will stay open. The result of dysfunctional narrative, as the poet Lawrence Joseph has suggested to me, is sorrow; I would argue that it is sorrow mixed with depression or rage, the condition of the abject, but in any case we are talking about the psychic landscape of trauma and paralysis, the landscape of, for example, two outwardly different writers, Don DeLillo (in most of *Libra*) and Jane Smiley (in the last one hundred pages of *A Thousand Acres*).

Jane Smiley's novel has been compared to *King Lear*, and its plot invites the comparison, but its real ancestors in fiction are the novels of Émile Zola. *A Thousand Acres* is Zola on the plains. Like Zola, Jane Smiley assembles precisely and carefully a collection of facts, a naturalistic pileup of details about—in this case—farming and land use. As for characters, the reader encounters articulate women (including the narrator, Rose) and mostly frustrated inarticulate men driven by blank desires, like Larry, the Lear figure. Lear, however, is articulate. Larry is not. He is like one of Zola's male characters, driven by urges he does not understand or even acknowledge.

Somewhat in the manner of other naturalistic narratives, *A Thousand Acres* causes its characters to behave like mechanisms, under obscure orders. Wry but humorless, shorn of poetry or any lyric outburst, and brilliantly observant and relentless, the novel at first seems to be about 1980s greed and the destruction of resources that we now associate with Reaganism, a literally exploitative husbandry. Such a story would reveal clear if deplorable motives in its various characters. But no: The book is about the essential criminality of furtive male desire. With the revelation of Larry's sexual abuse of his daughters, in a recovered memory scene not so much out of Zola as *Geraldo*, it shifts direction toward an account of conspiracy and memory, sorrow and depression, in which several of the major characters are acting out rather than acting, and doing their best to find someone to blame.

The characters' emotions are thus preordained, and the narrator gathers around herself a cloak of unreliability as the novel goes on. It is a moody novel, but the mood itself often seems impenetrable, because the characters, including the men, are not acting upon events in present narrative time but are reacting obscurely to harms done to them in the psychic past from unthinkable impulses that will go forever unexplained. Enacting greed at least involves making some decisions, but in this novel, the urge to enact incest upon one's daughter is beyond thought, if not the judicial system, and, in turn, creates consequences that are beyond thought. Rose herself lives in the shadow of thought. Throughout much of the book she is unaccountable, even to herself, by virtue of having been molested by her father. This is dysfunctional narrative as literary art, a novel that is also very much an artifact of *this* American era.

Watergate itself would have remained narratively dysfunctional if the tapes hadn't turned up, and, with them, the "smoking gun"—notice, by the way, the metaphors that we employ to designate narrative responsibility, the naming and placing of the phallically inopportune protagonist at the center. The arms-for-hostages deal is still a muddled narrative because various political functionaries are taking the fall for what the commander in chief is supposed to have decided himself. However, the commander in chief was not told; or he forgot; or he was out of the loop; or he didn't understand what was said to him. The buck stops here? In recent history, the buck doesn't stop anywhere. The buck keeps moving, endlessly. Perhaps we are in the era of the endlessly recirculating buck, the buck seeking a place to stop, like a story that cannot find its own ending.

We have been living in a political culture of disavowals. Disavowals follow from crimes for which no one is capable of claiming responsibility. Mistakes and crimes tend to create narratives, however, and they have done so from the time of the Greek tragedies. How can the contemporary disavowal movement not affect those of us who tell stories? We begin to move away from fiction of protagonists and antagonists into another mode, another model. It is hard to describe this model but I think it might be called the fiction of finger-pointing, the fiction of the quest for blame. It often culminates with a scene in a court of law.

In such fiction, people and events are often accused of turning the protagonist into the kind of person the protagonist is, usually an unhappy person. That's the whole story. When blame has been assigned, the story is over. In writing workshops, this kind of story is often the rule rather than the exception. Probably this model of storytelling has arisen because sizable population groups in our time feel confused and powerless, as they often do in mass societies when the mechanisms of power are carefully masked. For people with irregular employment and mounting debts and faithless partners and abusive parents, the most interesting feature of life is its unhappiness, its dull constant weight. But in a commodity culture, people are *supposed* to be happy. It's the one myth of advertising. You start to feel cheated if you're not happy. In such a consumerist climate, the perplexed and unhappy don't know what their lives are telling them, and they don't feel as if they are in charge of their own existence. No action they have ever taken is half as interesting to them as the consistency of their unhappiness.

Natural disasters, by contrast—earthquakes and floods—are narratively satisfying. We know what caused the misery, and we usually know what we can do to repair the damage, no matter how long it takes.

But corporate and social power, any power carefully masked and made conspiratorial, puts its victims into a state of frenzy, a result of narrative dysfunction. Somebody must be responsible for my pain. Someone *will* be found. Someone, usually close to home, *will* be blamed. TV loves dysfunctional families. Dysfunctional S&Ls and banks and corporate structures are not loved quite so much. They're harder to figure out. They like it that way. In this sense we have moved away from the naturalism of Zola or Frank Norris or Dreiser. Like them, we believe that people are often helpless, but we don't blame the corporations anymore. We blame the family, and we do it on afternoon TV talk shows, like *Oprah*.

Afternoon talk shows have only apparent antagonists. Their sparring partners are not real antagonists because the bad guys usually confess and then immediately disavow. The trouble with narratives without antagonists or a counterpoint to the central character—stories in which no one ever seems to be deciding anything or acting upon any motive except the search for a source of discontent—is that they tend formally to mirror the protagonists' unhappiness and confusion. Stories about being put-upon almost literally do not know what to look at. The visual details are muddled or indifferently described or excessively specific in nonpertinent situations. In any particular scene, everything is significant, and nothing is. The story is trying to find a source of meaning, but in the story everyone is disclaiming responsibility. Things have just happened.

When I hear the adjective "dysfunctional" now, I cringe. But I have to use it here to describe a structural unit (like the banking system, or the family, or narrative) whose outward appearance is intact but whose structural integrity has been compromised or has collapsed. No one is answerable from within it. Every event, every calamity, is unanswered, from the S&L collapse to the Exxon Valdez oil spill.

So we have created for ourselves a paradise of lawyers: We have an orgy of blame-finding on the one hand and disavowals of responsibility on the other.

All the recent debates and quarrels about taking responsibility as opposed to being a victim reflect bewilderment about whether in real life protagonists still exist or whether we are all minor characters, the objects of terrible forces. Of course, we are often both. But look at *Montel Williams*, or *Oprah*. (I have, I do, I can't help it.) For all the variety of the situations, the unwritten scripts are often similar. Someone is testifying because s/he's been hurt by someone else. The pain-inflicter is invariably present and accounted for onstage, and sometimes this person admits, abashedly, to inflicting the ruin: cheating, leaving, abusing, or murdering. Usually, however, there's no remorse or shame. Some other factor caused it: bad genes, alcoholism, drugs, or—the cause of last resort—Satan. For intellectuals it may be the patriarchy: some devil or other, but at least an *abstract* devil. In any case, the malefactor may be secretly pleased: s/he's on television and will be famous for fifteen minutes.

The audience's role is to comment on what the story means and to make a judgment about the players. Usually the audience members disagree and get into fights. The audience's judgment is required because the dramatis personae are incapable of judging themselves. They generally will not say that they did what they did because they wanted to, or because they had *decided* to do it. The story is shocking. You hear gasps. But the participants are as baffled and as bewildered as everyone else. So we have the spectacle of utterly perplexed villains deprived of their villainy. Villainy, properly understood, gives someone a largeness, a sense of scale. It seems to me that this sense of scale has probably abandoned us.

What we have instead is not exactly drama and not exactly therapy. It exists in that twilight world between the two, very much of our time, where deniability reigns. Call it therapeutic narration. No verdict ever comes in. Every verdict is appealed. No one is in a position to judge. The spectacle makes the mind itch as if from an ideological rash. Hour after hour, week after week, these dysfunctional narratives are interrupted by commercials (on the Detroit affiliates) for lawyers.

But wait: Isn't there something deeply interesting and moving and sometimes even beautiful when a character acknowledges an error? And isn't this narrative mode becoming something of a rarity?

Most young writers have this experience: They create characters who are imaginative projections of themselves, minus the flaws. They put this character into a fictional world, wanting that character to be successful and—to use that word from high school—*popular*. They don't want these imaginative projections of themselves to make any mistakes, wittingly or, even better, unwittingly, or to demonstrate what Aristotle thought was the core of stories, flaws of character that produce intelligent misjudgments for which someone must take the responsibility.

What's an unwitting action? It's what we do when we have to act so quickly, or under so much pressure that we can't stop to take thought. It's not the same as an urge, which may well have a brooding and inscrutable quality. For some reason, such moments of unwitting action in life and in fiction feel enormously charged with energy and meaning.

It's difficult for fictional characters to acknowledge their mistakes, because then they become definitive: They *are* that person who did *that* thing. The only people who like to see characters performing such actions are readers. They love to see characters getting themselves into interesting trouble and defining themselves.

Lately, thinking about the nature of drama and our resistance to certain forms of it, I have been reading Aristotle's *Poetics* again and mulling over his definition of what makes a poet. A poet, Aristotle says, is first and foremost a maker, not of verses, but of plots. The poet creates an imitation, and what he imitates is an action.

It might be useful to make a distinction here between what I might call "me" protagonists and "I" protagonists. "Me" protagonists are largely objects—objects of impersonal forces or the actions of other people. They are central characters to whom things happen. They do not initiate action so much as receive it. They are largely reactionary, in the old sense of that term, and passive. They are figures of fate and destiny, and they tend to appear during periods of accelerated social change, such as the American 1880s and 1890s, and again in the 1980s.

The "I" protagonist, by contrast, makes certain decisions and takes some responsibility for them and for the actions that follow from them. This does not make the "I" protagonist admirable by any means. It's this kind of protagonist that Aristotle is talking about. Such a person, Aristotle says, is not outstanding for virtue or justice, and s/he arrives at ill fortune not because of any wickedness or vice, but because of some mistake that s/he makes. There's that word again, "mistake."

Sometimes—if we are writers—we have to talk to our characters. We have to try to persuade them to do what they've only imagined doing. We have to nudge but not force them toward situations where they will get into interesting trouble, where they will make interesting mistakes that they may take responsibility for. When we allow our characters to make mistakes, we release them from the grip of our own authorial narcissism. That's wonderful for them, it's wonderful for us, but it's best of all for the story.

A few instances: I once had a friend in graduate school who gave long, loud, and unpleasantly exciting parties in the middle of winter. He and his girlfriend usually considered these parties unsuccessful unless someone did something shocking or embarrassing or both—something you could talk about later. He lived on the third floor of an old house in Buffalo, New York, and his acquaintances regularly fell down the front and back stairs.

I thought of him recently when I was reading about Mary Butts, an English writer of short fiction who lived from 1890 to 1937. Her stories have now been reissued in a collection called *From Altar to Chimneypiece*. Virgil Thomson, who was gay, once proposed marriage to her, and says the following about her in his autobiography:

> I used to call her the "storm goddess," because she was at her best surrounded by cataclysm. She could stir up others with drink and drugs and magic incantations, and then when the cyclone was at its most intense, sit down at calm center and glow. All of her stories are of moments when the persons observed are caught up by something, inner or outer, so irresistible that their highest powers and all their lowest conditionings are exposed. The resulting action therefore is definitive, an ultimate clarification arrived at through ecstasy.

As it happens, I do not think that this is an accurate representation of Mary Butts's stories, which tend to be about crossing thresholds and stumbling into very strange spiritual dimensions. But I am interested in Thomson's thought concerning definitive action because I think the whole concept of definitive action is meeting up with considerable cultural resistance these days.

Thomson, describing his storm goddess, shows us a temptress, a joyful, worldly woman, quite possibly brilliant and bad to the bone. In real life people like this can be insufferable. Marriage to such a person would be a relentless adventure. They're constantly pushing their friends and acquaintances to lower their defenses and drop their masks and do something for which they will probably be sorry later. They like it when anyone blurts out a sudden admission, or acts on an impulse and messes up conventional arrangements. They like to see people squirm. They're *gleeful*. They prefer Bizet to Wagner; they're more Carmen than Sieglinde. They like it when people lunge at a desired object, and cacophony and wreckage are the result.

The morning after, you can say, "Mistakes were made," but with the people I've known, a phrase like "Mistakes were made" won't even buy you a cup of coffee. There is such a thing as the poetry of a mistake, and when you say, "Mistakes were made," you deprive an action of its poetry, and you sound like a weasel. When you say, "I fucked up," the action retains its meaning, its sordid origin, its obscenity, and its poetry. Poetry is quite compatible with obscenity.

Chekhov says in two of his letters, ". . . shun all descriptions of the characters' spiritual state. You must try to have that state emerge from their actions. . . The artist must be only an impartial witness of his characters and what they said, not their judge." In Chekhov's view, a writer must try to release the story's characters from the aura of judgment that they've acquired simply because they're fictional.

In an atmosphere of constant moral judgment, characters are not often permitted to make interesting and intelligent mistakes and then to acknowledge them. The whole idea of the "intelligent mistake," the importance of the mistake made on an impulse, has gone out the window. Or, if fictional characters do make such mistakes, they're judged immediately and without appeal. One thinks of the attitudes of the aging Tolstoy and of his hatred of Shakespeare's and Chekhov's plays, and of his obsessive moralizing. He especially hated King Lear. He called it stupid, verbose, and incredible, and thought the craze for Shakespeare was like the tulip craze, a matter of mass hypnosis and "epidemic suggestion."

In the absence of any clear moral vision, we get moralizing instead. Moralizing in the 1990s has been inhibiting writers and making them nervous and irritable. Here is Mary Gaitskill, commenting on one of her own short stories, "The Girl on the Plane," in a recent *Best American Short Stories*. An account of a gang rape, the story apparently upset quite a few readers.

> In my opinion, most of us have not been taught how to be responsible for our thoughts and feelings. I see this strongly in the widespread tendency to read books and stories as if they exist to confirm how we are supposed to be, think, and feel. I'm not talking wacky political correctness. I'm talking mainstream. . . . Ladies and gentlemen, please. Stop asking "What am I supposed to feel?" Why

would an adult look to me or to any other writer to tell him or her what to feel? You're not supposed to feel anything. You feel what you feel.

Behind the writer's loss of patience one can just manage to make out a literary culture begging for an authority figure, the same sort of figure that Chekhov refused for himself. Mary Gaitskill's interest in bad behavior and adulthood is that of the observer, not the judge. Unhappy readers want her to be both, as if stories should come prepackaged with discursive authorial opinions about her own characters. Her exasperation is a reflection of C. K. Williams's observation that in a period of dysfunctional narratives, the illogic of feeling erodes the logic of stories. When people can't make any narrative sense of their own feelings, readers start to ask writers to tell them what they are supposed to feel. They want moralizing polemics. Reading begins to be understood as a form of personal therapy or political action. In such an atmosphere, already moralized stories are more comforting than stories in which characters are making complex or unwitting mistakes. In such a setup, *Uncle Tom's Cabin* starts to look better than any other nineteenth-century American novel.

Marilynne Robinson, in her essay "Hearing Silence: Western Myth Reconsidered," calls the already moralized story, the therapeutic narrative, part of a "mean little myth" of our time. She notes, however, that "we have ceased to encode our myths in narrative as that word is traditionally understood. Now they shield themselves from our skepticism by taking on the appearance of scientific or political or economic discourse. . . ." And what is this "mean little myth"?

One is born and in passage through childhood suffers some grave harm. Subsequent good fortune is meaningless because of this injury, while subsequent misfortune is highly significant as the consequence of this injury. The work of one's life is to discover and name the harm one has suffered.

This is, as it happens, a fairly accurate representation of the mythic armature of *A Thousand Acres*.

As long as this myth is operational, one cannot act, in stories or anywhere else, in a meaningful way. The injury takes for itself all the meaning. The injury *is* the meaning, although it is, itself, opaque. All achievements, and all mistakes, are finessed. There is no free will. There is only acting out, the acting out of one's destiny. But acting out is not the same as acting. Acting out is behavior that proceeds according to a predetermined, invisible pattern created by the injury. The injury becomes the unmoved mover, the replacement for the mind's capacity to judge and to decide. One thinks of Nixon here: the obscure wounds, the vindictiveness, the obsession with enemies, the acting out.

It has a feeling of Calvinism to it, of predetermination, this myth of injury and predestination. In its kingdom, sorrow and depression rule. Marilynne Robinson calls this mode of thought "bungled Freudianism." It's both that and something else: an effort to make pain acquire some comprehensibility so that those who feel helpless can at least be illuminated. But unlike Freudianism it asserts that the source of the pain can never be expunged. There is no working through of the injury. It has no tragic joy because, within it, all personal decisions have been made meaningless, deniable. It is a life fate, like a character disorder. Its politics cannot get much further than gender injury. It cannot take on the corporate state.

Confronted with this mode, I feel like an Old Leftist. I want to say: The Bosses are happy when *you* feel helpless. They're pleased when you think the source of your trouble is your family. They're delighted when you give up the idea that you should band together for political action. They'd rather have you feel helpless. They even like addicts, as long as they're mostly out of sight. After all, addiction is just the last stage of consumerism.

And I suppose I am nostalgic—as a writer, of course—for stories with mindful villainy, villainy with clear motives that any adult would understand, bad behavior with a sense of scale that would give back to us our imaginative grip on the despicable and the admirable and our capacity to have some opinions about the two. Most of us are interested in characters who willingly give up their innocence and start to act like adults, with complex and worldly motivations. I am fascinated when they do so, when they admit that they did what they did for good and sufficient reasons. At such moments the moral life becomes intelligible. It also becomes legibly political. If this is the liberal fallacy, this sense of choice, then so be it. (I know that people *do* get caught inside systems of harm and cannot maneuver themselves out—I have written about such situations myself—but that story is hardly the only one worth telling.)

It does seem curious that in contemporary America—a place of considerable good fortune and privilege—one of the most favored narrative modes from high to low has to do with disavowals, passivity, and the disarmed protagonist. Possibly we have never gotten over our American romance with innocence. We would rather be innocent than worldly and unshockable. Innocence is continually shocked and disarmed. But there is something wrong with this. No one can go through life perpetually shocked. It's disingenuous. Writing in his journals, Thornton Wilder notes, "I think that it can be assumed that no adults are ever really 'shocked'—that being shocked is always a pose." If Wilder's claim is even half true, then there is some failure of adulthood in contemporary American life. Our interest in victims and victimization has finally to do with our constant ambivalence about power, about being powerful, about wanting to be powerful but not having to acknowledge the buck stopping at our desk.

Romantic victims and disavowing perpetrators land us in a peculiar territory, a sort of neo-Puritanism without the backbone of theology and philosophy. After all, *The Scarlet Letter* is about disavowals, specifically Dimmesdale's, and the supposed "shock" of a minister of God being guilty of adultery. Dimmesdale's inability to admit publicly what he's done has something to do with the community—i.e., a culture of "shock"—and something to do with his own pusillanimous character.

The dialectics of innocence and worldliness have a different emotional coloration in British literature, or perhaps I am simply unable to get Elizabeth Bowen's *The Death of the Heart* out of my mind in this context. Portia, the perpetual innocent and stepchild, sixteen years old, in love with Eddie, twenty-three, has been writing a diary, and her guardian, Anna, has been reading it. Anna tells St. Quentin, her novelist friend, that she has been reading it. St. Quentin tells Portia what Anna has been doing. As it happens, Portia has been writing poisonously accurate observations about Anna and her husband, Thomas, in the diary. Anna is a bit pained to find herself so neatly skewered.

Bowen's portrait of Portia is beautifully managed, but it's her portrayal of Anna that fascinates me. Anna cannot be shocked. A great character you would never think of describing as "nice" or "likable," she is only what fictional characters should be—interesting. Everything she has done, she admits to. In the sixth chapter of the novel's final section, she really blossoms: Worldly, witty, rather mean, and absolutely clear about her own faults, she recognizes the situation and her own complicity in it. She may be sorry, but she doesn't promise to do better. Portia is the one who is innocent, who commands the superior virtues. Speaking of reading private diaries, Anna says, "It's the sort of thing I do do. Her diary's very good—you see, she has got us taped. . . . I don't say it has changed the course of my life, but it's given me a rather more disagreeable feeling about being alive—or, at least, about being me."

That "disagreeable feeling" seems to arise not only from the diary but from Anna's wish to read it, to violate it. Anna may feel disagreeable about being the person she is, but she does not say that she could be otherwise. She is honorable about her faults. She is the person who does what she admits to. As a result, there is a clarity, a functionality to Bowen's narrative that becomes apparent because everybody admits to everything in it and then gives their reasons for doing what they've done. Their actions have found a frame, a size, a scale. As bad as Anna may be, she is honest.

Anna defines herself, not in the American way of reciting inward virtues, but in a rather prideful litany of mistakes. In her view, we define ourselves at least as much by our mistakes as by our achievements. In fictional stories, mistakes are every bit as interesting as achievements are. They have an equal claim upon truth. Perhaps they have a greater one, because they are harder to show, harder to hear, harder to say. For that reason, they are rare, which causes their value to go up.

Speaking of a library book that is eighteen years overdue, but which she has just returned, the narrator of Grace Paley's story "Wants" says, "I didn't deny anything." She pays the thirty-two-dollar fine, and that's it. One of the pleasures of Paley's stories derives from their freedom from denial and subterfuge. Their characters explain themselves but don't bother to excuse themselves. City dwellers, they don't particularly like innocence, and they don't expect to be shocked. When there's blame, they take it. When they fall, they have reasons. They don't rise. They just get back on their feet, and when they think about reform, it's typically political rather than personal. For one of her characters, this is the "powerful last-half-of-the-century way." Well, it's nice to think so. Free of the therapeutic impulse, and of the recovery movement, and of Protestantism generally, her characters nevertheless *like* to imagine various social improvements in the lives of the members of their community.

Dysfunctional narratives tend to begin in solitude and they tend to resist their own forms of communication. They don't have communities so much as audiences of fellow victims. There is no polite way for their narratives to end. Richard Nixon, disgraced, resigned, still flashing the V-for-victory from the helicopter on the White House lawn, cognitively dissonant to the end, went off to his enforced retirement, where, tirelessly, year after year, in solitude, he wrote his accounts, every one of them meant to justify and to excuse. The title of his last book was apt: *Beyond Peace.*

CHARLES BAXTER *was born in Minnesota and teaches at the University of Michigan. He is the author of several books of fiction, including* Believers, A Relative Stranger, Shadow Play, Through the Safety Net, First Light, *and* Harmony of the World, *a poetry collection,* Imaginary Paintings, *a collection of essays* Burning Down the House, *and the editor of the anthology* The Business of Memory. *Baxter was also recently honored with an Academy Award in Literature from the American Academy of Arts and Letters.*

MARTHA BERGLAND

A Farm under a Lake

Dancing with a Dying Man

What I was trying not to think about was Carl Hawn whom I knew had lived for years alone in the house where he grew up. Shirley left him for good not long after Jack and I left the farm and now the house was falling down around him, the land rented out or lost to the bank. What I was trying not to think about was Jack Hawn sitting at the kitchen table in a condominium that could be anywhere, in a town where we don't know anyone. What I was trying to keep my mind off of was that fork in the road ahead of me. My foot was in that road.

After supper May and Ina and I went for a walk. I saw right away that Ina did not live, as I at first thought she did, in a settled and secure old neighborhood that would always be this way. At the end of her block was a convenience store, a gas station, and on the next block a feed mill whose smell of rotting soybeans was overpowering, she said, when the wind was right "or wrong." Many of these big old houses were at one time rooming houses and now were divided into apartments, but still some were pretty and there were lots of families with children. We had to step around a Big Wheel on almost every block, and little children, who had worn the grass off the yards just like chickens do, came off the porches to stare or smile at us. I liked it here and found myself wondering which of these places Jack and I could live in when we lost the condominium.

Later, while Ina bathed May and got her ready for bed, I tried to call Jack again, but there was no answer. There was no one to call to check on him. What a way to live! We had to get out of there. Without me, Jack had no one there. And I had no one without him. I knew Jack would not kill himself; my worry for him was not that, but that he would somehow permanently embarrass himself from need. From frustration. From getting a look at his own loneliness.

I called the Half Moon Hotel to tell Dad that I would be there tomorrow afternoon, but he was out, too. The girl at the desk said she would give him the message. She said he was probably at the Dairy Queen getting his nightly hot fudge sundae.

Around ten o'clock, Ina and I decided to try to get May to go to bed. We led her to it and pulled back the covers and Ina patted the bed like you do a chair you want a dog to jump up on. May got in the bed just fine, without reluctance, and Ina and I looked at each other in triumph. Now, if we can just get her to stay there. I sat with her while Ina got a basket of buttons and ribbons and sewing odds and ends that she had saved from years and years ago. Maybe it had been May's mother's; Ina wasn't sure. Then, while May sat in bed with a shawl around her shoulders and played with the odds and ends—taking them out and putting them back as she had the basket of things from Fan Butcher and the Ohio Motel—Ina and I sat on the couch under the windows in May's bedroom and waited. After a little bit, Ina started telling me a story about where she'd gotten the green-and-white-striped ticking to cover the couch and about the upholsterer she'd talked into doing the work for sixty dollars, but this time I was only half listening. I was thinking ahead to seeing my father again and to being in Half Moon and I was wondering where I would stay there; I hadn't given it any thought. I was seeing some places in the road near home, a farmhouse with no trees around it in the center of a field; a hedgerow; a house with windows that looked like eyebrows; a graceful crab apple tree in a valley near Sugar River; a rock on a corner fence post by a stop sign; the curve in the road near the elevator at Greene; and then the first view of Half Moon, "The Town on Five Hills," after that curve.

The night air coming in the windows was chilly and smelled like fields. Ina got up and closed them both most of the way, dimmed the light by May's bed, and brought me a sweater and us both an afghan. "Put your feet up," she said, "and put this over your legs." So we both settled in at each end of the sofa with our feet in the middle covered by the same afghan.

It was soothing sitting there in the near-dark while May played with those sewing things, as it is to sit in a room with a man or woman intent on making something. I remember one afternoon in Carl and Shirley's kitchen not long after Jack and I were married Shirley and I were putting up the last of the tomatoes and we were working quickly without talking, trying to get finished. I remember our hands slipping the skins off the scalded tomatoes and stuffing them in the quart jars and I remember Carl, his chin on his hands there at the table watching our hands. He had work to do—Jack had already gone back out to the field—but Carl sat a long time and just watched us. He seemed so content in the kitchen with Shirley and me canning tomatoes. It was nice, too, having him there, though neither of us said so; his watching gave grace to the small and repeated actions of our hands. I wondered how much contentment like that Carl had had since those days. From the sound of things, according to my father, not very much. As I sat with Ina and watched May's hands, I realized that I was facing east, the farm; I felt that I was on the circumference of the circle that the farm was the center of; from the edge of this circle it was a straight line to the house and to Carl; I was in range of Carl.

After a while I asked Ina, "Do you think it would have been better if May had stayed with John Ash?"

Ina, in a voice more contemplative than her daylight voice, finally answered. "I don't know. I don't think so, really. It didn't make any sense, her and John Ash. Doesn't it have to make sense? I mean, isn't that what marriage, the whole business, is for—to make some small amount of sense of the world? Albert and I made no sense together."

May dumped all the buttons and bows out again on the bed and some of the buttons fell on the floor. Ina and I crawled around retrieving them, then settled down again to wait for May to sleep. "Tell me about your husband, Janet. Is he a good man?"

"Oh yes, he's good, but he is . . . I don't know the word for it." I saw Jack again in my mind's eye, a good, just man sitting at the kitchen table— stalled and without the vision to see, this time, his way out. I saw myself next to him, exasperated with his plight which was somehow no longer mine. I saw myself leave him yesterday, saw the distance widen between us, as it widens between flotsam caught in two different currents of the same river. I saw, as if from a great distance, Jack going under. "There is a phrase for it, though. Jack is a farmer with a farm under a lake." And I found the voice to tell Ina the story my grandfather Orin Check had told us kids over and over about the hired man that Grandpa "Deecy" Hawn had called "the preacher Eldgrim." Deecy was Jack and Carl's grandfather.

I told Ina that one early summer day in the late twenties, Deecy Hawn and Orin Check were sitting on Deecy's back step, getting ready to go back out to work when they saw a tall man walking across Deecy's field. At the end rows the man's strides were wide as he tried every other furrow, then too short and comical when he stepped on the top of each one. "Whoever that man is, he's no farmer," Deecy said to my grandfather. The man came right up to them and introduced himself as Warren Eldgrim, and he said he was looking for work.

"Everybody's looking for work," one of them said, probably Deecy. And the other said that there's plenty of work everywhere you look; there's just no money for doing it. Eldgrim had just acquired some land, but he had no money and no skill in making money and he had no knowledge of farming, so he wanted to work for Deecy Hawn to learn to farm; he had heard that Deecy Hawn was the farmer, who, if there was one dollar to be made in farming, would be the one to make that dollar. He would work for Deecy for a year for room and board, so that he could go back to his land, then farm it himself. It was good river-bottom land, he said, though there wasn't much of it. Eldgrim was a serious man, with white hands, and he was, my grandfather said, a bit "poetical" in his speech.

Eldgrim stayed fourteen years at the Hawns and never went home to Hull because a government dam project put Eldgrim's land at the bottom of Sugar Lake. He never preached around Half Moon, though now and then women with trouble would go and wait in Deecy Hawn's wife's dark parlor, and they'd cry there while she went out to the field to bring back Eldgrim for their solace. The Hawn family got bigger, some said with help from

Eldgrim, but other than that, there was no more story to Eldgrim's life, just silence, endurance, shame. He just worked for Deecy Hawn, then died one spring of an influenza that killed young or old or weak ones. He was a preacher with no church, a bookish man who never read, a farmer with a farm under a lake.

I still remembered the story. Each next part of that story appeared in front of me like the next part of a familiar road. Though I couldn't picture the whole road, at each point where the story turned, I remembered which way it went. "My grandfather had a funny way of telling those stories—a funny formal way with those stories."

"I liked it," Ina said. "I like your grandfather's voice." Ina was looking at me curiously. "What does that tell me about your husband?"

"Not much really, but it tells you where he comes from, and it tells you that Jack is like that farmer with a farm under a lake. Jack is also a man out of context, away from the place where his people are, a man separated all his adult life from doing the work he wanted to do, living the life he wanted to live."

"It's terribly *sad*," said Ina, leaning forward, "and these days—all these damaged men—it's awfully common."

"I know," I said, but I laughed when I said it.

"How could it be funny?" Ina asked, a little indignant.

We both were watching May who was now leaning back on the fat pillows. Her eyes were closed, but her hands were still busy in that basket.

"Oh Jack's situation isn't funny; it's just something I remembered about the Preacher Eldgrim, something I haven't thought about for, I bet, thirty years. We kids who grew up together," I told Ina, "Jack, and Joyce, and Carl and I, had somehow got it in our heads that Eldgrim was the bogey man— a combination fool and fiend—and our worst insult was "*You* are the *bastard grandchild* of the preacher Eldgrim!" It was probably just the name that was funny to us, but we made him into a ghost—the one who preceded us and the one who would come after us. I remember arguments that lasted for hours about which bedroom on the square mile Eldgrim had died in. We found out at some point that he had died in a little hired man's house that had been torn down for years, but, even knowing that, we still liked to choose one of the four of us to pick on for a while and construct evidence that proved conclusively that it was, for example, *Joyce's room* where Eld-grim had died in horrible agony, cursing the Hawns and their progeny."

As I told Ina about Eldgrim, I saw the four of us kids on the back step at the Hawns bickering away an afternoon—the same back step on which our grandfathers sat when they first caught sight of poor Warren Eldgrim, the same back step where Joyce as a little girl sang to the cats, the same step where Carl stood so many years before listening to his wife bathe his chil-dren. The step was still there and the house, and Carl was still in the house, though everything else—our house and the people and most of the out-buildings and the fences and the hedges and the ownership of most of the land—was gone.

I stood up. Carl was still there. The house was there and the yard and the back step and the back porch that probably still smelled like cats and the garden and greasy overalls. I was eighty miles away from this place that was not just an idea we had lost, but a real place. While I was in this room with May and Ina, Carl was in one of the rooms of that house. And Carl was real; he was not just an idea of myself I had given up.

I turned to Ina. "I'm going to go back there right now. I know it's rude, but I don't mean to be rude. It's only an hour and a half or so from here." We looked at May. She was lying back on the pillows; her hands were still and her eyes were closed. She might be asleep. "Ina, don't even get off the couch." Disentangling my feet from the afghan, I stood in front of her and held her hands. "You are my friend and I will not let you and May fall out of my life. I'll be back to see you. I intend to keep you for a friend until I'm dead."

"More likely I'll be dead first, but I know what you mean, honey. Now you go do what you have to do. You know where to find me and you know you're welcome any time." She squeezed my hand, and then I kissed May lightly on the cheek, and I left.

All these damaged men—that's the phrase Ina had used. I heard it as I drove and I drove fast. There was no one on the two-lane roads, no car lights ahead of me or behind me, and there were few lights out there on all that flat land, except for the occasional pale green glow of a small town. There were no fences anymore or hedges or rows of cedars to stop the wind or the light or the eye—even in the dark. The land was a low black factory all around me, boiling with the slow green seethe that is a field in summer. There were almost no people left on this prairie that was now square-mile fields, but on the road in the dark at midnight I felt them around me. *All those damaged men.* Men driving alone. Men sitting in bars constructing atmospheres with beer and talk. Men awake alone in kitchens. Men watching movies on TV. Men damaged by war and work and no work and work in the wrong place for the wrong people. Men working for the wrong reasons, to take care of the wrong women. Men—and women, too—out of place, out of time, out of luck, alone.

I thought again of the best woman I had ever heard of. I'd heard about her from other nurses who took care of the aged in their homes. I don't know her name; she was a woman in her fifties, taking care of a frightening man—tall and wild-eyed and mean with what we used to call senility. He would not rest or eat or stop cursing or even sit down when she first went to his home, but she noticed right away that when music was on he seemed more calm and he seemed to move his body to the music. One day she put on a record—I don't know what music—and she asked him to dance with her. And he did. It clearly gave him pleasure and peace; then he could rest. After that the woman danced every day with this apparition, this skeleton in pajamas who scared away the young nurses. She danced with him every day three and four hours at a time until it seemed that he could rest. She danced with this dying man every day until almost the day he died. Whenever I thought of her, she gave me courage.

I drove very fast on the almost empty highway and got to the turnoff to the farm in a little more than an hour. Then I drove slowly on the gravel road and I drove clear around the square-mile section, clear around what had been the Hawns' and the Checks' farms. There is the part of darkness that filled in the room where the preacher Eldgrim died. That is the darkness that the hedge trees used to thrash and windmills used to fan, there is where Jack's and Nelda's arms used to conjure the future, and there is where our house used to be. From that spot on earth we used to spy on the Hawns.

I could feel the house in my chest, an ache as though the corners of the house pressed inside of me. How could it mean so much and yet be gone? How can that which is only inanimate be animated merely by association, by messages sent from the outside, through the senses, through the skin? I want to study the relationship of the surface of the body to the air. I want to know how it is that that which is commonest—the air and the light we walk in—can give up so much to us and yet still be not enough. How do we get so much through the surfaces of our bodies from the turn of the bird in the air, from the breezes and clouds that go on by, from walls and dishes and sheets, from kisses and caresses, from the touch of another's skin on ours? How is it that our surfaces are so permeable, so insubstantial, so alert, so passive, so hungry? How is it that mere colors and mere breezes and mere kisses can go through the skin to the heart?

Though the yard light was not on at Carl's, there were lights in the house. I parked the car where everyone had always parked, and, reaching out in the dark, felt the gate where my hand and arm still knew it was. My feet remembered the walk and the steps and the porch floor. My back remembered to catch the outside door before it slammed. The porch smelled like the same Hawn mingling of animal and vegetable and mineral—this vestibule between animal and human. I was sure of what I knew, and happy. I opened the inside door to the kitchen and called, "Carl?" The house smelled unfamiliar—smoky and male and closed. There was no answer, but I could hear the television on low in the front room. I went on into the kitchen. Two big, pale cats jumped down off the counter and disappeared into the pantry. "Carl?" In the dining room there were men's clothes folded on the table and hanging on the chairs. Carl must live downstairs, in these three rooms; this is where he kept his clothes. I stood in the doorway to the front room and there was Carl, just the way I imagined him to be, only worse. He was lying on the sofa asleep, facing away from me and the television. One arm was over his eyes, his nose was mashed against the back of the sofa and his mouth was open; he was snoring. He looked bad—he was unshaven, his hair long and dull, his skin pale.

I turned off the TV, and left on the little lamp behind the sofa, but Carl didn't wake up. I moved aside a few empty beer cans and ashtrays and sat down on the footlocker that Carl used for a coffee table. For a long time I just sat there and looked at him; I was looking for the young Carl I used to know, for his resemblance to Jack, and both were there. Now Carl looked more like the Jack I married than Jack did; the broad bones of his face made me remember the younger Jack, though the skin under his eyes, too, was thin and revealing. Carl seemed to be revising himself back toward his bones while Jack was putting on weight like it was real estate. Carl slept on, his breathing hard. I moved his arm away from his face and moved his face away from the back of the sofa so his breathing was easier. He still didn't wake up. He was very drunk.

I watched him as he slept, saw him as no one wants to be seen, but as everyone wants to be loved—dirty and coarsened and grey, in the midst of trying on death. I didn't want him to wake up; I didn't know what to say to him. If you don't talk to people, you forget how: I think I said this out loud, but Carl didn't wake up. In my mind I listed all the languages I had once known, but had lost from disuse—the French language and the language of family and friendship, the private local language of childhood, and the sweet language of the body in love.

I lifted Carl's heavy right arm and laid it across my lap. Under the brown skin of his forearm there was movement as there is in any live thing; his arm was reacting, I guess, to me and to a dream and to the spinning of the earth through space. Carl's fingers were relaxed and graceful, though his nails were broken, and when I put my fist under his warm dry palm, his hand closed on mine and held it for a moment in his sleep. When his hand let go again, I touched the back of it and his wrist; then with my thumb and fore-finger, I traced the bones along the outside of his hand and his arm, where the broad hand joins the narrow wrist. No matter what someone says or doesn't say or wants you to know about himself, that branching of long bones and muscle and skin into thumb and fingers says—involuntarily—something true. I think I can read there the balance of delicacy with strength. I remembered Carl's hands on steering wheels and Jack's hands too. The backs of Jack's hands were prideful and vulnerable and eloquent; Carl's hands were more knowing and they caught the air. I loved both of these Hawns.

In his sleep Carl turned toward the back of the sofa, pulled his arm away from my hands and drew his hand under his face. I stood up and from the corner of my eye saw something shining at me from the dark. Cats' eyes. The two cats had silently settled into the big chair by the window behind me and were watching me watch Carl. Some bank of air had shifted and now the night air came through the open windows—not in little breezes, but pouring in like rivers of cold water. I should have been cold, but then and there I would have been at home in a wide range of climates. I covered Carl with the ratty red blanket I found on the floor beside the sofa, one that the teen-aged Hawn boys used to keep in the trunk of the green Ford.

Then I moved the cats aside and sat down in their big chair where I could see both Carl and the night sky. The cats settled down again on my lap. They didn't care who I was; anyone warm would do.

A lot had been lost—money and land and time and parts of families, but this house and this farm were still *inhabited*. We had almost lost everything, but there was enough here, I thought, to fan to life. There was Carl and the Carl who used to be and the old man Carl who wouldn't given up on the others. I knew that. I knew what Carl was doing here: There was an old farmer he had a vision of; he was determined to grow into that skinny taciturn old man.

As I sat watching, the room began to be crowded, not with ghosts, but with presences from the past and future—guardians. The young, smart Jack and the wise man he could become. Ghostly Joyce, the three Carls. I was there, too, at sixty—bossier, quicker, fatter—a little like Nelda and like Ina and my own mother. And beyond was one who scared me—a paling eighty-year-old woman who, like May, had lost her words which, as I thought about it, were all that connected the spirit to the body, our earth to all that sky. And, oddly, watching over us all was the girl Janet at twenty who knew things then that she never spoke about even to herself, who knew things about the body and the earth and the air that all of us had forgotten. I saw that at forty I had been trying to simplify as Jack had always simplified for us: Who and how did I love twenty years ago? Was I wrong to marry Jack? Who do I love more? But all of us Janets together know that those questions cannot really be answered, only acknowledged. We all should have acknowledged, perhaps even spoken of, love and want and doubt and fear.

I sat there a long time and when the night was deepest and coldest and most quiet, I knew that I was really here and I was reinhabited by all my other selves and my voice. I pushed the cats off my lap and went into the kitchen. I took the phone into the pantry the way Jack used to when he was a teen-ager and talked on the phone to me for hours. I shut the door and sat down on the floor and called Jack.

I could hear that he answered before he was awake and before he controlled the fear in his voice. "Oh, Jan, where are you? Are you OK, honey? Is it an accident?"

"No, Jack, I'm fine. There's nothing wrong."

"Oh, thank God. Thank God." Jack was sitting up in bed now and I could hear him switch on the light and try to slow down his breathing. I knew that he was looking right at our clock when he asked me, "What the hell time is it? Where are you? What's going on?"

"I just called to hear your voice, Jack. To hear what's in it. You *do* miss me, don't you. I could hear it."

"Of course I do. Where are you now? At the old lady's daughter's?" Now I could hear Jack's situation crowding into his voice, pinching it. He was remembering that he had no work and no real place, that I was, at best, remote from him and so was his family.

"Jack, I'm at your place. The Hawn place. Carl's."

There was a long silence. I listened to Jack's breathing while he tried to figure the possibilities and what to say. He decided he needed more information. "Who else is there?" he asked me.

"Just Carl."

"What is going on, Janet?" He didn't know, so this time he just *asked* me. Twenty years ago he just assumed he knew what it was and twenty years ago the last thing he wanted was to hear me talk about it. And twenty years ago, talk was the last thing I could do.

Then I told him what had happened: that I had been sitting there talking to Ina Weaver and all of a sudden I had to be here at the farm, I had to see Carl and this place. I came here and found him drunk and asleep, and I sat and thought about some things for awhile.

"What am I supposed to think about this? Or do? I don't know what's going on in your head right now."

"You never did, Jack, but that's not just your fault. I'll just tell you." And I did. I told him I wasn't coming back there; I was staying here in Illinois. I told him that he should come here too. "Believe me, Jack, you're needed here. There's work to do here."

"There may be work to do, but there's no money in the work. Be realistic, Janet. Talk sense."

"We can figure out something. We can live here. We need to be here, to start over."

In Jack's voice I could hear the undercurrent of excitement that was beginning to sweep him away, that he wanted to be swept away by, but I could also hear his surface sense, the veneer of bitter experience in his words. "Janet, I have an interview in Sturgeon Bay the day after tomorrow. It's a good job. I have a good shot at this one. I can't just walk out like this and you can't either—walk out on me."

"We're nowhere there. We need to be here. Remember how visible the future was when we were here? Remember the garden I was going to make you with only blue flowers in it? Remember the orchards we would have and . . ."

"For Christ *sake*, you *have* to be realistic, just a little. You know and I know, though I will not mention any names, that others have dreamed that dream and killed themselves doing it. And Carl doesn't seem to be doing too good there with that idea. You haven't even *talked* to him about this."

Then I listed for him all the things that needed doing, just the things that I could see. I knew Jack. "Listen," I said, "most of the storm windows aren't even off yet and the fence is falling down; the porch needs new screens; there's just piles of things all over the downstairs here and outside there's a big branch half fallen off one of the maples, it landed on the porch, and sparrows are nesting in the eaves. Besides, there's not a thing to eat in this pantry and it's full of mouse droppings, even with two cats in the house."

After a moment and very slowly he said, "You and I and Carl? Carl?"

"Not here, Jack, in this house. Not the three of us. I was coming to that. You and Carl here and me in town at the hotel or someplace. I want to live by myself again for a while. But I want to work on this place with you and Carl. I want to start over."

For a long time he didn't say anything, but after a while I could hear that his breathing was beginning to churn itself into sobs, deep and hard. I just talked and talked to him, nonsense really, but words of love. I called him by all my old love names for him and told him what to bring and to be sure and not forget the cat and how the cat would like these two cats maybe and things would be OK again, Jack, really, things would be all right. "I'm not leaving you, Jack, Jack; I'm trying to get you back home. If I were leaving you, I'd never call you like this, from this phone that probably has some of your teen-aged spit still on it."

Then Jack laughed a little and said he had to go to that interview in Sturgeon Bay; he couldn't pass it up. But when I hung up the phone I knew he would come home. I just didn't know when.

It was getting light. In the dark kitchen the windows hung like grey pictures on the walls. I went to look at Carl again. He was still asleep on his side, one cat curled in the curve of his chest, the other behind his knees. I left the house quietly and drove slow into town with the car window open.

Later that morning I was sitting on a green bench with my dad under the big trees in front of the Half Moon Hotel. My father was the same as he had always been, only over the years he had gotten tinier and more pink and white, his hair finer, his memory sometimes fuzzy. He had just taken me to his new favorite place in town for breakfast—there were only four or five choices—and then we had been just sitting there on the bench for a while enjoying the summer sun. There were no buses in Half Moon, but we must have looked like people waiting for a bus and enjoying the wait. We must have looked like May.

"Listen to this, Janet, I heard a guy say this the other day. He was talking about when he was in the Korean War, I think. Anyway, he was talking about some foreign place a long way from here. He said, 'Their flying ants are as big as what we have here for wasps.' Get it, Janet? 'What we have here for wasps'? As if there was some empty place in creation the size and shape of wasps and we Americans were the ones with the good sense to fill that hole with wasps!"

It *was* funny and Dad laughed and slapped my knee to get me to laugh more.

But in a way, I knew how that man was thinking. Only here in this Illinois were there spaces in creation for Carl and Jack and I, spaces the size and shape of each of us grown and old and good.

"Is it Saturday?" Pop asked.

"No, Dad, it's Monday."

"Oh, too bad."

"Why, what is it about Saturday?"

"Well, the Catholics, they do this procession thing when they have their weddings." Pop clapped me on the knee again. "But you know that! You were in one. Oh my god, and it was a good one too! Do you remember what happened?"

"Of course I remember. How could I forget a thing like that. A girl doesn't forget that her skirt came off in her wedding procession." We both laughed and then Dad told the story again, as if I hadn't been there, as if it hadn't happened to me.

We sat there looking at the place where the Catholics could turn onto this street if it were Saturday and if any of them were getting married today. At the end of the street were the fields of corn.

After a while Pop asked me, "What are we doing, setting here, Janet?"

I could answer him. "Waiting for Jack."

MARTHA BERGLAND *is the author of* Idle Curiosity *and* A Farm under a Lake. *She currently teaches English at Milwaukee Area Technical College.*

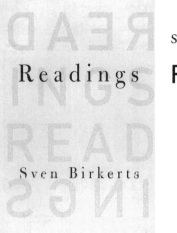

SVEN BIRKERTS

Readings

The Millennial Warp

Sometimes my writing students come to me to say that they are stuck or unable to get started or otherwise at a loss, at which point I am compelled to give them some version of my "return to the core" speech. I ask them to get into a meditative mode and then to monitor themselves carefully, to find out where their thoughts go when they are left to find their own level. "Look to those places," I urge them, "because that's where your best subjects and energies will most likely be found."

Physician, heal thyself! I have now spent the better part of a year in the tangles of a project, a very particular sort of memoir, the point of which is not to indulge my recollections for their own sake, but rather to present them selectively in such a way that the reader will grasp my real point, which is that in the past fifty years or so something in the nature of time—or in our experience of it—has changed radically; that, in other words, the shape of the very frame of things has altered. This is not an everyday sort of intuition. Indeed, to remark it is to admit to being in an unbalanced condition. Where do you draw the lines of definition? How do you begin to approach others for correction or corroboration?

I do bring the idea forth—tentatively—to certain people and find a fairly predictable sort of response. Most will concede that there have been astonishing changes on nearly every front in the past half century; that our ways of living have been transformed to an extraordinary degree. Everyone has a fund of available anecdotes on the subject. "I can remember," they begin. Or: "My father can still recall . . ." But nearly all view the process as one of accumulated innovation and cultural and societal acceleration. Brows ascend skeptically when I offer that we may have reached some condition of critical mass, that degree increments have brought us into the first stages of a change in kind. Simply: that our old understandings of time—and, therefore, of life itself—are in many ways useless.

This is my peculiar project. Yet even as I have a concept and an array of corroborating arguments, something in the nature of the topic has me getting lost again and again. I have bursts of local clarity, frequent accesses of new evidence, and these I coax to the page eagerly enough. But the backdrop, the larger point of it all, keeps slipping from me. I cannot easily hold the specific and the general in the right equilibrium. And so, often, much more than ought to be necessary under most writerly circumstances, I make myself heed my own precept. I ease up on the pressure, let the daydreams in; I look to reconnect with the originating impulse. I walk around in the world and see what thoughts I generate when there is no pressure to produce. The process usually works. I seem to be sufficiently self-consistent to end up once again revolving the same few notions in my thoughts. This must be me, I think, confirmed again. I am able to go back to sifting through the specific memories I have gathered.

But these do not concern me here. Just now I want to confront the sponsoring impulse itself, that special complex of intuitions and anxieties that keeps me fixated on the idea that the human time experience may be undergoing a fundamental mutation. By which I do not simply mean that we feel ourselves to have less and less of it, though this is, of course, part of what is happening, never mind the fact that we are surrounded by labor saving technologies on every front. But how to present the evidence?

My own way of posing the matter to myself can be figured as a rapid back-and-forth turning of the head—not so rapid as to make me dizzy, but rapid enough to allow the contrast between what I see on either side to be vivid. I am, in effect, looking from one end of my life to the other, from the past that came just before and into which I arrived, suddenly present, to the future, parts of which I have faith I will see, but which will more properly be the time my children will claim as theirs. Rapid shifts of focus, then. On one side, the world of my grandparents and parents—the lore of the old country I absorbed so deeply from their stories, the evidence of their gestures and ways of doing things, and my own awakening perceptions of the early 1950s, a time before television, a time of young stay-at-home mothers and briefcase-toting fathers driving off to work. On the other side, the sound- and image-saturated *now*, my bemusement and unease at the complexly decontextual way the world presents itself, and how confused I am to see my children adapting to it so readily. "Things have always gone so," I mutter to myself, and I wonder, honestly, whether my whole conception of a deep-down renovation of things might not just be the grumpy reactions of aging in a disguised form.

The head-turning operation is, I grant it, dissociative in its very nature: The contrast emerges when the connective tissue has been cut away. But of course we *live* the connective tissue—the whole point of it is *connection*. I am, moreover, skewing things by being so selective in what I view. That is, I look at only those phenomena that will show me something about changes in our time experience. I do not consider the other evidence, the constants— childbirth, say, or the recurrence of irrepressible bonding urges—that might belie my insistence. Besides, one might argue, looking back and forth this way over any fifty-year period is guaranteed to induce time shock. Things change, and they have always changed.

But no. My very point is that the acceleration, the gathering of momentum, over this fifty-year period is something new, that it runs so far in excess of historical expectations of change, and does so on so many different levels at once, that we cannot lay it to rest by calling it just more of the same. If nothing else—and there is much else—this is the first epoch in which all-encompassing shifts in the way life was lived have been recorded—by photograph, by film, by video, by recording machines—and then fed back to us, slowly at first, then as a part of such a cataract of data and imagery that the reflection of life can itself be seen to be one of the most pronounced features of life. It has been in this most recent period, which we are now and perhaps henceforth immersed in, that we finally have seen the creature succeed in swallowing its own tail—this is the first time, ever, that the perceptions of events and the transmission of the perceptions have become as important as the events themselves. It is not enough to say that life has simply evolved and gotten more complicated. Life—the "it"—is now in some crucial ways a new substance, and this basic fact must be contemplated deeply.

When I look back and forth between the early post–World War II years and the premillennial present, I often feel a kind of vertigo overtake me. Much is, of course, the same—people wear clothes, ride buses, eat in restaurants, play baseball—but the sameness is not what is striking. I feel, rather, that the present is a lingering transition moment between that past and a future that offers an entirely unfamiliar aspect to the comparative anthropologist. The elements are still recognizable, but they are part of a momentum that will imminently alter their nature. And time, that grand abstraction, has everything to do with this.

The first thing that any disinterested historian-anthropologist would notice about this period is the astonishing increase and acceleration on all fronts: more people, more things, and rates of activity undreamed of by the most animated of philosophers. It is as if we were all molecules in a liquid that had been subjected to a sudden high heat. One could, I suppose, approach this statistically, citing increases in population, production, consumption, automotive and airline travel, and so on. My impulse is different. I want to grasp at the change subjectively—to remember, admittedly with a child's senses, what it felt like to be in downtown Birmingham, Michigan, on a Saturday afternoon circa 1956, and then to focus in on impressions from recent visits. How else do we study these things—in our souls, I mean?

What I fetch up from them is the inside picture of a very different world. In this quieter, smaller town, people drove their cars right into the center and parked in a metered space on the street. Kids lined up down the block to get into the afternoon movie. Stores—I could almost close my eyes and name them—tended to feature so-called necessities, and these were finite in number. But these are not really the things I remember. What I preserve is an overall feeling, a sense of the essential pace of things. This embraced everything, from the movement of people on the sidewalks to the way adults kept encountering one another and lingering to talk; it also embraced the tempo of transactions, the air given off by shop owners and employees, and—to sound crotchety now—the absence of piped-in music: Many more things seemed to take place against a backdrop of natural ambient noise, nothing more.

Nowadays, returning to visit, I find the place more than doubled in size. Going to town means jockeying to get into a parking lot and adjusting to the sidewalk flow between pricey boutiques; it means, as often as not, laying down plastic for a purchase and having the shopping contact limited to the clerk's rapid-fire verification of the card. I exaggerate—or do I? I am guilty of nostalgia, sure, but to use that word is not to invalidate the perception. The world has speeded up in a thousand ways, and that acceleration has come to comprise a significant part of a person's interaction with society. A change in the rate of interaction is, let's face it, a change in the nature of the interaction.

This molecular agitation, it should be noted, embraces everyone. Even children and the elderly—two groups formerly safe from the ethos of busyness—are now ensnared, racing to clubs, sports, support groups, and lessons. In the collective judgment, expressed through everything from advertisements for pain medication to the gestural inflections of news show anchors, to hold a valid ticket to being, one must be busy.

A direct consequence of this massive systemic speedup is the thinning out, the near disappearance, of the intermediary layer. Leisure, silence, stillness—formerly the stresses of labor were cushioned. There were kinds of time, and the counterpart to busyness was rest. When the sun went down, or the church bells rang, a slowness of the kind we now find intolerable swept in. The entertainment options were fewer: One might read, listen to the radio, play cards. Now the expectation is that entertainment, the right to it, is inalienable. The structure of entertainment—its massive and variegated presence—now fills what were formerly preserves of open time, those often monumentally boring periods when little or nothing stood between the self and the grainy presence of the world. Certainly there was boredom, but there was also nearness to the primary world. Before the great mediation, a person had only to pause in a task or sit calmly in order to be in contact, however fleetingly, with the ground of nature, to feel its rhythms, its essential peacefulness. No longer. We have put between ourselves and the natural world so many layers of signals, noises, devices, and habits that the chance for such connection is very limited. More often than not, a person finding himself suddenly in an uncontaminated natural setting will register a body shock, a tremor of extreme displacement.

Dramatic increases not only in the rate of activity but also in the kinds of activities available—everything from affinity groups to workshops to therapies to lessons to Internet cruising—have naturally affected the way in which we engage events. The more there is to do in a finite period of time, the more likely it is that a person will rationalize the task and divide the time. Indeed, we are now deeply immersed in the perception of life as a set of scheduled events—a kind of actuarial decathlon that has us hitting specific marks at regular intervals through the day as well as at all of the appointed stages of life's way. A vast and intricate grid has been superimposed on our older way of being, and it's hard now to conceive that things were ever really different. Time comes in blocks and everything runs to plan. The awareness is no longer enforced just externally, it penetrates every consciousness. Only young children are—blessedly and, alas, briefly—unaware. The rest of us are completely enshrouded, from the beeping of the morning alarm, to the radio reminders every few minutes, to the giant hourglass that is the urban and suburban traffic pattern; from the opening of offices and shops, to the scheduling of classes, to the programming of our TV shows. We move through the day in lockstep with the clock, far removed from our ancestors—and I don't even mean the cave dwellers—who had no commute, no media, and who, even when they had clocks, were more apt to tune their time awareness to the changes of the light.

The insidious thing is, of course, this internalization, the way we absorb a structure and then bend to its dictates. We have all experienced the vacation syndrome—how the first three or four days of our two-week break find us struggling to escape the hold of habit. We carry the suddenly useless scaffolding with us even as we know we are paying dearly for the privilege of leaving it behind. The longer we work, the more we participate in the societal expectation, the more deeply we absorb a structure that has no organic basis, that was rationalized to serve the interests of commerce. How sad, too, that while it takes so many days to relinquish the work habits, the vacation reflexes disappear as quickly as the taste of brine on our lips.

But it is not simply our relation to time that has been altered here, it is our relation to situation, to event, to life itself. As we become creatures of outward obedience to order and inwardly suppressed impulse, we also take an ever greater role in scripting events, in planning situations so that they will conform to expectation. How indolent and fanciful it seems now that in the era of slower travel and patchwork communications, people would, in going from place to place, get off the grid; could, in effect, wander, or at least proceed without the sense of being enslaved by schedule; could be free of that peculiarly late-modern feeling, call it the "panopticon effect," of somehow always being seen. Or think of the now mythic figure of the flaneur, that unique phenomenon of nineteenth-century Paris, the individual who idled about the urban center in open defiance of the newly minted tyrannies of time.

Or listen to Milan Kundera, who in the opening pages of his wonderfully named novel, *Slowness*, asks: "Why has the pleasure of slowness disappeared? Ah, where have they gone, those loafing heroes of folksong, those vagabonds who roam from one mill to another and bed down under the stars?" Our only contact with this vanished spirit comes during the all-too-infrequent blizzards, which alone, by paralyzing our cars, have the power to overwhelm our planning strategies. Although the radio and TV reports present these events essentially as disasters, a great many people experience them as the only true holidays they have. I can think of few days more liberated and celebratory than those on which the whole neighborhood has been kept from its daily business. Adults appear in the street like bears coming out of caves; children run up and down in packs, alert in every sense to the suspension of routine. But these are the rare exceptions, and their special atmosphere, that electric truancy, is purchased with the internalized expectations of dailyness.

Rhythms have changed, expectations have changed, and so too, with what feels in historical terms like instantaneousness, have the things that people do—the fundamental actions that get performed in the course of an average day. We can contemplate—and this is but a single instance—how many ways in which technological innovations have short-circuited our physical involvement in tasks. From kneading dough to opening the garage door, and from carrying a suitcase to mowing the lawn, there is scarcely a physical operation that has not been simplified, streamlined, or eliminated entirely by some invention. We explain to our incredulous children that telephones once had dials that had to be turned, and that people used to get up from the couch every time they wanted to change the television channel. We do not tell them that there was a time before television even existed.

This technological intervention means many things, among them a worrisome loss of the sense of how things work and, more abstractly, a further change in our understanding of the time of things. For it used to be that the measurement of a task was in terms of how long it took the body to do it. People spoke confidently of a half-day's work, or a week's work, and the centrality of the working self was assumed. Now as tasks are divided and machines are implicated at every level, there is little correlation between the day and the operations one performs in it.

Of the innumerable technologies that have revolutionized our sense of time and our experience of daily life and labor, certainly the computer has had the greatest range of effects. On the most obvious level, the processing power of the microchip and the organizational capacities of software programs have not only transformed how we handle information—transplanting paper and print functions to keyboard and screen—they have changed our relation to information itself. Static print archives—data files—have been rendered potentially dynamic. The drudgery of rote retrieval and transcription, former clerical functions, has yielded to a new ease of access and agency. Energy has been released into the system. Watch individuals at their terminals—at travel agencies, in banks, at service counters—and you can see not only their dependence on the powerful tools they now command but also their delight in working the combinations, at taking part in the dynamic magic of information flow.

Obviously, then, there is much about the arrival of the computer in the workplace that is liberating. The overall change in the relation to information, which these search-and-retrieve operations only hint at, has other kinds of significance as well. For one thing, computers not only put enormous quanta of data into play, but they also, through options of linkage, situate the user in what is a potential infinity. In the blink of an eye, the formerly vast but comprehensible body of information symbolized by banks of paper files has become an incomprehensible totality, an ocean whose shores may never be located—incomprehensible, that is, to the individual, but navigable by technology. And thus we accept the prosthesis, move it into the center of our lives, and grant it the powers we cannot possess. In the process of handing ourselves over, we enact a subliminal self-diminution, tacitly admitting that we no longer have command of the data we manipulate.

This is somewhat general. But haven't we all witnessed the revealing instances, seen how the same agent or teller who at one moment clicks confidently at the keyboard, presiding over some portion of our fate, is suddenly reduced to shakes of the head and dumb shrugs when the mainframe goes down? Take away the prosthesis and the person does not even have the former paper props to fall back on. In the moment of the loss of power we glimpse the differential. Just as when the storm knocks out the power to our houses, we feel ourselves living as in a parenthesis, waiting, unable to carry on with our lives as we know them, never mind that the power we rely on has only been available for the briefest little part of our species' life. The fact is, we not only rely on it practically, we have *defined* ourselves in terms of it; and the same is already becoming true of our relationship with computers. We define our sense of who we are in part through a recognition of what we can do. And our sense of what we can do is being very rapidly altered by the technology we have brought into our midst.

Some will say, "So what?" The fact is that we *have* computers now—they are here to stay—much as we have our circuits, our electricity, and the astonishing know-how that has changed the way we live once and for all. I will propose shortly that the matter is not quite so simple, that such attainments have levied an extraordinary pressure, and that our definitional sense of ourselves may be more than a little affected. But there are certain preliminary implications that need to be considered.

We must consider, for example, that the awareness of the infinite interconnectedness of information made possible by the computer is both literal—is the sensation of potentiality felt by the user at the terminal—and figurative. That is, we now—owing to computers as well as broadcast media—grasp the world as hypersaturated. Too many channels, too many facts, too many images—too much that thrusts itself at us. Who does not, now, inhabit a world at once infinite and absolutely incomprehensible? The once narrow aperture defined by place and time, by the cognitive limits of the unassisted senses—William Blake's "windows"—has been forced open. Globalness and instantaneity are our new lot. Never mind that we still live, bodily, in one place and still relate ourselves to our environment with our bodily senses; that inhabiting, once the core of our self-conception, our at-homeness in the world, has become schizophrenic. To simple actuality has been added perpetual possibility. Upon the evidence present to immediacy has been superimposed an invisible realm of event—the ever-present awareness of elsewheres and of the impossibly complex ways in which they impinge on our here and now.

This is not, strictly speaking, an entirely new condition. It has been with us since the telegraph first breached the barriers of distance and began bringing the news from elsewhere into our lives. But the momentum that began with the newspaper and intensified with network television has now, just very recently, escalated past our already overstrained capacities of response. We cannot avoid it, blinker ourselves as we may, for the movement of the world all around us is in a thousand ways orchestrated by incessant global awareness. The moment-by-moment fluctuation of global financial markets impinges on us whether we own stocks or not. Everything is connected.

We humans, of course, are not capable of the kind of receptivity and response that a global information environment would seem to require. As Sigmund Freud astutely suggested, "For a living organism, protection against stimuli is an almost more important function than the reception of stimuli." To put it another way: The radical refinement of the microchip, measured in generations defined by specific operational capability, is not matched by the adaptational capacity of the human organism. Yet it is the rate of evolution of the microchip that is, in significant ways, determining the nature of our information environment.

Human, overwhelmed, we reply to the rapidly mutating conditions of life by editing. We take in what we can, double up our functioning when we need to; we willfully turn away from many kinds of information, of stimuli, because we instinctively grasp that our response mechanisms would be overtaxed. And we flee from saturation—an ever more common sensation—into the decompression of entertainment. The perfect counterbalance to a day spent navigating the perpetual overflow of the present is an evening given over to the mindless absorption of images and music. The spring that is tightened past its natural bent must be allowed to recoil.

This is, I would venture, something new in the world—the overall sense that so many people have of being in arrears; of moving in the midst of data ramified past all true comprehensibility; of living partially with no hope of gaining the ground to wholeness.

Yet, and here is a terrible paradox, at the very same time that the world is felt to be overwhelming, there is also a poignant sense of its limitation. We have created a sphere of endless news, imagery, and information—a sort of world within the world—but the other world, the one that greets our natural senses and imaginations, seems depleted, exhausted. We have eliminated the physical, the geographical, frontiers. There are no more endless tracts or unknown lands to compel the imagination. And what there is of variousness and remoteness is being rapidly stripped of aura and homogenized. Bring the rain forest into the living room enough times and it loses its otherness. Crowd the extremities of earth (what were once the extremities of earth) with Burger Kings and cinemas showing *Die Hard II* and the sense of possibility begins to vaporize. Is it too obvious to note that the two developments are deeply linked, that the infinity of information has in some ways been purchased at the price of the terrestrial unknown and the sense of mystery it once housed? That the sphere of information takes its exponential growth at the expense of the actual, which nowadays appears to be shrinking, losing force?

All of this, of course, relates in specific ways to the human time experience. There is ever less difference between local and global communications—the same near instantaneousness governs both—and this has subjected our older sense of the time of things to a disfiguring pressure. For until quite recently we understood time as being, at least in one sense, in dynamic relation to distance. But when a signal can travel to the other side of the world in a second—easily and cheaply, that is, no longer requiring the voodoo of the long-distance telephone call—then our sense of these two abstractions, once etched so deeply into our reflexes, our very being, must alter. The ground feels different under our feet than it felt to our forebears, as does the distance our eyes gaze into feel different.

These imponderables are what I am finally concerned with—our sense of the ground under and around us, our understanding of what *far away* is, or could be, or what we register when we speak of "long ago" or "tomorrow" or "a year from now." These are, as it were, the bright A-B-C blocks of our being in the world, and they are not the same as they were for so many generations preceding ours. The primary elements—the undercurrents of meaning and the feeling tones—are mysteriously changing.

While I cannot begin to assess what might be the ultimate effects of these subtle alchemizings of the ordinary, it seems clear that they have already wreaked some havoc on our sense of where it is in time we find ourselves. Which is to say, our relation—individually and collectively—to the idea of past, present, and future has been radically modified. A great many people now live with the feeling that both the historical and the personal past exist on the other side of a widening gulf, while the future seems to press down with a palpable urgency. Obviously there is no objective source for such a pronouncement. I take my evidence from talking to people— older people, peers, and students. From the older people I gather that things felt quite a bit different in the past. Although changes came steadily in the old days, too (new inventions, changes in the workplace) and sometimes with unexpected force (the depression, the war), the line of continuity was never ruptured. The idea of tradition still prevailed; the past was felt to be linked to the present as a source, and the future, the perennial unknown, was felt to be a kind of new land that everyone moved slowly into, individually and en masse.

No more. The past, so different from everything we see happening around us—different in kind, not just in degree—appears quaint and irrelevant, fodder for periodic recycling as nostalgia. At the same time, we feel ourselves hurtling toward the future. Everything feels provisional. No product, no artistic work, no initiative carries any hint of permanence. Rather, we are fixated by the seasonal rotation, the fashion. The music will last for a moment; the computer will be upgraded shortly; and it is cheaper just to throw away the old appliance and get a new one. The idea of repair itself belongs to the past. And the future, the millennium, is the destination. There the time line, the last vestiges of the old orientation, will self-destruct. There, somehow, we will all begin to live in a new configuration. We are pulled inexorably toward that apotheosis.

I will grant that my extrapolations are sketchy and will seem fanciful to some, arbitrary to others. But they are, for better or for worse, the things I keep thinking about; they are what my own experience has thrust into relief. Although I present them sequentially, in my awareness they are all entangled. And I cannot honestly contemplate the future for very long without feeling a swarming sense of angst. Not so much for myself anymore, but for my children. My dread is custodial: I have to wonder what their world, their life experience, will be like. And I ask myself if I should be readying them to adapt to the new order of things, or, contrarily, equipping them with lore about the old. Is the past in this sense a bequest or a burden? It is in asking these very questions that I grasp the profound implications of what we are living through.

Quite recently I had an illumination of sorts. Two very different insights—metaphors, really—from two very different thinkers combined, and all at once I seemed to understand the deeper structure, if not the problem, then at least of my own fear.

The first notion, which reached me only when the lengthy fuse had burned down, came by means of Arthur Danto's recent book, *After the End of Art*. And while the whole book galvanized my thinking about our late-modern circumstance, it was one of its opening passages that figured most suggestively in my thinking:

> At roughly the same moment, but quite in ignorance of one
> another's thought, the German art historian Hans Belting and
> I both published texts on the end of art. Each of us had arrived at a
> vivid sense that some momentous historical shift had taken place in
> the productive conditions of the visual arts, even if, outwardly
> speaking, the institutional complexes of the art world—the gal-
> leries, the art schools, the periodicals, the museums, the critical

establishment, curatoriat—seemed relatively stable. Belting has since published an amazing book, tracing the history of devotional images in the Christian West from late Roman times until about a.d. 1400, to which he gave the striking subtitle *The Image before the Era of Art*. It was not that those images were not art in some large sense, but their being art did not figure in their production, since the concept of art had not as yet emerged in general consciousness, and such images—icons, really—played quite a different role in the lives of people than works of art came to play when the concept at last emerged and something like aesthetic considerations began to govern our relationship to them.

Danto goes on to theorize as follows:

If this is at all thinkable, then there might be another discontinuity, no less profound, between the art produced during the era of art and art produced after that era ended. The era of art did not begin abruptly in 1400, nor did it end sharply either, sometime before the mid-1980s when Belting's and my texts appeared respectively in German and in English. Neither of us, perhaps, had as clear an idea as we might now have . . . of what we were trying to say, but, now that Belting has come forward with the idea of art before the beginning of art, we might think about *art* after the end of art, as if we were emerging from the era of art into something else the exact shape and structure of which remains [*sic*] to be understood.

Danto's idea—that we may now be making art after the end of art— affected me profoundly. It brought back at least part of the disturbance I had felt long ago when I understood—grasped viscerally—what Friedrich Nietzsche meant about living after the death of God. How different was the backdrop—suddenly—against which all things were seen. So, too, I registered the end of art as being the end, the expiration, of another way of believing, as the end of the myth of aesthetic investigation and progress. For Danto did not mean, of course, that there is to be no more expressive making, only that individual expressions no longer have a chance of adding up to something larger, something perceived to be substantially related to human experience in important ways. The ground of that mattering, he believes, is gone.

Given the long-standing assumption in many quarters that the deeper expressions of art were bound integrally to the spirit of the times—to the historical moment—one cannot help but wonder whether the end of art might not be consequent upon the end of something in the world itself, something that art had so diversely reflected and drew its fundamental purpose from. An unnerving suggestion, this, but one to which I will need to return.

The other concept, which has steadily haunted me for several years now, and which was, by way of obvious association, brought forth again by my reading of Danto, comes from Bill McKibben's *The End of Nature*. McKibben's idea, or realization, is disturbingly simple. It is that with the growth of world population, urbanization, the spread of mechanization, and, more recently, with the invisible saturation of all airspace with electronic signals, we have effectively eliminated the idea of nature as an entity that exceeds us and to which we belong. Now, and henceforth, we believe and act as if nature belongs to us. All natural environments are either enclosed by or critically influenced by human doings. McKibben asserts:

> When I say that we have ended nature, I don't mean, obviously, that natural processes have ceased—there is still sunshine and still wind, still growth, still decay. Photosynthesis continues, as does respiration. *But we have ended the thing that has, at least in modern times, defined nature for us—its separation from human society.* . . .
>
> We can no longer imagine that we are part of something larger than ourselves—that is what all this boils down to. We used to be. When we were only a few hundred million, or only a billion or two, and the atmosphere had the composition it would have had with or without us, then even Darwin's revelations could in the end only strengthen our sense of belonging to creation; and our wonder at the magnificence and abundance of that creation. And there was the possibility that something larger than us—Francis's God,

Thoreau's Benefactor and Intelligence, Peattie's Supreme Command—reigned over us. We were as bears—we slept less, made better tools, took longer to rear our young, but we lived in a world that we found made for us. . . . But now *we* make that world, affect its every operation.

Why Danto should have called McKibben to mind is easy to see. The titles alone—*After the End of Art* and *The End of Nature*—signal their kinship. Both propose the recognition of a core transformation, manifest as the loss of a primary human concept, and both ask how we propose to live on in what amounts to a new order. I almost wrote "live on bereft," but very likely few people have any awareness that something may have happened—many, indeed, live on as if Copernicus had not come along. That is, their conceptions of art and nature, insofar as they have such conceptions, remain intact. Nature equates to wooded landscapes and national parks, art to paintings in museums, full stop. But even the unreflective must feel at times a sense of great barometric shifts taking place in the atmosphere they inhabit, and they cannot be entirely unanxious about what such shifts may signify.

Danto's and McKibben's scenarios combined in my thoughts with forceful consequence. No doubt they exacerbated my own tendency to pessimistic brooding about the future. I know that I woke one day with a pressing conviction: that if there is any figurative truth to these two assessments, then we must think about the possibility of a third, a kind of summa. And this would be that in spite of the fact that various biological constants remain—the human need for food, shelter, and procreation—and despite the nominal survival of any number of fundamental social institutions, enough has changed, *is* changing, at a root level to allow us to say that human life as we have known it and characterized it in our figures of speech, our collective myths, our movies and novels and advertisements, scarcely exists anymore. We are in a new system, a new arrangement, one that has become estranged from the defining former norms, even as we continue to look back at them for orientation and solace.

This is, granted, wide-eyed, and so general as to seem useless, and anyone who cares to will be able to name enough things that are unchanged to make the assertion—and its proponent—seem unbalanced. But might it not, for many others of us, serve to underscore a feeling we share all too often, that something in the fundamental order of things has slipped out of plumb? It won't be the first time a change like this has been noted. Think of Virginia Woolf's famous observation that "on or about December, 1910, human character changed." Did it? Who will say? What criteria will we invoke? The questions are not to be answered. We only know that her words corresponded enough to what many others thought, or felt, that they were much repeated—indeed, became one of the best-known diagnostic assessments of the modern period.

Let this be the spirit and the frame of reference. I am not saying that human life or human possibility has ended, only that the terms are no longer those assumed in our central artistic expressions since at least the Renaissance.

With this strange yoking of Danto and McKibben I have honed in on my own fear, which is that in some way that vitally impinges on the psyche, we are coming to live in an "after the end" period; that the collective sense of the millennium itself may be shaped by this strange apprehension. What does it mean?

To understand "living after the end" we must see that what has ended is not any one thing but the whole ordering—the dynamics of scale and connectedness—that had become the basis of meaning and of our idea of the human. Within that organic complex were woven deep assumptions about time, space, nature, human autonomy, societal connectedness, and a good many other things. These, separately and together, have in a short period of time sustained an unprecedented pressure.

And yet we remain—do we not?—recognizably the same basic creatures. And we persist in holding to the idea of continuity, in refusing the possibility that, in William Butler Yeats's words, "All's changed, changed utterly." That doggedness of refusal may itself be taken as an impulse to cohesion— a conservatism—mightier than any transfiguration. This, too, is an exciting thought: that we may yet prevail as ourselves, even as we move, individually and collectively, into an electronic connectedness that has us sacrificing attributes and reflexes one would have thought absolutely defining. Maybe the citizen of the near future, maneuvering among apparatuses and devoting his day to circulating data through far-flung circuits, is more like than unlike his preelectronic counterpart who moved real things with his hands and inhabited a silence, an isolation, that was deep and resonant. Who will say? And how far would we need to move into the realms of the virtual before that resemblance really changed?

When I was younger I was fascinated by a philosophical riddle of sorts that I had encountered in Miguel de Unamuno's *The Tragic Sense of Life*. There he described a ship that left its home port and sailed around the world. At every port of call, some parts of the vessel were replaced, until, finally, not an original nail remained. Only the name was the same. Was it, Unamuno demanded, the same ship? And if so, why?

I see that I am worrying a similar problem these days. How much change can the fundamental human prototype—whatever that might be—take before we have to retire the old terminologies and come up with something new? Can we sustain indefinitely a divorce from the natural world—its seasons, its creatures, its original wildness—and the breaching of our essential solitude in a condition of dissolved interconnectedness? Can we lose track entirely of the space-time perceptions that were so long believed to be hardwired into our cognitive engines? Can we mutate endlessly in adaptation to a riot of new forces, moving with each step further from our origins, and still harken to the old paradigmatic images and expressions of the human? Is it silly to be asking these questions?

Let me conclude with two passages drawn from E. M. Forster's hair-raisingly dystopic story, "The Machine Stops," wherein he has imagined a future gone virtual in the extreme. Individuals live in hexagonal cells, their every need secured, and devote themselves almost exclusively to the exchange of information and ideas by means of a peculiar apparatus that can put them into instant contact with others anywhere in the world. The totality of technologies and operations is called "the machine," and although it is known by all to be a human, not a godly, creation, after a time people begin to revere it as if it were, indeed, a deity.

The conflict in the story is between a mother, Vashti, who has become a believer, and her son, Kuno, who alone has rebelled, seeking out the mysteries of the world so long ago transcended. Returning from the aboveground realm to which he has journeyed, Kuno reports:

> You know that we have lost the sense of space. We say 'space is annihilated,' but we have annihilated not space, but the sense thereof. We have lost a part of ourselves. I determined to recover it and I began by walking up and down the platform of the railway outside my room. Up and down, until I was tired, and so did recapture the meaning of 'near' and 'far.' 'Near' is a place to which I can get quickly *on my feet*, not a place to which the train or air-ship will take me quickly. 'Far' is a place to which I cannot get quickly on my feet. . . . Man is the measure. That was my first lesson. Man's feet are the measure for distance, his hands are the measure for ownership, his body is the measure for all that is lovable and desirable and strong.

Vashti will not accept Kuno's understanding, not until the very end, when the machine—the whole imponderable totality of it—breaks down. Universal horror and anguish ensue. Mother and son, finding one another, burst into tears; they reconcile:

> They wept for humanity, those two, not for themselves. They could not bear that this should be the end. Ere silence was completed their hearts were opened, and they knew what had been important on earth. Man, the flower of all flesh, the noblest of all creatures visible, man who had once made god in his image, and had mirrored his strength on the constellations, beautiful naked man was dying, strangled in the garments he had woven. Century after century he had toiled, and here was his reward. Truly the garment had seemed heavenly at first, shot with the colours of culture, sewn with the threads of self-denial. And heavenly it had been so long as it was a garment and no more, so long as man could shed it at will and live by the essence that is his soul, and the essence, equally divine, that is his body.

And this, I believe, is where the line gets drawn, where we determine whether change has been integrated or has led to deformation. Can we differentiate those essences of soul and body from the garment we have woven? I have faith that we still can, though not as naturally and effortlessly as we once may have. If we have a millennial task, it will be to keep the blade of discrimination whetted.

SVEN BIRKERTS *is the author of* The Gutenberg Elegies: The Fate of Reading in an Electronic Age, Readings, *and the editor of* Graywolf Forum One: Tolstoy's Dictaphone: Technology and the Muse. *He teaches at Mount Holyoke College, is a member of the core faculty of the Bennington Writing Seminars, and lives in Arlington, Massachusetts.*

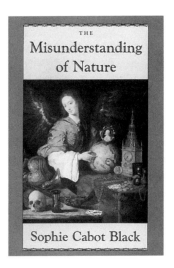

SOPHIE CABOT BLACK

The Misunderstanding of Nature

The Converted

When those doves come for their evening weep
And the last sun kneels till the lawn is lit
From underneath,

When the tiny bats begin their arcs around the porch
And the older goats remember,
Running for the stable door,

The sky cracks again; the inexhaustible pours in.

Breezes swing down into fields, amulets.
Leaves chatter against the flagstone. Each house steadies
Into night like an airplane, silver propellers of light

Nosing out. The dog stands in front of the TV: Heston
Is Moses and Moses in color. Suddenly all is conspiracy.
Night dark pushes out the cold stone of moon; each lightbulb

Chooses a star to convert, to bring down.

If Only for a Little While

I dream of a crowded street where I break
A kiss into your mouth; instead my windows
Are darkened with curtains and in fear

I want to hide you, your sigh, my hand
Cupping your fast breath so those who walk by
Will not hear. We do even this honest thing

Wrong and lie down again in the necessary
Doubt of our age, believing we should have been
Braver at the start, when in some bewildering

Moment I began to move fingers down
Through a moss so original it became secret,
Became home. To stay just awhile, to stay awake

For now as your throat trembles I hold you
All the way through, to finish what's begun.

The Misunderstanding of Nature

I cannot stop watching her and thinking
Of ways to follow. Against the window
Her urgent spring buds strangle,

Summer aches with what longs to loosen,
A wet fall leaf hits clapboards. By winter
She pulls back into ice, but even then gives herself away;

To push myself right up to her, looking hard into
What it is she leaves behind. I believed I'd learn
How to change my life, like getting in a car and slamming the pedal

Until it goes into beauty then beyond
Beauty, then staying there until my blood also starts
To give itself away. Only I am still

In my own room, talking myself into a new gratitude.
Each evening a transaction breaks the landscape:
A child at the door, the cow crossing to the barn.

Only then does the light finally change. The child
Wants to know about trees not growing to the sky,
About rivers running north, about the length of night;

The cow makes deep sounds, the old complaint,
And the light falls suddenly like that,
Down into patient arms

Yet has been falling all afternoon, giving itself away: the great
Wheel turns, gently passes over mountains,
Over their dark green breath, over my blood

That curls and uncurls waiting, over all that time
I was sure something was wrong,
Over those democracies she will always bring

Of cow, ice, light, and child.
Each with a gift for the other: it is perhaps
Without waiting or corresponding to anything at all.

SOPHIE CABOT BLACK's *first collection of poetry is* The Misunderstanding of Nature, *winner of the Poetry Society of America's Norma Farber First Book Award. Among her awards and honors are the Grolier Poetry Prize and the John Masefield Memorial Award from the Poetry Society of America. She lives in New York City.*

LOUIS EDWARDS

Ten Seconds

And He Was 27 Years Old...

He is standing at the back entrance to the shop. He has just walked in from
the field. The shop is a big tin shed of a building where the machinists do
their work and where all of the craftsmen—carpenters, pipefitters, welders,
and machinists, too—have their lockers, a place where they all congregate
when they're on breaks, during any free time. The workers call it "the
house." When it is almost quitting time, a man still in the field might look
at his watch and say to his partner, "Let's head for the house." The ceiling is
high above, so the shop isn't nearly as hot as it might be. The floor is a deep
gray marble-smooth concrete. A long ten-foot-wide path runs north-south
through the middle of the shop, front to back. The north half of the shop,
the front end, the end closest to the entrance gate of the refinery, is mainly
the locker area. There are pale green benches about eighteen inches off the
floor placed in front of each row of lockers. The men sit here and drink cof-
fee from Styrofoam cups and tell jokes during the breaks. Another path
runs east-west, dividing this area from the machinists' work area. This
walkway leads to an air-conditioned trailer outside, on the west side of the
shop, about twenty yards away across a gravel lot where the workers pick up
their paychecks every other Tuesday. To the east, this walkway leads to dou-
ble doors that open to a dark, stuffy hall that turns to the right. About mid-

way down the hall on the left are the restrooms; at the end is light—the lunchroom. The south half of the shop is the area where the machinists work. It is a danger area. Even if there were no caution signs, drilling sounds, buzzing saws, or shooting sparks and flying iron filings, the missing fingers would be warning enough. The wide garagelike rear entrance, the one Eddie has reached, places you right in this area. He has been standing, just outside the shop, kicking gravel. His eyes have been staring down for a few seconds through safety glasses at his black work boots, following them as they move like the feet of a procrastinating child, one digging under the rocky surface, then the other swinging lightly over the gravel, both becoming coated with the floury gravel dust. He is afraid to look up (though he knows he is about to) and into the machinists' area, where they are still working (there are still a few minutes before the last break). He is afraid that if he looks up he will see all kinds of ugly memories. He will see what resembles to him a kind of war zone. A scene complete with a frightening clamor, buddies falling, and teamwork with an obscured purpose. To him it is not a house; it is a hell. (When someone in the field says to him, "Let's go to the house," he thinks to himself, "Okay, if we must, let's go to hell.") If he looks up he will not see men smiling beneath hard hats and behind safety glasses saying "Howdy" like in the films they show sometimes. He will see men struggling. Men fighting for survival. He will see blood. The blood of those who did not make it. Men like Malcolm. Malcolm fell so quietly, they told Eddie later, that it must have been five minutes before Moonie looked down and saw him lying still, unconscious on the floor, blood oozing from a hole in his chest made by a drill bit as thick as a finger. "Jesus!" Moonie yelled. "Somebody help me! Somebody help me!" No one heard him over the din and through the earplugs, but his arms were flailing so wildly that he drew Clem Landry's attention. Clem rushed over to where Malcolm lay, followed quickly by Roger Hebert, Joe Phillips, and the rest of the shop. Then the place was complete madness. Screaming. Men running to Safety to get the doctor and the nurse. Others hurrying to tell the foremen who were in their offices at the two front corners of the shop. The blood was beginning to spread across the floor, so the crowd around Malcolm kept a five-foot radius between him and themselves. They were silent. Some of them exchanged glances with one another, then they looked over at Roger Hebert, the senior machinist under whom Malcolm was an apprentice. They shook their heads. Hadn't the dumb-ass shown the man how to operate the fuckin' drill properly? Probably not, knowing him. Yep, it looked like another classic fuck-up by old R. H. He hadn't long ago taken his own left index finger and two years ago his pinky on the same hand. Johnny Dixon always told the story about how R. H. had once tried to use a welder's torch to cut some old scrap metal to take home from the plant, and he had somehow managed to burn his right foot in half. R. H. always swore that the ugly, crescent-shaped scar on his right forearm was from when he was in the war, but no one believed him. And now this. This was too much for even old R. H. A lot of guys didn't have fingers, but they had never killed anybody. And there was no doubt: Malcolm was dead.

Moonie was apparently the only one who thought about Eddie out in the field not knowing. He waited for the doctor to get there, confirm things, and send for the ambulance, then whispered to his foreman that he was going out to tell Eddie. Moonie, a good old guy, pushing fifty. Just about the only one Eddie thought didn't have "nigger" on the tip of his tongue. (The graffiti on the bathroom walls told you what they were thinking.) They had worked together a couple of times on the same jobs, Eddie helping to reconnect some engines Moonie had repaired. They got along well. Once, Moonie even sat with Malcolm and Eddie at one of the black tables in the lunchroom. It was no big deal, didn't make anybody give any funny looks their way or anything like that. It was just that nobody ever did it. But Moonie was different. He had picked up on the friendship between Eddie and Malcolm and wanted Eddie to find out as soon as possible.

Eddie was out at the Cat Cracker removing the giant nuts that held on the heads of the filtering vessels, so that the lines and the screens could be cleaned out. He fought with the hydraulic wrench that clack-clacked away at the stubborn nuts. Sweat drained from his forehead into his eyes, blurring his vision. Only eleven o'clock and already hot as hell. The acid air of the plant made it hard for him to breathe. He felt he would never get used to this air. He'd been working here for seven years, and it still choked him sometimes. As he wiped away the sweat from his eyes, he looked up and saw Moonie running in the direction of the Cat Cracker. Automatically he knew something was wrong. Nobody ever ran while out in the field, at least not in the direction Moonie was running and not at eleven in the morning. If anybody ran, it was only someone unlucky enough to be still in the field when the whistle blew to signal the day's end—and then he ran toward the gate. He didn't even have his toolbox, so he wasn't headed to work on an emergency job. Eddie started to lock the wrench on another nut, keeping a view of Moonie in the corner of his eye. He slowed to a jog as he got closer to the Cat Cracker. Then he stopped. Eddie could feel his stare. He turned and faced Moonie. Mouth wide open, the aging, overweight man was huffing up a storm. He doesn't even run to the gate at quitting time, Eddie thought. He gripped his side and bent over for a moment, squinting his eyes, trying to shield himself from sunlight and pain. Then he straightened up a little and waved for Eddie to come to him. Eddie released the pressure in the wrench. Whatever it was that was wrong had something to do with him. He hopped off the platform that held the wrench and half-smiled his way over to Moonie. No one who was watching would know his fear. He slapped Moonie on the back. "What's up, old man?" "Eddie," he said, "there's been a real bad accident at the shop. Malcolm. He's hurt real, real bad. Well, he's not gonna make it. I mean he didn't make it. Malcolm is dead. It just now happened. We don't know how. I just turned around and looked and saw him on the ground. A drill bit some kinda way in his chest. A freak accident." They started to run toward the shop together. "I'm sorry I'm the one to have to tell you. But I just wanted you to find out right away. I mean I figured you'd want to know right away. Dr. Moore is there and it's an ambulance on the way." Moonie stopped running. "You go on," he shouted at Eddie's back.

Eddie heard "Malcolm is dead" over and over again as he ran. Malcolm is dead. And as he ran, he saw his best friend and himself sitting at the bar of their favorite nightclub, The Landing. Just last week. It was Thursday. Ladies' Night. A couple of married men, twenty-seven-year-olds, watching the ladies. Even though Malcolm had been separated from Pam for a while now, Eddie still considered them together. He would always see them together. Somehow the security of his own relationship with Betty depended on Malcolm and Pam still being together. When Eddie thought about their separation, he would see Malcolm and Pam dancing together or laughing or holding hands, and he would hear his own voice, muted, chanting in his head like a Greek chorus: "It's a shame. It's a damned shame. It's a shame. It's a damned shame." He preferred to think of Malcolm the way he was now, sitting here watching the babes. The two of them with wives waiting at home. Yes, he and Malcolm were just two old married men up to no good, the way they should be. They were drinking beer, smoking cigarettes, just a warm-up for later. Eddie had some good smoke in the car. Malcolm didn't usually get high, but he didn't mind if Eddie did. He always talked about how good it smelled. Eddie was saying what he wanted to do to this cute little light-skinned chick standing over by the DJ's booth. Malcolm just nodded and laughed his big happy laugh, like a boy, those lines jutting down from his cheeks and almost meeting at his chin. "Yeah, right," he said. "You're nothin but talk, buddy. Betty would kill you." No, she'd just leave me, Eddie thought beneath his "Nigger, you must be crazy." She had said many times she would and he believed her. (She had ways of making him believe her when she said certain things.) That's why he had to keep secrets, even from Malcolm. He couldn't take the chance of telling even Malcolm. And he felt a real sense of guilt about this, too. It was his obligation to give the details to his buddies. He had shared information with the fellas for as long as he could remember. That was part of the sport as he knew it.

But Malcolm didn't give Eddie the details of his affairs—if, indeed, he had any. (Malcolm had *never* told, though; he was, for reasons Eddie had no inclination to question, exempt from this part of their code. He had always been.) If Malcolm had never been with any woman other than Pam, it would not have surprised Eddie, because Malcolm could be so conservative about certain things. Like not smoking marijuana. And all he ever drank was light beer. If Eddie didn't have marijuana in the car, he'd be drinking Chivas Regal on the rocks. They had already graduated from high school by the time Malcolm started saying the word "fuck" with anything close to conviction. Nope. Maybe he wasn't keeping any secrets from Eddie. Maybe he'd never been to the Chelsea Motel on Hawkins Street in the north end of the city, not four blocks from his own house and Lancaster Park. Maybe Malcolm had never been there at all. Fifteen dollars for four hours. More time than you ever needed. "Nigger, you must be crazy."

"No," said Malcolm. "I'm not crazy and neither is Betty."

"Don't worry about me, chief. I can take care of *my* house—" Eddie tried to stop himself, but it had already slipped out sounding just that way, with ugly implications. Fucking light beer. Not enough real stuff in his system yet to keep him from being clumsy and dangerous. "I didn't mean—" he tried to clean it up. "I didn't mean it like that, Malcolm, you know."

"It ain't no big deal, Eddie," Malcolm said. "Why do you have to make it such a big deal? You don't see me cryin about it." He smiled, a V starting at his chin. "Did you see me cry one day about it?" Eddie just shrugged. "No," Malcolm said. "That's because I never did. There was nothing to cry about. It was just time to go our separate ways."

"Yeah, but shit, man," Eddie started slowly. "I-I-I don't understand. I mean what about the baby? Don't you want to, you know, be around? Watch him grow up and shit?"

"It's not like I left town without telling anybody. I see them all the time. I keep in touch. Hey—I don't brag about it but, you know, I'm really not a bad father. I'm really kinda good to tell you to the truth."

Eddie sipped his beer and turned to watch the people out on the dance floor. There was nothing for him to say. He was in no position to give anyone any advice. Malcolm probably was a good father, a better one than Eddie was living in the same house with his children. He took Betty and his kids for granted, he knew. Talking to Malcolm like this might make him go home tonight and tiptoe or stumble into his children's bedroom, still kind of high, and kiss them, but tomorrow or Saturday for sure, he'd be out here again. Home was too restrictive, too small, without enough chances for adventure. Out here was the place to be. Wide open. Out here anything could happen. There was always the chance to catch a high. There were friends, there was booze, there was dope. There were women. They were chances, too; they could be the best highs. There was a hotel he could afford. This was his life. Maybe he would outgrow it someday—and according to Betty he would have to—but right now, he could not resist it. Out here was the place to be. And yet—he couldn't see himself ever giving up Betty the way Malcolm had given up Pam. His life with her was a long way from being hopeless. He needed her. When he was away from her, like now, her restrictiveness became reassuring, like a safety net. And a lot of times, after their arguments, she was a high.

Malcolm tapped him on his shoulder. "Come on. Let's go. I feel like smoking a J."

"You?" Eddie teased. "What is the world coming to?"

They walked outside and stood in front of the club, breathing good air, the music sounding muffled, only the boom-boom of the bass drum filtering out to them. A well-lit corner on the strip. Just hangin' out. All of the chances. And Malcolm chuckling beside him like a boy for no reason, stumbling off the curb as they crossed the street, tipsy off of a couple of light beers, asking for a joint just to make Eddie happy. And, yes, he was happy, because for him, this moment represented the only kind of perfection he knew. He wanted to stand here on this street corner, just helping Malcolm gather his footing and stand up straight, forever.

"Malcolm is dead," Eddie kept hearing as he raced to the shop. As he got closer, he saw the flashing lights, and the siren that had been only an eerie, barely audible musical accompaniment to his thoughts began to register as belonging to an ambulance and not as being a regular plant alarm. He knew that he would not cry no matter how awful it was; he never cried. That was one thing he never had to worry about. If one of them had to be killed here, it was better that it was Malcolm—because if Eddie had been killed, Malcolm would have cried like a baby. You couldn't trust him about things like that. He didn't care enough about what they thought. If Eddie would start bitching to him about something one of them had said to him under his breath or a dirty look one of them had given him, Malcolm would always end up trying to calm him down and say that none of it really mattered. He would start talking about something else. Eddie could tell that he genuinely believed that it didn't really matter. Malcolm had acquired an attitude about a year ago that said nothing on earth really mattered. It wasn't a cynical attitude, however, and, as far as Eddie could tell, it had nothing to do with religion. It was as though he had found the answer to all of his problems. When he and Pam split up, he hadn't missed a beat. The separation seemed to make him happy somehow. He seemed to accept it as part of the plan for his life. That was, it seemed, how he had started to take everything—just as part of the plan for his life. Eddie had yearned for Malcolm to explain it all to him, to tell the source of his ability to look at the world this way. But he knew they never talked about such things; they only put out signals for each other to read. Even Eddie's yearning to know Malcolm's secret was so quiet that he wasn't really aware of the existence of his own desire, which, though only a whisper, amounted to desperation. Still, Eddie had thought that somehow Malcolm would manage to share with him what seemed to be a liberating truth. But no—not now. Malcolm is dead, and he will never be able to reveal to Eddie in some moment filled with one of their silent dialogues what he believed now, while caught in the throes of this tragedy, might have been the key to life, maybe to death, salvation.

But whatever Malcolm's new vision had been, it didn't stop him from crying; Eddie had seen him. At a movie, for Christ's sake. And if Eddie had been lying dead in the shop, Malcolm would definitely have cried, because it didn't matter what they thought. And they would have eaten it up. See the monkey cry. "The only place for a nigger is the zoo with his (pri)mate." That's what the bathroom wall said.

Eddie slowed up as he reached the shop. He could see the paramedics carrying the stretcher because the wheels wouldn't roll on the gravel. Malcolm lay upon it with the metal protruding up from his chest. Eddie walked closer, close enough to touch the body. The paramedics stopped; something about Eddie said they had to. Eddie could feel the eyes upon him. He would not cry. He looked at Malcolm's face and let the blankness he saw there move into the deepest part of himself, shielding his soul from the bombardment of his emotions. From this moment on, even in the most private times, he would never be able to grieve deeply for Malcolm. The paramedics said there was nothing they could do; they were taking him to St. Patrick's. It was the procedure; they were sorry. Then they slid the stretcher into the ambulance, slammed the doors, and drove off. Nobody said anything about Eddie's riding to the hospital, so he figured that doing so must not be the way these things worked. Not part of the procedure. He tried not to think of Malcolm's chest, but it remained fixed in his mind, a shot through the heart, blood soaking through in one massive, dark, wet patch on his old faded green T-shirt. An ugly wound. John Parker, the pipe fitter foreman, came over and told Eddie to come with him to his office; it might be better if he went on home. They walked through the back entrance of the shop. Parker tried to block the puddle from Eddie's view, but it was no use. It was the only spot in the shop that mattered. The flies knew. Eddie stopped. "They're gonna clean it up right away," Parker said. "Jerry!" he yelled too loudly into the unusual silence. "Get Cooper over here to clean this up!" The eyes of the other men nudged Eddie along, and he walked away from the puddle.

Yes, Malcolm is dead, he is thinking, standing with his head down, watching his boots, but about to look up. Dead almost two months. When he looks up he will feel it all, this one time. He will see it all in even greater detail than those who were actually there. Even Moonie had not seen Malcolm fall, but Eddie will. He will see Malcolm fall, and he will see Moonie turning and seeing him lying on the ground. He will see the crowd gather around Malcolm and he will see the eyes accusing R. H. He will see the blood and he will see the flies. He will see it all. And he will hear everything, too. All of the clanging and banging, the metallic buzzing, a scream perhaps. And it will all amount to one sound—the sound of the single shot, Malcolm's, which no one heard: *Pow*!

Now he looks up. Oh, no. Oh, yes. He has seen this all before.

LOUIS EDWARDS *is the author of* N: A Romantic Mystery *and* Ten Seconds. *He grew up in Lake Charles, Louisiana, and worked for many years for the New Orleans Jazz & Heritage Festival and the JVC JAZZ Festival—New York.*

PERCIVAL EVERETT

Watershed

Landscapes Evolve Sequentially

except under extraordinary provocation, or in circumstances not at all to be ap-prehended, it is not probable that as many as five hundred Indian warriors will ever again be mustered at one point for a fight; and with the conflicting interests of the different tribes, and the occupation of the intervening country by advanc-ing settlements, such an event as a general Indian war can never occur in the United States. (Edward Parmelee Smith, 1873)

༈

My blood is my own and my name is Robert Hawks. I am sitting on a painted green wooden bench in a small Episcopal church on the northern edge of the Plata Indian Reservation, holding in my hands a Vietnam-era M-16, the butt of the weapon flat against the plank floor between my feet. There are seven other armed people sitting on the floor, backs against the paneled walls, or pacing and peering out the windows—stained and clear— at the armored personnel carrier some hundred yards away across the dirt and gravel parking lot, and at the pasture where two sad-looking bulls stand, their sides, black and gray, flat against the sky behind them. Out there, there are two hundred and fifty police—FBI, all clad in blue windbreakers with large gold letters, and National Guardsmen, looking like the soldiers they want to be. There is an FBI agent sitting in a chair opposite me; his hands are bound with yellow nylon cord; his mouth is ungagged; his feet are bare and rubbing against each other in this cold room. The hard look he had worn just hours ago has faded and, although his blue eyes show no fear, the continual licking of his lips betrays him. His partner, a shorter, wider man, is face down on the ground outside; his blood and last heat having melted the snow beneath him. He lies dead between two dead Indians, brothers, twins.

That I should feel put out or annoyed or even dismayed at having to tell this story is absurd since I do want the story told and since I am the only one who can properly and accurately reproduce it. There is no one else in whom I place sufficient trust to attempt a fair representation of the events—not that the events related would be anything less than factual, but that those chosen for exhibition would not cover the canvas with the stain or underpainting of truth—and of course truth necessarily exists only as perception and its subsequent recitation alters it. But I can tell it, my own incriminations aside.

⁊

The insignificant point of light on the ceiling seemed to dilate as I watched, and I wondered how it was that the perforation would not let in enough light to illuminate even a section of the poorly lit room, but could allow in enough water to ruin the entire house; how it had to be in some way dark to see the distending prick, but water would always find me in there. I slapped myself for pondering like an idiot and did the only thing that made any sense: I grabbed my vest, the box of flies I'd tied the previous night, and my sixty-year-old Wright and McGill bamboo rod that no one could believe I actually got wet, much less used, and went fishing.

⁊

Nymphs are meant to be fished near or on the bottom of the water and so must absorb moisture and/or be weighted so they get to the bottom quickly. The mate-

rials of their construction must give the appearance of life, suggesting the movement of a living insect in its larval or nymphal stage, its pulsing, vibrating. The fish get close to it, without the concern of the surface predators, and take a good look, and so it must be lifelike.

⅋

My father had never liked fishing. It seemed enough to him that my grandfather, his father, hunted and fished. My grandfather never pushed the idea on him, however. In fact, he confided in me that he understood my father needed the difference between them as a necessary point of divergence. "We're so much alike," he would say, then make a cast or load his rifle or rip the guts out of a fish in one quick motion. Indeed, he and my father looked enough alike to be brothers and to my mind, in matters all but those having to do with the outdoors, they shared the same beliefs. They were both physicians and both well liked, though to hear them speak you'd have assumed they found people objectionable and you would have been right, but it was people, not persons, who were problematic, they would articulately point out. They hated America, policemen, and especially churches. Their outright detestation for Christianity—it was much more than a simple disregard—had ended their marriages: my grandfather had known full well that his wife was a member of the AME Church but had hoped that he could live with it; my father claimed that my mother had found religion and bushwhacked him one day with a prayer at the dinner table. My grandmother died when I was ten and we went to the funeral, Christian service and all, and my aunt shouted at my grandfather, called him a heathen. She then turned to my father and said, "You're just as bad." She then knelt in front of me and tried to be nice, offering me a Lifesaver—I said, "Blow it out your barracks bag." After my parents' divorce I lived with my mother, and the religious stuff weighed heavily on me, my being convinced that one had to be in some way born Christian because there was not a genuflecting bone in my body, and so my mother and I lived with our horns locked. The religious stuff became a lot more important than it should have been, as I did not actively dislike it, but simply did not care. When I was twelve, I went to live with my father and grandfather, whom "I was just like," and for four and a half years until I left for college, I watched the two of whom it would sccm I was a pretty faithful copy.

ॐ

The fishing turned out to be slow—I took three trout in a couple of hours, all on a store-bought Royal Coachman. I hated the generalized flies, the ones that didn't look like some particular insect native to the water but that because of their color or glitter caused the fish to strike them out of interest or anger or whatever, but I enjoyed following the green-and-red fly whiz through the air and light with its stark white calf-hair wings on the surface of the water. Anyway, the fish were small and I let them go. I switched to a hare's ear nymph and began to have pretty good success, starting on a string of keepers.

ॐ

Before I came out here to the cabin, to fish and think and be alone, I was in the city with Karen, a woman I had been fucking. I decided on this term for our interaction, having found disfavor with the term relationship and seeing that I had simply and stupidly fallen into something out of convenience and, sadly, habit and, as with most things entered into easily, extricating myself turned out to be decidedly more difficult. Her voice grated on me, as did her attitudes and disposition, and finally her smells, but still I would lie between her legs again and again, pathetically seeking release or simply seeking.

"This is not a good time to go fishing," Karen had said, sitting at the kitchen table in my apartment, drumming her nails against the Formica, her index finger striking the place that had been chipped when I dropped my binoculars some months earlier. I just stood there, in sort of agreement, sort of nodding. We had been arguing, about what exactly was unclear now, but it had come, as it always did, to my defending myself by telling her that I did indeed care about her and that I did want to make her happy. As the discussion wore on I realized my lie and wanted to tell her that indeed I was not in love with her, never had been in love with her and, further, believed completely that she was too insane to be capable of love herself. Karen was a smart person and not unreasonable, but she wouldn't let me talk, wouldn't take a breath, and, sadly, as I was forced to listen now, was saying nothing new. "So, are you going fishing?" she had asked. Her drumming stopped.

Her words had sounded exactly like, "I dare you to go fishing." I studied her eyes and felt sick to my stomach at how I, in some way, genuinely detested her and her ways and here she was again daring me to do what I had done so many times before. I had been chanting in my head, and perhaps she heard it, that this was the last time, that this time I meant it, that there was no coming back, that I was turning the corner, no longer the weak man I had proven myself to be. I had said, "Yes."

"Why!?" she had screamed, her voice much louder than her size. "Because you need to get away from me? Am I that awful?"

"No, because I want to go fishing. I like fishing. It relaxes me."

"And I don't relax you?!"

ॐ

That had been some weeks ago, just more than a month, when I had left Karen for the third and last time and come to the mountains. The weather was turning colder, with stiff winds from the northwest pressing through the canyons. I wondered if the fishing was relaxing me. It made the days pass and I was at least obliged to use my hands, for repairs on the cabin and tying flies—my hands needing the work, my eyes needing the attention to detail. And the fish didn't yell at me. They more often than not ignored me, but they didn't yell at me. I watched the no. 12 hare's ear I had tied the night before land and sink beneath the surface of the water.

ॐ

Hook: Mustad 9674
Thread: Reddish or dark brown
Tail: Brown or ginger hackle fibers (1½ gap widths in length)
Rib: Fine gold tinsel
Abdomen: Hare's mask and ear dubbing fur blend

Wing case: Gray duck-wing quill section (folded over)
Thorax: Same as abdomen
Legs: Guard hairs plucked from under thorax with a dubbing needle

❦

I had a string of six decent browns wrapped in newspaper. I took them down to the little store at the junction of the highway and the road off which I lived, hoping I could trade them for sundries.

"Hi, hon," Clara said as I walked in. She was a rough-looking woman with a soft, pleasant voice that came from beneath a massive mound of white hair and from behind oversized, red-framed bifocals. The glasses were new, one in a long line of pairs, as it seemed the woman was unable to locate her glasses once removed from her narrow face and set on some surface.

"Clara." I greeted her at the old brass-scrolled register she sat behind in the front of the store. Light found its way through the collecting clouds and into the store through the painted window beside her. "I brought you some trout. What do you say? Six fish for milk, butter, and eggs?"

"Why them ain't trout," she said, giving the fish a look, lifting her glasses and squinting, then gazing through both lenses of her bifocals. "Them's minnows."

"They told me they were trout."

"It's a deal then," Clara said, no smile, her lips tight. "But remember, I'm doing you a favor."

I felt the woman watching me as I collected the items from the refrigerator on the other side of the store, the air outside the unit fogging up the door as I held it open. I walked back toward her, smiling.

She said, as I dropped the butter on the counter with a thud, "You're pretty ugly for a young feller." She entered the routine smoothly, the same line as always; I assumed she reserved it for all younger men.

"Precocious."

"I call 'em likes I see 'em."

"A fine quality in anyone." I grabbed a loaf of rye bread from the unstable wire rack beside me and took some fruit, three bananas and ten apples, from the big wicker basket on the counter.

"How long do you think that many bananas are going to last you?" Clara asked.

"They get ripe too fast," I told her. "I like them while they're still a little green."

"Go figure ugly guys." She tallied in her head, her eyes disappearing behind the change in her lenses. "Let's call it two bucks."

I gave her the money.

"By the way, your lady friend called," Clara said, opening a paper sack with a snap and setting it on the counter. She looked at the message book she kept by the phone. "Let me see. She said call her back." My hands found the groceries and began to bag them. "You're welcome," she said. She watched me load the fruit into the bag. "So, you gonna call her?"

"What do you think I should do?"

"A feller what looks like you? I think you should call."

"You're probably right." I shook my head. "Still, I don't know. I don't know what to say. Suppose you were a woman, what would you want to hear me say?"

"That's why I like you," Clara laughed, then coughed, roughly. "Tell her to cut the crap and get the hell up here so you can frolic and cavort in the deep woods in your all-together. Either that or you go back down there where you can have anxious sex next to a banging radiator and traffic clatter outside the window."

"You do have a way of putting things." But, of course, I was not uncertain whether I should return the call. I felt the easiness of assured resolve, knowing and trusting, finally, my decision to abandon the sickness, as it were.

Clara nodded. "So what are you going to do?"

"I'm going to go home and fix the hole in my roof."

"What is that, some kind of metaphor?"

"Probably."

⅍

The Half-breeds of said tribes, and those persons, citizens of the United States who have intermarried with Indian women of said tribe and continue to

*maintain domestic relations with them, shall not be compelled to remove to said
reservation, but shall be allowed to remain undisturbed upon the lands herein
above ceded and relinquished to the United States.*

⁂

Outside, I fell in behind the wheel of my pickup, turned the key, and heard
the engine try but fail to start. I pumped the gas pedal and turned the key
again. A third time. A fourth. I sighed and leaned forward to rest my head
on the steering wheel. I didn't feel anxious or even put out; that was what
the mountain did for me. So the car wouldn't start—the car could be fixed.
It might take a little time, but time was free and it might take a little money,
but money was just money.

"Pop the hood," a small voice said. I looked out the open window and
saw no one, then glancing slightly downward I found a very short woman.
The woman was the size of a child, with her dark hair pulled tightly back
exposing a largish, almost hooked nose and oddly flat cheekbones. "Pop the
hood," she said again.

"Doesn't need to be popped," I told her and watched her walk around to
the front of my truck. I could see the top of her head as she searched for,
then found and released the hood latch. Then I couldn't see her, but I heard
her climbing onto the bumper as she pushed open the hood, heard her
fumbling around on my engine. I stayed put and waited.

"Try it now," she called.

I turned the key and the truck fired up. The small woman walked
around to the back of the truck. I watched in my mirror as she picked up
a knapsack and stowed it in the bed just behind the cab. She opened the
passenger-side door and climbed in beside me, scooting her butt back into
the seat and fastening the belt. The shoulder strap bothered her face and so
she put it under her arm.

"Thanks," I said to her. "I guess I do owe you a ride. Where am I taking
you?"

"Just go wherever you were going."

"I live twenty-five miles up the road," I said, expecting that to give her
pause.

"That's fine."

"You don't want to go to my house. And there's nothing else up there."

"No, just get me close to the lake."

I looked back over my shoulder into the bed at her pack, red with yellow pockets. She was diminutive, so her clothes were no doubt little, but still her pack seemed slight: no tent, no pad, no sleeping bag. "You don't have much gear," I said. "You know, it gets cold up there."

"Let's just go."

"So, what was wrong with my engine?" I asked, backing away from the planking of the store's porch and driving out onto the road.

"I don't know. I just jiggled a do-hickey."

"You'll have to show it to me. The do-hickey. In case that ever happens again." I glanced at her briefly. "It sounded like the distributor wire was loose." I looked at her again, but she kept her eyes straight ahead. "You know the old trick where you disable a car and then fix it so the person will give you a ride?"

"That's an old trick?" She didn't look at me.

"I've never heard of anybody doing it. Actually, I just thought it up."

"So what you're telling me is that you're paranoid."

"It doesn't sound good when you say it," I said.

The woman laughed. "My name is Louise."

"Robert." I shook her hand, her little bones feeling unreal in my grasp, feeling as though they might break, rolling together under my thumb the way I had once felt my mother's roll together when she was old. After another glance at her gear I asked, "Just planning a hike back down the trail?"

"Yes," Louise said quickly, too quickly, quickly enough to tell me to shut up, quickly enough to raise if not concern, then my curiosity.

I observed her canvas sneakers with their white, semicircled rubber toes, then looked at the slate sky. "You realize it's likely to snow today. I haven't heard the report, but it looks like snow."

Louise looked at the sky, leaning her small frame forward, her dark eyes searching.

"I mention it because of your shoes."

"Oh, I've got boots in my pack."

"I see."

I felt her uneasiness and so I backed off, attending to my driving, putting both hands on the wheel. I hoped that I had not made her feel that I was interested in her. I felt somewhat badly that her size, or lack thereof, had caused me to believe she was not quite capable of taking care of herself. It was a stupid thing to think, but I couldn't deny it, and I recognized and acknowledged once again one of my problems—my inability to deny conveniently some stupidity of mine, even momentarily. It seemed that, at every opportunity, I examined closely the nature, structure, and philosophical ramifications of my stupid feelings, a kind of over-the-top second-order thinking that turned out to be a detaching device rather than a constructive exercise.

I pulled off to the side of the road and stopped. "Well," I said, "my place is a couple of miles down this muffler-buster. The lake and trail head are just half a mile on. Would you like me to drive you the rest of the way?"

"No, that won't be necessary. Thanks for the ride." And she lifted the handle and pushed open the door and got out. She closed the door, went to the back of the truck, and leaned her body over the bed wall to retrieve her pack. She stepped away and waved to me.

I drove on down the lane, watching her grow even smaller in my mirror. She was still standing there when I rounded the bend and lost sight of her.

PERCIVAL EVERETT *is the author of fourteen books of fiction, including* Frenzy, Watershed, *and* Glyph. *His collection of short stories,* Big Picture, *was the recipient of the PEN Oakland-Josephine Miles Award for Excellence in Literature. He is a professor of English at the University of Southern California.*

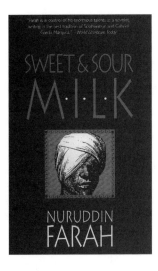

NURUDDIN FARAH

Sweet & Sour Milk

Prologue

Like a baby with a meatless bone in his mouth, a bone given him by his mother to suck while she is in the kitchen minding the pot which has now begun to sing. . . .

There was something very disturbing about his features today, there was something which suggested an untidiness of a sort—rather like a cotton dress washed in salty water and worn until it reeks of human sweat. There was something very vulnerable about his looks, something quite restless. He breathed billows his lungs' size. His tongue, swollen and red, rolled in the discharge of pain. Soyaan held his mother's hand, held it lovingly and tightly, and he pressed it.

"Drink this," she said. "It will do you a lot of good."

A beetle entered, and cut the heat-waves of the room. The beetle headed upwards, it dog-fought with another there, returned and, for a while, circled just a few inches away from Soyaan's eyes. He closed and opened them. This pained his eyes. And the beetle was gone.

"Please drink it up."

But he wouldn't drink the medicinal concoction his mother held in front of his unseeing eyes. Nor would he give a plausible explanation of why he had come home with a stomach disorder. What had he eaten? With whom had he been? What poisonous food had he been given? He had feared that his mother's persistent queries would make a rent in his defensive armour, he had feared that his sister's appeal would make a small tear or two in his cloak of privacy. No fear of that now. For he had become inarticulate with the groans of pain. He need not offer answers to their questions. "Soyaan, my son," his mother had said.

Soyaan: healthy as the antimony of her kohled vision. Never had she known him to fall ill. Never had she known him unwell for long. Unlike Loyaan, his twin brother, unlike his sister Ladan, unlike them both, Soyaan had been a catapult of order; all three were quite unlike their father Keynaan, who was the epitome of hypochondria. But what had Soyaan eaten? What unearthly potions had he taken? What had he come into contact with, whom? Why had he vomited a colourful mixture of vegetables, meat and spaghetti? His skin, for one thing, had turned unpleasantly pale, almost anaemic. His head had become unduly heavy for the rest of his body: to lift it from the pillow, he needed to be helped.

"With your mother's blessing . . . ," she said.

He shook his head. No. He wouldn't take it.

"Please."

She held a straw fan in her hand. With it, she chased away the flies. With it she also dispersed the heat. As she fanned, some of the flies fled, some stirred but remained where they had been, while those which she had struck landed on the floor. They made a pattern there, a pattern ugly and unhealthy.

He wondered if the room could be sprayed. All these flies, mosquitoes. Where there were flies, there were health hazards, inconveniences.

He motioned to her to help him lift his head off the pillow. She put one of her arms under his head and with her other supported the weight of his body—frail and yet heavy-boned. She suffered the painful effort of watching him place a pillow conveniently under his back. She stood back and eased her features into a relaxed smile when she saw him accomplish, with maintained grace, the difficult task of remaining in a propped-up position. Then she nodded an acknowledgment when he mumbled a word of gratitude.

She sighed as she took her seat again. She felt a pain in her back, a pain which reminded her of childbearing and other complications. But she took refuge in the menopausal safety of her age. Thank the Lord: three child-births and a near-fatal fourth; and a terror for a husband. She remembered that Soyaan had vomited all she had forced down his throat. A friend of his, a Dr Ahmed-Wellie, had come and provided another long list of prescriptive remedies. Qumman picked up the straw fan again. She worked herself into a mood of fury, she fanned and she fanned. Abruptly she stopped to inquire if Soyaan would take at least a few spoonfuls of the yogurt he had originally requested.

"No, thank you."

"What is wrong with it?" She looked strangely at the bowl in her hand. She brought it nearer her nose and smelt it. Maybe to sense if he, too, had scented the dash of herbs the traditionalist savant had administered to the yogurt.

Her tone of voice became desperate: "You haven't had anything since yesterday."

That wasn't quite true and she knew it. He had taken a little salted yogurt. When he couldn't stand the taste, he had asked for it to be sugared. But then he still didn't want any of it.

"Loyaan will be here any time now," she told him.

This alerted his tired senses, though his reaction to the news about his twin brother's arrival wasn't instantaneous. First he smiled his pleasure. A little later the lines of his face were cast in a mould of cheer. They hadn't met for several months.

"He should be here any time now."

As Soyaan breathed, his nostrils issued a whistle. His mother helped herself to the yogurt. The family's economy couldn't afford the slightest waste. The house in which they were had only just been paid for. *My precious son*, she said to herself, *we cannot afford to lose you.*

"Before I go, is there anything you specially want me to get for you?" she asked as she touched him, feeling his temperature.

"No."

Her hand pressed his stomach which in reaction made a noise something like a belch. He knitted his brow as though from a fresh start of pain. She smoothed his wrinkles with her open palm.

"All these when you are only twenty-nine!" she commented.

"Please." He pointed at a table by the door. His voice was feeble, his stare pale and unfocused.

On the table to which he pointed there lay, as though on display, an assortment of bottles of various groupings and dimensions. But his mother shook her head determinedly. No, she wouldn't get them for him. No. She wouldn't pass the bottles to him. Not before he promised her something. What? He knew that she had little faith in the miracles of modern medicines. He knew that she would exhaust what little faith she had in them long before the curded taste of malaria tablets melted flat out on the tongue which had drenched them. Qumman made no secret of this. She would argue with sustained passion that she favoured traditional medicines; in the event that they didn't work, then Allah's providential cures. Her sons and daughters found it inexplicably curious that she nevertheless tolerated injections when it really came to making the ultimate choice.

"You don't need any of these," she said.

She went to the table and stood there for a while. She took two of the bottles, one in each hand, and studied them. She held them in front of her and stared at them. Knowing she couldn't read the instructions on the bottles, Soyaan wondered what it was that made her look at them in that strange, bewitched manner.

"If only you heard yourself. Of course, you weren't lucid, and your gaze was fixed on the unclear mist of the mad. Your temperature was exceptionally high. The inconsistencies you speak in your sleep—the obscenities your disturbed sleep utters. Is it that woman who gave you whatever has upset you so terribly?"

"What woman?"

Qumman's mouth opened but closed after only having softly pronounced the first letter of that woman's name. Her tongue had stumbled on the vowel-formation of the name, but she rose, with dignity, before she tripped over the wire trap of unuttered thoughts.

"Decency, mother—and I should like to quote your own words," said Soyaan, "doesn't hide only in the skirt-folds of a young lady of perfumed modesty, whose movements are inconspicuous, unpretentious, a young lady who is discreet. If you pull the string, once you undo the hem—the nude is too obscene and too commonplace whatever the sex. Decency."

She moved away a little, quiet as dust. Her mind settled with and wouldn't do away with the choice she had made. She would not waver like agitated air between this and that pocket of the wind's pressure. She would stay firm.

"You always lose hold of your own reality," she said. "You are very sick. So I suggest you put your trust in us and we will, in no time, loosen *her* grip on your soul."

"Come to the point, Mother."

"You're bewitched, my son."

"No, no. I meant, what was it I said in my disturbed, bewitched sleep?"

"Inconsistencies."

"Be specific, Mother."

"Ask Ladan. Ask your sister." She held the bottles in front of her as before.

"Please," he appealed, looking at the bottled tablets.

"These haven't done you any good, anyhow."

"Just pass them to me." He looked at his watch. Time he took the hourly prescription Ahmed-Wellie had approved of. He should tell her that medicine takes a long time for its effect to work; but he dared not. "Please."

She set the bottles down on the table again. She walked back towards her chair. The floor stirred under her feet. There was a small breeze in the room now that the wind had pushed the window open.

"How about this," his mother challenged: "if I pass them to you and I let you take them, will you do something for me in return?"

"Let's hear it."

"When the sheikh arrives, will you promise not to make a mock of his efforts or deride mine? The Koran is all we know that cures without complications. We'll forget about the yogurt, as a compromise," she bargained.

No word from Soyaan. There was a light scatter of dust falling on the aluminium roof. Qumman looked up at the ceiling while she waited for his response. He looked up from his Neruda. Against the bottles, he noticed now, there stood the family copy of the Koran.

"Promise," he said.

She went out of the room to tell the sheikh to prepare.

Whereupon Soyaan searched for further clues to life's mysteries as he focused his stare on a gecko which moved, with consummate grace, up and down the uneven crevices of the wall in front of him. The silence helped lift the weight off his thoughts. He slowed down. He let his mind sail away. He spread his sailcloth at a very convenient spot. He lay there—feeling light as a sail, fleeing from all but *her*, feeling wanted. *Do enter if you will. I am spread like water. Come into me but slowly, lovingly. . . .*

༄

The water was knee-high. They were in the shallow edge of the sea. Soyaan's friend was fully clothed, as the law of the land required of women. Her dress, recently tailored to order, was low-cut in the front. Her large breasts showed every now and again. The water lapped against her shapely thighs. And the waves, tamed by the shallowness of the water, made her dress detour slightly, made her skirt climb up at the back and stay glued to her gorgeous body. The contours of her beautiful figure mapped their sexual geography.

He had known her for one and a half years, or nearly. He would admit he had enjoyed every moment of it. But there were difficulties to this relationship. Yes, although neither spoke the name, there was another. A man important enough to be recognised in public at every gathering in Mogadiscio. So whenever Soyaan met her, they did so in private.

Now she held him by the ankles. Soyaan's strokes were well-timed. He swam like a professional. He let his long arms descend upon the water from as far and as high as he could stretch them. He dived and remained under the water for as long as his lungs could hold out. The solidity of his body in the water's transparency flowed into ripples of fantasy. She pulled him upwards, catching him by the hair. They embraced. She gently kissed him. When she let him go, he swam away, his strokes superbly executed. She went over to where he now was.

"I've enjoyed reading it," she said.

"I was wondering how you found it." But he didn't wait to say any more.

He made a dive, improvised and clumsy. She followed him in. She couldn't stay under for as long as he did. The sea spat her out. Up and out, and she panted. She waited for him to re-emerge.

When he did, she asked, "Has anybody else seen it?"

"Why?"

"Dangerous stuff."

"Do you think so?"

"It certainly is a strong political statement."

He made no comment. He swam away doing the butterfly. He returned. He joined her where the water had been breast-high. They swam together. He stopped. He splashed water up at the heavens. He swallowed a mouthful.

"Can you hold on to it for me?

"Of course."

They came out. They still believed they had the beach to themselves.

§

She wrote his name on the sand. The sea washed away her writing. They silently watched the water recede. He wished he could read her message in the water receding. She wished she could make him see reason about the political statement he had made. Would he?

"You haven't shown it to anybody else, have you?"

He didn't reply. He tugged at the string of his swimming-suit tied tightly around his waist. He was a hairy man. Tall. Slim. And handsome. She was a few inches shorter than he. When they both stretched their arms out, side by side with their shoulders nearly touching, it appeared that they were the same height. He dug his big toe into the sand. And he was ready to change the topic.

"How is the little angel?" he asked.

"Growing wings of youth, independence and teeth."

A spatter of water fell on to Soyaan's forehead. He looked up. No, to describe accurately: he started. He stared up in surprise. There was a small child dripping sandy water, a child barely two who stood above him. The child's smile lit a fire of delight in Soyaan's eyes whose lids had opened to reveal sparkles of his memory's dotage. The little angel had grown wings of youth, independence and teeth. But the newly arrived child wouldn't go, nor would he speak and explain how he came to be there. Soyaan gazed up at the child. His sight was now misted with unexplained mysteries and the child's sudden appearance from nowhere. The child did not return Soyaan's solicitous greetings. Nor did he respond to the woman's queries, but milled around without speaking. The name of a man came to Soyaan's and her mind, a name which both found convenient to immediately consign to the outskirts of their busy brain-centres. The child went away as quietly and as mysteriously as he came without saying anything. Soyaan wondered if the beach was really as private as he had thought. He wondered if there were other persons, adults, in the area. Neither spoke for a long while. Only much, much later when they had made love behind the bushes:

"The emaciated poor upon whom feed the hungry lice. Well-put that," she commented.

"But you've forgotten."

"What?"

"Once in a while the police gather these beggars as though they were a season's pick."

They lay side by side. The shadow of the clouds spread a short-lived umbrella all along the shore. Way down on the horizon, a couple of swallows chased each other playfully.

"When they finally come, having broken the pride of dawn, they will find me prepared. No, I don't belong to the class of the humiliated. I shall have readied myself like a woman who awaits her lover."

A defiant look from him. Her gaze avoided his: she appeared offended. And for an instant, she thought she saw a vulture perched on the precipice at the far end of the shore. She called back to her mind the apparition of the child who'd come and who'd gone. Her cheeks poured wet with a cataract of tears. She was up and on her feet. She ran away from him. She went to wash her hot tears in the salted water of the sea.

The sheikh had consulted his concise concordance. He had chosen which passages to read, which Suras of the Koran would suit the occasion, and he chanted them. Soyaan, as promised, made no comment nor mocked their efforts. The incense pot which she placed in the doorway burned an odorous mixture of frankincense and myrrh. Soyaan's sensitive nose detected something bizarre in the smell. Should he ask his mother to name what she had in that pot? What ungodly odour was that? Hair burning? Did she really think he had been bewitched by that woman?

His father was announced. The sheikh withdrew as Keynaan entered.

⁊℅

Of late, the two had been on very bad terms. Soyaan had cut the small allowance which used to be earmarked for the maintenance of Keynaan and his other wife, Beydan. He told his mother and sister that he had done this in order to pay for the house of which, it turned out, Mother would eventually take full possession. There was, however, another untold reason. Soyaan had learned that the old man had been courting a young girl Ladan's age and he had spent on her what money he had received for Beydan, despite the fact that Beydan was heavy with nine months' pregnancy. Of course, Soyaan didn't inform Beydan about this; nor his mother, sister or twin brother. Keynaan would feel the pinch, had said Soyaan to himself. He would speak. He would explain. He would say what had happened. And he did. "My son has abandoned me to the wolves of shame and disgrace," he said. "He has listened to the counsel of women. A man who seeks and follows women's advice is a man ruined."

"I've applied for a job," Keynaan told Soyaan now.

Silence. He couldn't take it, Soyaan couldn't. His itching nerve, Soyaan's inner impatience hazarded a move: he switched the radio on. He turned the volume unnecessarily loud. Keynaan, to be heard, spoke at the top of his voice. When his throat pained, Keynaan turned the volume down. The two listened to Dulman, the country's most famous actress, sing the psalms of the General's praise-names. Soyaan rubbed his eyes harder. The smoke of burning incense had stung them. Anyway, was it worthwhile asking what job Keynaan had applied for? A former police inspector, a man forced to retire because of scandalous inconveniences he had created for the régime, what job might he qualify for? An informer, a daily gatherer of spoken indiscretions, an "ear-servant" of the National Security Service since he was semi-literate?

"I am sorry I wasn't there when you came to Afgoi. Beydan told me of your visit," Keynaan said.

"How is she?"

"Nine months. Heavy as guilt with the weight of her pregnancy."

Beydan, on one of their last encounters, spoke to Soyaan of a dream she had seen, a dream in which she, the centre figure, wasn't there. "Like a ghost," she said, "whose shadow isn't reflected in mirrors, I do not see myself in the dreams I dream." Poor woman. "Neither are you there, my Soyaan. No. Loyaan stands high among the pall-bearers, tall, sad, unsmiling." Poor woman! Keynaan, fidgety in his chair, looked visibly uneasy. Was he, too, now thinking the same thoughts? Dulman's praise-songs of the country's Grand Patriarch provided him with a pretext for changing the subject of their conversation, supplied him with a cue.

"Listen to these ludicrous eulogies of the General," Soyaan said. "The father of the nation. The carrier of wisdom. The provider of comforts. A demi-god. I see him as a Grand Warden of a Gulag."

"I won't ask you to unsay that. But I suggest you be careful. It seems you take too many things for granted. If I were you, I wouldn't do that. I would be more careful if I were you. Gulag or no, you are doing well. I don't see why it is you who puts a neck out. Why you? Where are the others? Why must you carry the standard? Why must you be its bearer?"

"I am no bearer of anybody's banner. But I feel humiliated, I feel abused, daily, minutely. A friend of mine is in for anti-Soviet activities. But where are we? What era is this? Is this Africa or is this Stalin's Russia? I am disgusted. As soon as I feel better, I promise you. . . ." He hiccupped.

"I warn you."

"As soon as I feel better, I *hic* will *hic.* . . ."

"Have a glass of cold water."

Hiccup. "No."

Soyaan switched off the radio. He thus strangled the singer in the middle of a syllable, made Dulman choke on the consonants of sycophancy.

But just before either had time to think of things to say, there came the voice of a beggar chanting alms-songs.

Keynaan went out. Soyaan returned to Neruda's *Machu Picchu.*

※

"Read it to me, please."

"Which sonnet?"

"Number X."

Gestures of love and tenderness: Ladan. Yes, of such gentle gestures were loving sisters made, thought Soyaan as he listened to the cadences of her beautiful voice, as she lifted her head and looked at him, as she rolled her eyes in tears of tenderness. She had just returned home from school where for the past four or so months she had taught, this being part of her two-year National Service. Before her, there had come and gone several other persons, her mother told her. There was Dr Ahmed-Wellie who had stayed by him for a very long time. There was "Siciliano." There was Keynaan. Plus some others. There were women from the neighbourhood who suggested that the family brand the body of the ailing with the cauterants of studied medical traditions. Once when Ladan had stolen in on them like a shadow, she thought she overheard a conversation in which the name of Koschin occurred more than twice. Wasn't the man "Il Siciliano," the one who was extremely courteous and who bowed as he took leave, as he bid them farewell? She finished reading the sonnet and sat silently, her feet heavy—like the cold wetness of a sweaty dream. Come what might, she told herself, she would contain the secret, she wouldn't repeat to him what he had spoken in his sleep. Yes, she would keep under control her alchemy of emotions.

She turned a page. The wick of her memory had lit, with a fresh flash, a page of her past. She read to herself the lyrics of love. A chapter of gratitude dedicated to Soyaan; another of sympathetic understanding to her mother; a third of assurances to Loyaan; a sonnet of love to Koschin, which especially rhymed with that name. There was no mention of Keynaan, no reference to him. To Ladan, Soyaan was the braille of her otherwise unguided vision; to her, Loyaan was the brother who enabled her to sow her moons and bright days with nightly stars.

Soyaan turned towards her and said: "Mother says that I speak in my sleep."

"Does she?"

He took Neruda's book from her and put it aside. "She says I utter inconsistencies."

"You know what Mother is like."

"No, Ladan dearest. Tell me. Do I?"

She now had his hand in hers. She kissed it. "One has tumultuous moments and intervals of lucidity when one is ill, with a temperature as high as yours. So what does it matter what you've said and what you haven't?"

"What did I say?"

"Nothing of importance."

"What did I say?"

A tender smile framed her worried look. But she remained silent as curtainfall for a very long time. She looked away. She let his hand go. The air in the room was heavy as the gas a stove emits. Then:

"You spoke of pale ghostly beings which jabbed you with needles."

He regarded her with renewed interest.

"Yes, you said that," she assured him.

Pale ghostly beings jabbing him with needles? He changed the position in which he had lain: these injections, thought he to himself, how they pained! He remembered a scene in a hospital room, white as death and dull as a knife gone rusty. Or was he dreaming? They had tied him to a chair, there were three men, and they gave him an injection.

"What else?"

"You uttered obscenities about the General. But these were moments of tumultuous confusion and high fever. I was there. So was Mother. 'The Koran, the Holy Koran,' she once shouted. 'Read a passage, let us take refuge in the word of God.'"

"Anything else?"

"That was sufficient evidence, she argued, that you were bewitched. She interpreted it this way: the pale ghostly beings you saw were none but the masters of the *mingis*-bewitching ceremonies, the men who, for the performance of the rite, smear their black faces with the powder of lime-ash."

Another pause. Whispered asides. Inaudible murmurs. Soyaan's. Then there was a noise, which, although feeble, made Soyaan turn and open his eyes. The noise came from behind Ladan. She turned round. The robed angels of her dreams: heaven's God. *What do I see?* It was Loyaan. Loyaan in person. For a good five minutes, no one would recall who did what, who said what, who hugged or kissed whom.

Ladan left the twins together to talk things over.

⟩⟨

A beggar's chant: the singing voice of a youth which alternated with that of an old man. Even beggars had classes, Soyaan was thinking, as he allowed his brother to take his temperature and ask questions for which he would get no answers. There were those in white, in clean robes, who were learned and who professionally chanted only religious incantations; these were usually considered as pupils of a principal sheikh, an imam at a mosque and were thus treated well. There were the others who wore tatters, whose manners were uncouth and harsh as their voices. They were treated as were street cats and masterless dogs.

"Feed the hungry tongues of the needy with the fats of the
    Almighty.
Wet the dry mouths of famine with the waters of the Wondermaker.
Give and God will offer you more in return and also in abundance."

Ladan and Qumman went to fill the beggars' stomachs and empty containers with mouthfuls of residuals. *Pray for the sick among us, pray for the souls of the dead relative and Muslim anywhere they may be found.*

Meanwhile: Loyaan had felt Soyaan's pulse and taken his temperature. At first he got nowhere with his persistent questions about where his brother had been, with whom and what he had eaten. It transpired after an hour's talk, however, that Soyaan had been to Beydan's and had eaten something there. It also became clear that he had seen a doctor at the Military Hospital. The doctor's suggestions were on the table, Loyaan could read the instructions himself. But who was the doctor? Soyaan, however, dragged the conversation on to topics of the day's politics. On the spree of improvised vitality, surprising Loyaan and himself too, he embarked on a long-winded monologue about how the General was serving up a cocktail of poisonous contradictions to the masses. He said, with sufficient conviction, that if a small group, with a small following, were to organise, say, a picket or a sit-in of a sort, if this small group informed the masses of what really was happening, information being essential in a country where everything was censored . . . hiccup. . . .

"Come, come, now. Hold your breath. Inhale."

"A knock on the door at *hic* dawn. The Security take the man away *hic* and leave behind him a wife *hic* who suffers from the insomnia of restless nights *hic*."

"Come, come now. Hold your breath. Inhale."

But he wouldn't hold his breath. There was no cold water either. Should Loyaan resort to the traditional method? Should he shock him, tell him the most horrid of news? "Your love is dead." Who? Who was Soyaan's love? Did he have one? What was her name? Or should he resign himself to one simple fact: that he knew hardly anything of Soyaan's private life, who his closest friends were. Hiccup.

"How is Beydan?"

The saliva in the floor of Soyaan's mouth soured into anger at the mention of her name, anger at himself more than at anybody else. He should do something for that woman. Would Loyaan please help give her some money? Would he please see to it that she got it in person? No. He chose not to tell even Loyaan about the young woman whom Keynaan intended to marry. That would only make things worse. Soyaan: a man of intrigue, rhetoric, polemic and politics. Loyaan: a man of melodramatic scenes, mundanities and lost tempers. Loyaan would insist, for instance, on removing all inverted commas from phrases like "revolution in Africa," "socialism in Africa," "radical governments," whereas Soyaan was fond of dressing them with these and other punctuational accessories; he was fond of opening a parenthesis he had no intention of closing. Years ago as a matter of fact it was Soyaan who had suggested that Loyaan should avoid politics as should a patient unprescribed drugs: "You stay where you are, in that region of Baidoa, you do your job well and you are the most revolutionary of revolutionaries"—inverted commas removed! Hiccup. Soyaan lay quiet under the sheet like a tucked-in child. Hiccup.

"And how is Father?"

"He was *hic* here a while ago."

"How is he?"

"A powerless *hic* patriarch, the grandest of them *hic* all. We are on the worst *hic* of terms."

"On account of Beydan?"

"Not only that."

"What?"

"The politics of confront-*hic*-tation."

"I don't understand."

"The demystifica-*hic*-tion of in-*hic*-formation. Tell the *hic* masses in the simplest *hic* of terms what is happening. Demystify *hic* politics. Empty those heads filled with tons of rhetoric. Uncover whether hiding *hic* behind pregnant letters such as KGB, CIA, or other *hic* wicked alphabet of mysteries *hic*. Do you *hic* understand now *hic*?"

Soyaan's eyes were trained on Loyaan. "I am not sure I do."

A smile. A hiccup. Then:

"You will in *hic* time."

Loyaan's silence elicited a further comment from Soyaan. The aluminium sheet rattled as a MiG-21 flew past overhead.

"Koschin, by the way, *hic*, is in terrible *hic* need of help."

"Where are they keeping him?"

"In the underground prison *hic* the East Germans *hic* have constructed. A super-prison *hic* as aid from one Soviet *hic* satellite to *hic* a fake socialist but really *hic* fascist Somalia."

"How can I be of any help?"

"Ask Ahmed-Wellie. He will know."

Loyaan's chair sat in the perforation of the sun's needle of rays. Soyaan's knees stood out as they strained against the sheets which covered him. He changed position and was ready to change topic of conversation as well. But Loyaan was somewhere else. He had gone back to and was walking the passageways of a past he had forgotten. . . . The twins were at play; there was a sandy beach; Merca; sandy castles under construction. Yes, out of the hidden depths emerged a ball with illustrations drawn on it, a globe, a world map, complete with the physical as well as the political colouring of colonies, mountains and lakes. This came and for a long while stayed hung in front of him brightly like a lantern. Keynaan was there as well. Keynaan the grand patriarch, Keynaan with a knife in hand, feet in boots, Keynaan heartless, gutless, and the knife tore into the ball. "A world round as a ball. Whoever heard of that?" Hiccup.

Soyaan lay silent and spreadeagled. Under one of his arms, there was a copy of Machiavelli's *The Prince*. Loyaan picked up the book. He read out a passage Soyaan had underlined:

"There is nothing more difficult to take in hand, more perilous to conduct, or more uncertain in its success than to take the lead in the introduction of a new order of things. Because the innovator has for enemies all those who have done well under the old conditions, and lukewarm defenders in those who may do well under the new."

When Loyaan stopped reading, he saw that Soyaan had fallen asleep.

৯৫

An hour later. Soyaan awoke and found him still seated there. They discussed serious as well as banal topics which concerned the family's life, politics of the General, et cetera. Then suddenly Soyaan's eyes, like the sun's light in the room, dimmed. Soyaan hiccupped a series of involuntary spasms of breathlessness. He looked all the more disturbed as he stretched his hand out to Loyaan who took it and held it in his. He repeated and repeated and repeated Loyaan's name in between these spasms of breathlessness.

First, the warmth went out of Soyaan's hand. Then the brightness out of his eyes. Everything assumed an artificial quietness, for an unbroken fraction of a second.

And Soyaan hiccupped his last.

NURUDDIN FARAH *of Somalia was named the 1998 Laureate of the Neustadt International Prize for Literature. He is the author of three books comprising the trilogy* Variations on the Theme of an African Dictatorship (Sweet & Sour Milk, Sardines, Close Sesame), *and his most recent book is* Secrets.

TESS GALLAGHER

Amplitude

New and Selected Poems

Instructions to the Double

So now it's your turn,
little mother of silences, little
father of half-belief. Take up
this face, these daily rounds
with a cabbage under each arm
convincing the multitudes
that a well-made-anything
could save them. Take up
most of all, these hands
trained to an ornate piano
in a house on the other side
of the country.

I'm staying here
without music, without
applause. I'm not going
to wait up for you. Take
your time. Take mine
too. Get into some trouble

I'll have to account for. Walk
into some bars alone
with a slit in your skirt. Let
the men follow you on the street
with their clumsy propositions, their
loud hatreds of this and that. Keep
walking. Keep your head
up. They are calling to you—slut, mother,
virgin, whore, daughter, adultress, lover,
mistress, bitch, wife, cunt, harlot,
betrothed, Jezebel, Messalina, Diana,
Bathsheba, Rebecca, Lucretia, Mary,
Magdelena, Ruth, you—Niobe,
woman of the tombs.

Don't stop for anything, not
a caress or a promise. Go
to the temple of the poets, not
the one like a run-down country club,
but the one on fire
with so much it wants
to be done with. Say all the last words
and the first: hello, goodbye, yes,
I, no, please, always, never.

If anyone from the country club
asks if you write poems, say
your name is Lizzie Borden.
Show him your axe, the one
they gave you with a silver
blade, your name engraved there
like a whisper of their own.

If anyone calls you a witch,
burn for him; if anyone calls you

less or more than you are
let him burn for you.

It's a dangerous mission. You
could die out there. You
could live forever.

Under Stars

The sleep of this night deepens
because I have walked coatless from the house
carrying the white envelope.
All night it will say one name
in its little tin house by the roadside.

I have raised the metal flag
so its shadow under the roadlamp
leaves an imprint on the rain-heavy bushes.
Now I will walk back
thinking of the few lights still on
in the town a mile away.

In the yellowed light of a kitchen
the millworker has finished his coffee,
his wife has laid out the white slices of bread
on the counter. Now while the bed they have left
is still warm, I will think of you, you
who are so far away
you have caused me to look up at the stars.

Tonight they have not moved
from childhood, those games played after dark.

Again I walk into the wet grass
toward the starry voices. Again, I
am the found one, intimate, returned
by all I touch on the way.

Conversation with a Fireman from Brooklyn

He offers, between planes,
to buy me a drink. I've never talked
to a fireman before, not one from Brooklyn
anyway. Okay. Fine, I say. Somehow
the subject is bound to come up, women
firefighters, and since I'm
a woman and he's a fireman, between
the two of us, we know something
about this subject. Already
he's telling me he doesn't mind
women firefighters, but what
they look like
after fighting a fire, well
they lose all respect. He's sorry, but
he looks at them
covered with the cinders of someone's
lost hope, and he feels disgust, he just
wants to turn the hose on them, they
are that sweaty and stinking, just like
him, of course, but not the woman he
wants, you get me? and to come to that—
isn't it too bad, to be despised
for what you do to prove yourself
among men
who want to love you, to love you,
love you.

Willingly

When I get up he has been long at work,
his brush limber against the house.
Seeing him on his ladder under the eaves,
I look back on myself asleep in the dream
I could not carry awake. Sleep
inside a house that is being painted,
whole lifetimes now only the familiar cast
of morning light over the prayer plant.
This "not remembering" is something new
of where you have been.

What was settled or unsettled in sleep
stays there. But your house
under his steady arm is leaving itself
and you see this gradual surface of
new light covering your sleep
has the greater power.
You think now you felt brush strokes or
the space between them, a motion
bearing down on you—an accumulation
of stars, each night of them
arranging over the roofs of entire cities.

His careful strokes whiten the web,
the swirl of woodgrain blotted
out like a breath stopped
at the heart. Nothing has changed
you say, faithlessly. But something has
cleansed you past recognition. When
you stand near his ladder looking up
he does not acknowledge you,
and as from daylight in a dream you see

your house has passed from you
into the blessed hands of others.

This is ownership, you think, arriving
in the heady afterlife of paint smell.
A deep opening goes on in you.
Some paint has dropped onto your shoulder
as though light concealed an unsuspected
weight. You think it has fallen through
you. You think you have agreed to this,
what has been done with your life, willingly.

TESS GALLAGHER

Moon Crossing Bridge

Now that I Am Never Alone

In the bath I look up and see the brown moth
pressed like a pair of unpredictable lips
against the white wall. I heat up
the water, running as much hot in as I can stand.
These handfuls over my shoulder—how once
he pulled my head against his thigh and dipped
a rivulet down my neck of coldest water from the spring
we were drinking from. Beautiful mischief
that stills a moment so I can never look
back. Only now, brightest now, and the water
never hot enough to drive that shiver out.

But I remember solitude—no other
presence and each thing what it was. Not this raw
fluttering I make of you as you have made of me
your watch-fire, your killing light.

Fresh Stain

I don't know now if it was kindness—we do
and we do. But I wanted you with me
that day in the cool raspberry vines, before
I had loved anyone, when another girl and I
saw the owner's son coming to lift away
our heaped flats of berries. His
white shirt outside his jeans so
tempting. That whiteness, that quick side-glance
in our direction. We said nothing,
but quickly gathered all the berries we could, losing
some in our mirth and trampling them
like two black ponies who only want to keep their backs
free, who only want to be shaken with
the black night-in-day murmur of hemlocks
high above. Our slim waists, our buds
of breasts and red stain of raspberries cheapening
our lips. We were sudden, we were
two blurred dancers who didn't need paradise. His shirt,
his white shirt when the pelting ended, as if
we had kissed him until his own blood
opened. So we refused every plea and
were satisfied. And you didn't touch me then, just
listened to the cool silence after. Inside,
the ripe hidden berries as we took up our wicker baskets
and lost our hands past the wrists
in the trellised vines. Just girls with the arms of
their sweaters twisted across their hips, their laughter
high in sunlight and shadow, that girl
you can almost remember as she leans into the vine,
following with pure unanswerable desire, a boy
going into the house to change his shirt.

I Stop Writing the Poem

to fold the clothes. No matter who lives
or who dies, I'm still a woman.
I'll always have plenty to do.
I bring the arms of his shirt
together. Nothing can stop
our tenderness. I'll get back
to the poem. I'll get back to being
a woman. But for now
there's a shirt, a giant shirt
in my hands, and somewhere a small girl
standing next to her mother
watching to see how it's done.

TESS GALLAGHER *is a poet, short fiction writer, and essayist. Among her many books are* Moon Crossing Bridge, Amplitude: New and Selected Poems, At the Owl Woman Saloon, The Lover of Horses, *and* A Concert of Tenses. *Gallagher acted as consultant to Robert Altman on the film* Short Cuts, *based on the short stories of her late husband Raymond Carver. She lives in Port Angeles, Washington.*

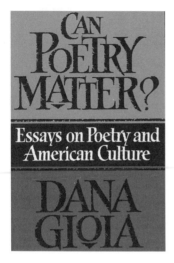

DANA GIOIA

Can Poetry Matter?

*Essays on Poetry and
American Culture*

Can Poetry Matter?

American poetry now belongs to a subculture. No longer part of the mainstream of artistic and intellectual life, it has become the specialized occupation of a relatively small and isolated group. Little of the frenetic activity it generates ever reaches outside that closed group. As a class, poets are not without cultural status. Like priests in a town of agnostics, they still command a certain residual prestige. But as individual artists they are almost invisible.

What makes the situation of contemporary poetry particularly surprising is that it comes at a moment of unprecedented expansion for the art. There have never before been so many new books of poetry published, so many anthologies or literary magazines. Never has it been so easy to earn a living as a poet. There are now several thousand college-level jobs in teaching creative writing, and many more at the primary and secondary levels. Congress has even instituted the position of poet laureate, as have twenty-five states. One also finds a complex network of public subvention for poets, funded by federal, state, and local agencies, augmented by private support in the form of foundation fellowships, prizes, and subsidized retreats. There has also never before been so much published criticism about contemporary poetry; it fills dozens of literary newsletters and scholarly journals.

The proliferation of new poetry and poetry programs is astounding by any historical measure. Just under a thousand new collections of verse are published each year, in addition to a myriad of new poems printed in magazines both small and large. No one knows how many poetry readings take place each year, but surely the total must run into the tens of thousands. And there are now about 200 graduate creative-writing programs in the United States, and more than a thousand undergraduate ones. With an average of ten poetry students in each graduate section, these programs alone will produce about 20,000 accredited professional poets over the next decade. From such statistics an observer might easily conclude that we live in the golden age of American poetry.

But the poetry boom has been a distressingly confined phenomenon. Decades of public and private funding have created a large professional class for the production and reception of new poetry, comprising legions of teachers, graduate students, editors, publishers, and administrators. Based mostly in universities, these groups have gradually become the primary audience for contemporary verse. Consequently, the energy of American poetry, which was once directed outward, is now increasingly focused inward. Reputations are made and rewards distributed within the poetry subculture. To adapt Russell Jacoby's definition of contemporary academic renown from *The Last Intellectuals*, a "famous" poet now means someone famous only to other poets. But there are enough poets to make that local fame relatively meaningful. Not long ago, "only poets read poetry" was meant as damning criticism. Now it is a proven marketing strategy.

The situation has become a paradox, a Zen riddle of cultural sociology. Over the past half century, as American poetry's specialist audience has steadily expanded, its general readership has declined. Moreover, the engines that have driven poetry's institutional success—the explosion of academic writing programs, the proliferation of subsidized magazines and presses, the emergence of a creative-writing career track, and the migration of American literary culture to the university—have unwittingly contributed to its disappearance from public view.

To the average reader, the proposition that poetry's audience has declined may seem self-evident. It is symptomatic of the art's current isolation that within the subculture such notions are often rejected. Like chamber-of-commerce representatives from Parnassus, poetry boosters offer impressive recitations of the numerical growth of publications, programs, and professorships. Given the bullish statistic on poetry's material expansion, how does one demonstrate that its intellectual and spiritual influence has eroded? One cannot easily marshal numbers, but to any candid observer the evidence throughout the world of ideas and letters seems inescapable.

Daily newspapers no longer review poetry. There is, in fact, little coverage of poetry or poets in the general press. From 1984 until this year the National Book Awards dropped poetry as a category. Leading critics rarely review it. In fact, virtually no one reviews it except other poets. Almost no popular collections of contemporary poetry are available except those, like the *Norton Anthology*, targeting an academic audience. It seems, in short, as if the large audience that still exists for quality fiction hardly notices poetry. A reader familiar with the novels of Joyce Carol Oates, John Updike, or John Barth may not even recognize the names of Gwendolyn Brooks, Gary Snyder, or W. D. Snodgrass.

One can see a microcosm of poetry's current position by studying its coverage in the *New York Times*. Virtually never reviewed in the daily edition, new poetry is intermittently discussed in the Sunday *Book Review*, but almost always in group reviews where three books are briefly considered together. Whereas a new novel or biography is reviewed on or around its publication date, a new collection by an important poet like Donald Hall or David Ignatow might wait up to a year for a notice. Or it might never be reviewed at all. Henry Taylor's *The Flying Change* was reviewed only after it had won the Pulitzer Prize. Rodney Jones's *Transparent Gestures* was reviewed months after it had won the National Book Critics Circle Award. Rita Dove's Pulitzer Prize–winning *Thomas and Beulah* was not reviewed by the *Times* at all.

Poetry reviewing is no better anywhere else, and generally it is much worse. The *New York Times* only reflects the opinion that although there is a great deal of poetry around, none of it matters very much to readers, publishers, or advertisers—to anyone, that is, except other poets. For most newspapers and magazines, poetry has become a literary commodity intended less to be read than to be noted with approval. Most editors run poems and poetry reviews the way a prosperous Montana rancher might keep a few buffalo around—not to eat the endangered creatures but to display them for tradition's sake.

Arguments about the decline of poetry's cultural importance are not new. In American letters they date back to the nineteenth century. But the modern debate might be said to have begun in 1934, when Edmund Wilson published the first version of his controversial essay "Is Verse a Dying Technique?" Surveying literary history, Wilson noted that verse's role had grown increasingly narrow since the eighteenth century. In particular, Romanticism's emphasis on intensity made poetry seem so "fleeting and quintessential" that eventually it dwindled into a mainly lyric medium. As verse—which had previously been a popular medium for narrative, satire, drama, even history and scientific speculation—retreated into lyric, prose usurped much of its cultural territory. Truly ambitious writers eventually had no choice but to write in prose. The future of great literature, Wilson speculated, belonged almost entirely to prose.

Wilson was a capable analyst of literary trends. His skeptical assessment of poetry's place in modern letters has been frequently attacked and qualified over the past half century, but it has never been convincingly dismissed. His argument set the ground rules for all subsequent defenders of contemporary poetry. It also provided the starting point for later iconoclasts, such as Delmore Schwartz, Leslie Fiedler, and Christopher Clausen. The most recent and celebrated of these revisions is Joseph Epstein, whose mordant 1988 critique "Who Killed Poetry?" first appeared in *Commentary* and was reprinted in an extravagantly acrimonious symposium in *AWP Chronicle* (the journal of the Associated Writing Programs). Not coincidentally, Epstein's title pays a double homage to Wilson's essay—first by mimicking the interrogative form of the original title, second by employing its metaphor of death.

Epstein essentially updated Wilson's argument, but with important differences. Whereas Wilson looked on the decline of poetry's cultural position as a gradual process spanning three centuries, Epstein focused on the past few decades. He contrasted the major achievements of the Modernists—the generation of Eliot and Stevens, which led poetry from moribund Romanticism into the twentieth century—with what he felt were the minor accomplishments of the present practitioners. The Modernists, Epstein maintained, were artists who worked from a broad cultural vision. Contemporary writers were "poetry professionals," who operated within the closed world of the university. Wilson blamed poetry's plight on historical forces; Epstein indicted the poets themselves and the institutions they had helped create, especially creative-writing programs. A brilliant polemicist, Epstein intended his essay to be incendiary, and it did ignite an explosion of criticism. No recent essay on American poetry has generated so many immediate responses in literary journals. And certainly none has drawn so much violently negative criticism from poets themselves. To date at least thirty writers have responded in print. Henry Taylor published two rebuttals.

Poets are justifiably sensitive to arguments that poetry has declined in cultural importance, because journalists and reviewers have used such arguments simplistically to declare all contemporary verse irrelevant. Usually the less a critic knows about verse the more readily he or she dismisses it. It is no coincidence, I think, that the two most persuasive essays on poetry's presumed demise were written by outstanding critics of fiction, neither of whom has written extensively about contemporary poetry. It is too soon to judge the accuracy of Epstein's essay, but a literary historian would find Wilson's timing ironic. As Wilson finished his famous essay, Robert Frost, Wallace Stevens, T. S. Eliot, Ezra Pound, Marianne Moore, E. E. Cummings, Robinson Jeffers, H. D. (Hilda Doolittle), Robert Graves, W. H. Auden, Archibald MacLeish, Basil Bunting, and others were writing some of their finest poems, which, encompassing history, politics, economics, religion, and philosophy, are among the most culturally inclusive in the history of the language. At the same time, a new generation, which would include Robert Lowell, Elizabeth Bishop, Philip Larkin, Randall Jarrell, Dylan Thomas, A. D. Hope, and others, was just breaking into print. Wilson himself later admitted that the emergence of a versatile and ambitious poet like Auden contradicted several points of his argument. But if Wilson's prophecies were sometimes inaccurate, his sense of poetry's overall situation was depressingly astute. Even if great poetry continues to be written, it has retreated from the center of literary life. Though supported by a loyal coterie, poetry has lost the confidence that it speaks to and for the general culture.

One sees evidence of poetry's diminished stature even within the thriving subculture. The established rituals of the poetry world—the readings, small magazines, workshops, and conferences—exhibit a surprising number of self-imposed limitations. Why, for example, does poetry mix so seldom with music, dance, or theater? At most readings the program consists of verse only—and usually only verse by that night's author. Forty years ago, when Dylan Thomas read, he spent half the program reciting other poets' work. Hardly a self-effacing man, he was nevertheless humble before his art. Today most readings are celebrations less of poetry than of the author's ego. No wonder the audience for such events usually consists entirely of poets, would-be poets, and friends of the author.

Several dozen journals now exist that print only verse. They don't publish literary reviews, just page after page of freshly minted poems. The heart sinks to see so many poems crammed so tightly together, like downcast immigrants in steerage. One can easily miss a radiant poem amid the many lackluster ones. It takes tremendous effort to read these small magazines with openness and attention. Few people bother, generally not even the magazines' contributors. The indifference to poetry in the mass media has created a monster of the opposite kind—journals that love poetry not wisely but too well.

Until about thirty years ago most poetry appeared in magazines that addressed a nonspecialist audience on a range of subjects. Poetry vied for the reader's interest along with political journalism, humor, fiction, and reviews—a competition that proved healthy for all the genres. A poem that didn't command the reader's attention wasn't considered much of a poem. Editors chose verse that they felt would appeal to their particular audiences, and the diversity of magazines assured that a variety of poetry appeared. The early *Kenyon Review* published Robert Lowell's poems next to critical essays and literary reviews. The old *New Yorker* showcased Ogden Nash between cartoons and short stories.

A few general-interest magazines, such as the *New Republic* and the *New Yorker*, still publish poetry in every issue, but, significantly, none except the

Nation still reviews it regularly. Some poetry appears in the handful of small magazines and quarterlies that consistently discuss a broad cultural agenda with nonspecialist readers, such as the *Threepenny Review*, the *New Criterion*, and the *Hudson Review*. But most poetry is published in journals that address an insular audience of literary professionals, mainly teachers of creative writing and their students. A few of these, such as *American Poetry Review* and *AWP Chronicle*, have moderately large circulations. Many more have negligible readerships. But size is not the problem. The problem is their complacency or resignation about existing only in and for a subculture.

What are the characteristics of a poetry-subculture publication? First, the one subject it addresses is current American literature (supplemented perhaps by a few translations of poets who have already been widely translated). Second, if it prints anything other than poetry, that is usually short fiction. Third, if it runs discursive prose, the essays and reviews are overwhelmingly positive. If it publishes an interview, the tone will be unabashedly reverent toward the author. For these journals critical prose exists not to provide a disinterested perspective on new books but to publicize them. Quite often there are manifest personal connections between the reviewers and the authors they discuss. If occasionally a negative review is published, it will be openly sectarian, rejecting an aesthetic that the magazine has already condemned. The unspoken editorial rule seems to be, Never surprise or annoy the readers; they are, after all, mainly our friends and colleagues.

By abandoning the hard work of evaluation, the poetry subculture demeans its own art. Since there are too many new poetry collections appearing each year for anyone to evaluate, the reader must rely on the candor and discernment of reviewers to recommend the best books. But the general press has largely abandoned this task, and the specialized press has grown so overprotective of poetry that it is reluctant to make harsh judgments. In his book *American Poetry: Wildness and Domesticity*, Robert Bly has accurately described the corrosive effect of this critical boosterism:

> We have an odd situation: although more bad poetry is being published now than ever before in American history, most of the reviews are positive. Critics say, "I never attack what is bad, all that

will take care of itself," . . . but the country is full of young poets and readers who are confused by seeing mediocre poetry praised, or never attacked, and who end up doubting their own critical perceptions.

A clubby feeling also typifies most recent anthologies of contemporary poetry. Although these collections represent themselves as trustworthy guides to the best new poetry, they are not compiled for readers outside the academy. More than one editor has discovered that the best way to get an anthology assigned is to include work by the poets who teach the courses. Compiled in the spirit of congenial opportunism, many of these anthologies give the impression that literary quality is a concept that neither an editor nor a reader should take too seriously.

The 1985 *Morrow Anthology of Younger American Poets*, for example, is not so much a selective literary collection as a comprehensive directory of creative-writing teachers (it even offers a photo of each author). Running nearly 800 pages, the volume presents no fewer than 104 important young poets, virtually all of whom teach creative writing. The editorial principle governing selection seems to have been the fear of leaving out some influential colleague. The book does contain a few strong and original poems, but they are surrounded by so many undistinguished exercises that one wonders if the good work got there by design or simply by random sampling. In the drearier patches one suspects that perhaps the book was never truly meant to be read, only assigned.

And that is the real issue. The poetry subculture no longer assumes that all published poems will be read. Like their colleagues in other academic departments, poetry professionals must publish, for purposes of both job security and career advancement. The more they publish, the faster they progress. If they do not publish, or wait too long, their economic futures are in grave jeopardy.

In art, of course, everyone agrees that quality and not quantity matters. Some authors survive on the basis of a single unforgettable poem—Edmund Waller's "Go, lovely rose," for example, or Edwin Markham's "The Man With the Hoe," which was made famous by being reprinted in hundreds of newspapers—an unthinkable occurrence today. But bureaucracies, by their very nature, have difficulty measuring something as intangible as literary quality. When institutions evaluate creative artists for employment or promotion, they still must find some seemingly objective means to do so. As the critic Bruce Bawer has observed,

> A poem is, after all, a fragile thing, and its intrinsic worth, or lack thereof, is a frighteningly subjective consideration; but fellowships, grants, degrees, appointments, and publications are objective facts. They are quantifiable; they can be listed on a résumé.

Poets serious about making careers in institutions understand that the criteria for success are primary quantitative. They must publish as much as possible as quickly as possible. The slow maturation of genuine creativity looks like laziness to a committee. Wallace Stevens was forty-three when his first book appeared. Robert Frost was thirty-nine. Today these sluggards would be unemployable.

The proliferation of literary journals and presses over the past thirty years has been a response less to an increased appetite for poetry among the public than to the desperate need of writing teachers for professional validation. Like subsidized farming that grows food no one wants, a poetry industry has been created to serve the interests of the producers and not the consumers. And in the process the integrity of the art has been betrayed. Of course, no poet is allowed to admit this in public. The cultural credibility of the professional poetry establishment depends on maintaining a polite hypocrisy. Millions of dollars in public and private funding are at stake. Luckily, no one outside the subculture cares enough to press the point very far. No Woodward and Bernstein will ever investigate a cover-up by members of the Associated Writing Programs.

The new poet makes a living not by publishing literary work but by providing specialized educational services. Most likely he or she either works for or aspires to work for a large institution—usually a state-run enterprise, such as a school district, a college, or a university (or lately even a hospital or prison)—teaching others how to write poetry or, at the highest levels, how to teach others how to write poetry.

To look at the issue in strictly economic terms, most contemporary poets have been alienated from their original cultural function. As Marx maintained and few economists have disputed, changes in a class's economic function eventually transform its values and behavior. In poetry's case, the socioeconomic changes have led to a divided literary culture: the superabundance of poetry within a small class and the impoverishment outside it. One might even say that outside the classroom—where society demands that the two groups interact—poets and the common reader are no longer on speaking terms.

The divorce of poetry from the educated reader has had another, more pernicious result. Seeing so much mediocre verse not only published but praised, slogging through so many dull anthologies and small magazines, most readers—even sophisticated ones like Joseph Epstein—now assume that no significant new poetry is being written. This public skepticism represents the final isolation of verse as an art form in contemporary society.

The irony is that this skepticism comes in a period of genuine achievement. Gresham's Law, that bad coinage drives out good, only half applies to current poetry. The sheer mass of mediocrity may have frightened away most readers, but it has not yet driven talented writers from the field. Anyone patient enough to weed through the tangle of contemporary work finds an impressive and diverse range of new poetry. Adrienne Rich, for example, despite her often overbearing polemics, is a major poet by any standard. The best work of Donald Justice, Anthony Hecht, Donald Hall, James Merrill, Louis Simpson, William Stafford, and Richard Wilbur—to mention only writers of the older generation—can hold its own against anything in the national literature. One might also add Sylvia Plath and James Wright, two strong poets of the same generation who died early. America is also a country rich in émigré poetry, as major writers like Czeslaw Milosz, Nina Cassian, Derek Walcott, Joseph Brodsky, and Thom Gunn demonstrate.

Without a role in the broader culture, however, talented poets lack the confidence to create public speech. Occasionally a writer links up rewardingly to a social or political movement. Rich, for example, has used feminism to expand the vision of her work. Robert Bly wrote his finest poetry to protest the Vietnam War. His sense of addressing a large and diverse audience added humor, breadth, and humanity to his previously minimalist verse. But it is a difficult task to marry the Muse happily to politics.

Consequently, most contemporary poets, knowing that they are virtually invisible in the larger culture, focus on the more intimate forms of lyric and meditative verse. (And a few loners, like X. J. Kennedy and John Updike, turn their genius to the critically disreputable demimonde of light verse and children's poetry.) Therefore, although current American poetry has not often excelled in public forms like political or satiric verse, it has nonetheless produced personal poems of unsurpassed beauty and power. Despite its manifest excellence, this new work has not found a public beyond the poetry subculture, because the traditional machinery of transmission—the reliable reviewing, honest criticism, and selective anthologies—has broken down. The audience that once made Frost and Eliot, Cummings and Millay, part of its cultural vision remains out of reach. Today Walt Whitman's challenge "To have great poets, there must be great audiences, too" reads like an indictment.

To maintain their activities, subcultures usually require institutions, since the general society does not share their interests. Nudists flock to "nature camps" to express their unfettered lifestyle. Monks remain in monasteries to protect their austere ideals. As long as poets belonged to a broader class of artists and intellectuals, they centered their lives in urban bohemias, where they maintained a distrustful independence from institutions. Once poets began moving into universities, they abandoned the working-class heterogeneity of Greenwich Village and North Beach for the professional homogeneity of academia.

At first they existed on the fringes of English departments, which was probably healthy. Without advanced degrees or formal career paths, poets were recognized as special creatures. They were allowed—like aboriginal chieftains visiting an anthropologist's campsite—to behave according to their own laws. But as the demand for creative writing grew, the poet's job expanded from merely literary to administrative duties. At the university's urging, these self-trained writers designed history's first institutional curricula for young poets. Creative writing evolved from occasional courses taught within the English department into its own undergraduate major or graduate-degree program. Writers fashioned their academic specialty in the image of other university studies. As the new writing departments multiplied, the new professionals patterned their infrastructure—job titles, journals, annual conventions, organizations—according to the standards not of urban bohemia but of educational institutions. Out of the professional networks this educational expansion created, the subculture of poetry was born.

Initially, the multiplication of creative-writing programs must have been a dizzyingly happy affair. Poets who had scraped by in bohemia or had spent their early adulthood fighting the Second World War suddenly secured stable, well-paying jobs. Writers who had never earned much public attention found themselves surrounded by eager students. Poets who had been too poor to travel flew from campus to campus and from conference to conference, to speak before audiences of their peers. As Wilfrid Sheed once described a moment in John Berryman's career, "Through the burgeoning university network, it was suddenly possible to think of oneself as a national poet, even if the nation turned out to consist entirely of English Departments." The bright postwar world promised a renaissance for American poetry.

In material terms that promise has been fulfilled beyond the dreams of anyone in Berryman's Depression-scarred generation. Poets now occupy niches at every level of academia, from a few sumptuously endowed chairs with six-figure salaries to the more numerous part-time stints that pay roughly the same as Burger King. But even at minimum wage, teaching poetry earns more than writing it ever did. Before the creative-writing boom, being a poet usually meant living in genteel poverty or worse. While the sacrifices poetry demanded caused much individual suffering, the rigors of serving Milton's "thankless Muse" also delivered the collective cultural benefit of frightening away all but committed artists.

Today poetry is a modestly upwardly mobile, middle-class profession—not as lucrative as waste management or dermatology but several big steps above the squalor of bohemia. Only a philistine would romanticize the blissfully banished artistic poverty of yesteryear. But a clear-eyed observer must also recognize that by opening the poet's trade to all applicants and by employing writers to do something other than write, institutions have changed the social and economic identity of the poet from artist to educator. In social terms the identification of poet with teacher is now complete.

The first question one poet now asks another upon being introduced is "Where do you teach?" The problem is not that poets teach. The campus is not a bad place for a poet to work. It's just a bad place for all poets to work. Society suffers by losing the imagination and vitality that poets brought to public culture. Poetry suffers when literary standards are forced to conform to institutional ones.

Even within the university contemporary poetry now exists as a subculture. The teaching poet finds that he or she has little in common with academic colleagues. The academic study of literature over the past twenty-five years has veered off in a theoretical direction with which most imaginative writers have little sympathy or familiarity. Thirty years ago detractors of creative-writing programs predicted that poets in universities would become enmeshed in literary criticism and scholarship. This prophecy has proved spectacularly wrong. Poets have created enclaves in the academy almost entirely separate from their critical colleagues. They write less criticism than they did before entering the academy. Pressed to keep up with the plethora of new poetry, small magazines, professional journals, and anthologies, they are frequently also less well read in the literature of the past. Their peers in the English department generally read less contemporary poetry and more literary theory. In many departments writers and literary theorists are openly at war. Bringing the two groups under one roof has paradoxically made each more territorial. Isolated even within the university, the poet, whose true subject is the whole of human existence, has reluctantly become an educational specialist.

To understand how radically the social situation of the American poet has changed, one need only compare today with fifty years ago. In 1940, with the notable exception of Robert Frost, few poets were working in colleges unless, like Mark Van Doren and Yvor Winters, they taught traditional academic subjects. The only creative-writing program was an experiment begun a few years earlier at the University of Iowa. The modernists exemplified the options that poets had for making a living. They could enter middle-class professions, as had T. S. Eliot (a banker turned publisher), Wallace Stevens (a corporate insurance lawyer), and William Carlos Williams (a pediatrician). Or they could live in bohemia supporting themselves as artists, as, in different ways, did Ezra Pound, e.e. cummings, and Marianne Moore. If the city proved unattractive, they could, like Robinson Jeffers, scrape by in a rural arts colony like Carmel, California. Or they might become farmers, like the young Robert Frost.

Most often poets supported themselves as editors or reviewers, actively taking part in the artistic and intellectual life of their time. Archibald MacLeish was an editor and writer at *Fortune*. James Agee reviewed movies for *Time* and the *Nation*, and eventually wrote screenplays for Hollywood. Randall Jarrell reviewed books. Weldon Kees wrote about jazz and modern art. Delmore Schwartz reviewed everything. Even poets who eventually took up academic careers spent intellectually broadening apprenticeships in literary journalism. The young Robert Hayden covered music and theater for Michigan's black press. R. P. Blackmur, who never completed high school, reviewed books for *Hound & Horn* before teaching at Princeton. Occasionally a poet might supplement his or her income by giving a reading or lecture, but these occasions were rare. Robinson Jeffers, for example, was fifty-four when he gave his first public reading. For most poets, the sustaining medium was not the classroom or the podium but the written word.

If poets supported themselves by writing, it was mainly by writing prose. Paying outlets for poetry were limited. Beyond a few national magazines, which generally preferred light verse or political satire, there were at any one time only a few dozen journals that published a significant amount of poetry. The emergence of a serious new quarterly like *Partisan Review* or *Furioso* was an event of real importance, and a small but dedicated audience eagerly looked forward to each issue. If people could not afford to buy copies, they borrowed them or visited public libraries. As for books of poetry, if one excludes vanity-press editions, fewer than a hundred new titles were published each year. But the books that did appear were reviewed in daily newspapers as well as magazines and quarterlies. A focused monthly like *Poetry* could cover virtually the entire field.

Reviewers fifty years ago were by today's standards extraordinarily tough. They said exactly what they thought, even about their most influential contemporaries. Listen, for example, to Randall Jarrell's description of a book by the famous anthologist Oscar Williams: it "gave the impression of having been written on a typewriter by a typewriter." That remark kept Jarrell out of subsequent Williams anthologies, but he did not hesitate to publish it. Or consider Jarrell's assessment of Archibald MacLeish's public poem *America Was Promises*: it "might have been devised by a YMCA secretary at a home for the mentally deficient." Or read Weldon Kees's one-sentence review of Muriel Rukeyser's *Wake Island*— "There's one thing you can say about Muriel: she's not lazy." But these same reviewers could write generously about poets they admired, as Jarrell did about Elizabeth Bishop, and Kees about Wallace Stevens. Their praise mattered, because readers knew it did not come lightly.

The reviewers of fifty years ago knew that their primary loyalty must lie not with their fellow poets or publishers but with the reader. Consequently they reported their reactions with scrupulous honesty, even when their opinions might lose them literary allies and writing assignments. In discussing new poetry they addressed a wide community of educated readers. Without talking down to their audience, they cultivated a public idiom. Prizing clarity and accessibility, they avoided specialist jargon and pedantic displays of scholarship. They also tried, as serious intellectuals should but specialists often do not, to relate what was happening in poetry to social, political, and artistic trends. They charged modern poetry with cultural importance and made it the focal point of their intellectual discourse.

Ill-paid, overworked, and underappreciated, this argumentative group of "practical" critics, all of them poets, accomplished remarkable things. They defined the canon of Modernist poetry, established methods to analyze verse of extraordinary difficulty, and identified the new mid-century generation of American poets (Lowell, Roethke, Bishop, Berryman, and others) that still dominates our literary consciousness. Whatever one thinks of their literary canon or critical principles, one must admire the intellectual energy and sheer determination of these critics, who developed as writers without grants or permanent faculty positions, often while working precariously on free-lance assignments. They represent a high point in American intellectual life. Even fifty years later their names still command more authority than those of all but a few contemporary critics. A short roll call would include John Berryman, R. P. Blackmur, Louise Bogan, John Ciardi, Horace Gregory, Langston Hughes, Randall Jarrell, Weldon Kees,

Kenneth Rexroth, Delmore Schwartz, Karl Shapiro, Allen Tate, and Yvor Winters. Although contemporary poetry has its boosters and publicists, it has no group of comparable dedication and talent able to address the general literary community.

Like all genuine intellectuals, these critics were visionary. They believed that if modern poets did not have an audience, they could create one. And gradually they did. It was not a mass audience; few American poets of any period have enjoyed a direct relationship with the general public. It was a cross-section of artists and intellectuals, including scientists, clergymen, educators, lawyers, and, of course, writers. This group constituted a literary intelligentsia, made up mainly of nonspecialists, who took poetry as seriously as fiction and drama. Recently Donald Hall and other critics have questioned the size of this audience by citing the low average sales of a volume of new verse by an established poet during the period (usually under a thousand copies). But these skeptics do not understand how poetry was read then.

America was a smaller, less affluent country in 1940, with about half its current population and one sixth its current real GNP. In those pre-paperback days of the late Depression neither readers nor libraries could afford to buy as many books as they do today. Nor was there a large captive audience of creative-writing students who bought books of contemporary poetry for classroom use. Readers usually bought poetry in two forms—in an occasional *Collected Poems* by a leading author, or in anthologies. The comprehensive collections of writers like Frost, Eliot, Auden, Jeffers, Wylie, and Millay sold very well, were frequently reprinted, and stayed perpetually in print. (Today most *Collected Poems* disappear after one printing.) Occasionally a book of new poems would capture the public's fancy. Edwin Arlington Robinson's *Tristram* (1927) became a Literary Guild selection. Frost's *A Further Range* sold 50,000 copies as a 1936 Book-of-the-Month Club selection. But people knew poetry mainly from anthologies, which they not only bought but also read, with curiosity and attention.

Louis Untermeyer's *Modern American Poetry*, first published in 1919, was frequently revised to keep it up to date and was a perennial best-seller. My 1942 edition, for example, had been reprinted five times by 1945. My edition of Oscar Williams's *A Pocket Book of Modern Poetry* had been reprinted nineteen times in fourteen years. Untermeyer and Williams prided themselves on keeping their anthologies broad-based and timely. They tried to represent the best of what was being published. Each edition added new poems and poets and dropped older ones. The public appreciated their efforts. Poetry anthologies were an indispensable part of any serious reader's library. Random House's popular Modern Library series, for example, included not one but two anthologies—Selden Rodman's *A New Anthology of Modern Poetry* and Conrad Aiken's *Twentieth-Century American Poetry*. All these collections were read and reread by a diverse public. Favorite poems were memorized. Difficult authors like Eliot and Thomas were actively discussed and debated. Poetry mattered outside the classroom.

Today these general readers constitute the audience that poetry has lost. United by intelligence and curiosity, this heterogenous group cuts across lines of race, class, age, and occupation. Representing our cultural intelligentsia, they are the people who support the arts—who buy classical and jazz records; who attend foreign films, serious theater, opera, symphony, and dance; who read quality fiction and biographies; who listen to public radio and subscribe to the best journals. (They are also often the parents who read poetry to their children and remember, once upon a time in college or high school or kindergarten, liking it themselves.) No one knows the size of this community, but even if one accepts the conservative estimate that it accounts for only two percent of the U.S. population, it still represents a potential audience of almost five million readers. However healthy poetry may appear within its professional subculture, it has lost this larger audience that represents poetry's bridge to the general culture.

But why should anyone but a poet care about the problems of American poetry? What possible relevance does this archaic art form have to contemporary society? In a better world, poetry would need no justification beyond the sheer splendor of its own existence. As Wallace Stevens once observed, "The purpose of poetry is to contribute to man's happiness." Children know this essential truth when they ask to hear their favorite nursery rhymes again and again. Aesthetic pleasure needs no justification, because a life without such pleasure is one not worth living.

But the rest of society has mostly forgotten the value of poetry. To the general reader, discussions about the state of poetry sound like the debating of foreign politics by émigrés in a seedy café. Or, as Cyril Connolly more bitterly described it, "Poets arguing about modern poetry: jackals snarling over a dried-up well." Anyone who hopes to broaden poetry's audience—critic, teacher, librarian, poet, or lonely literary amateur—faces a daunting challenge. How does one persuade justly skeptical readers, in terms they can understand and appreciate, that poetry still matters?

A passage in William Carlos Williams's "Asphodel, That Greeny Flower" provides a possible starting point. Written toward the end of the author's life, after he had been partly paralyzed by a stroke, the lines sum up the hard lessons about poetry and audience that Williams had learned over years of dedication to both poetry and medicine. He wrote,

> My heart rouses
> thinking to bring you news
> of something
> that concerns you
> and concerns many men. Look at
> what passes for the new.
> You will not find it there but in
> despised poems.
> It is difficult
> to get the news from poems
> yet men die miserably every day
> for lack
> of what is found there.

Williams understood poetry's human value but had no illusions about the difficulties his contemporaries faced in trying to engage the audience that needed the art most desperately. To regain poetry's readership one must begin by meeting Williams's challenge to find what "concerns many men," not simply what concerns poets.

There are at least two reasons why the situation of poetry matters to the entire intellectual community. The first involves the role of language in a free society. Poetry is the art of using words charged with their utmost meaning. A society whose intellectual leaders lose the skill to shape, appreciate, and understand the power of language will become the slaves of those who retain it—be they politicians, preachers, copywriters, or newscasters. The public responsibility of poetry has been pointed out repeatedly by modern writers. Even the arch-symbolist Stéphane Mallarmé praised the poet's central mission to "purify the words of the tribe." And Ezra Pound warned that

> Good writers are those who keep the language efficient. That is to say, keep it accurate, keep it clear. It doesn't matter whether a good writer wants to be useful or whether the bad writer wants to do harm. . . .
>
> If a nation's literature declines, the nation atrophies and decays.

Or, as George Orwell wrote after the Second World War, "One ought to recognize that the present political chaos is connected with the decay of language. . . ." Poetry is not the entire solution to keeping the nation's language clear and honest, but one is hard pressed to imagine a country's citizens improving the health of its language while abandoning poetry.

The second reason why the situation of poetry matters to all intellectuals is that poetry is not alone among the arts in its marginal position. If the audience for poetry has declined into a subculture of specialists, so too have the audiences for most contemporary art forms, from serious drama to jazz. The unprecedented fragmentation of American high culture during the past half century has left most arts in isolation from one another as well as from the general audience. Contemporary classical music scarcely exists as a living art outside university departments and conservatories. Jazz, which once commanded a broad popular audience, has become the semi-private domain of aficionados and musicians. (Today even influential jazz innovators cannot find places to perform in many metropolitan centers—and for an improvisatory art the inability to perform is a crippling liability.) Much serious drama is now confined to the margins of American theater, where it is seen only by actors, aspiring actors, playwrights, and a few diehard fans. Only the visual arts, perhaps because of their financial glamour and upper-class support, have largely escaped the decline in public attention.

The most serious question for the future of American culture is whether the arts will continue to exist in isolation and decline into subsidized academic specialties or whether some possibility of rapprochement with the educated public remains. Each of the arts must face the challenge separately, and no art faces more towering obstacles than poetry. Given the decline of literacy, the proliferation of other media, the crisis in humanities education, the collapse of critical standards, and the sheer weight of past failures, how can poets possibly succeed in being heard? Wouldn't it take a miracle?

Toward the end of her life Marianne Moore wrote a short poem called "O To Be a Dragon." This poem recalled the biblical dream in which the Lord appeared to King Solomon and said, "Ask what I shall give thee." Solomon wished for a wise and understanding heart. Moore's wish is harder to summarize. Her poem reads,

> If I, like Solomon, . . .
> could have my wish—
>
> my wish—O to be a dragon,
> a symbol of the power of Heaven—of silkworm
> size or immense; at times invisible.
> Felicitous phenomenon!

Moore got her wish. She became, as all genuine poets do, "a symbol of the power of Heaven." She succeeded in what Robert Frost called "the utmost of ambition"—namely, "to lodge a few poems where they will be hard to get rid of." She is permanently part of the "felicitous phenomenon" of American literature.

So wishes can come true—even extravagant ones. If I, like Marianne Moore, could have my wish, and I, like Solomon, could have the self-control not to wish for myself, I would wish that poetry could again become a part of American public culture. I don't think this is impossible. All it would require is that poets and poetry teachers take more responsibility for bringing their art to the public. I will close with six modest proposals for how this dream might come true.

1. *When poets give public readings, they should spend part of every program reciting other people's work*—preferably poems they admire by

writers they do not know personally. Readings should be celebrations of poetry in general, not merely of the featured author's work.

2. *When arts administrators plan public readings, they should avoid the standard subculture format of poetry only.* Mix poetry with the other arts, especially music. Plan evenings honoring dead or foreign writers. Combine short critical lectures with poetry performances. Such combinations would attract an audience from beyond the poetry world without compromising quality.

3. *Poets need to write prose about poetry more often, more candidly, and more effectively.* Poets must recapture the attention of the broader intellectual community by writing for nonspecialist publications. They must also avoid the jargon of contemporary academic criticism and write in a public idiom. Finally, poets must regain the reader's trust by candidly admitting what they don't like as well as promoting what they like. Professional courtesy has no place in literary journalism.

4. *Poets who compile anthologies—or even reading lists—should be scrupulously honest in including only poems they genuinely admire.* Anthologies are poetry's gateway to the general culture. They should not be used as pork barrels for the creative-writing trade. An art expands its audience by presenting masterpieces, not mediocrity. Anthologies should be compiled to move, delight, and instruct readers, not to flatter the writing teachers who assign books. Poet-anthologists must never trade the Muse's property for professional favors.

5. *Poetry teachers, especially at the high-school and undergraduate levels, should spend less time on analysis and more on performance.* Poetry needs to be liberated from literary criticism. Poems should be memorized, recited, and performed. The sheer joy of the art must be emphasized. The pleasure of performance is what first attracts children to poetry, the sensual excitement of speaking and hearing the words of the poem. Performance was also the teaching technique that kept poetry vital for centuries. Maybe it also holds the key to poetry's future.

6. *Finally, poets and arts administrators should use radio to expand the arts audience.* Poetry is an aural medium, and thus ideally suited to radio. A little imaginative programming at the hundreds of college and public-supported radio stations could bring poetry to millions of listeners. Some programming exists, but it is stuck mostly in the standard subculture format of living poets' reading their own work. Mixing poetry with music on classical and jazz stations or creating innovative talk-radio formats could reestablish a direct relationship between poetry and the general audience.

The history of art tells the same story over and over. As art forms develop, they establish conventions that guide creation, performance, instruction, even analysis. But eventually these conventions grow stale. They begin to stand between the art and its audience. Although much wonderful poetry is being written, the American poetry establishment is locked into a series of exhausted conventions—outmoded ways of presenting, discussing, editing, and teaching poetry. Educational institutions have codified them into a stifling bureaucratic etiquette that enervates the art. These conventions may once have made sense, but today they imprison poetry in an intellectual ghetto.

It is time to experiment, time to leave the well-ordered but stuffy classroom, time to restore a vulgar vitality to poetry and unleash the energy now trapped in the subculture. There is nothing to lose. Society has already told us that poetry is dead. Let's build a funeral pyre out of the desiccated conventions piled around us and watch the ancient, spangle-feathered, unkillable phoenix rise from the ashes.

DANA GIOIA *is an essayist, a translator, a librettist, an anthologist, and a poet. His two books of poetry are* The Gods of Winter *and* Daily Horoscope, *and his essay collection is titled* Can Poetry Matter? *Gioia has translated the* Mottetti *of Eugenio Montale, and is currently working on a libretto of* Nosferatu. *He lives and writes in California.*

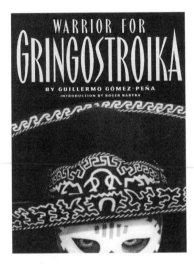

GUILLERMO GÓMEZ-PEÑA

Warrior for Gringostroika

Essays, Performance Texts, and Poetry

The Border Is . . .

A MANIFESTO / 1989

Border culture is a polysemantic term.

Stepping outside of one's culture is equivalent to walking outside of the law.

Border culture means boycott, complot, ilegalidad, clandestinidad, contrabando, transgresión, desobediencia binacional; en otros palabras, to smuggle dangerous poetry and utopian visions from one culture to another, desde allá, hasta acá.

But it also means to maintain one's dignity outside the law.

But it also means hybrid art forms for new contents-in-gestation: spray mural, techno-altar, poetry-in-tongues, audio graffiti, punkarachi, video corrido, anti-bolero, anti-todo: la migra (border patrol), art world, police, monocultura; en otras palabras y tierras, an art against the monolingües, tapados, nacionalistas, ex-teticistas en extinción, per omnia saecula speculorum . . .

But it also means to be fluid in English, Spanish, Spanglish, and Ingleñol, 'cause Spanglish is the language of border diplomacy.

But is also means transcultural friendship and collaboration among races, sexes, and generations.

But it also means to practice creative appropriation, expropriation, and subversion of dominant cultural forms.

But it also means a new cartography; a brand-new map to host the new project; the democratization of the East; the socialization of the West; the Third-Worldization of the North and the First-Worldization of the South.

But it also means a multiplicity of voices away from the center, different geo-cultural relations among more culturally akin regions: Tepito—San Diejuana, San Pancho—Nuyorrico, Miami—Quebec, San Antonio—Berlin, your home town and mine, digamos, a new internationalism ex centris.

But it also means regresar y volver a partir: to return and depart once again, 'cause border culture is a Sisyphean experience and to arrive is just an illusion.

But it also means a new terminology for new hybrid identities and métiers constantly metamorphosing: sudacá, not sudaca; Chicarrican, not Hispanic; mestizaje, not miscegenation; social thinker, not bohemian; accionista, not performer; intercultural, not postmodern.

But it also means to develop new models to interpret the world-in-crisis, the only world we know.

But it also means to push the borders of countries and languages or, better said, to find new languages to express the fluctuating borders.

But it also means experimenting with the fringes between art and society, legalidad and illegality, English and español, male and female, North and South, self and other, and subverting these relationships.

But it also means to speak from the crevasse, desde acá, desde el medio. The border is the juncture, not the edge, and monoculturalism has been expelled to the margins.

But it also means glasnost, not government censorship, for censorship is the opposite of border culture.

But it also means to analyze critically all that lies on the current table of debates: multiculturalism, the Latino "boom," "ethnic art," controversial art, even border culture.

But it also means to question and transgress border culture. What today is powerful and necessary, tomorrow is arcane and ridiculous; what today is border culture, tomorrow is institutional art, not vice versa.

But it also means to escape the current cooptation of border culture.

But it also means to look at the past and the future at the same time. 1492 was the beginning of a genocidal era. 1992 will mark the beginning of a new era: America post-Colombina, Arteamérica sin fronteras. Soon, a new internationalism will have to gravitate around the spinal cord of this continent—not Europe, not just the North, not just white, not only you, compañero del otro lado de la frontera, el lenguaje y el océano.

GUILLERMO GÓMEZ PEÑA *was born and raised in Mexico City and came to the U.S. in 1978. In his work, which includes performance art, video, audio, installations, poetry, journalism, critical writings, and cultural theory, he explores cross-cultural issues and North/South border relations. His books include* Warrior for Gringostroika, New World Border, *and* Codex Espangliensis.

LINDA GREGG

The Sacraments of Desire

Glistening

As I pull the bucket from the crude well,
the water changes from dark to a light
more silver than the sun. When I pour it
over my body that is standing in the dust
by the oleander bush, it sparkles easily
in the sunlight with an earnestness like
the spirit close up. The water magnifies
the sun all along the length of it.
Love is not less because of the spirit.
Delight does not make the heart childish.
We thought the blood thinned, our weight
lessened, that our substance was reduced
by simple happiness. The oleander is thick
with leaves and flowers because of spilled
water. Let the spirit marry the heart.
When I return naked to the stone porch,
there is no one to see me glistening.
But I look at the almond tree with its husks
cracking open in the heat. I look down

the whole mountain to the sea. Goats bleating
faintly and sometimes bells. I stand there
a long time with the sun and the quiet,
the earth moving slowly as I dry in the light.

The Color of Many Deer Running

The air fresh, as it has been for days.
Upper sky lavender. Deer on the far hill.
The farm woman said they would be gone
when I got there as I started down the lane.
Jumped the stream. Went under great eucalyptus
where the ground was stamped bare by two bulls
who watched from the other side of their field.
The young deer were playing as the old ate
or guarded. They all were gone, leaping.
Except one looking down from the top.
The ending made me glad. I turned toward
the red sky and ran back down to the farm,
the man, the woman, and the young calves.
Thinking that as I grow older I will lose
my color. Will turn tan and gray like the deer.
Not one deer, but when many of them run away.

The Conditions

You will have to stand in the clearing and see
your arms glow near ferns and roots. Hear things
moving in the branches heavy with black green.
You will be silvery, knowing death could capture
you in that condition of yielding. You will be alarmed
by everything real, even moisture. She will not
tell you there is nothing to fear. You will come
to see her and she will blaze upon you, stun you
with the radiance of a feral world. But she cannot
take you up into herself whenever you desire,
as the world can. She is the other nature,
and sexual in a way that makes the intervening flesh
thin as paper. You will feel your bones getting
lighter. You will feel more and more at risk.
You will think her shining drains you of meaning,
but it is a journey you must take. And when the sun
returns, when you walk from the forest to your world,
you will have known the land where your spirit lives.
Will have diagrams drawn by creases on your body,
and maps on your palms that were also there. Now
you will recognize them as geography. You will know
an unkempt singing you will never hear without her.

LINDA GREGG

Chosen by the Lion

Chosen by the Lion

I am the one chosen by the lion at sundown
and dragged back from the shining water.
Yanked back to bushes and torn open, blood
blazing at the throat and breast of me.
Take as meat. Devoured as spirit by spirit.
The others will return quickly to drink again
peacefully, but for me now there is only faith.
Only the fact that the tall windows I lived
with were left uncovered halfway up.
And the silence of those days I lived there
which were marked by your arrivals like
stations on a long journey. You write to say
you love me and lie awake in stillness
to avoid the pain. I remember looking
at you from within at the last moment,
with faith like a gift handkerchief, delicate
and almost fragile. This is the final thing.
Purity and faith, power and blood. Is there
nothing to see? Not memory even of forgetting?

Only the body eating the body? What of faith
when it meets death, being when it is hard
to account for? The nipples you bit
and the body you possessed lie buried in you.
My faith shines as the moon in the darkness
on water, as the sky in the day. Does it hover
in the air around you? Does it come like
a flower in your groin? Or is it like before
when you were alone and about to fall asleep
saying out loud in the darkness, "Linda,"
and hearing me answer immediately, "Yes!"

Asking for Directions

We could have been mistaken for a married couple
riding on the train from Manhattan to Chicago
that last time we were together. I remember
looking out the window and praising the beauty
of the ordinary: the in-between places, the world
with its back turned to us, the small neglected
stations of our history. I slept across your
chest and stomach without asking permission
because they were the last hours. There was
a smell to the sheepskin lining of your new
Chinese vest that I didn't recognize. I felt
it deliberately. I woke early and asked you
to come with me for coffee. You said, sleep more,
and I said we only had one hour and you came.
We didn't say much after that. In the station,
you took your things and handed me the vest,
then left as we had planned. So you would have
ten minutes to meet your family and leave.
I stood by the seat dazed by exhaustion

and the absoluteness of the end, so still I was
aware of myself breathing. I put on the vest
and my coat, got my bag and, turning, saw you
through the dirty window standing outside looking
up at me. We looked at each other without any
expression at all. Invisible, unnoticed, still.
That moment is what I will tell of as proof
that you loved me permanently. After that I was
a woman alone carrying her bag, asking a worker
which direction to walk to find a taxi.

Fishing in the Keep of Silence

There is a hush now while the hills rise up
and God is going to sleep. He trusts the ship
of Heaven to take over and proceed beautifully
as he lies dreaming in the lap of the world.
He knows the owls will guard the sweetness
of the soul in their massive keep of silence,
looking out with eyes open or closed over
the length of Tomales Bay that the herons
conform to, whitely broad in flight, white
and slim in standing. God, who thinks about
poetry all the time, breathes happily as He
repeats to Himself: There are fish in the net,
lots of fish this time in the net of the heart.

The Wind Blowing through a Tree

Clamour of amplitudes,
of the body's disunity, of carrying bread
home from the bakery and feeling
its heat gradually diminish
against the heart.
Learning the complexity. Picking up
pieces of ancient ceramic and seeing
they are not a thing but a mold
of the thing, and that thing
Aphrodite on her throne.
Four goats nearby and the water
shining down below.
The regal scent of eucalyptus
in the motionless summer heat.
It is not that the darkness
must be there, but that it sometimes is.

LINDA GREGG *is the author of* Things and Flesh, Chosen by the Lion, The Sacraments of Desire, Too Bright to See, *and* Alma. *Gregg divides her time between Marin County, California and Northhampton, Massachusetts.*

EAMON GRENNAN

Relations

New & Selected Poems

Night Driving in the Desert

Move fluent as water
Splashing brightness. Imagine
Jackal, badger, wild goat,
Fox-eyes glinting like broken glass:
Gingerly they sniff the sour exhaust.

Remember greenness; name
Its distant children: *ryegrass,*
Olive, avocado, fig—
First sweetness welling in the mouth.

Herbs the Arabs call *ashab*
Sprout inside a single rain,
Rush to blossom fruit seed,
Staining the sand with rainbows.

Imagine a procession of tanager dresses
Drifting through plaited shadow:

Women crossing the earth like water,
Sunlight splashing their skin to stars.

I know it is over in a flash and after
My heart is beating wildly, wildly for days.

Station

We are saying goodbye
on the platform. In silence
the huge train waits, crowding the station
with aftermath and longing
and all we've never said
to one another. He shoulders
his black dufflebag and shifts
from foot to foot, restless to be off, his eyes
wandering over tinted windows where he'll sit
staring out at the Hudson's platinum dazzle.

I want to tell him he's entering into the light
of the world, but it feels like a long tunnel
as he leaves one home, one parent
for another, and we both
know in our bones it won't ever
be the same again. What is the air at,
heaping between us then
thinning to nothing? Or those slategrey birds
that croon to themselves in an iron angle
and then take flight—inscribing
huge loops of effortless grace
between this station of shade and the shining water?

When our cheeks rest glancing against each other,
I feel mine scratchy with beard and stubble, his

not quite smooth as a girl's, harder, a faint fuzz
starting—those silken beginnings I can see
when the light is right, his next life
in bright first touches. What ails our hearts? Mine
aching in vain for the words
to make sense of our life together; his
fluttering in dread
of my finding the words, feathered syllables
fidgeting in his throat.

In a sudden rush of bodies
and announcements out of the air, he says
he's got to be going. One quick touch
and he's gone. In a minute
the train—ghostly faces behind smoked glass—
groans away on wheels and shackles, a slow glide
I walk beside, waving
at what I can see no longer. Later,
on his own in the city, he'll enter the underground
and cross the river, going home
to his mother's house. And I imagine
that pale face of his
carried along in the dark glass, shining
through shadows that fill the window
and fall away again
before we're even able to name them.

Pause

The weird containing stillness of the neighbourhood
just before the school bus brings the neighbourhood kids
home in the middle of the cold afternoon: a moment
of pure waiting, anticipation, before the outbreak of anything,

when everything seems just, seems *justified*, just hanging
in the wings, about to happen, and in your mind you see
the flashing lights flare amber to scarlet, and your daughter
in her blue jacket and white-fringed sapphire hat
step gingerly down and out into our world again
and hurry through silence and snow-grass
as the bus door sighs shut
and her own front door flies open and she finds you
behind it, father-in-waiting, the stillness in bits
and the common world restored as you bend
to touch her, take her hat and coat from the floor
where she's dropped them, hear the live voice of her
filling every crack. In the pause
before all this happens, you know something
about the shape of the life you've chosen to live
between the silence of almost infinite possibility and that
explosion of things as they are—those vast unanswerable
intrusions of love and disaster, or just the casual scatter
of your child's winter clothes on the hall floor.

Firefly

On my last night in the country, a firefly
gets stuck in the mesh of the windowscreen
and hangs there, revealing to me its tiny legs,
head like a miniscule metal bolt, the beige sac
jutting under its curl of a tail, splayed
on the fine wire and at intervals sparking,
the sac flashing lime-green, liquid, electric
— *on-off-on*, again *on-off-on*, then stop—
as if signalling to me in silence,
the trapped thing singing its own song.

For a while I watched it singing its own song
and then, when it went dark for a long time,
I leaned up close to the wire to become
a huge looming thing in its eyes and blew on it
gently, the way you'd blow a faint spark
to fire again—catching a dead leaf, a dry twig,
growing towards flame—and it started to flush
lime-green again, *on-off-on* again, deliberate
and slow, a brilliance beyond description
which filled my eyes as if responding to
the bare encouragement of breath I'd offered,
this kiss of life in a lighter dispensation,
as if I'd been part of its other world
for a minute, almost an element of air
and speaking some common tongue to it,   .
a body language rarefied beyond the vast
difference between our two bodies, both of us
simply living in this space and making
our own sense of it and, almost, one another.

It's how they talk what we call love to one another
over great distances, making their separate
presences felt in the dark, claiming whatever
the abrupt compulsions of the blood have brought
home to them, then seeking each other out
through the blind static that clogs up the night,
the mob of small voices and hungry mouths
coming between them, that grid of difficulty
they have to deal with if they want in every sense
to find themselves and decode in their own limbs
the complicated burden of this cold light
they've been, their whole excited lives, carrying.

Of course I don't understand their whole lives carrying
this cold light that might once have been a figure

for the soul, the soul at risk, worn on the sleeve,
its happenstance of chance and circumstance and will,
those habits of negotiation between its own
intermittent radiance and the larger dark; of course
the words I reach to touch it with are clumsy
and impertinent, nothing to the real purpose;
and of course it leads its subtle specific life
beyond such blunderings. But it was the smallest
of all those creatures I've come close to, looked—
however dumbly—into, and was still signalling
that last time I breathed its liquid fire to life,
blew my own breath into its brief body and it fell
from the wire like a firework spending itself
in blackness, one luminous blip of silence into
the surrounding night—the way a firework goes
suddenly silent at its height and drifts back down
in a dead hush, blobs of slow light growing fainter
as they fall into the flattened arms of the dark.

But for those moments it inhabited the dark
wired border zone between us, it seemed
as if it could be looking back at me, making
between my breath and its uncanny light
a kind of contact, almost (I want to think)
communication—short, entirely circumscribed,
and set in true perspective by the static-
riddled big pitch dark, but still something like
the way we might telegraph our own selves
in short bright telling phrases to each other—
on-off-on then stop—the whole live busy night
a huge ear harking to the high notes
of our specific music, and to the silence
that contains it as the dark contains the light.

Fenceposts

Inside each of these old fenceposts
fashioned from weathered boughs and salt-bleached branches
(knotholes, wormy ridges, shreds of bark still visible)
something pulses with a life that lies outside our language:
for all their varicose veins and dried grain lines,
these old-timers know how to stand up
to whatever weather swaggers off the Atlantic or
over the holy nose of Croagh Patrick to ruffle
the supple grasses with no backbone—which seem
endlessly agreeable, like polite, forbearing men
in a bar of rowdies. Driven nails, spancels
of barbed wire, rust collars or iron braces—the fenceposts
tighten their grip on these and hang on, perfecting
their art and craft of saying next to nothing
while the rain keeps coming down, the chapping wind
whittles them, and the merciless sun
just stares and stares: yearly the shore is eaten away
and they'll dangle by a thread until salvaged
and planted again in the open field, which they bring
to an order of sorts, showing us how to be at home
and useful in adversity, and weather it.

EAMON GRENNAN *is an Irish citizen and the Dexter M. Ferry, Jr. Professor of English at Vassar College. He is the author of the poetry collections* Relations: New & Selected Poems, So It Goes, As If It Matters, *and* What Light There Is & Other Poems, *the critical study* Facing the Music: Irish Poetry in the Twentieth Century, *and his translation,* Leopardi: Selected Poems. *He divides his time between New York and Ireland.*

JAN ZITA GROVER

North Enough

AIDS and Other Clear-Cuts

AIDS AND OTHER CLEAR-CUTS

JAN ZITA GROVER

Cutover

I stuff myself into the agent's ragtop Jeep and we shoot north, then east along a series of sand roads still partly covered with snow. Arctic air seeps through the cracks and holes in the Jeep's ragtop and sears my lungs. Despite the compass of bright spring sun, I lose all sense of direction as we careen from one short patch of light to shadow down unmarked roads. The sky is almost purple, and the low banks of the road are fretted with the attenuated shadows of shrubs.

For mile upon mile of northwestern Wisconsin, tree plantations cast blocks of deep shade over the sunlit snow; light strobes through the tree rows like sun piercing a picket fence. "You don't have to worry about the paper mills harvesting these trees and leaving big dead patches around here," the agent yells over rushing air. "Wisconsin law makes them leave strips along the roads now"—a cosmetic illusion to hide clear-cuts that I soon learn the Canadians call idiot strips. Behind the scrim of bushy trees, a prickly rash of young aspens, the northern forest's most symptomatic response to clear-cutting, pokes leaflessly above the snow.

From the road, the tree farms look appealing—dense, dark, sheltering. Early-returning hawks soar above them, and ravens and crows. But when I have the chance to stop seeing the plantations as distant prospects and manage to peer down their serried rows, I can see that they provide no cover or browse for four-legged animals: the ground beneath them is smooth and cleared of pine needles (harvested for commercial mulch), and their trunks are pruned of lateral branches so they will grow straight and tall. Viewed up close, the pulpwood plantations are a DMZ, not much of a home for forest creatures.

For miles of numbing cold and skidding turns, we roar past tree plantations, bogs of black spruce and tamarack, hillsides of anonymous hardwoods. In its prespring bleakness, the landscape looks more like a candidate for reclamation than the stately northern retreat I am seeking. Where are the murmuring pines and hemlocks, the loons on gelid lakes? The agent's bright promise of excellent birding along the St. Croix Flowage increasingly sounds like pie in the sky, her enthusiasm for this burned-over district demented. So I cower low in the passenger seat, tugging my headband over my ears. Soon, I promise myself, soon it will be over, and I can return to Minneapolis and rethink this project of finding that proverbial northwoods grail, The Cabin on the Lake.

Two hours and several inspections later, we shoot across a bridge alongside a low concrete dam and up a hill to a sharp, rocking stop. In the sudden stillness, the agent smiles and points slowly across the road. I follow the arc of her finger toward a small pond about thirty feet down a steep slope. In the center of the pond is a tiny island. On the island stands a log cabin scaled so cunningly that I can almost fool myself into believing that I am flying miles above an islanded lake, looking down on that diminished roof. Only by pulling my reluctant eyes back to the surrounding hills and roadway do I recognize the visual joke and see the cabin's scale for what it is: an inch-to-a-foot miniature set down on a bathmat-sized island on some unnamed northern pond.

No, the agent doesn't know who built the cabin: it has been here as long as she's lived up north and is widely loved. It sits there, illusorily sturdy and big, magical in origin and purpose. My mind begins purring more favorably toward the bleak landscape around us.

I travel with my dead; Perry has been dead for six months, and I wonder what he would think of this landscape, still so unreadable to my California eyes. I cannot imagine it green and refulgent, shoots and crosiers and leaves scrambling over the scars. I try to see it through his eyes, but I cannot; he is like a faraway station, flickering in, fading out. I cannot think of anyone else who can help me imagine this place whole, who has willed damage into wholeness as thoroughly as he did.

I want a place I can explore slowly, slowly, like a lover's body, like a body I will tend—what, after all, has become more familiar?—but that will last longer than any body. I am new to Minnesota, which is more like a new country than a new state to me. I have no lover, and my cumulative terrors keep me from seeking one. *Nothing lasts forever*, Perry often said, only reminding me of what we all profess to know but what most of us refuse to accept. Unlike me, he inhabited that difficult truth: his body rotted, sloughed its beauty, liquesced. He sunk deeper and deeper in his bed, as if growing roots, extruding layers like a clam, blanket upon blanket, until he was little more than a finely carved mask with the high white nose of the dead, surrounded by petals of bedding. A still face surrounded by sheets in a high narrow room.

Today I sit in a drafty four-wheel-drive looking out over a place as visibly damaged, as compromised, as he was, but permanent in ways we forked creatures are not: *Perry, is this worth my taking a chance on?*

He does not answer, and I am surprised to realize I no longer expect him to—he probably wouldn't answer if I were sitting across from him on one of his black couches, except perhaps to rasp out, "*You* want to escape to the north woods, but you expect *me* to provide you with the rationale?"

Decisions hang on so little. I stare at the fine magic of the tiny cabin centered on a frozen pond and agree to look at just one more place.

It is the kind of logged-out, burned-over district that makes westward migration seem like a sensible idea. Miles of black oak and jack pine, much of it dead and down. Sand roads lined with scrub. Beaten-down trailers and perpetually unfinished houses, their composition walls dulling to gray, then black, as the seasons pass. Hills and grades scraped nude, gullies branded into the thin sand soils by all-terrain vehicles (ATVs). A place visited mostly when the bogs freeze over and hunters from cities to the south fan out across the scratchy hills in search of bear and white tails.

The Minnesota and Wisconsin cutovers are northern counties that were logged over several times between 1860 and 1920. Never particularly habitable on a permanent basis, their soils were too thin or too sandy or too acid for farming, their growing seasons too short. But as pines and then hardwoods and then tamaracks and spruces were successively logged off, the timber and railroad companies set out to create a market for the land they had depleted and defaced. In Scandinavia, Germany, and in northern and eastern American cities, northern Minnesota and Wisconsin were touted as rich farmlands, and the ignorant and the desperate came to homestead. Two or three growing seasons, and the thin soils were exhausted. By 1921, taxes on one million acres in the Wisconsin cutover were delinquent; over 40 percent of the tax deeds remained unsold. By 1927, over 2.5 million acres were delinquent and 80 percent of tax deeds were unsold. The University of Wisconsin Experiment Station reported that the total acreage under cultivation in the "resettled" cutover was only 6 percent. Conditions in Minnesota were similar or even worse: much of the cutover there were peatlands, which were drained at great expense with county bonds. Farmers in the peatlands could not pay the steadily rising taxes on their ditched and drained land with what they earned from their poor crops (hay, rye). Most of Minnesota's cutover was abandoned by its homesteaders before the Dirty Thirties even came along.

Then came the Depression. The federal Resettlement Administration (later the Farm Security Administration [FSA]) assessed the plight of cutover settlers and concluded that their farms were too marginal to succeed. Many of those who had stuck it out farming in northern Minnesota and Wisconsin were resettled by the FSA to the experimental Matanuska Colony in southeastern Alaska. City squatters occupied the land after that, then moved on. Families were frozen out. As more and more of the land fell under federal, state, and county ownership through tax default, much of the cutover was reseeded to pine, spruce, and fir. Forest appeared to be the only practicable use for a land that had become depopulated and had failed as farmland.

Douglas County, Wisconsin, offers a bar for seemingly every resident— bars hidden back on sand roads, bars tucked back in the trees. My neighbor says the impressive ratio of bars to people gives fresh meaning to the phrase "Build it, and they will come."

They're out here for a reason.

The long glacial hills sliding away from the road are densely covered in knee-high popple. Beyond lie moraines bereft even of seedlings—denuded pine barrens with sandy orange soil, piled slash, and the crisscross indicia of earthmovers' treads. Stumps like broken orange beaver teeth. Only under snow cover does such a landscape approach conventional beauty.

The sand road to the last cabin we look at winds past pulp-tree plantations. Turning onto County Road 50, we dip past thickets of black oak and aspen toward a low, boggy bay of Crystal Lake. This is no managed landscape. It bears all the signs of a neglect neither benign nor malign, merely indifferent. Downed pine and oak everywhere. The few small birch choked by anonymous, weedy shrubs. With the exception of several near dead red pines, not a tree is over fifteen feet tall. A dead porcupine lies across the road, its viscera turned out on the tar surface like items at a yard sale. The hole in its abdomen is as smooth as a surgical incision.

We flash past the body, my doubts increasing. Up ahead someone has planted idiot strips of red and white pine. Their soughing beauty makes the jacks and black oak behind them look even less northwoods idyllic.

The jack pine that predominates here is a humble tree, lacking the breathtaking height of reds and whites; as it ages, its branches rise popple-like toward the sky, diminishing its profile. Unlike the reds and whites, with their soft fans of needles in threes and fives, jacks produce blunt, short-bristled clusters and cones that recoil on themselves in tight gnarls. Like the black oak, its sand-barrens companion, the jack has a modest architecture: it does not require a lot of space, sharing equitably with other trash trees and shrubs. At sixty years, a jack pine is ancient, ready to fall; at sixty, a red or white pine is just attaining adulthood.

But jacks are the first conifers to reestablish themselves after a fire. Intense heat melts the resinous glue of their crescent-shaped cones, which then open like blowsy flowers, scattering their seed to the hot winds. The result is an initial growth of heavy jack-pine seedlings "thick as the hair on a dog's back," as foresters put it. Jacks are the toughest and most adaptable of northern pines, boreal trees that can thrive on the thin sand soils left behind by glaciers as far north as the tree line. Rangers celebrate the jack's tenacity and homeliness in doggerel—"There, there, little jack pine, don't you sigh. You'll be a white pine by and by"—but the cutover's loggers despised it. The wood is soft and light, unsuitable for timber, unworthy of the loggers' art, useful only for pulping. Whatever else it may be, the jack is a survivor.

Perry recognized my homesickness before I did. We had met only once before, several weeks after my move to Minnesota from California, and now we sat sweating in the all-or-nothing heat of my rented house. Even in the room's feverish heat, Perry was still cold. He curled conchlike into himself, tan and blond but shivering, wrapped in his afghan. I had been told that he had once been one of Minneapolis's great beauties, black leathered and dangerous, back in his drinking days. But that had been almost a decade ago; although his face was still handsome and mostly delicate, pale blue shadows bloomed there and one eye was swollen shut, edematous.

It was an early March afternoon in Minneapolis. Outside the windows sunlight glittered deceptively. The climate struck me as deceitful: *How could it be so cold when it looked so warm?* We spent the afternoon concocting elaborate descriptions of the flowers and light we could be enjoying right now, this very minute, if we were in California instead. Perry was a writer, and porous. Our tongues clattered free, our imaginations sparked and mated, and we became besotted with each other's language. Perry invoked the poisonous, beautiful datura that overhung pastel doorways in San Diego, where he hoped to spend his future winters. I summoned up the purple iris that bloomed along the brick walks of San Francisco General in January, the water blue wisteria that overhung Berkeley's Julia Morgan houses, and the long golden light of February. We spun scenarios of almost pornographic detail as the cold northern sun sluiced down the sky.

A week later, he called me up. "Would you like to go to the Home and Garden Show?" His voice cracked; new lesions in his throat.

Home and Garden Show? Lawn mowers, tractors, redwood hot tubs, and gazebos? Double-glazed install-them-yourself windows and battery-operated screwdrivers? It sounded about as appealing as a sales meeting. But I would have followed Perry's kindness, his supple heart, anywhere.

"Sure," I said.

"I'll pick you up at seven. Watch for a white Volvo."

He rang the bell instead. For a moment, standing there top-lit on the porch, he was a *calavera* figure. I didn't recognize him. He was bald from chemotherapy and wore a jaunty little tocque on his gleaming skull. Like Rudolf, his fine nose was tipped now with a huge red bulb, a lesion. He wore a black-and-white keyboard-patterned neck scarf and a purple-and-black cotton sweater that matched his KS lesions exactly, the sweater I wear now as I write. He handed me a big sheaf of French tulips. He was smiling.

"Ready?" he said.

Seeing the cabin for the first time, I know nothing of the cutover, of the north woods' sad history. I am innocent of the urge to metaphorize every tree, shrub, lichen. I know only that the land seems vaguely distressed, the forest mournful and neglected—not at all what I had hoped to find. Against the hard white April snow, the scabby forest lacks any beauty I can understand. Scoriatic bark, rheumatoid branches, the torn flags of last season's leaves. I sense such trees are the result of the damage done here, but I am not sympathetic to their homeliness. I am seeking an unblemished north woods of tall, stately trees. I want no part of these scarred veterans or of the opened earth, the trailer camps back in the trees, the sandbanks riven by ATVs. I am eager to move on without wasting any more time.

The cabin lies at the end of a sand road alongside a bay still opaque with ice. Far out on the horizon, something black and liquid dips and loops, pouring itself under the ice, then reappearing in a skivvying line. With binoculars, the dark coil resolves into an otter. The agent brightens at my new show of interest and quickly piles on other points in the property's favor: bald eagle, bobcat, bear.

I hear her as if from a great distance. Already something completely unexpected is working in me: a slight, almost imperceptible intimation that this ruined land can become my teacher if only I will agree to become its pupil. What surrounds me I can see now only conventionally, but I sense that one day, through love and knowledge, I may find this place beautiful. I am eager to be schooled, to stimulate what twitches of feeling I still possess.

There are dangers in reading landscapes and other cultural artifacts as texts. The meaning of any text greatly exceeds the words used to constitute it: this is what intertextuality is about—the excess of cultural baggage we bring to reading something seemingly circumscribed and specific. The references we bring tend to be from other textual systems—films, music, literature—that for all their differences are still a particular kind of human artifact: symbolic representations of real acts.

Land is not only a representation. It is also a physical palimpsest upon which complex human, animal, and geologic acts, most of which are not primarily symbolic, have been written in flesh and tree and rock. While most landscapes are unquestionably cultural, it does not follow that theories devised for analyzing cultural representations are particularly applicable to reading them. The cutover is a "deep" cultural landscape: even if I look back no further than the arrival of the first documented Europeans—the *voyageurs*—that still leaves almost four centuries of European, Ojibway, and Dakota actions on the land to account for and interpret. These woodlands have been fretted by the pathways of peoples moving west and south, then north and east, then south and west again. If the European settlers' arrival and displacement of earlier inhabitants seems to us now somehow more decisive, more tragic, than the Ojibway's displacement of the Dakota, it is partly because it is more recent and better documented *as text*. But anguish is kept alive in landscape as well as in writing by both the displacer and the displaced, and heightened by the cultural differences between the victor and the vanquished.

Suppose I choose to look deeply at the area surrounding the cabin: what then do I call such a search? A textual reading? I might instead call it landscape study or a species of cultural studies, with all that the latter term implies about eclectic methods and intentions. Does it matter at all what I call this project? Well, yes: depending on how I conceive it, certain data, certain methods, suggest themselves. My observations might turn toward the jack pine's life cycle in one case and the history of European American logging in another.

I ask myself why I find a landscape this damaged so beautiful, or at any rate so touching. Answering this question brings me to the lip of the abyss, to the six years I chose to live under the whip of AIDS.

I no longer believe there will be time enough for what I want to do. That I can control many events. That my culture's standards of beauty are attainable or even desirable. How easy it is to stand outside my own body and watch it strain toward feeling, any feeling, at any cost! I have learned to find beauty in places where I never would have searched for or found it before—an edematous face, a lesioned and smelly body, a mind rubbed numb by pain. Pain. A burned-over district. Mortal lessons: the beauty of a ravished landscape. Now middle-aged, I find mortality doubly my possession, keeper and kept.

The diminishment of this landscape mortifies and disciplines me. Its scars will outlast me, bearing witness for decades beyond my death to the damage done here. Fat-tired ATVs and their helmeted riders lay the land bare, ream it continuously until it runs red and open, as disease has defaced the bodies of my friends. I learn to love what has been defaced, to cherish it for reasons other than easy beauty. I walk after the ATVs now, collecting beer cans and plastic leech tubs from the banks of the bass hole, tutor myself in the difficult art of loving what is superficially ugly. Beauty flashes out unexpectedly. I try not to anticipate its location, merely to trust its imminence.

Exceptions: Curving in a hook southeast of the cabin is a point crowned by a stand of ancient red and white pines beneath which time itself seems stilled. An eagle couple lives there, wheeling over the adjoining bog each dawn and sunset. The pines on the point survived the felling of millions of their fellows because they were too difficult to haul out, protected by a wide bog thick with the improbable creatures that live on its floating mat: tamarack, sundew, pitcher plant, leatherleaf, bog rosemary, Labrador tea.

There is no more lesson in the pines' survival than in why some people with HIV live for ten or twelve years while others die after only three. Survival no longer has much intrinsic meaning to me. These things happen. I have learned to be deeply suspicious of metaphor, resistant to the pretty conceits that once satisfied my need to explain pain. When I look south to the surviving pines, I try to abjure the lessons that spin so readily to mind, like files summoned from a whirling disk. If I choose to find meaning in any of this, I must remember it is *my* meaning, just as the comfort I drag from friends' deaths—heavy, cold, resistant as wet laundry—is for and by myself.

The damage here is subtle, or so I am told. Hillsides damaged by ATVs. Yet pines continue to double over in the northwest winds and blueberries to fruit underfoot. In late fall, old beater pickups prowl the sand roads, jammed with camo'd guys and galvanized kennels of bawling coonhounds, sound and spunk as ancient as the music of cranes. Deer still flash across the bog like glimpsed dreams. The woods are reputedly full of bear, the sky thick with waterfowl, the lakes clear and deep and filled with muskie and pike. In fall, oak leaves flutter oxblood against navy sky, and the bay water shines black with cold. Natural, natural, all so natural.

And yet.

So *what's the problem?*—why my heart-stopping conviction of measureless damage? I am not alone in feeling the force of disaster; a friend febrile with infection visited me here for only an afternoon and felt, as deeply and potently as I do, the profound damage done here. It is as if the land secretes pheromones testifying to its abuse, detectable only by those who are themselves damaged.

Landscape presents itself as an epistemological puzzle. Can we understand it by recurring to what it once was? The sentimental response to this would be Yes: merely invoke the "pre-invasion" or pre-European forest as a measure of what has been lost, and the job is apparently done. But it is not: *which* pre-European forest shall we mourn the loss of? Forests in this sandskinned country succeed each other at a variety of paces, depending on whether or not fire is involved. If the cutover's most visible recent damage was caused by European American logging, it is also true that lightning-caused fires alter these northern forests as dramatically, as conclusively, as loggers do. As does wind: on the Fourth of July, 1977, a 200 mph straight-line wind flattened miles of forest just south of the cabin as thoroughly as any logging operation ever did. The scraped hills of that blowdown are now covered with ten-foot popple indistinguishable from those succeeding a clear-cut. In the spin of centuries, metasuccession for some species may barely register the damage done by nineteenth-century European settlers and loggers. For other species, logging and farming were decisive: they have vanished. So for what forest or part of the forest am I mourning? Whose deaths?

Today on a dawn walk, I see for the first time a small meadow obscured during summer by a snarl of shrubs along the road. Now I crash through the leafless bramble to look at it more closely. I stand knee-deep in frost-stiffened grass, and this is what I see: a former beaver pond, perfectly round and silted up, wind- and animal-seeded, moving slowly through the ordinations of succession. It is on its way to becoming a forest clearing, then a patch of forest. But what kind of forest? Jack pine and black oak? Surrounding it are a fringe of aspen and birch—a hardwood thicket, what foresters call an asbestos forest. That means the soil here is probably moister and deeper than it is sixty yards away among the jacks. A small conundrum for people a hundred years from now, who may puzzle over this unexplained ring of deep-soil hardwoods surrounded by dryland jacks and oaks.

Like that small meadow, the bay is slowly transmuting. It is becoming a bog; already it is lapidary with peat eruptions that maroon unwary canoeists when the water draws down in midsummer. If the next century is unusually dry and warm, the breakdown of water plants in the bay will accelerate, and the bog along the western shore will expand. Centuries from now, the bog will dry to meadow, at which point trees will move in from the edges. Swamp forest.

Do I call this process damage, do I call it succession? What model—too inappropriate, too human—do I use when embracing this landscape and calling it damaged, imperfect? According to whose sense of time?

I am watching the resident vulture soar on wings stiff as ironing boards, rocking faintly on a thermal. I think about Perry's leg.

One night shortly before he died, I got my first look at it. I had been uncomfortably aware of his leg lesions for several weeks—a faintly sweet, overripe smell in the house, an undertone of rot.

Perry was reluctant to let me change his bandage. "Are you sure you want to do this? It can wait until morning. Are you sure? Are you *very* sure?"

I wanted to do it. It comforted me to think of him going to bed dry and clean when I could do so little else for his dying blond beauty. I knelt before him and slowly peeled away his pant leg from the soaked bandage, yards and yards of puke green gauze. I unwound and heaped them in a reeking pile.

How much of the world could I find in something that was dying—in a leg no longer smooth, intact, encased in a tan skin? In a leg now erupted, returning to orderless matter?

It did not look like a leg. It looked like freshly turned soil, dark and ruptured. Like something I did not associate with the living, with bone and tendon and ligament, muscle and skin.

I was tempted to touch it, to find out what something so formless-looking could possibly feel like. Were there still nerve endings in this mass of dead and sloughing cells? Did it feel, this leg?

Could I learn to see his leg as a creation as well as a destruction? Its world was entropic: moist, swirling with energy turned on itself, no longer producing orderly structures. Dermis, epidermis, capillary, vein, artery, ganglion. Gone. Instead, hyperbolic replication that guttered out needed systems, flooding cells. Drowned them. The surface looked like deep night sky, dark, starred with drops of serum winking back my reflection, the room, me kneeling there.

Light gathered up chaos, shaped it. Perry's leg shaped death: here was where it most visibly entered my friend, through this swollen log. He hauled his death around with him; it came this way. The leg, or what used to be the leg, midwifed urgent talk. *Talk death*, it urged. *It's present; you can smell it, you can see it.* It created a faint sweet stench deep as formalin. Ineradicable, deeply remembered.

Perry sat on the edge of his bed in jolly green clothes. Small, still, tired. I debrided his lesions with hydrogen peroxide much as I would pour soda over a ham or meat loaf. The bubbles winked back at me, catch-lit; they might have been stars wheeling in an unfamiliar galaxy.

Perry talked disparagingly about his leg.

I asked him, "How does it feel, seeing your leg like that?"

"Sometimes I simply can't bear it." As if he could not believe it was his.

"What do you do then?"

He opened his still-beautiful mouth.

And as quickly as he answered, I forgot what he said. It plunged fast, sunk deep. I have tried to remember, fallen asleep hoping to catch his answer when it bobs unguarded from sleep's deep hole. But I cannot. His reply lies rockbound in some shaded place, guarded against memory.

Perhaps he did not answer me at all. Soon afterward he told me he had developed a high tolerance for pain. And perhaps that was his only answer: he had learned to dissociate himself from the slow dying of his body. But Perry did not apportion himself into those cold-war blocs, body and soul. He knew that the KS festering in his left leg had also laid hold of his lungs, liver, esophagus, soul. None of him was unaffected by what then macerated his flesh. He was turning into something else, rich and strange—a dead organism, human peat. Dear bog.

I rewound his leg's burial sheet.

JAN ZITA GROVER *is a transplant from San Francisco who now lives in Duluth, Minnesota. She is the author of* Northern Waters *and* North Enough.

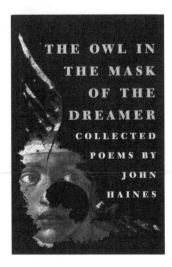

JOHN HAINES

The Owl in the Mask of the Dreamer

Collected Poems

The House of the Injured

I found a house in the forest,
small, windowless, and dark.

From the doorway came the close,
suffocating odor of blood
and fur mixed with dung.

I looked inside and saw
an injured bird
that filled the room.

With a stifled croaking
it lunged toward the door
as if held back
by an invisible chain:

the beak was half eaten away,
and its heart beat wildly
under the rumpled feathers.

I sank to my knees—
a man shown the face of God.

Listening in October

In the quiet house
a lamp is burning
where the book of autumn
lies open on a table.

There is tea with milk
in heavy mugs,
brown raisin cake, and thoughts
that stir the heart
with the promises of death.

We sit without words,
gazing past the limit
of fire into the towering
darkness . . .

There are silences so deep
you can hear
the journeys of the soul,
enormous footsteps
downward in a freezing earth.

The Stone Harp

A road deepening in the north,
strung with steel,
resonant in the winter evening,
as though the earth were a harp
soon to be struck.

As if a spade
rang in a rock chamber:

in the subterranean light,
glittering with mica,
a figure like a tree turning to stone
stands on its charred roots
and tries to sing.

Now there is all this blood
flowing into the west,
ragged holes at the waterline of the sun—
that ship is sinking.

And the only poet is the wind,
a drifter
who walked in from the coast
with empty pockets.

He stands on the road
at evening, making a sound
like a stone harp
strummed
by a handful of leaves . . .

The Snowbound City

I believe in this stalled magnificence,
this churning chaos of traffic,
a beast with broken spine,
its hoarse voice hooded in feathers
and mist; the baffled eyes
wink amber and slowly darken.

Of men and women suddenly walking,
stumbling with little sleighs
in search of Tibetan houses—
dust from a far-off mountain
already whitens their shoulders.

When evening falls in blurred heaps,
a man losing his way among churches
and schoolyards feels under his cold hand
the stone thoughts of that city,

impassable to all but a few children
who went on into the hidden life
of caves and winter fires,
their faces glowing with disaster.

Cicada

I

I sank past bitten leaves,
tuning in a shell my song
of the absent and deaf.

And that pain came alive
in the dark, shot

with the torment of seeds,
root-ends and wiry elbows.

II

A whisper, dry and insane,
repeating like a paper drum
something I was,
something I might become:

a little green knife
slitting the wind upstairs,
or a husk in the sod.

III

It was late summer
in the grass overhead.
I wanted wings and a voice,

my own tree to climb,
and someone else to answer,
clear across
loud acres of sun.

The Owl in the Mask of the Dreamer

Nothing bestial or human remains
in all the brass and tin
that we strike and break and weld.

Nothing of the hand-warmed stone
made flesh, of the poured heat
filling breast, belly, and thigh.

The craft of an old affection
that called by name the lion shape
of night, gave rain its body

and the wind its mouth—the owl
in the mask of the dreamer,
one of the animal stones asleep . . .

By tinker and by cutting torch
reduced to a fist of slag,
to a knot of rust on a face of chrome.

So, black dust of the grinding wheels,
bright and sinewy curl of metal
fallen beneath the lathe:

Speak for these people of drawn wire
striding toward each other
over a swept square of bronze.

For them the silence is loud
and the sunlight is strong.

No matter how far they walk
they will never be closer.

Night

Do not wake me, for I am not ready
to speak, to break the spell
fixed in these sleeping stones.

Go quietly here. Whisper to wise men
what you cannot speak aloud.
Quiet the metal of doors.

It is the time of earth-changes,
of vanishing rainfall,
and the restless barking of dogs.

Divided is the man of hidden
purpose, and evil his redemption.

Harness the wind and drive the water,
you that govern,
who yoke and stride the world . . .

And then be still.

Leaves of the one standing tree
fall through the twilight;
the nightborn images rise, the owl

in the mask of the dreamer wakes:
Who is the guest?
Who is it who knocks and whispers?

As one calmed in his death-dream
would never return
to this hunted world—

one more key to the clockwork
that drives the stunned machine,
another cry under the wheel . . .

But calmed and stationed aloft,
delight in his distance,
to see on the star-pavilions

the bright, imperial creatures rise,
ascend their thrones, rule
and prosper. The thrones darken,

earth in the moon-shadow fails,
and he alone in that cold
and drifting waste keeps alight

memorial constellations . . .

So I in this quiet sleep of stone
can say to you: Leave to me
this one sustaining solace—

my night that has more night
to come. To the sun that has set,
whose dawn I cannot see . . .

Mute in my transformation,
and do not wake me.

JOHN HAINES *is the author of several major collections of poetry, essays, and memoirs. His books include* The Owl in the Mask of the Dreamer, Fables and Distances, The Stars, the Snow, the Fire, *and* Living Off the Country. *He has spent most of his life in Alaska and is currently living in Montana.*

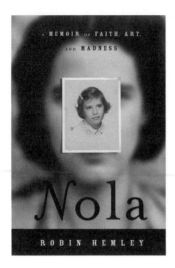

ROBIN HEMLEY

Nola

*A Memoir of Faith, Art,
and Madness*

Prologue: Larceny

ADMISSIBLE EVIDENCE

My parents seemed to believe in letting everyone do whatever they wanted until they became very good at it or died. My father, Cecil Hemley, was a poet, novelist, editor, and translator of Isaac Bashevis Singer's work. He was also a good smoker and that's what he died of when I was seven. My older brother Jonathan used to be good at everything, from languages to sports to the sciences, but over the last twenty years he's specialized—in Orthodox Judaism, and lives with his eight children and wife in L.A. My sister Nola was good at everything, too, art and language, but especially things of the spirit—and that, in a sense, is what she eventually died from. My mother Elaine Gottlieb is a short story writer and teacher. She's good at surviving. As for myself . . . I've always had a larcenous heart.

As I get older, the thief diminishes, but still there is something inside me essentially untrustworthy, someone hard and calculating, egged on by the deaths of my father and sister, someone who will not always accept responsibility for his actions. I remember a camp counselor at Granite Lake Camp in New Hampshire telling me one night that he was on to me. He called me conniving. I pretended I didn't know what he was talking about, and was silent. He was one of the only people who saw through me like that, or at least one of the few who ever told me directly. I wonder about confession, this nagging need. When I confess, I make myself vulnerable. Some people will like me for it and others will arm themselves with my admissions and hurl them back. One time I told my mother what this counselor had said about me and the next time we argued, she said, "Your counselor was right. You are conniving." After that, I resolved to bury myself deeper, to hide this other person where even I wouldn't be able to recognize him. Sometimes I think it's too late, that he has already stolen away the things my sister gave me—things of the imagination and spirit that he pawned to support his habit.

INADMISSIBLE EVIDENCE

I'm looking through a drawer of a desk in my room at my grandmother's house. I'm seventeen and I'm looking for something to steal—loose change would be great or an antique paperweight or letter opener.

Inside one of the drawers, I come across a legal-sized document with a rusty paper clip attached. It's titled POINT OF ERROR #1 and reads "The Finding that 'No marriage between Elliot Chess and Elaine Gottlieb (also known as Elaine Hemley) was ever entered into at any time or at any place' is contrary to the evidence and against the weight of the evidence. Appellees proved the contract of marriage." That's as far as I read. I'm not sure what this document is or how it pertains to me, but I know I have to have it, and I know that I can't tell anyone about it. It has something to do with Nola, who's been dead three years.

DISCOVERY

Uncovering the facts, not even the facts but the feelings of my sister and mother's lives, has become a detective story for me. It started out before I even knew it was a detective story, when I was seventeen and found some court documents about my mother and Nola's father, Elliot Chess, in a drawer at my grandmother's house. The remarkable thing about finding these documents was that I never told anyone I'd found them and never read them until now. For years, I kept them in a box and never looked at them. But now that I've read them, now that I understand things about my mother's life, things perhaps that she wouldn't want me to know, the revelations follow quickly, one upon the other. And the more I uncover, the more I realize that one of these days I'm going to have to tell my mother about the court papers I found. Eventually, I'll confess. But the documents keep multiplying. Everyone in my family, or connected with it, it seems, has written about the events I want to write about—although not in a way that gives an overall picture of who we are. Every day, I seem to learn about new documents. I'm drowning in them. My mother tells me little by little about their existence, almost as though she's teasing me. But this is how she's always been. Rarely does she volunteer information about her life, although if asked a direct question, she'll sometimes answer. She's known a lot of famous writers and artists: Isaac Singer, Joseph Heller, Robert Motherwell, Weldon Kees, Louise Bogan, Conrad Aiken, John Crowe Ransom, but she almost never mentions any of them: It's not important to her.

My mother has kept a journal for years. I never knew this until I stumbled upon the fact New Year's Eve, 1994, when I asked her nonchalantly whether she'd ever kept a journal.

"Sure, I've been keeping a journal since I was sixteen."

I was stunned. "Do you have anything from your time in Mexico with your first husband?"

"Sure, I have a lot about Mexico."

"I need it all," I told her.

She laughed.

"Do you know where it is?"

"I was just looking at it the other day."

"Mom, I'm always amazed how I just find out these things about you by chance."

She laughed again.

That night, she and I sat on her bed and sorted through her journal, hundreds of loose-leaf typed pages dating from the thirties. She let me have whatever I wanted, but she also said, "I don't think you should know everything."

"I have to," I said, half laughing. "I want to know everything."

I keep thinking that it's my right to know all this, that she should volunteer everything she knows, as though this is a court case and she'll be accountable for what she doesn't divulge. It says something new about my relationship with my mother that for years everything was too painful to divulge to me, but now nothing is. My mother, since learning about my project, has been sending me steady streams of old photos, journal excerpts, letters.

THE PRESENT

My mother is working on a novel, two novels really, a mystery about a trip we took to England when I was eighteen and another one whose subject I'm unsure of. She's been working on a novel for years, ever since I can remember—her second novel. Her first was published in 1947, the year of my sister Nola's birth. Almost every time I speak to her she's working on a new novel, having abandoned each previous one after a couple of drafts or a few chapters. Every few years she rediscovers her old novels and realizes they were pretty good. She'll work feverishly on a rediscovered novel with renewed vigor until another loss of faith, and then she's off to a new project. In between she writes short stories. For many years they were published in some of the best literary journals and anthologies.

I find myself trying to make time to read her new stories between my busy teaching schedule, doing my own writing, spending time with my own family. Everything produces guilt. I look at my daughters and realize I'm not spending enough time with them. I try to give everyone encouragement. "Just keep sending them out, Mom." "Why don't you just finish this one before moving on? I like the idea of this one."

"I'll get back to it," she tells me.

But I know that after she dies, I'll find a dozen or so novels in various stages of completion, and I won't know what to do with them. Should I find the best ones and try to edit them? Should I send them out as is? Why am I worrying about this now? It's strange to think of your family leaving you documents, but that's what my family leaves behind: stories, novels, poems. Documents. Half-truths. Fiction. It's what my family was built on, what we've always believed in. We've always been suspicious of fact, frightened of it. My grandmother, on her deathbed, delirious, asking for the impossible— to just go home and sit outside for a while on her porch, started ranting, according to my mother, about a supposed case of incest in a branch of our family that happened two hundred years ago, and begged that the family line be stopped. Facts, even two hundred years old, haunt our family.

"Fictionalize it," my mother says. "Why don't you fictionalize it?"

THE PAST

My father has been dead six months. Heart attack. I'm spending the summer with my grandmother Ida, and she enrolls me at Atlantic Beach Day Camp a few blocks from where she lives. I hate swimming, so during swim period I organize a pickpocket ring. I don't know how I learned to pickpocket, but I'm pretty good, so I teach a small group at the camp how to do it. At first, we lift combs from back pockets, but then we start taking wallets. We're finally caught and lined up by the pool where the head counselor interrogates us.

"I know you're good kids," he says. "You wouldn't do this on your own. There's one bad apple among you. Tell me who it is and I'll let the rest of you go."

I turn to the boy in line next to me, a fat kid named Bernard who reluctantly joined the ring, and who seems to think I'm cool. "Why don't you tell them it's you?" I say to Bernard, as though this would be a very good thing for him to do.

He blinks at me and tugs his hair.

"Tell them it's you," I say.

"Why?" he whispers.

"You'll be a hero," I say.

The counselor waits. He moves down the line, looking at the tops of our heads. More than anything, I don't want Ida to know what I've done. She wouldn't be able to believe it. She thinks I'm a good kid and so does my mother, and I can't bear the thought of them being told what I've done.

Bernard glances over at me and gives me an unsure and suffering look. "Go ahead," I say. "Be a hero."

He raises his hand.

"What?" the counselor says.

"It's me," Bernard says. "I'm the ringleader."

The counselor looks a bit surprised, but then a smug look replaces the other and he grins. He reaches over and yanks Bernard by the arm. Bernard cowers in front of us.

"I thought so," the counselor says. "I knew it was you."

The counselor takes Bernard away and that's the last I ever see of him. Another counselor dismisses us. No one says a word to our parents, or in my case, my grandmother, and those of us involved never speak of the pickpocket ring or Bernard again. Maybe they think they've scared us enough or maybe they don't want our parents to think Atlantic Beach Day Camp gives its campers enough idle time to organize pickpocket rings.

The next day I'm idling by one the buildings listening with a whole group of idlers to a transistor radio. We're entranced by a new Beatles song. Someone has called me over to hear it, and we gather around the radio as though hearing the first transmission from a distant universe. Across from us, the good campers, the nonidlers, the Boy Scouts, the Penny-saved-is-a-penny-earned boys are playing softball. I glance up for a second and see something white coming down on me. It knocks me flat. The other idlers laugh at me and the softball group runs over to where I lie, mildly concussed. They argue whether or not it was a home run or fan interference on my part. I don't care. I know it's punishment. A knock on the head from heaven.

A counselor named Herman takes me under his wing. He thinks I'm a good kid and he feels sorry for me that my dad has died. He spends extra time with me, even after the day camp has closed. With my grandmother's permission he takes me to the boardwalk one night. We ride the Ferris wheel. He buys me cotton candy and a potato knish. It's a strange night because there's been a tidal wave the night before, and it's flooded the normally wide beach all the way to the street under the boardwalk. The boardwalk is fine, but you can hear the small waves roiling against the support beams, even catch glimpses of the water through the slats. As we're walking along he picks me up and dangles me over the railing. I see the water, the ocean right beneath me, a dark slapping sea.

He laughs. "Should I drop you over?"

"No," I say, laughing, too, confident that he wouldn't dare.

"I'm going to drop you," he says, and for a moment I can feel it. I'm lost. I'm gone out to sea, pulled far from anything solid. I scream.

Still, he holds me over.

"Don't you wish you learned how to swim?" he says.

Does he know, I wonder? Does he know that I was the ringleader? I'm dangling over the railing by one foot. "I've got you," he says. "I've got you," and I wonder what he means by that.

THE NONFICTIONAL

My mother returns my call on Thanksgiving. I left a message on her machine. I know she's there—probably upstairs in her study writing, but she can't hear me because she's turned her hearing aid down. One of her former students invited her for Thanksgiving dinner, but my mother declined, preferring these days to celebrate holidays by writing.

"Did I tell you I'm working on a mystery?" she asks.

"Yes." She's told me a dozen times already.

"With Nancy Cowgil," she says. "It's about our trip to England."

"I'm writing, too," I say. "I hope Jonny won't hate me when I finish this." But that's not what I really mean to say. What I really mean to say is, "I hope you won't hate me."

"Why's that?"

"I'm not holding anything back."

"You can always soft-pedal the facts," she says. "I found a photo of Nola for you, but it's from when she was twenty."

"I'm going to be writing about you and Elliot Chess."

"What do you know about us? I haven't told you much."

"But that's part of it. I've done a little . . . investigating." I think about what she said about soft-pedaling. I think about the document I have that she doesn't know about, what I found when I was seventeen. I didn't even read it until this summer. While preparing to write this, I remembered the papers and started searching for them, tearing through my files, coming up with nothing, thinking with despair, "I couldn't have thrown them out. Why would I throw them out?" Finally, I found them in my attic, in a corner, at the very bottom of a file box filled with assorted papers. There's so much in these papers that my mother doesn't know I know. I keep hinting that I know more than she's told me, but I just can't make a clean confession. I think about what she said the last time we spoke about this, "God, I'm going to have to become a hermit after you write this." I want to confess. I want more than anything to tell her what I have, but I know that she'd want to see it, that she'd say, "Fictionalize. Don't embarrass me," and I'd have to say, "There's nothing to be embarrassed about. It happened fifty years ago. These things happen every day now." But I know that wouldn't do a thing to diminish her pain, the pain of abandonment and betrayal. And now, here I am—am I betraying her? Do I have any right to say what I know, to tell the facts, private facts from public documents? I know that if I had grown up in a different family, a family of architects, the answer would have been no. All of my writing friends urge me to wait until the manuscript is done before I show it to my mother. One of them tells me, "Thomas Wolfe never would have written *Look Homeward, Angel*, if he'd sought his mother's approval first."

THE FICTIONAL

I come from a family of writers, and the pain that comes from words is not diminished, necessarily, by a fictionalized stance. I grew up as the subject of or a character in my mother's published stories. I was told that I shouldn't be angered by this, that fiction transforms. And I wasn't bothered, except by momentary twinges when I saw revealed in a story, my late thumb-sucking, for instance. I still believe we have the right, the obligation, to write about the world as we see it. Of course, it's always transformed. There's a story by Donald Barthelme, "The Author," in which a famous writer uses her children as the models for all her stories, and when they come to complain to her about telling all their secrets, they ask what gives her the right and she blithely answers, "Because you're mine." But the flip side of that is that they own her, too. The children own the mother and father, whether they know it or not. At times, I want to cry as I'm writing. At times, I want to do wrong, knowingly, to get at what's right.

THE LIES

In Ida's room while she's in the kitchen, I open the clasp of her pocketbook and start digging for her purse. The pocketbook is stuffed with sugar packets she's taken from restaurants, salt and pepper packets, moist towelettes, tissues, combs, her compact, and finally down at the bottom, the little cowhide change purse where she keeps her bills crumpled up together in a wad. I open it and feel the bills. All of them come up in my hand together. I've done this many times. The money is for comic books. I'm fourteen. I don't plan on taking all her money, just a few dollars, maybe five, depending on how much she has and how much I think she'll miss.

As I'm sorting through the mass of wadded bills, Ida walks into the room.

"What are you doing?" she asks. For some reason, she doesn't look surprised.

"I was looking for something," I tell her.

"In my purse?"

I'm holding the wadded bills still, gently, as if I don't know what to do with them, like they're some wounded bird I've found.

"A pen," I say. "I was just looking for a pen."

There's a bit of a whine in my voice, even a threat, not physical, but emotional. I'll do whatever necessary to protect and preserve this lie. I stare at her. I hate her right now for finding out about me. And this is something she can't stand. She looks afraid for a second and says quietly, "I'll help you find one." Only then do I put the money back where I found it and neither of us say a word about this to anyone nor to each other, nor, I'm sure, to ourselves.

THE SPOKEN

Nola was my half sister from my mother's previous marriage, eleven years older than me, a brilliant young woman who graduated Phi Beta Kappa and then studied for her Ph.D. in philosophy at Brandeis. She was also interested, obsessed actually, with spiritual and psychic phenomenon and apprenticed under her Guru, Sri Ramanuja.

Sometimes I still miss Nola keenly. I miss her most when I'm with my daughters, Olivia and Isabel, and it's just us, and I wish they could know their aunt, someone who played the Irish harp, who knew Sanskrit and Greek and French and German and Hebrew, who would teach them Shakespearean songs and sing with them—someone so impractical and imaginative that nearly anything seemed possible to me in her presence.

Anything that had to do with the hidden, with the magical, Nola was interested in, and she cultivated this interest in me. I was her darling baby brother, and she wanted my life to be rich with what was hidden and most inaccessible about the world. In the summer, Nola made a garland of flowers and placed it in my hair, then danced around the yard with me.

She was always telling me stories, Irish folktales, Tolkien, Greek myths, or we sang folk songs, and her songs, like her stories, brimmed with possibility—even to say brimmed, suggests a container, but there was none that I could see. She learned to make animals out of balloons for me and birds out of paper. She loved transformation. She loved metamorphosis. Everything was changing and vibrant in her world, and she tried to show me that in all she made for me. The most ordinary earthbound thing could be made into something that could fly away.

In 1973, she died.

The last several years of her life were spent in and out of mental hospitals, where she was diagnosed with schizophrenia.

She and I had been close until her illness manifested itself and I started to detest her. Before I had a chance to grow up, to mature, to understand, she vanished. It wasn't suicide, I was told, although she had tried to kill herself before. It was a horrible accident, a doctor's mistake. He'd prescribed too much Thorazine and her body had shut down, kidney failure. She went into a coma and died two days later.

THE UNSPOKEN

I've never written about my sister, except in the most oblique way. Every time I've tried head-on, I've failed. For some reason, I can't seem to recreate on the page who my sister was. The people I know the best elude me when I try to describe them. The writing friends whom I admire the most are those who seem to be able to write completely recognizable portraits of their sisters, their fathers, their friends. I've never written about my closest living relatives—never touched my brother or my mother, not even in a fictional way, even though I could avoid issues in fiction that I can't avoid in this. I wonder if you can feel bereavement for the living as well as the dead. That's close to what I feel for my brother.

Jonathan boycotted my wedding because I married a woman of Scotch/Irish/German descent, not Jewish. A couple of weeks before my wedding a rabbi from L.A. called me and told me he was an emissary from my brother. He wanted, he said, to fly to my home and spend a day with me to "tell me the great spectacle of Jewish history."

I thanked the rabbi and told him that the spectacle of Jewish history, while interesting, I'm sure, would not affect the outcome of my marriage. Finally, the rabbi gave up, but before he left me he extracted a promise I'd tell my brother that he'd tried. For some reason, he also seemed intent that I remember his name, which I repeated three times, like something out of Rumpelstiltskin, and promptly forgot the next day.

I know I have not always been the best brother myself. I have often been neglectful. I never bought him a wedding present when he married in 1980, for instance. I wonder if bereavement and guilt are inextricably linked, if in some way you have betrayed the memory of the one bereaved simply by continuing on your own without them. My brother, who is five years older than me, became my father figure after my father died. I always followed his lead until he chose his Orthodox path. He's hurt me as I'm sure I've hurt him. What hurt me the most was a conversation my mother reported to me last year. She said that she had told Jonny she wished we could become close again and Jonny replied, "We were never that close." I wondered if that could be true, if my memory could be so misleading—if his version of the truth or mine is the right one, or if the years of silence between us have stolen the truth away from us forever.

NOT GUILTY

I try not to feel guilty about any of this, any of these thefts. I've felt guilty in the past, but not now. In a way, I feel proud. I'm telling you "Look what I got away with." I cheated death. I escaped madness. I stole before I was stolen. I want you to know that this is what it's really about. This is about the stories we're allowed to tell and the ones we lock away. I'm telling you this is what I've become good at. The other morning I saw that word "Larceny" scrawled in a dream like a film title. The words scrolled in front of me like the beginning of an old movie that establishes a different time and place through words, not images: "Paris, 1797. Anarchy reigned in the streets!" But these words wouldn't have made sense to a movie-theater crowd, wouldn't have set any scene: "Stolen property. Your sister Nola. A search of many years ensued."

An acquaintance of mine, another writer, recently suggested that all writers should be virtuous. He was drunk at the time, but I'll assume it was an honest sentiment. I guess I don't believe it in any case, at least not in the traditional sense of virtue. Outwardly, I'd like for people to think of me as virtuous, but inwardly, I don't care. There's something inside me that still wants to be the thief. For me, the truth is not a matter of virtue. It's something to be stolen, co-opted, appropriated—hot-button words that make the virtuous cringe and yell, "What gives you the right?" The answer is nothing, no right, but what's best about the world did not always spring from the brow of virtue. Pat your pocket. Show me the location of what you value most

ROBIN HEMLEY *is the author of several works of fiction and nonfiction, including* Nola: A Memoir of Faith, Art, and Madness; Turning Life into Fiction; The Last Studebaker; All You Can Eat; *and* The Big Ear. *He presently teaches creative writing at Western Washington University in Bellingham.*

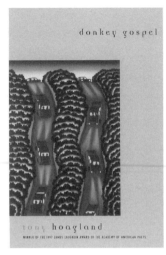

TONY HOAGLAND

Donkey Gospel

Reading Moby-Dick *at 30,000 Feet*

At this height, Kansas
is just a concept,
a checkerboard design of wheat and corn

no larger than the foldout section
of my neighbor's travel magazine.
At this stage of the journey

I would estimate the distance
between myself and my own feelings
is roughly the same as the mileage

from Seattle to New York,
so I can lean back into the upholstered interval
between Muzak and lunch,

a little bored, a little old and strange.
I remember, as a dreamy
backyard kind of kid,

172

Donkey Gospel | 173

tilting up my head to watch
those planes engrave the sky
in lines so steady and so straight

they implied the enormous concentration
of good men,
but now my eyes flicker

from the in-flight movie
to the stewardess's pantyline,
then back into my book,

where men throw harpoons at something
much bigger and probably
better than themselves,

wanting to kill it, wanting
to see great clouds of blood erupt
to prove that they exist.

Imagine being born and growing up,
rushing through the world for sixty years
at unimaginable speeds.

Imagine a century like a room so large,
a corridor so long
you could travel for a lifetime

and never find the door,
until you had forgotten
that such a thing as doors exist.

Better to be on board the *Pequod*,
with a mad one-legged captain
living for revenge.

Better to feel the salt wind
spitting in your face,
to hold your sharpened weapon high,

to see the glisten
of the beast beneath the waves.
What a relief it would be

to hear someone in the crew
cry out like a gull,
Oh Captain, Captain!
Where are we going now?

Brave World

But what about the courage
of the cancer cell
that breaks out from the crowd
it has belonged to all its life

like a housewife erupting
from her line at the grocery store
because she just can't stand
the sameness anymore?

What about the virus that arrives
in town like a traveler
from somewhere faraway
with suitcases in hand,

who only wants a place
to stay, a chance to get ahead
in the land of opportunity,
but who smells bad,

talks funny, and reproduces fast?
What about the microbe that
hurls its tiny boat straight
into the rushing metabolic tide,

no less cunning and intrepid
than Odysseus; that gambles all
to found a city
on an unknown shore?

What about their bill of rights,
their access to a full-scale,
first-class destiny?
their chance to realize

maximum potential?—which, sure,
will come at the expense
of someone else, someone
who, from a certain point of view,

is a secondary character,
whose weeping is almost
too far off to hear,

a noise among the noises
coming from the shadows
of any brave new world.

Hearings

Autumn, and the trees decide again they don't
                                             need leaves.
Mothers add more blankets to the bed.
Yellow lights in windows of the junior high

mean that night school is back in session,
tired grown-ups sitting at the plastic desks,
learning to bisect the hypotenuse,
how to say *spreadsheet* in Japanese.

This week on the televised hearings,
we get to watch our congressmen
nervously pronounce the word *homosexual*
in public—the committee trying to determine
whether queers are good enough

       to pull the triggers
on machines designed to foreclose lives
contrary to the national well-being.

But the congressman can't
pull the trigger on his own tongue
to fire out the word without
tripping over it—fumbling, stumbling
into the ditch between *home* and *sexual.*

You might say his defense industry is troubled,
as if he had a subterranean suspicion
that to say it might mean, just a little,
to *become* it—

    which might be right,

since language uses us
the way that birds use sky,
the way that seeds and viruses
braid themselves into a mammal's fur
and hitchhike toward the future.

When you say a word,
you enter *its* vocabulary,
it's got your home address, your phone number
and weight—it won't forget,

—the way that parents, who finally
bring themselves to say *lesbian*,
enter, through that checkpoint,
the country where their daughter lives.

Tonight, all over Washington, senators in mirrors
will practice until they are as fluent
saying *homosexual*
as they already are at saying *Mr. President*,
and *first-strike option.*

Sometimes we think the truth
is the worst thing that could happen
but the truth is not the worst thing that could happen.

Now it is autumn and in stores
the turquoise wading pools
spangled with bright starfishes and shells
are stacked against the walls, on sale,

implying what was costly yesterday
is cheap today, and might be free tomorrow—
All our yearnings, all our fears:
so many seahorses,
galloping through bubbles.

Are You Experienced?

While Jimi Hendrix played "Purple Haze" onstage,
scaling his guitar like a black cat
up a high-voltage, psychedelic fence,

I was in the parking lot of the rock festival,
trying to get away from the noise and
looking for my car because

I wanted to have something familiar
to throw up next to. The haze I was in
was actually ultraviolet, the murky lavender

of the pills I had swallowed
several hundred years before,
pills that had answered so many of my questions,

they might as well have been guided tours
of miniature castles and museums,
microscopic Sistine Chapels

with room for everyone inside.
—But now something was backfiring,
and I was out on the perimeter of history,

gagging at the volume of raw data,
unable to recall the kind and color
of the car I owned,

and unable to guess, as I studied
the fresco of vomit on concrete,
that one day this moment

cleaned up and polished
would itself become
a kind of credential.

TONY HOAGLAND *is the author of* Donkey Gospel, *winner of the 1997 James Laughlin Award of The Academy of American Poets and* Sweet Ruin, *winner of the 1992 Brittingham Prize in Poetry. He teaches creative writing at New Mexico State University in Las Cruces and in the Warren Wilson College low-residency M.F.A. program.*

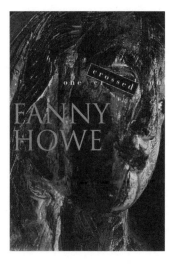

FANNY HOWE

One Crossed Out

Basic Science

One cadaver said to the other
cadaver, "You're my cadaver."

The conversation ended there
but not its effects.

Their souls had evaporated.

It was up to love to raise them
from their litters and let them

arrive as the living poor
at the surface of earth. It did.

At first the maculate pair
poked and picked through refuse.

Denials were their daily breads.
Then they were sold to those

who found their fertility a bonus.
Owned then by the living with names

and fortunes, with lovers who say,
"Lover, I'm your lover,"

cadavers were still the majority.
They kept creation going and love

as well—like hands on a cold
or sunburned back—a weight

with properties that animate.

My Broken Heart

On the 85th night of 19— there were 280 days left in the year.
The cure began. Just as Pascal carried the date of his revelation
in his breast pocket, I began to carry a dated hanky next to my heart.
Healing is a job that requires a mop.

This arm I am leaning on is perfectly suited to mine.
(I always wanted to say that.) Now cold winds have come
and the doctor has determined that my hope was full of holes.
"But holes in the universe are made of matter."

On the 305th night of 19— there were 60 days left in the year.
The cure began. Beauty of style depends on similarity.
Snow for instance is a perfect show, because the sky
opens like a flower shaking out its secrets.

This time of year reminds me of the dot that completes my name.
The dot over the letter that pertains to the first person
singular is a symbol for me of my head.
I always put on my dot when I'm already out of the word.

At last I only have hope for heaven.
Like a person who has "come to" after fainting,
I now know the meaning of the question:
"Where in the world?"

Women should sit down like me—
wherever they are standing now—and refuse to move.
I always wanted to say that.
Whoa! Is someone here, or is this, like, a hat tossed in the air?

Am I really better at being crushed than I was before?

Starlet

That terrible day my heart took a blow that nearly killed
it. While silver lilac shivered in the Hollywood Hills,
I packed and prepared to fly. My heart, once red as a
valentine, seemed to contract and blacken like a prune.

If you want to know the truth, I missed happiness by
inches. A meeting (planned for seven years) never took
place. The person lost me. I could not find him. As a
result, my personal pulse dropped the formula for
survival. I fled the city of colors, emptying, with each
mile, my will to go on.

On the night freeway my heart felt like a body in a pine
box, calling "Preacher, keep it short, for God's sake."

Every minute was a sort of monument in a mortuary.

1. To be lost is to be undiscovered.
2. To find is to discover what was already lost and waiting.

But where is the object of desire in fact?
Is it really out there, waiting?
How can it be there, when it requires time to find it?
And if the time required to get there doesn't yet exist, how
do I know it's there at all?

Everything's a Fake

Coyote scruff in canyons off Mulholland Drive. Fragrance of sage and rose-
mary, now it's spring. At night the mockingbirds ring their warnings of cats
coming across the neighborhoods. Like castanets in the palms of a dancer,
the palm trees clack. The HOLLYWOOD sign has a white skin of fog across it
where erotic canyons hump, moisten, slide, dry up, swell, and shift. They
appear impatient—to make such powerful contact with pleasure that they
will toss back the entire cover of earth. She walks for days around brown
trails, threading sometimes under the low branches of bay and acacia. Bit-
ter flowers will catch her eye: pink and thin honeysuckle, or mock orange.
They coat the branches like lace in the back of a mystical store. Other de-
viant men and women live at the base of these canyons, closer to the city
however. Her mouth is often dry, her chest tight, but she is filled to the
brim with excess idolatry. It was like a flat mouse—the whole of Los Ange-
les she could hold in the circle formed by her thumb and forefinger. Tires
were planted to stop the flow of mud at her feet. But she could see all the
way to Long Beach through a tunnel made in her fist. Her quest for the per-
fect place was only a symptom of the same infection that was out there, a
mild one, but a symptom nonetheless.

FANNY HOWE *is the author of over twenty books of poetry and fiction, including* One
Crossed Out, Saving History, Famous Questions, *and* The Quietist. *She is a professor of
Writing and American Literature at the University of California at San Diego.*

JANET KAUFFMAN

Characters on the Loose

Eureka in Toledo, Weather Permitting

She says I'm matter-of-fact, but she's sure as hell not. If Eureka's matter-of-anything, and it's hard to know what that means, that *matter*, you'd have to say she's matter-of-weather. You notice I don't say matter-of-Mad-Hatter, although she'd like that. She's no dummy.

With Eureka, weather is not small talk: it's her motive, her parentage, her explanation. Science and eros; roof and floor.

On the steps of the Capitol, in sunlight, within minutes of meeting her, she told me one longish story, and I got the picture.

One September day, Eureka said, it was simple. She sat on the wood boards of the back porch of her house, her head against the brick wall. The sun moved across her face through the day, side to side. It heated her hair, one side of her head, then her forehead, then the rest of her hair. She felt the sun on both knees.

She said there wasn't much to see: a field of weeds, a loop of sky. Overhead, birds passed. She heard cars behind her on the road, the noise through the house. She saw dust blow over the roof and settle down. She stared beyond the backyard, and only a couple of things moved: leaves, dry grasses, intermittent clouds.

She just wanted to sit for a while in the sun. But time passed. She stuck it out, and as the day went along, she decided not to move until it was dark.

Eureka, she said to herself. Eureka.

After dark, Eureka walked into the house through the back door. The rooms were full of air.

She walked out the front door. More air.

The sun was still on her arms, she could smell it. She put her nose on her forearm and smelled it.

And it didn't matter, after that, if she was inside a house or out. She was herself, Eureka Upright. She could handle the backbone name of her father, and its mismatch with a bathtub shriek—a name also drawn from the full-page ads, those vacuum cleaners with power-sweep brushes, attachments attached.

Clean sweep was the phrase she kept in mind from then on. The mental action she saw, whenever she heard her name.

On my way to see Jesse Helms, yes indeed, I first saw Eureka Upright on the steps of the Capitol. She sat there, her head thrown back, her eyes shut. She didn't look right. Too calm, much too calm. She wore a white T-shirt, white shorts, and she'd stuffed an oversize tapestried sack under her knees.

I floated a pamphlet into her lap—"Environmental Clean-Up: Big Business for Big Business."

She wasn't aware. Or she was. I couldn't know.

On the way back, though, she clipped my leg, one friendly chop to the kneebone when I passed—she recognized me, or remembered the smell of my skirt, who knows—and she said, "I read this. Sit down and talk."

It's easy to talk to a human being. I know. I talk, I lobby. I try to per-suade Senator Helms that cleaning up the junk in the environment could be a boon to the North Carolina economy—business deals big as defense deals. Same companies, same contracts. It's reasonable. You don't have to be on the side of nature to see the opportunities, I tell him.

I don't get far. But he says a few things, and I say some more, and that's how talk goes. It's all you can hope for.

Outside the Capitol, Eureka Upright wanted to talk. She didn't want coffee. She wanted to sit on the steps where she was. And had been. All right with me.

She looked like a poor soul, and maybe that's what she was. But her voice was calm, airy. And there was a reasonable rasp to it, and edges to her phrases. I didn't mind listening. I thought, all right, let *her* talk.

She said what she wanted to talk about was the words of her name and the weather.

I asked her her name. Well, okay, no question, I sat down and said, "Sure. Talk about the words of your name and the weather."

We sat there an hour, two o'clock to three, then another hour. I don't know anybody else who could sit around that long, without thinking ahead about what to do next. She said she had nothing to do next.

When she talked, she twisted her hair, she braided the twists. It looked like an interest, experimental, in the possibilities, given different conditions. She pulled a braid into her mouth, licked it wet. Then she blew the braid back toward her ear, out of the way. Or, she untwisted everything and pulled her hair in a heap on the top of her head, divided it all in two, and tied it in a knot up there.

Her voice made me think of woodwinds—air moving through reeds. She lurched through words, fell back, picked up a story somewhere else. She wasn't incoherent, but freewheeling, I would say, in tracking her recollections of days, the connections she made between rainfall one day in Texas, for instance, and some kind of similar fog in Alaska.

Apparently she got around. She said she liked to move.

Eureka leaned back on the steps as if they were cushions, and stretched out, with the complicated look on her face of those women in circuses strapped to circles of wood, happy to have knives flying at them, at the edges of their bodies. Eureka, I believe, was overly trusting of circumstances. Or a good judge of a situation. She didn't look worried.

"We're all named," she said. "Unlike the lizards or grasses." Eureka unknotted her hair. "It's the same after any human birth," she said. "They sign the certificate. And after that you can't find any word or any weather that's pure or plain."

When Eureka Upright discovered it was possible to sit a whole day in the sun without eating or washing a dish, she did it. She was certainly doing it when I met her.

But how long can you live, basking? At the end of the several hours, I asked Eureka if she needed a job. She said, yes, she always needed a job.

"Well, okay," I said, "if you want to go to Toledo, you've got a summer job." And that's how she ended up—why not?—cleaning my parents' house, the one I'd inherited and had no intention of living in. The one my sister in Memphis said we ought to keep anyway.

"Make it a festival house," my sister said. "We don't have to have a family to have a feast."

It had somehow come to sound like a good idea. My sister could bring Chris along at Thanksgiving, and Claudine. LaLonda, in my Washington office, was always looking for someplace to go for the holidays. Hell, maybe Senator Helms would want some turkey.

"Go. Gut the place," I said to Eureka. "Clean sweep. Do what you have to do."

The next weeks, postcards arrived at the office in Eureka's emphatic, large-print handwriting. LaLonda taped them on the door:

"Hot. Hot. Sultry, not at all sulky. Eureka."

"Temperature is 98 degrees. White light off one white cloud—explodes. Eureka."

"Is she all right?" LaLonda asked.

On my vacation, I drove to Ohio to help. Off the turnpike, north, then west, the turn onto Route 2, off that onto the gravel road. I could see from the driveway, my parents' house, gone—good—gone for good. Eureka'd erased the details. The house was there, the same house, of course, white frame, concrete block chimney, but Eureka had moved every scrap out of the yard, the barrels, the stacks of boards, the cartons off the porches, all of it somewhere, ditched or into the barn. She'd cut the grass.

She opened the front door, pointed inside. Just took my hand and pushed me into the hallway.

There wouldn't be much to do. She'd already scraped off paint, steamed off paper, torn out carpet. She had the place down to the barest bones, plaster and spackle, white paint, bone bone. My God, the rooms were huge. She led me into the living room—nothing—wall-to-wall.

But you know how it is. It was a labor not to see what wasn't there: brown drapes, the furnishings, the striped wallpaper, blue carpet into every corner. There were holdover waftings of everyday aromas, recollections of ceramic plates, glassy objects, things cut like snowflaked paper.

"It still feels packed," I said.

"Air in a room is as dense," Eureka said, "as soil to the worm-eye."

I sat down on the floor. Eureka brought two glasses of beer.

"Altoona," she said. "I was born there. Altoona. Listen to it. *That's* got some empty space in it."

The next day, too hot to paint, we drove to Lake Erie, those marshlands near Sandusky and the nuclear power plant. We sat on a breakwall slab of concrete, all afternoon into the evening. We ate egg salad sandwiches and Eureka said the summer in Toledo had been the driest on record.

"Fine with me," she said. She picked up a shell and rubbed it like a comb down her arm. "Shine—or rain," she said, "out of a house, it's always easy to have a good time."

"Is it?" I said.

She handed me the shell.

"There's no escape from anything," she said.

"And that's good?" I asked.

"You said it," she said.

"All right. A day in the sun is all right," I said. "If the gunfire's someplace else."

"See, you've fallen in love with weather," she said.

"Eureka, I've fallen in love with you."

She sat up. "That hits the ear as melodramatic," she said. "Even in a voice as matter-of-fact as yours. It's the *Eureka*, you know, that does it," she said.

Before I went back to Washington, we held a barn sale. Everything sold, even bedsprings, even broken dishes. I saved out a card table. A set of folding chairs.

Eureka stayed on a few days, painting the last rooms upstairs, and then, she took off, too, sending a box number in Altoona.

At the office, sometime in October, a card arrived from Nova Scotia: "A bluish mist collects on skin. A person rains. Eureka."

I wrote to Altoona: "Join us in Toledo for Thanksgiving. Weather permitting."

The whole Washington office drove out—LaLonda, Harmon, Leland, Matilda, and their assorted others—carrying Thai spring rolls, enchiladas verdes, rye bread and cheese. I bought a fresh turkey in Toledo.

My sister arrived and brought a TV. She plugged it in, and the first things we heard from the kitchen were gunshots, ricocheting off the living room walls.

"It's okay," she yelled.

The empty rooms amplified everything. Matilda pinged cranberries into a bowl. LaLonda's boyfriend sang "Madame George," slow, off-key—it sounded pretty good.

By midafternoon, the rooms were echoing thunder. The clouds had turned gray-green, and it rained and stormed, a renegade warm front ripping up from the Gulf.

Eureka showed up, blew in?, in the heaviest downpour, with two friends on the porch in gray dresses, something like sackcloth, soaked. "I've hauled in a few more refugees," she said.

The women were from the highlands of Peru, as it turned out.

"They're in a religous order," Eureka said, "that worships things like waterfalls."

We gave the women some blankets from my sister's car, and Harmon opened the champagne.

I wanted to clink glasses with Eureka, but she'd stepped outside. She was out there in the rain, her hair tied up with a rubber band, straight up in sprigs, like a fountain, dripping from all the ends.

Inside, with cheers, then blah blah ordinary talk going on all through the house, it sounded like a crowd, enough to start a small country. One of the women from Peru sat down on the floor beside me. Her hair was soaked. Her eyes toured the empty room—she was looking for the right words. She took my hand and said, slowly, "Tell me, now, where are we?"

. .

JANET KAUFFMAN'*s books include* Characters on the Loose, The Body in Four Parts, Collaborators, Obscene Gestures for Women, *and* Places in the World a Woman Could Walk. *She lives in Hudson, Michigan.*

JANE KENYON

Otherwise

New & Selected Poems

Reading Aloud to My Father

I chose the book haphazard
from the shelf, but with Nabokov's first
sentence I knew it wasn't the thing
to read to a dying man:
The cradle rocks above an abyss, it began,
*and common sense tells us that our existence
is but a brief crack of light
between two eternities of darkness.*

The words disturbed both of us immediately,
and I stopped. With music it was the same—
Chopin's Piano Concerto—he asked me
to turn it off. He ceased eating, and drank
little, while the tumors briskly appropriated
what was left of him.

But to return to the cradle rocking. I think
Nabokov had it wrong. This is the abyss.
That's why babies howl at birth,

and why the dying so often reach
for something only they can apprehend.

At the end they don't want their hands
to be under the covers, and if you should put
your hand on theirs in a tentative gesture
of solidarity, they'll pull the hand free;
and you must honor that desire,
and let them pull it free.

Evening Sun

Why does this light force me back
to my childhood? I wore a yellow
summer dress, and the skirt
made a perfect circle.

                   Turning and turning
until it flared to the limit
was irresistible. . . .The grass and trees,
my outstretched arms, and the skirt
whirled in the ochre light
of an early June evening.

                   And I knew then
that I would have to live, and go on
living: what a sorrow it was; and still
what sorrow burns
but does not destroy my heart.

Thinking of Madame Bovary

The first hot April day the granite step
was warm. Flies droned in the grass.
When a car went past they rose
in unison, then dropped back down. . . .

I saw that a yellow crocus bud had pierced
a dead oak leaf, then opened wide. How strong
its appetite for the luxury of the sun!

Everyone longs for love's tense joys and red delights.

And then I spied an ant
dragging a ragged, disembodied wing
up the warm brick walk. It must have been
the Methodist in me that leaned forward,
preceded by my shadow, to put a twig just where
the ant was struggling with its own desire.

Briefly It Enters, and Briefly Speaks

I am the blossom pressed in a book,
found again after two hundred years. . . .

I am the maker, the lover, and the keeper. . . .

When the young girl who starves
sits down to a table
she will sit beside me. . . .

I am food on the prisoner's plate. . . .

I am water rushing to the wellhead,
filling the pitcher until it spills. . . .

I am the patient gardener
of the dry and weedy garden. . . .

I am the stone step,
the latch, and the working hinge. . . .

I am the heart contracted by joy. . .
the longest hair, white
before the rest. . . .

I am there in the basket of fruit
presented to the widow. . . .

I am the musk rose opening
unattended, the fern on the boggy summit. . . .

I am the one whose love
overcomes you, already with you
when you think to call my name. . . .

Let Evening Come

Let the light of late afternoon
shine through chinks in the barn, moving
up the bales as the sun moves down.

Let the cricket take up chafing
as a woman takes up her needles
and her yarn. Let evening come.

Let dew collect on the hoe abandoned
in long grass. Let the stars appear
and the moon disclose her silver horn.

Let the fox go back to its sandy den.
Let the wind die down. Let the shed
go black inside. Let evening come.

To the bottle in the ditch, to the scoop
in the oats, to air in the lung
let evening come.

Let it come, as it will, and don't
be afraid. God does not leave us
comfortless, so let evening come.

Peonies at Dusk

White peonies blooming along the porch
send out light
while the rest of the yard grows dim.

Outrageous flowers as big as human
heads! They're staggered
by their own luxuriance: I had
to prop them up with stakes and twine.

The moist air intensifies their scent,
and the moon moves around the barn
to find out what it's coming from.

In the darkening June evening
I draw a blossom near, and bending close
search it as a woman searches
a loved one's face.

Otherwise

I got out of bed
on two strong legs.
It might have been
otherwise. I ate
cereal, sweet
milk, ripe, flawless
peach. It might
have been otherwise.
I took the dog uphill
to the birch wood.
All morning I did
the work I love.

At noon I lay down
with my mate. It might
have been otherwise.
We ate dinner together
at a table with silver
candlesticks. It might
have been otherwise.
I slept in a bed
in a room with paintings
on the walls, and
planned another day
just like this day.
But one day, I know,
it will be otherwise.

Notes from the Other Side

I divested myself of despair
and fear when I came here.

Now there is no more catching
one's own eye in the mirror,

there are no bad books, no plastic,
no insurance premiums, and of course

no illness. Contrition
does not exist, nor gnashing

of teeth. No one howls as the first
clod of earth hits the casket.

The poor we no longer have with us.
Our calm hearts strike only the hour,

and God, as promised, proves
to be mercy clothed in light.

JANE KENYON *is the author of five collections of poetry:* Otherwise: New & Selected Poems, Constance, Let Evening Come, The Boat of Quiet Hours, *and* From Room to Room, *the translator of* Twenty Poems of Anna Akhmatova, *and the author of* A Hundred White Daffodils, *a posthumous collection of essays, translations, interviews, and a final poem. She lived and worked with her husband Donald Hall in Wilmot, New Hampshire, until her death in 1995.*

Owning It All

William Kittredge

WILLIAM KITTREDGE

Owning It All

"Owning It All" (excerpt)

Imagine the slow history of our country in the far reaches of southeastern Oregon, a backlands enclave even in the American West, the first settlers not arriving until a decade after the end of the Civil War. I've learned to think of myself as having had the luck to grow up at the tail end of a way of existing in which people lived in everyday proximity to animals on territory they knew more precisely than the patterns in the palms of their hands.

In Warner Valley we understood our property as others know their cities, a landscape of neighborhoods, some sacred, some demonic, some habitable, some not, which is as the sea, they tell me, is understood by fishermen. It was only later, in college, that I learned it was possible to understand Warner as a fertile oasis in a vast featureless sagebrush desert.

Over in that other world on the edge of rain-forests which is the Willamette Valley of Oregon, I'd gone to school in General Agriculture, absorbed in a double-bind sort of learning, studying to center myself in the County Agent/Corps of Engineers mentality they taught and at the same time taking classes from Bernard Malamud and wondering with great romantic fervor if it was in me to write the true history of the place where I had always lived.

Straight from college I went to Photo Intelligence work in the Air Force.

The last couple of those years were spent deep in jungle on the island of Guam, where we lived in a little compound of cleared land, in a quonset hut.

The years on Guam were basically happy and bookish: we were newly married, with children. A hundred or so yards north of our quonset hut, along a trail through the luxuriant undergrowth between coconut palms and banana trees, a ragged cliff of red porous volcanic rock fell directly to the ocean. When the Pacific typhoons came roaring in, our hut was washed with blowing spray from the great breakers. On calm days we would stand on the cliff at that absolute edge of our jungle and island, and gaze out across to the island of Rota, and to the endlessness of ocean beyond, and I would marvel at my life, so far from southeastern Oregon.

And then in the late fall of 1958, after I had been gone from Warner Valley for eight years, I came back to participate in our agriculture. The road in had been paved, we had Bonneville Power on lines from the Columbia River, and high atop the western rim of the valley there was a TV translator, which beamed fluttering pictures from New York and Los Angeles direct to us.

And I had changed, or thought I had, for a while. No more daydreams about writing the true history. Try to understand my excitement as I climbed to the rim behind our house and stood there by our community TV translator. The valley where I had always seen myself living was open before me like another map and playground, and this time I was an adult, and high up in the War Department. Looking down maybe 3,000 feet into Warner, and across to the high basin and range desert where we summered our cattle, I saw the beginnings of my real life as an agricultural manager. The flow of watercourses in the valley was spread before me like a map, and I saw it as a surgeon might see the flow of blood across a chart of anatomy, and saw myself helping to turn the fertile homeplace of my childhood into a machine for agriculture whose features could be delineated with the same surgeon's precision in my mind.

It was work which can be thought of as craftsmanlike, both artistic and mechanical, creating order according to an ideal of beauty based on efficiency, manipulating the forces of water and soil, season and seed, manpower and equipment, laying out functional patterns for irrigation and cultivation on the surface of our valley. We drained and leveled, ditched and pumped, and for a long while our crops were all any of us could have asked. There were over 5,000 water control devices. We constructed a perfect agricultural place, and it was sacred, so it seemed.

ॐ

Agriculture is often envisioned as an art, and it can be. Of course there is always survival, and bank notes, and all that. But your basic bottom line on the farm is again and again some notion of how life should be lived. The majority of agricultural people, if you press them hard enough, even though most of them despise sentimental abstractions, will admit they are trying to create a good place, and to live as part of that goodness, in the kind of connection which with fine reason we called *rootedness*. It's just that there is good art and bad art.

These are thoughts which come back when I visit eastern Oregon. I park and stand looking down into the lava-rock and juniper-tree canyon where Deep Creek cuts its way out of the Warner Mountains, and the great turkey buzzard soars high in the yellow-orange light above the evening. The fishing water is low, as it always is in late August, unfurling itself around dark and broken boulders. The trout, I know, are hanging where the currents swirl across themselves, waiting for the one entirely precise and lucky cast, the Renegade fly bobbing toward them.

Even now I can see it, each turn of water along miles of that creek. Walk some stretch enough times with a fly rod and its configurations will imprint themselves on your being with Newtonian exactitude. Which is beyond doubt one of the attractions of such fishing—the hours of learning, and then the intimacy with a living system that carries you beyond the sadness of mere gaming for sport.

What I liked to do, back in the old days, was pack in some spuds and an onion and corn flour and spices mixed up in a plastic bag, a small cast-iron frying pan in my wicker creel and, in the late twilight on a gravel bar by the water, cook up a couple of rainbows over a fire of snapping dead willow and sage, eating alone while the birds flitted through the last hatch, wiping my greasy fingers on my pants while the heavy trout began rolling at the lower ends of the pools.

The canyon would be shadowed under the moon when I walked out to show up home empty-handed, to sit with my wife over a drink of whiskey at the kitchen table. Those nights I would go to bed and sleep without dreams, a grown-up man secure in the house and the western valley where he had been a child, enclosed in a topography of spirit he assumed he knew more closely than his own features in the shaving mirror.

So, I ask myself, if it was such a pretty life, why didn't I stay? The peat soil in Warner Valley was deep and rich, we ran good cattle, and my most sacred memories are centered there. What could run me off?

Well, for openers, it got harder and harder to get out of bed in the mornings and face the days, for reasons I didn't understand. More and more I sought the comfort of fishing that knowable creek. Or in winter the blindness of television.

My father grew up on a homestead place on the sagebrush flats outside Silver Lake, Oregon. He tells of hiding under the bed with his sisters when strangers came to the gate. He grew up, as we all did in that country and era, believing that the one sure defense against the world was property. I was born in 1932, and recall a life before the end of World War II in which it was possible for a child to imagine that his family owned the world.

Warner Valley was largely swampland when my grandfather bought the MC Ranch with no downpayment in 1936, right at the heart of the Great Depression. The outside work was done mostly by men and horses and mules, and our ranch valley was filled with life. In 1937 my father bought his first track-layer, a secondhand RD6 Caterpillar he used to build a 17-mile diversion canal to carry the spring floodwater around the east side of the valley, and we were on our way to draining all swamps. The next year he bought an RD7 and a John Deere 36 combine which cut an 18-foot swath, and we were deeper into the dream of power over nature and men, which I had begun to inhabit while playing those long-ago games of war.

The peat ground left by the decaying remnants of ancient tule beds was diked into huge undulating grainfields—Houston Swamp with 750 irrigated acres, Dodson Lake with 800—a final total of almost 8,000 acres under cultivation, and for reasons of what seemed like common sense and efficiency, the work became industrialized. Our artistry worked toward a model whose central image was the machine.

The natural patterns of drainage were squared into drag-line ditches, the tules and the aftermath of the oat and barley crops were burned—along with a little more of the combustible peat soil every year. We flood-irrigated when the water came in spring, drained in late March, and planted in a 24-hour-a-day frenzy which began around April 25 and ended—with luck—by the 10th of May, just as leaves on the Lombardy poplar were breaking from their buds. We summered our cattle on more than a million acres of Taylor Grazing Land across the high lava-rock and sagebrush desert out east of the valley, miles of territory where we owned most of what water there was, and it was ours. We owned it all, or so we felt. The government was as distant as news on the radio.

The most intricate part of my job was called "balancing water," a night-and-day process of opening and closing pipes and redwood headgates and running the 18-inch drainage pumps. That system was the finest plaything I ever had.

And despite the mud and endless hours, the work remained play for a long time, the making of a thing both functional and elegant. We were doing God's labor and creating a good place on earth, living the pastoral yeoman dream—that's how our mythology defined it, although nobody would ever had thought to talk about work in that way.

And then it all went dead, over years, but swiftly.

You can imagine our surprise and despair, our sense of having been profoundly cheated. It took us a long while to realize some unnamable thing was wrong, and then we blamed it on ourselves, our inability to manage enough. But the fault wasn't ours, beyond the fact that we had all been educated to believe in a grand bad factory-land notion as our prime model of excellence.

We felt enormously betrayed. For so many years, through endless efforts, we had proceeded in good faith, and it turned out we had wrecked all we had not left untouched. The beloved migratory rafts of waterbirds, the green-headed mallards and the redheads and canvasbacks, the cinnamon teal and the great Canadian honkers, were mostly gone along with their swampland habitat. The hunting, in so many ways, was no longer what it had been.

We wanted to build a reservoir, and litigation started. Our laws were being used against us, by people who wanted a share of what we thought of as our water. We could not endure the boredom of our mechanical work, and couldn't hire anyone who cared enough to do it right. We baited the coyotes with 1080, and rodents destroyed our alfalfa; we sprayed weeds and insects with 2-4-D Ethyl and Malathion, and Parathion for clover mite, and we shortened our own lives.

In quite an actual way we had come to victory in the artistry of our playground warfare against all that was naturally alive in our native home. We had reinvented our valley according to the most persuasive ideal given us by our culture, and we ended with a landscape organized like a machine for growing crops and fattening cattle, a machine that creaked a little louder each year, a dreamland gone wrong.

One of my strongest memories comes from a morning when I was maybe 10 years old, out on the lawn before our country home in spring, beneath a bluebird sky. I was watching the waterbirds coming off the valley swamps and grainfields where they had been feeding overnight. They were going north to nesting grounds on the Canadian tundra, and that piece of morning, inhabited by the sounds of their wings and their calling in the clean air, was wonder-filled and magical. I was enclosed in a living place.

No doubt that memory has persisted because it was a sight of possibility which I will always cherish—an image of the great good place rubbed smooth over the years like a river stone, which I touch again as I consider why life in Warner Valley went so seriously haywire. But never again in my lifetime will it be possible for a child to stand out on a bright spring morning in Warner Valley and watch the waterbirds come through in enormous, rafting, vee-shaped flocks of thousands—and I grieve.

My father is a very old man. A while back we were driving up the Bitterroot Valley of Montana, and he was gazing away to the mountains. "They'll never see it the way we did," he said, and I wonder what he saw.

We shaped our piece of the West according to the model provided by our mythology, and instead of a great good place such order had given us enormous power over nature, and a blank perfection of fields.

❧

A mythology can be understood as a story that contains a set of implicit instructions from a society to its members, telling them what is valuable and how to conduct themselves if they are to preserve the things they value.

The teaching mythology we grew up with in the American West is a pastoral story of agricultural ownership. The story begins with a vast innocent continent, natural and almost magically alive, capable of inspiring us to reverence and awe, and yet savage, a wilderness. A good rural people come from the East, and they take the land from its native inhabitants, and tame it for agricultural purposes, bringing civilization: a notion of how to live embodied in law. The story is as old as invading armies, and at heart it is a racist, sexist, imperialist mythology of conquest; a rationale for violence—against other people and against nature.

At the same time, that mythology is a lens through which we continue to see ourselves. Many of us like to imagine ourselves as honest yeomen who sweat and work in the woods or the mines or the fields for a living. And many of us are. We live in a real family, a work-centered society, and we like to see ourselves as people with the good luck and sense to live in a place where some vestige of the natural world still exists in working order. Many of us hold that natural world as sacred to some degree, just as it is in our myth. Lately, more and more of us are coming to understand our society in the American West as an exploited colony, threatened by greedy outsiders who want to take our sacred place away from us, or at least strip and degrade it.

In short, we see ourselves as a society of mostly decent people who live with some connection to a holy wilderness, threatened by those who lust for power and property. We look for Shane to come riding out of the Tetons, and instead we see Exxon and the Sierra Club. One looks virtually as alien as the other.

And our mythology tells us we own the West, absolutely and morally—we own it because of our history. Our people brought law to this difficult place, they suffered and they shed blood and they survived, and they earned this land for us. Our efforts have surely earned us the right to absolute control over the thing we created. The myth tells us this place is ours, and will always be ours, to do with as we see fit.

That's a most troubling and enduring message, because we want to believe it, and we do believe it, so many of us, despite its implicit ironies and wrongheadedness, despite the fact that we took the land from someone else. We try to ignore a genocidal history of violence against the Native Americans.

In the American West we are struggling to revise our dominant mythology, and to find a new story to inhabit. Laws control our lives, and they are designed to preserve a model of society based on values learned from mythology. Only after re-imagining our myths can we coherently remodel our laws, and hope to keep our society in a realistic relationship to what is actual.

In Warner Valley we thought we were living the right lives, creating a great precise perfection of fields, and we found the mythology had been telling us an enormous lie. The world had proven too complex, or the myth too simpleminded. And we were mortally angered.

The truth is, we never owned all the land and water. We don't even own very much of them, privately. And we don't own anything absolutely or forever. As our society grows more and more complex and interwoven, our entitlement becomes less and less absolute, more and more likely to be legally diminished. Our rights to property will never take precedence over the needs of society. Nor should they, we all must agree in our grudging hearts. Ownership of property has always been a privilege granted by society, and revokable.

WILLIAM KITTREDGE *is the author of* Owning It All, We Are Not in This Together, Who Owns the West, Hole in the Sky, *and* Van Gogh Field and Other Stories. *He teaches creative writing at the University of Montana in Missoula.*

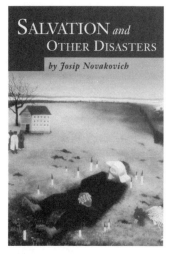

JOSIP NOVAKOVICH

Salvation and Other Disasters

Sheepskin

Since I can't tell this to anybody, I'm writing it, not just to sort it out for myself, but for someone nosy who'll rummage through my papers one day. In a way I want to be caught but I won't call this story a confession. I should pretend that it's somebody else's story, that it is fiction. I wish I could set it in a different country—outside Croatia and outside the former Yugoslavia—and that it was about somebody else, a former self, a formerly uninformed me. I don't mean that I want a complete break with my past—nothing as dramatic as suicide, although, of course, I've entertained thoughts of it, but the thoughts have not entertained me. I have survived knives and bombs: I should be able to survive thoughts and memories.

I'll start with a scene on a train in western Slavonia. Though it was hot, I closed the window. Not that I am superstitious against drafts as many of our people are. Dandelion seeds floated in, like dry snowflakes, and all sorts of pollens and other emissaries of the wild fields filled the air with smells of chamomile, menthol, and other teas. It would have been pleasant if I hadn't had a cold that made me sneeze and squint. The countryside seemed mostly abandoned.

I had never seen vegetation so free and jubilant. The war had loosened the earth, shaken the farmers off its back. Strewn mines kept them from venturing into the fields, but did not bother the flowers. The color intensity of grasses and beeches in the background gave me a dizziness I could not attribute to my cold. I saw a fox leap out of orange bushes of tea. Of course, it was not tea, but many of these wildflowers would be teas if broken by human hands and dried in the sun, mellifluous teas, curing asthma, improving memory, and filling you with tenderness. If we had stuck to drinking tea, maybe the war would have never happened.

I leaned against the wooden side of the train, but gave up, since the magnum I had strapped on my side pressed into my arm painfully. I would have probably fallen asleep, intoxicated with the fields and the musty oil, which doused the wood beneath the tracks. As a child I had loved the oily smell of rails; it had transformed for me the iron clanking of the gaps in the tracks into a transcontinental guitar with two hammered strings and thousands of sorrowful frets that fell into diminished distances. I'd have dozed off if every time I leaned against the vibrating wall of the train the gun hadn't pinched a nerve and shaken me awake. And just when I was beginning to slumber, the door screeched.

A gaunt man entered. I was startled, recognizing my old tormentor from the Vukovar hospital. He took off his hat and revealed unruly cow-licked hair, grayer than I remembered it. His thick eyebrows, which almost met above his nose, were black. I wondered whether he colored them.

The man did not look toward me, although he stiffened. I was sure he was aware of me. I had dreamed of this moment many times, imagining that if given the opportunity the first thing I'd do would be to jump at the man, grab his throat, and strangle him with the sheer power of rage. My heart leaped, but I didn't. I gazed at him from the corner of my eye. He looked a little thinner and taller than I remembered. I did not know his name, but in my mind I had always called him Milos. I ceased to believe we coexisted in the same world—imagined that he was in Serbia, off the map as far as I was concerned.

I looked out the window, and the sunlit fields glowed even more, with the dark undersides, shadows, enhancing the light in the foreground. The train was pulling into Djulevci. The Catholic church gaped open, its tower missing, its front wall and gate in rubble, the pews crushed, overturned, and the side wall had several big howitzer holes; only here and there pale mortar remained, reflecting the sun so violently that my eyes hurt. At the train station there was a pile of oak logs, probably a decade old, but still not rotten. And past the train station stood the Serb Orthodox church, pock-marked. It probably wouldn't be standing if there hadn't been guards around it, night and day. The Croatian government wanted to demonstrate to the world—although journalists never bothered to come to this village—how much better Croats were than Serbs, but that was a show. The Croat policemen sat on chairs, one wiggled a semi-automatic rifle, and the other tossed a crushed can of Coke over his shoulder.

There was a time when I would have thrown grenades into the church, owing to my traveling companion and other Serb soldiers who had surrounded and choked the city of Vukovar for months. Fearing that I would starve to death, I had minced my sheepskin jacket and made a soup out of it. The day before the soldiers invaded the city, I'd seen a cat struck in the neck with shrapnel. I picked her up and skinned her. I overgrilled her because I was squeamish to eat a cat, and once I had eaten most of her, I grew feverish. I wasn't sure whether the cat had gotten some disease from rats—I would not have been surprised if I had caught the plague this way—or whether it was sheer guilt and disgust with myself, that I had eaten a cat, that made me ill. My body, unused to food, just could not take it; I was delirious in the hospital, but there was no doubt what I saw was not a dream: soldiers laughing, crashing wine bottles on the chairs, dragging old men in torn pajamas out of their hospital beds. A man with black eyebrows and a gray cowlick that shot out trembling strands of hair above his forehead came to my side and spat at me. He pulled the sheet off my bed and stabbed my thigh with a broken wine bottle. I coiled and shrieked, and he uncoiled me, pulling my arms, and another pulled my legs, while the third one pissed over my wound and said, "This is the best disinfectant around, absolutely the best. *Na zdravlye!*"

"There, pig, you'll thank me one day, you'll see," said Milos, and stabbed my leg again.

Other soldiers came and dragged a wailing old woman down the stairs.

"How about this guy?" one of the soldiers asked about me.

"No, he's bleeding too much," said Milos. "I don't want to get contaminated by his shitty blood."

A tall French journalist came in and took pictures of me, and muttered in English.

"What are you staring at?" I asked. "There are worse sights around."

"Yes, but they are not alive," he said. He carried me out, while my blood soaked his clothes. He pushed me into his jeep, and we drove out and passed several checkpoints without any inspection. He took me to the Vinkovci hospital, which was often bombed. Two nurses pulled glass from my leg, tied rubber above and below the wound, stitched me up, wrapped the wound—all without painkillers. I wished I could swoon from the pain. I ground my teeth so hard that a molar cracked.

Thanks a lot for the pleasure, I thought now and looked at my silent companion on the train. At Virovitica, we'd have to change trains. Mine was going to Zagreb, and I did not know whether he was going there, or east, to Osijek.

He got out of the compartment first, and I did not want to be obvious about following him. Many peasants with loud white chickens in their pleated baskets filled the corridor between us.

When I jumped off the train into the gravel, his head covered with a hat slid behind a wall. His shadow moved jerkily on the gray cement of the platform, but I could not see the shadow's owner. Milos must have been behind the corner. Maybe he was aware of being followed.

I thought he could be waiting for me in ambush. People walked and stepped on his shadow, but they could not trample it, because as they stepped on it, it climbed on them, and I was no longer sure whether it was Milos's shadow, or whether they were casting shadows over each other. Not that it mattered one way or another, but I suppose that's part of my professional photographer's distortion and disorientation that I look at light and shadow wherever I turn, and I frame what I see in rectangular snatches; I keep squaring the world, in my head, to some early and primitive cosmology of a flat earth, where nothing comes around.

I rushed past the corner. There was a kiosk stocked with cigarettes and many magazines featuring pictures of naked blondes. I stopped and pretended to be reading the train schedule posted at the station entrance so I could observe Milos's reflection on the glass over the departures schedule. He rolled the magazine he had bought into a flute, and entered a restaurant.

I followed. There was an outdoor section under a tin roof, with large wooden tables and benches. A TV set was blaring out a sequence of Croatian President Tudjman kissing the flag at the Knin fort, after his forces captured Knin. The President lifted his clenched fist to the sky. What kind of kiss was it, from thin bloodless lips sinking through the concave mouth of a politician? I detest flags. Anyhow, I was not in a loving mood right then, toward anybody. In Vukovar we thought that Tudjman had abandoned us. Maybe he was partly responsible for my wantonly following a stranger down the stairs, to the lower level of the country dive. Milos sat below a window with fake crystal glass that refracted light into purple rays. I did not sit right away, but walked past him, following arrows to the bathroom across a yard with a fenced family of sheep with muddy feet, who eyed me calmly. I walked back and sat at a round table about two yards from his.

He ordered lamb and a carafe of red wine in a perfect Zagreb accent. In Vukovar I remembered him using long Serb vowels, ironically stretching them. Maybe he was now afraid to be taken for a Serb. I couldn't blame him for that. Still, a man who could dissemble so well was dangerous, I thought.

I ordered the same thing. When I pronounced my order, I used the same wording as Milos, in my eastern Slavonian leisurely way, which to many people outside my region sounded similar to Serbian.

Milos looked at me for the first time and, hearing my voice, gave a start. The waiter, slumping in his greasy black jacket with a napkin hanging out of his pocket, eyed me contemptuously. His mouth was curled to one side, and one silver tooth gleamed over his shiny fat lower lip.

He brought one carafe to Milos and one to me along with empty glasses. Milos drank, I drank. He opened his magazine to the centerfold of a blonde with black pubic hair, and then he stared at me. What was the point? Did he pretend that he thought I was a homosexual stalking him and about to proposition him, so this was his way of telling me, No, I'm not interested? If he imagined he could confuse me this way so I would not be positive I had recognized him, he was dead wrong.

I had a postcard in my pocket; I pulled it out and began to write—I did not know to whom. To my ex-wife, who'd left me at the beginning of the war to visit her relatives in Belgrade? They had filled her head with nonsense about how Croats were going to kill her, and how even I might be a rabid

Croat who would cut her throat. The nonsense actually served Miriana well; she got out right before the city was encircled by Serb troops and bombed. From what I hear she now lives with a widowed cardiologist whose Croatian wife died of a heart attack. Miriana used to visit Belgrade frequently even before the war; she had probably had an affair with the cardiologist. Her running away from the fighting may have been simply a pretext for leaving me. Anyway, I didn't have her address, so I couldn't write to her—no big loss.

I wrote to my dead father instead, although this made no sense either. He had died of stomach cancer last year in Osijek, perhaps because of the war. Without the anxiety he could have lived with the latent stomach cancer for years.

"Hi, my old man. I wish you were here. Not that there'd be much to see—in fact, Virovitica has to be one of the dreariest towns in Slavonia. But the wine is good. . . ."

My meal arrived. I folded the postcard and put it in my pocket. The meat was lukewarm. Who knows when it was cooked—maybe days ago, and it stayed in the refrigerator. I grumbled as I cut.

Milos swore too, as he struggled. He asked for a sharper knife.

"This is awful! They charge so much and give you only the bone!" he said to me.

If he thought he could engage me in a conversation and thus appease me, he was wrong, although I did answer. "Yes, they figure only travelers would eat here anyway, and once they get our money and we're gone, they can laugh at us."

He gulped wine.

I navigated my blade through the stringy meat.

"Where are you from?" he asked me.

I called the waiter. "You forgot the salad."

"You haven't asked for it."

He was probably right, but I still said, "Yes, I did."

He soon brought me a plate of sliced tomatoes and onions, with oily vinegar. That helped subdue the heavy and rotten lamb taste. Funny how finicky I'd become in a hurry—not long before, I had chewed on a sheepskin jacket, certain that I'd starve to death, and now I behaved like a jaded gourmet.

Milos bent down to search through his luggage. Maybe he's going to draw a gun? I thought. I slid my hand into my jacket.

Milos took out three dolls, the Lion King hyenas. What, is this possible? My torturer is buying toys for kids? He put the magazine and the hyenas into his traveling bag. Maybe that was his way of saying, I am not a guy who'd stab anybody, I'm a kind, family man.

He looked toward me, and I felt self-conscious with my hand in my jacket. So it wouldn't look as though I was pulling a gun, I fumbled in the pocket and took out my pigskin wallet. The waiter eagerly came to my table. I gave him fifty kunas, certainly more than the meal was worth. "I need no change," I said.

"Excuse me, four and a half more kunas, please," asked the waiter. I gave him five coins.

"Preposterous, isn't it?" Milos said. "How can they charge that much for this? If I had known, I'd have controlled my appetite, could have bought another toy for my kids."

Was he appealing to me again? I had no sympathy for family men. My marriage failed perhaps because I had no kids. My business failed because the likes of Milos bombed my town, and here I sat as a twitching mass of resentment. I took another gulp of wine. I first used a toothpick and then whistled through my teeth to clean out bits of meat that got stuck there.

Milos looked at me with annoyance. He clearly didn't like my whistling. So what, I thought. If it bothers you, I'll do more of it. And who was he to complain? He slurped wine as though it were hot soup. And with his sharp knife, sharper than mine, he cut through more lamb, and I couldn't escape remembering again how he'd cut into my leg.

I scratched my swollen scar through the woolen fabric of my pants. It itched to the point of my wanting to tear it.

"Do you think there are fleas here?" I asked loudly, as if to excuse my scratching, but looked at nobody.

The waiter strutted and dumped tiny coins on my table ostentatiously, probably to make a statement that it was beneath him to take my tip. The rattle of the change scared two turquoise flies off my plate.

"Flies are all right," I said. Not much had changed since communism. I used to think that rudeness was a matter of fixed salaries, no incentive. But here, I was pretty sure the waiter was part-owner of this free enterprise establishment, and he was still rude, and did his best to disgust his customers. And, of course, customers hadn't changed either. They used to be rude, and I would continue to be rude. But before I could think of another insulting question, Milos asked one. "Hey, my friend, do you think I could buy a sheepskin jacket anywhere around here?"

This may have been a jab at me. But how could he have known I'd eaten a sheepskin jacket in Vukovar?

The waiter answered: "Maybe in a couple of hours. We are just getting some ready."

"Could I see them?" Milos was standing and picking up a thick cloth napkin that looked like a towel from his lap.

The waiter grabbed a large hair dryer from among plum brandy bottles on the shelf and waved to Milos to come along. Although I was not invited, I followed. They had identical bald spots on their heads.

Behind the sheep stall, in a shed filled with hay, on thick clothes wires hung two sheepskins, dripping blood into aluminum pots on the dusty dirt floor.

I wondered why the waiter collected the blood, why not simply let it soak the ground. Maybe he made blood sausages; maybe he drank it, like an ancient Mongolian horseman.

The waiter aimed the blow dryer at a sheepskin, filling it with air. Rounded like a sail full of wind, the skin gave me a spooky impression that an invisible sheep was beginning to inhabit it.

"This'll be a terrific jacket," the waiter said. "Give it an hour, if you can spare."

"But what about the pattern?" Milos said. "What about the buttons?"

"Fuck buttons. You can get those anyplace. But fine sheepskin like this, nowhere. Two hundred kunas, is that a deal?"

Milos stroked the sheepskin's tight yellowish curls.

"The winter's going to be a harsh one," said the waiter.

"Yes, but sheep won't save us from it," I said.

Milos quit stroking, and as he turned around, he stepped on the edge of a bowl, and blood spilled over his jeans and white socks and leather shoes.

"Seeing this is enough to make one become a vegetarian," I said to the waiter. I was nauseated.

"I'll be passing through town in two days again," said Milos. "Could I pick it up then?"

"No problem." The waiter walked back, Milos followed. The waiter pushed in a silvery CD, and Croatian pop came on, tambourines with electric organs that shook the speakers. The music was cranked beyond the point of clarity—blasted. No conversation was possible.

Milos walked into the backyard. I thought that his Serb soul wouldn't let him listen to Croat music. He gave me a look and winked. I wondered what he meant. The waiter smirked, perhaps thinking there was a gay connection established between Milos and me. Milos went into the toilet, an outhouse next to the sheep stall.

I went behind the outhouse. There was a hole in the gray wood through which I could see his back. I put the gun in the hole and shot through his spine. His body jolted forward and then fell back, right against the wall. I shot again. Blood flowed through the spacing between dry planks. Because of the music, I was sure the waiter couldn't hear the shots.

I rushed away from the tavern yard through the rear gate. A train was whistling into the station. I jumped on the train even before it stopped. I wondered why I was running away. I should have been able to explain my deed—revenge against a war criminal. I went straight into the train toilet and shaved off my droopy mustache that made me look melancholy and forsaken. Now in the mirror I looked much younger, despite my receding hairline and the isolated widow's peak.

I thought I'd feel triumphant after my revenge. And I did feel proud as I looked at my cleared lip. Great, I am free from my sorrow, from the humiliation. I won.

But as I sat in the soft seat of the first-class coach and looked around holes burnt into the velvet seat by cigarette butts, my heart pounded and I could barely draw a breath. The smell of stale tobacco and spilled beer irritated me. I turned the ashtray over, cleaned it with a paper towel, and threw it out the window. The awful mutton seemed to be coming up to my throat. I was afraid.

If I was caught, and there was a trial, public sympathy would be with me. Many people want personal revenge. Forget institutional revenge, forget the International War Crimes Tribunal in Den Haage.

When I got off in Zagreb policemen in blue uniforms with German shepherds strolled on the platform but they did not stop me. They probably did not look for me. The war was going on in Krajina; one more civilian dead in the North made no difference.

Drunken people frolicked all over town, beeping their car horns, the way they did when their soccer clubs won. As I walked I expected a hand on my shoulder, from somewhere, perhaps the sky. It did not happen. But what happened was worse. At the tram stop, I saw a man exactly like Milos. I thought it was him. Were my bullets blanks? But where had the blood come from? How could Milos have made it to the train? When he saw me, I thought I noticed a fleeting recognition, the cowlick on his head shook, but that was too little reaction for what had happened in Virovitica. It was not Milos from the restaurant. This man was a little shorter and plumper. He looked genuinely like the man from Vukovar who had stabbed me, more than my Milos from Virovitica did. What if I had killed the wrong man? We rode in the same tram car. I forgot to buy my ticket, I was so stunned. He had his punched in the orange box near the entrance and stood, with one arm holding on to a pole. What to do? I wondered, as the tram jangled us around curves, and slim young ladies with tranquil made-up faces stood between us. I could not just kill the man, although this was probably the one that I should have killed in the first place. He got off at Kvaternik Square. Now I could blame him not only for my injury but for the death of an innocent man, his double. But I could have been wrong, again. I couldn't trust my "recognitions" anymore. I hadn't felt particularly ecstatic after my first murder, not for long anyway, and I was not looking for ecstasy. So I did not follow this man. I was crazed enough that I could have killed him too, but I wanted to be alone. Enough stuffy trams, oily tracks, expressionless people.

I walked home, near the zoo, just south of the stadium. In the streets I saw another Milos look-alike. Was I hallucinating? It was getting dark, true, but I looked at this third Milos keenly. They all had the same gait, same graying and trembling cowlick, same heavy black brow. I was glad I hadn't killed the man on the tram. How many men would I have to shoot to get the right one? It was absurd, and I was afraid that I was going insane.

I watched TV in my messy efficiency. Crime, if this was crime, was no news. Only Serb mass exodus from Krajina and Croat mass exodus from Banja Luka and Vojvodina made the news along with Mitterand's prostate. I drank three bottles of warm red wine and still couldn't fall asleep.

Next morning, sleepless and hungover, on my way to buy a daily, I thought I saw a Milos look-alike, leaning against the window of an espresso café, staring vacantly, as though he were the corpse of my traveling companion from Virovitica.

In the papers I saw the picture of my man, "Murdered by an Unidentified Traveler": Mario Toplak, Latin teacher at the Zagreb Classical Gymnasium, survived by his wife, Tanya, son Kruno, and daughter Irena. Clearly, I got the wrong man. This one was Croatian, judging by his name. But then, even the man in the Vukovar hospital could have been a Croat. He could have been drafted. The fact that he did not kill me and did not drag me out onto a bus to be shot in a cornfield now gave me the idea that wounding me may have saved me. I could not walk, and since I gushed blood it would have been too disgusting for anybody to carry me onto the bus, so I was left alone. He may have been a Serb, and he saved me nevertheless. Why hadn't I thought of that possibility before? Maybe I should have sought out the man to thank him. But thirst for revenge makes you blind. Is this a real thought? I'm probably just paraphrasing "Love makes you blind." I'm filling in the dots in prefab thoughts. Can I think?

At Toplak's funeral there were almost a hundred people, so I felt I was inconspicuous in the chapel. His wife wept, and his son, about four, and daughter, about five, did not seem to understand what was going on. "Where is Daddy? I want my daddy!" shouted Kruno.

"He's going to visit the angels in heaven, so he could tell us what it's like there. He'll bring back some tiny clouds who can sing in foreign tongues, you'll see." The widow whispered loudly. Maybe she was proud of how well she was shielding her kids from the truth.

"How can Daddy fly to heaven from here?" asked Irena.

I could see why she worried about that. The chapel was small, stuffy with perfume—I detest perfume, as though breathing wasn't hard enough without it!—and too cramped for any Ascension to take place. Tanya looked pathetic, tragic, dignified with her dark auburn hair, pale skin, and vermilion lips. Her skirt was slightly above the knee; she had thin ankles, a shapely waist with round, sexily tilted hips. She was in her mid-thirties. After the funeral, I gave her a white carnation, which had fallen in front of me from a precariously laid bouquet during the prayer. (I wondered, could you make tea from carnations, at least for funerals?) "I knew your husband," I said. "I'm so sorry."

She took the flower mechanically and put it in her purse.

"Could I give you a call, to share memories of him with you?" I said.

"Not for a while. What would be the point anyway?" She gave me a look through her eyelashes, grasped her children's hands, and walked toward the chapel door. Kruno turned around, looked at the varnished casket, and asked, "How come the box has no wings? How will it fly?"

Toplak was in the phone book. I called her a month later but when she answered I put the receiver down. I was too excited, I couldn't talk. I feared that I wanted to confess to her. On several occasions I waited for hours not far from her house and followed her. Every Saturday morning she went to the neighborhood playground with her kids.

In the meanwhile, I had grown crazed and lucky in everything I did. I can't say that I was a shy man—I used to be, but photography, shoving my eyes into everybody's business and intimacy, freed me from that affliction. At the end of August 1995 I took on loans, sold a small house in Djakovo I had inherited from my father, rented a shop, and photographed a lot of weddings, funerals, births. I accosted couples in the park who seemed to be on the verge of getting married, got their phone numbers; I put up ads in all the funeral parlors, crashed funeral parties with my camera. I hired an assistant, made a lot of money. The country seemed to follow the same mood swings as I did. After Krajina was conquered, and all the transportation lines in Croatia were opened again, and there were no threats of bombing in Zagreb, everybody was on the make. Optimism, investment, spending—many people seemed to have money, while months before hardly anybody did. If I had talked to Tanya a couple of days after the funeral, I would have had nothing to show for myself, but just two months later, when I approached her at the playground while her kids were jumping up and down the slides, I could boast. It was a superb day, with leaves turning color and fluttering in the slanted rays of the afternoon sun.

I came up to her bench, camera slung around my neck, and said, "Hello, you look beautiful. Would you mind if I took several pictures of you?"

"Oh come on, that's an old line. Thanks for the compliment, but I don't think so." She did not even look at me, but laughed.

"I'm serious. I don't mean nudes, though I'm sure they would be wonderful too, but just your face, your figure, dressed. Your expression, your mood, that's art."

Here, she was taken aback by my speech, and she looked up at me, raising one of her pencil-defined eyebrows. I was standing against the sun, casting a shadow over her left shoulder but letting the sun blaze into her eyes—her hazel irises glowed with emerald undertones, like moss in a forest in the fall. Her eye colors composed well with the turning leaves, as the soul of raving colors. I wasn't lying—I did want to take her picture, and it would have been terrific.

"Do I know you?" she asked.

"Slightly. I came up to you at your husband's funeral and gave you a carnation."

"Oh yes. And even then you were about to offer something. What did you want to talk about then?"

"I was on the train with your husband that day," I said—actually, blurted out.

"Yes?" she said, and then looked over to the playground to see whether her kids were safe.

I waited and didn't say anything for several seconds. I did not want to give away any clues, but her husband was the only ostensible link I had with her—I wanted to use it, so she would not evade me and leave as a stranger. My desire for her was stronger than my impulse toward safety.

"We chatted briefly," I told her. "He told me how much he loved his family, you and the kids, particularly how crazy he was about you, how lucky to have such a beautiful wife. But that's not why I came to the funeral, to see how voluptuous you are." She grinned as though she understood that I was lying and waited for me to go on. "He went off to the restaurant, he was hungry. I was surprised when I did not see him come back to the train station, but I figured the meal must have been great if he'd miss the train out of that God-forsaken station for it. I hope, for his sake, that it was."

"Really, he talked to you about how much he loved me? I wish he'd told me he loved me. Anyway, I don't believe that he said it."

"Maybe he was shy with you."

"And not with you?" she said. "Maybe you're right. He was a moody self-obsessed mathematician. Anyhow, he was a homosexual. We hadn't slept together in two years. I don't know why I'm telling you all this, maybe just to let you know that I have reasons not to believe you."

"You seem to resent him." I was amazed. I had thought Milos was defending himself from a possible gay stalker in the restaurant, but he was actually trying to pick me up. The waiter may have been partly right to smirk and think there was a lewd connection being established.

"I know, it's irrational, but in a way I blame him for leaving us like this. Now I have to work full-time, support the family, the kids are a mess, as though we didn't have enough problems."

"Did he serve in the army during the war? I've heard that in post-traumatic stress, many straight men go through a gay phase." I was bull-shitting, just to appear natural, and also, to find out whether her husband was in Vukovar as a soldier, after all.

"That's interesting. Yes, he was in the army, in Zadar, and was wounded." She was studying me, and nibbling on a pencil eraser.

"What army?"

"Funny question."

"What work do you do?" I asked.

"Curious, aren't we? I teach English, mostly private lessons, and I teach at a school."

"Could I sign up for an intensive program?" I asked.

"That depends," she said.

"Don't you want to make money?"

"Sure, but there's something strange about you . . . I didn't mean it to come out like that. What I mean is, I don't know you."

"Do you have to be intimate with people before you give them lessons?"

I joked. It was not a good joke, but she laughed, perhaps because we were both tense.

She let me take pictures of her kids, I took several lessons, and paid well. She allowed me to take pictures of her, in her funeral dress, with the red lipstick. She could not be as pale as she'd been during the funeral, so we touched up her face with white powder to intensify the contrast with her hair. I don't know why I hadn't taken pictures at her funeral; it hadn't occurred to me then.

That was three weeks ago. I've taken her and the kids to the movies, to the zoo, and now that the first snow has fallen, I'll take them skiing. Tonight I paid for a baby-sitter and Tanya and I took a walk in the old town, past the lanterns, in narrow cobbled streets. A cold wind chapped my lips, and they hurt, until I kissed her in a dark corridor, a moist, tingling kiss. We trembled.

When I got home, I saw that I had vermilion lips. I had forgotten to wipe them. I am still filled with tenderness, and I'm drinking red wine. I'm looking forward to another date, tomorrow night, hoping to make love to her.

I don't know why I'm having success with her—perhaps too many men are in the army, many have been killed, and there's a shortage that may be working to my advantage. Maybe she's stringing me along, maybe she's suspecting me and investigating the case. I think my guilt gives me extraordinary confidence—I have nothing to lose. I am tempted to expose myself to her, and this temptation thrills me just as much as the erotic seduction does. I am dizzy from her images—and his—swarming in my head. I should go back to the western Slavonian fields, and gather wildflowers, bury myself in their scents and colors. Then I would not need to remember and rave on the page from a strange desire to be caught. I would live like a fox in a bush of red tea.

JOSIP NOVAKOVICH *is a Croatian-born fiction writer and essayist. He currently is an assistant professor of English at the University of Cincinnati, and his published work includes* Salvation and Other Disasters, Yolk, Apricots from Chernobyl, *and* Fiction Writer's Workshop. *He is the recipient of a 1997 Whiting Writers' Award, an Ingram Merrill Award, the Richard Margolis Prize for Socially Important Writing, and an NEA Fellowship for Fiction Writing. He lives in Blue Creek, Ohio.*

CARL PHILLIPS

Cortège

Teaching Ovid to Sixth-Graders

Easy enough, now,
listening to this uneven rustle
of sleeved arms over paper,

to imagine what Ganymede heard,
desire, and the new life to be spent
bending

for a body that already had undone
so many,
on wings approaching.

I look at their arms,
things I sometimes have thought
I would not mind learning,

in my own way, to love, and I wonder—
even now, after Ganymede
and all the other names I have told them

for the flesh in defeat—
what do these bodies know, really,
that I wanted them to,

how any myth
is finally about the lengths the mind will
carry a tale to, to explain what the body

knows already, and so never answers:
that there *is* no way to explain
what can happen,

what can take a life
that does not mean harm
just as suddenly and terribly

down, for all that.
Pacing the aisles,
I dream my mouth to each ear,

the lesson beginning
all over again,
but different.

Freeze

The only light in the room,
moonlight, was
enough,

gave to his body on the bed
the suggestion of
stone drawn,

in relief, up from the stone
rest of itself,
what art

always wants, to pull somehow
a life from what
isn't. At

the window, the first snow had
begun, early. Watching
its shadow

pass, slow, down his back, in
the same way my hand
sometimes

does—that unnoticed, that
determined to, anyway,
do it—

I began thinking elsewhere, of
a life from before.
I wondered

if the snow fell there, too.

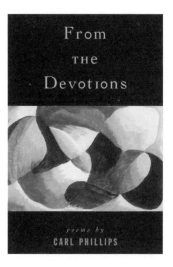

CARL PHILLIPS

From the Devotions

Alba: Failure

If the bare trees at the glass were kings
really, I would know they bend over in grief,
mourning their lost brilliant crowns that

they can only watch, not reach as, beneath them,
they let go of all color all flash all sway,
it would be better, I wouldn't have to say *no*

they are not kings, they are trees, I know this,
and if they bend it is wind only, it is nature,
isn't it also indifference? Passing yesterday

the bodies that, wrapped and wrapped, lay
sprawled above the steam as it left the vents
of my city, I could only fumble for the words

(*dead lamb, dead lamb*) to some song to sing
parts of, I gave, but what I gave—is it
right to say it helped no one, or can I say

I brought lullaby, sealed a thin life,
awhile longer, in sleep? What is failure?
Having read how there were such things as

orchard lamps for keeping the good fruit, on
colder nights, from freezing, I was curious
for that kind of heat go the lines from

a poem I never finished. The shorter version
is: once, twice, in a difficult time, I have
failed you. No poetry corrects this. But

does it mean we don't love? In the last poem
of you waking, I am any small bird, unnoticed,
above, watching; you are the traveler who

can't know (there is fog, or no stars, a steep
dark) that the all but given up for impossible
next town is soon, soon. Come. We turn here.

From the Devotions

I.
As if somewhere, away, a door had slammed shut.
—But not metal; not wood.

Or as when something is later remembered only
as something dark in the dream:

torn, bruised, dream-slow
descending, it could be anything—

tiling, clouds,
you again, beautifully consistent, in no

usual or masterable way   *leaves, a woman's*
shaken-loose throat, shattered

eyes of the seer, palms, ashes, the flesh
instructing; you, silent.

A sky, a sea requires crossing and, like that,
there is a boat or, like that, a plane:

for whom is it this way now, when
as if still did I lie down beside, still

turn to, touch
                I can't, I could not save you?

II.
Not, despite what you believed, that
all travel necessarily ends here, at the sea.

I am back, but only because.
As the sun only happens to meet the water

in such a way that the water becomes
a kind of cuirass: how each piece takes

and, for nothing, gives back whatever light—
sun's, moon's. A bird that is not a gull

passes over; I mark what you would: underneath,
at the tip of either wing, a fluorescent-white

moon, or round star. Does the bird itself
ever see this? According to you *many have*

had the ashes of lovers strewn here,
on this beach on this water that now beats at,

now seems to want just to rest alongside.
The dead can't know we miss them Presumably,

we were walking *that we are walking*
upon them.

III.
All night, again,
a wind that failed to bring storm—

instead, the Paradise dream: the abandoned
one nest at a bad angle—in danger,

and what it is to not know it;
the equally abandoned one tree that,

for the time being, holds it—alone,
and what it is to not know it.

All morning, it has been the fog
thinning at last,

as if that were the prayer,
the streets filling with men *as if they*

were divine answer and not just
what happens. Do I love less, if less is

all I remember? Your mouth, like a hole
to fly through. What you understood

of the flesh: how always first are we
struck down. *Then we rise; are astounded.*

CARL PHILLIPS *is the author of four poetry books:* From the Devotions, *a finalist for the 1998 National Book Award in Poetry;* Cortège, *a finalist for both the National Book Critics Circle Award and the Lambda Literary Award for Gay Men's Poetry;* In the Blood, *winner of the Morse Poetry Prize; and the forthcoming* Pastoral. *He is an associate professor of English and African and Afro-American Studies at Washington University in St. Louis.*

Wise Poison

Welcome, Fear

For one thing I'm glad
the goal of enlightenment means being stupid
enough to slip out the door
each morning & live. With no second-guessing,
no poses,
just this leaning & slouching
the experts term hope.
So people like me cannot be held guilty.
In our travels
we'd never laugh at the passing streets,
we're not like those grins they have
plastered to the sides of every bus.
But what do I do, what am I supposed to
do when I want someone
to hold me? How easy it is, & inevitable
and paramount & sweet, to recall
how you would dress before the mirror—
in those minutes before a blouse
started to button itself on,

when sunlight from the window might rest
briefly on your back, & I'd begin
by tipping my mouth to your skin
the way the first imagined oar dipped
into an unimaginable sea.

Now nothing seems right. Between us everything
either finished or unfinishable.
Whatever I once wrote to you fills me,
torn into many small pieces. Sometimes
it seems as if that mirror I mentioned
has been lost, perhaps stolen, but by men I'd hired
myself, mistakenly.
I am my own bad influence.
Many things have gone wrong.
And I will never be what you wished me to be.
You will always lean toward the mirror,
putting on lipstick, kissing the air,
but since the mirror has been revoked
the kiss collects in the shape of space attempting
to kiss itself. Well
the tragic can go fuck itself. Even if, once,
in the middle of the night, I woke
because a smoke detector went off, signaling
its batteries were dying. Even if it's like that. Fear,
like that: walking naked
through a cold house, moving from alarm
to alarm, unable to find the right one. Even if it's like that.

What Kind of Times?

What kind of times? When we still seem to want
     what we've already gotten,
influence & coin, acumen & verve, got, & given

again whatever's due us after getting, the esteem,
     the song, the necessary
snakeskin, the necessary drug, say six breeds

of dog that insinuate power, or the tan of her
     shoulders, a meticulous tan, & silk
black & loose as it falls from her shoulders.

Whatever it is, without completion or calm.
     What can never be enough.
Whether you stand on the curb at First & 6th,

snapping an imaginary whip, or the gift possessed
     by your hands begins
to recede, the stalk of hyacinth, freshly cut,

its scent, unlikely to overwhelm for longer
     than a beat. If you breathe here
now. In the praxis of attainables. American.

Curious Forces

The party spills outside, & for a short time, overhead,
the stars look trapped, like travelers attacked
by bandits, but dead-drunk, so loaded
they hardly act surprised. The air cool,
though I don't want a coat. And none would fit anyway,
nothing in the closet looks familiar, everything—

even my leather jackets—seems shrunk.
As if the rains got endless. As if my greatcoat,
the camel hair my brother loaned, smartened-up
and stalked back to him. But you were the one
who ripped the raglan sleeves,
and snapped off all the buttons.
Sometimes for one last time I am
the small space between your tongue & lips,
a December morning, tears, our teeth chattering.
Even then, I don't want a coat, & don't now.
And isn't this the way it always starts—without need,
first going out coatless, then
joking, the way I do, offering for five bucks
to buy a thirty-year-old blazer,
the olive-gold & green-that-is-mostly-
a-bewitching-black polyester worn by a woman
who resembles you
only if she whispers. The silk lining is ripped,
the lapels stained by wine in one or two places.
When will my life begin again?
Sometimes your smile drifts through my veins,
a raft I float to safety on. I stand outside on a wooden deck,
offering to buy a jacket.
Tenderness is amazed.
The deck descends toward the river.
And you are two thousand miles away,
while my sad cough, my indigenous sadness, loiters,
stuck, on some nearby stairs.
In Tucson, once, there was a man who
thinking you turned tricks
came over to your table & left his business card,
all because of a leopard-skin skirt & makeup.
How blank his breath as you threw back the card,
the lettering raised & black.
Sometimes I have wished to be that card. Tonight

I ask too many questions of the woman
I stand with, her blond, centripetal hair enlivening
the curious forces of the party, & of course
I make another offer on her jacket,
as if donning it might make me clear enough
to understand if our marriage had ended,
if I were really leaving you
and the love of the last twelve years.
Sometimes I have wished to be
ink, black on white, & flung.

Change My Evil Ways

Some days it is my one wish to live
alone, nameless, unfathomable,
a drifter or unemployed alien.
But that day the movie was over.
I found myself walking
in Cambridge, & on the Common
there were some conga players, as well as the guys
with xylophones, with fingerpianos & tambourines.
Have you ever seen minnows flopping
from shallow to shallow, doing somersaults?
The drummers' hands were pale fish,
like guppies thrashing light in a clear plastic bag,
as blurred as children careening around
lawn sprinklers in the careening mercuric blue dusk of August.
Dulse wavering! Hair shook out while somebody dances.
Some days it isn't a life alone I need
but one that supplies the luxury
of forgiveness. It was a day like that,
luckily. Past the tobacconist,
a kid sang his song about changing

my evil ways, & strummed
a three-chord blues, plugged into a boom box
that lay at his side like a wolfhound.
And I put my ear close to his snout,
and—a little
cautious at first—I began to listen.

DAVID RIVARD *is the author of two books of poetry:* Wise Poison, *winner of the 1996 James Laughlin Award of The Academy of American Poets, and* Torque, *winner of the Agnes Lynch Starrett Poetry Prize. He teaches at Tufts University and in the M.F.A. in Writing Program at Vermont College.*

MERCÈ RODOREDA

The Time of
the Doves

Translated by David H. Rosenthal

Julieta came by the pastry shop just to tell me that, before they raffled off the basket of fruit and candy, they'd raffle some coffeepots. She'd already seen them: lovely white ones with oranges painted on them. The oranges were cut in half so you could see the seeds. I didn't feel like dancing or even going out because I'd spent the day selling pastries and my fingertips hurt from tying so many gold ribbons and making so many bows and handles. And because I knew Julieta. She felt fine after three hours' sleep and didn't care if she slept at all. But she made me come even though I didn't want to, because that's how I was. It was hard for me to say no if someone asked me to do something. I was dressed all in white, my dress and petticoats starched, my shoes like two drops of milk, my earrings white enamel, three hoop bracelets that matched the earrings, and a white purse Julieta said was made of vinyl and a snap shaped like a gold shellfish.

When we got to the square, the musicians were already playing. The roof was covered with colored flowers and paper chains: a chain of paper, a chain of flowers. There were flowers with lights inside them and the whole roof was like an umbrella turned inside out, because the ends of the chains were tied much higher up than the middle where they all came together. My petticoat had a rubber waistband I'd had a lot of trouble putting on with a crochet hook that could barely squeeze through. It was fastened with a little button and a loop of string and it dug into my skin. I probably already had a red mark around my waist, but as soon as I started breathing harder I began to feel like I was being martyred. There were asparagus plants around the bandstand to keep the crowd away, and the plants were decorated with flowers tied together with tiny wires. And the musicians with their jackets off, sweating. My mother had been dead for years and couldn't give me advice and my father had remarried. My father remarried and me without my mother whose only joy in life had been to fuss over me. And my father remarried and me a young woman all alone in the Plaça del Diamant waiting for the coffeepot rattle and Julieta shouting to be heard above the music "Stop! You'll get your clothes all wrinkled!" and before my eyes the flower-covered lights and the chains pasted on them and everybody happy and while I was gazing a voice said right by my ear, "Would you like to dance?"

Without hardly realizing, I answered that I didn't know how, and then I turned around to look. I bumped into a face so close to mine that I could hardly see what it looked like, but it was a young man's face. "Don't worry," he said. "I'm good at it. I'll show you how." I thought about poor Pere, who at that moment was shut up in the basement of the Hotel Colón cooking in a white apron, and I was dumb enough to say:

"What if my fiancé finds out?"

He brought his face even closer and said, laughing, "So young and you're already engaged?" And when he laughed his lips stretched and I saw all his teeth. He had little eyes like a monkey and was wearing a white shirt with thin blue stripes, soaked with sweat around the armpits and open at the neck. And suddenly he turned his back to me and stood on tiptoe and leaned one way and then the other and turned back to me and said, "Excuse me," and started shouting, "Hey! Has anyone seen my jacket? It was next to the bandstand! On a chair! Hey . . ." And he told me they'd taken his jacket and he'd be right back and would I be good enough to wait for him. He began shouting, "Cintet . . . Cintet!"

Julieta, who was wearing a canary-yellow dress with green embroidery on it, came up from I don't know where and said, "Cover me. I've got to take off my shoes. . . . I can't stand it anymore." I told her I couldn't move because a boy who was looking for his jacket and was determined to dance with me had told me to wait for him. And Julieta said, "Then dance,

dance. . . ." And it was hot. Kids were setting off firecrackers and rockets in the street. There were watermelon seeds on the ground and near the buildings watermelon rinds and empty beer bottles and they were setting off rockets on the rooftops too and from balconies. I saw faces shining with sweat and young men wiping their faces with handkerchiefs. The musicians happily playing away. Everything like a decoration. And the two-step. I found myself dancing back and forth and, like it was coming from far away though really it was up close, I heard his voice: "Well, so she *does* know how to dance!" And I smelled the strong sweat and faded cologne. And those gleaming monkey's eyes right next to mine and those ears like little medallions. That rubber waistband digging into my waist and my dead mother couldn't advise me, because I told him my fiancé was a cook at the Colón and he laughed and said he felt sorry for him because by New Year's I'd be his wife and his queen and we'd be dancing in the Plaça del Diamant.

"My queen," he said.

And he said by the end of the year I'd be his wife and I hadn't even looked at him yet and I looked him over and then he said, "Don't look at me like that or they'll have to pick me up off the ground," and when I told him he had eyes like a monkey he started laughing. The waistband was like a knife in my skin and the musicians "TararI tararI!" And I couldn't see Julieta anywhere. She'd disappeared. And me with those eyes in front of me that wouldn't go away, as if the whole world had become those eyes and there was no way to escape them. And the night moving forward with its chariot of stars and the festival going on and the fruitbasket and the girl with the fruitbasket, all in blue, whirling around. . . . My mother in Saint Gervasi Cemetery and me in the Plaça del Diamant. . . . "You sell sweet things? Honey and jam . . ." And the musicians, tired, putting things in their cases and taking them out again because someone had tipped them to play a waltz and everyone spinning around like tops. When the waltz ended people started to leave. I said I'd lost Julieta and he said he'd lost Cintet and that when we were alone and everyone shut up in their houses and the streets empty we'd dance a waltz on tiptoe in the Plaça del Diamant . . . round and round . . . He called me Colometa, his little dove. I looked at him very annoyed and said my name was Natalia and when I said my name was Natalia he kept laughing and said I could have only one name:

Colometa. That was when I started running with him behind me: "Don't get scared . . . listen, you can't walk through the streets all alone, you'll get robbed. . . ." and he grabbed my arm and stopped me. "Don't you see you'll get robbed, Colometa?" And my mother dead and me caught in my tracks and that waistband pinching, pinching, like I was tied with a wire to a bunch of asparagus.

And I started running again. With him behind me. The stores shut with their blinds down and the windows full of silent things like inkwells and blotters and postcards and dolls and clothing on display and aluminum pots and needlepoint patterns. . . . And we came out on the Carrer Gran and me running up the street and him behind me and both of us running and years later he'd still talk about it sometimes: "The day I met Colometa in the Plaça del Diamant she suddenly started running and right in front of the streetcar stop, blam! her petticoat fell down."

The loop broke and my petticoat ended up on the ground. I jumped over it, almost tripping, and then I started running again like all the devils in hell were after me. I got home and threw myself on the bed in the dark, my girl's brass bed, like I was throwing a stone onto it. I felt embarrassed. When I got tired of feeling embarrassed, I kicked off my shoes and untied my hair. And Quimet, years later, still talked about it as if it had just happened: "Her waistband broke and she ran like the wind. . . ."

It was very mysterious. I'd put on my pink dress, a little too light for the weather, and I got goosebumps waiting for Quimet on a corner. After I'd been standing around for a while doing nothing, I felt like someone was watching me from behind some shutters, because I saw the slats on one side move a little. Quimet and I had agreed to meet near Güell Park. A man came out of the building with a revolver in his belt and holding a shotgun and went by, brushing against my skirt and calling out, "Meki, meki. . . ."

Someone pushed down the slats, the shutters flew open and a man in pajamas went "Pst! pst!" and, crooking his finger, motioned me to come closer. To make sure, I pointed to myself and, looking at him, whispered, "Me?" Without hearing he understood and nodded his head, which was very handsome, and I crossed the street and came closer. When I was right below the balcony he said, "Come on in and we'll take a little nap."

I blushed bright red and went away furious—mainly with myself—and feeling very nervous because I could feel him staring right into my back through my clothes and skin. I stood where the young man in pajamas couldn't see me but I was afraid that, since I was half hidden, it was Quimet who wouldn't see me. I decided to wait and see what happened because it was the first time we'd arranged to meet outside a park. That morning at work I'd been thinking so much about the afternoon that I'd done all kinds of dumb things. I felt so nervous I thought I'd go out of my mind. Quimet had said we'd meet at three thirty and he didn't show up until four-thirty; but I didn't say anything because I thought maybe I hadn't heard him right and it was me who'd made a mistake and since he didn't say even half a word of apology . . . I was afraid to tell him my feet hurt from standing up so long because I was wearing very hot patent leather shoes and how a young man had taken liberties with me. We started walking up the hill without saying a single wretched word and when we got to the top I didn't feel cold anymore and my skin went back to being smooth like usual. I wanted to tell him I'd broken up with Pere, that everything was settled now. We sat down on a stone bench in a corner out of sight, between two slender trees with long, thin leaves, and a blackbird who kept flying up into them and went from one to the other giving harsh little chirps. We'd sit for a while without seeing him and then he'd fly down onto the ground just when we'd forgotten about him and he kept doing the same thing over and over again. Without looking straight at him, out of the corner of my eye I saw that Quimet was looking at the little houses in the distance. Finally he said, "Doesn't that bird scare you?"

I told him I liked the bird, and he said his mother had always told him how birds that were black, even ordinary blackbirds, brought bad luck. All the other times I'd gone out with Quimet, after that first day in the Plaça del Diamant, the first thing he'd asked me, leaning his whole body forward, was whether I'd broken up with Pere yet. And that day he didn't ask and I didn't know how to begin to tell him I'd told Pere it was all over between us. And I felt worried about having said it, because Pere had flamed up like a match when you blow on it. And when I thought about leaving Pere it hurt me inside and the hurt made me realize I'd done something wrong. I was sure of it, because I'd always felt comfortable inside, and when I thought about Pere's face I felt a pain that hurt deep inside me, as if in the middle of the peace I'd felt before a little door had opened that was hiding a nest of scorpions and the scorpions had come out and mixed with the pain and made it sting even more and had swarmed through my blood and made it black. Because Pere, with his voice choked up and his eyes full of tears and shaking, had said I'd wrecked his life. That I'd turned it into a little clot of mud. And while he was looking at the blackbird, Quimet began to talk about Senyor Gaudí. How his father had met Gaudí the day he was run over by a streetcar, how his father had been one of the people who'd taken him to the hospital, poor Senyor Gaudí, such a good person, what a horrible way to die . . . And how there was nothing in the world like Güell Park and the Holy Family Church and the Pedrera apartment house. I told him that, all in all, there were too many spires and waves. He hit my knee with the edge of his hand and made my leg fly up with surprise and said if I wanted to be his wife I had to start by liking everything he liked. He delivered a long sermon about men and women and the rights of the one and the rights of the other and when I was able to cut in I asked him:

"What if I just can't bring myself to like something?"

"You've got to like it, because that means it's something you don't understand."

And another sermon, very long. He brought up lots of people in his family: his parents, an uncle who had a little chapel and a prayer stool, and Ferdinand and Isabella's mothers who he said were the ones who'd shown the right path.

And then—at first I didn't get the point because he mixed it up with so many other things he was saying—he said, "Poor Maria. . . ." And again Ferdinand and Isabella's mothers and how maybe we could get married soon because he had two friends who were already looking for an apartment for him. And he'd make some furniture that would floor me because he wasn't a carpenter for nothing and he was like Saint Joseph and I was like the Virgin Mary.

He said it all very happily and I was thinking of what he'd meant when he said, "Poor Maria . . ." and my mind was getting further away like the fading light. The blackbird never got tired. He was always popping out on

the ground and flying from one tree to another and popping out under-
neath as if there was a whole flock of blackbirds working on it.

"I'll make a wardrobe for both of us out of bottle-tree wood, with two
compartments. And when the apartment's all furnished, I'll make a little
bed for our kid."

He told me he liked children and he didn't, that he'd never been able to
make up his mind. The sun was going down and where it no longer reached
the shadows were turning blue and it was strange-looking. And Quimet
kept talking about different kinds of wood, which one to use, jacaranda or
mahogany or oak or holly. . . . It was then—I remember it and I'll always re-
member it—that he kissed me. And when he started kissing me I saw Our
Lord up above in his house inside a puffed-up cloud with bright orange
edges that was changing color on one side, and Our Lord spread his arms
wide—they were very long—and he grabbed the sides of the cloud and shut
himself up in it like it was a cupboard.

"We shouldn't have come today."

And the first kiss faded into another and the whole sky clouded up. I
saw a big cloud moving away and other smaller ones come out and they all
started following the puffed-up one and Quimet's mouth tasted like coffee
and milk. And he shouted, "They're closing!"

"How do you know?"

"Didn't you hear the whistle?"

We got up, startling the blackbird who flew away. The wind whipped up
my skirts . . . and we followed the paths downward. There was a girl sitting
on a bench made out of ceramic tiles who was picking her nose and rubbing
her finger against an eight-point star on the back of the bench. Her dress
was the same color as mine and I told Quimet. He didn't answer. When we
got to the street I said, "Look, people are still going in . . ." and he said,
"Don't worry, they'll throw them out soon." We walked down through the
streets and just when I was about to tell him, "You know, Pere and I have
broken up," he suddenly stopped and stood in front of me. He took hold of
my arms and said, looking at me like there was something weird about me,
"Poor Maria."

I was about to tell him not to fret and to tell me what was eating him with this Maria . . . but I didn't dare. Then he let go of my arms and started walking beside me again toward the center of town till we got to the corner of Diagonal and the Passeig de Gràcia. We started walking around the block. My feet were killing me. When we'd been going round and round for half an hour he stopped and took hold of my arms again. We were standing under a streetlight, and just when I was expecting him to say "Poor Maria" again and holding my breath waiting for him to say it, he said angrily:

"If we hadn't gotten out of there so quickly, between the blackbird and everything else, I don't know what would have happened! . . . But don't trust me. The day I catch you I'll hobble you for life."

We walked around the block till it was eight o'clock without saying a word to each other, as if we'd been born mute. When he said goodbye and I was alone again I looked at the sky and it was all black. And I don't know . . . all together, it was very mysterious . . .

MERCÈ RODOREDA *was born in Barcelona in 1908, and fled into exile at the end of the Spanish Civil War. She is the author of* My Christina & Other Stories, Time of the Doves, *and* Camelia Street. *Finally able to return to Barcelona, she died there in 1983.*

R. A. SASAKI

The Loom

And Other Stories

Ohaka-Mairi

The car turns smoothly under my father's hand. Silently, it slips onto the freeway, heading south.

"Too cold back there?" my father asks, glancing at me in the rearview mirror and rolling up his window.

"No." The air is suddenly close.

"Jo hasn't been to see her yet," my mother says. "She should once, before she goes away in the fall."

It has been two years, after all. But why must we go to this long-ago place, this place left behind in windswept memories? Until now, I have grieved for her in my own way, in my own places.

I don't know whether something in the air carried a silent message discernible only to my mother, or whether it was some inner clock at work that only she possessed, but about two or three times a year she would suddenly say to the rest of the family: "Mo, it's about time we went ohaka-mairi." *And we would go that weekend.*

We would all pile into the car and head south, out of the city. From San Francisco, Sunday drives with the family could take us in any of three directions. Each direction had special significance, emotional coloring. North was a warm, sunny direction. It meant crossing the Golden Gate Bridge. It meant rolling hills and sleepy harbor towns. It almost always meant an ice cream cone. East meant getting up before dawn and going to Yosemite. We did this every summer. South was chilly, south was sad. The fog always made us hunch down in our seats, shivering. South meant either the airport, to say good-bye, or the cemetery.

My father is looking at me in the rearview mirror. My hands tingle, bloodless. I am sitting on them.

I want to remember her as she was the night she brought Jeff home with her. She came through the front door like a fresh wind, fire-cheeked and blooming, hair a hopeless tangle falling to her waist. I laughed, and my fingers became trapped in the knotted black mass as I tried to untangle it. She laughed, and stopped moving just long enough for me to get my fingers out. She was home.

But Jeff was there. He stood between the living room where my father sat and the kitchen floor where my mother was putting away her apron, looking as though he had brought all of outdoors in with him. But all of outdoors did not fit into our house. Standing in our entryway against black lacquer and flowered scrolls, beard bristling over ruddy skin, boots crusted with the dried earth of another world, he was like a giant redwood among the potted bonsai of my father's house. My mother came hurrying from the kitchen, bowing instinctively. I retreated to the stairway, from which I could see my father sitting in his armchair, perfectly still.

The next time I saw Jeff was after she died.

The cemetery was like a city of tombstones, laid out in neat rows with intersections and streets along which neither cars nor people moved, only dust. It was always windy. We would stop at one of the flower shops along the side of the road, where my father would buy flowers—usually carnations, because they are a hardy flower and last a long time after cut. Then we would turn into the cemetery and park on the dusty road. My mother and father would clip the hedge that grew on my grandparents' plot, pour water over the headstone, rake the dead leaves. My sisters and I would play hide-and-seek among the tombstones. Some of them were big enough to stand behind.

On the day she died, relatives came and went like figures in a dream. I sat alone in the house, watching out the window, hearing the voices of aunts and uncles downstairs stifling the laughter of children and worrying about lunch. The doorbell kept ringing, and I would open the door and stare blankly at whoever stood outside until my aunt came to usher them in.

The coroner's report spoke only of an inanimate object. Date, time, place, injuries sustained, cause of death.

Our car eases into the exit lane. We leave the freeway, and pass a row of drive-ins. A large red and white barrel floats by. My father catches my eye in the rearview mirror. Perhaps he is remembering that last early-morning fishing expedition, when she and I filled a Kentucky Fried Chicken bucket with sand crabs. We went shrieking along the beach after the scuttling crabs, and the only reason I got myself to pick one up was because she did it first. At the end of the day, we left the racks of our *zori* entwined in the wet sand. The bucket was still full. Let them go, my father had said. We were reluctant. All that work. We vowed to do this again, next weekend if possible. But we didn't.

We met with Jeff two months after the funeral, my sisters and I. It was just lunch, a sandwich eaten outside on the grass. It was the third and last time I saw him, the second being at the banquet after my sister's funeral when my father, in fury mixed up with grief, had ordered him to leave. We had not had a chance to get to know Jeff, and now it seemed too late. He was a stranger. I searched his face, looking for whatever it was that my sister had loved. There were so many questions I wanted to ask, but I thought of the night he had spent trapped, alone on that ledge after she fell, and I could not ask them. We spoke of unimportant things, even made a few jokes. Then we said good-bye. A year later, he went away, to Canada. Now I am leaving, too.

Flower shops begin appearing along the side of the road. We are almost there. We pull into the parking lot of one of the shops. The window is filled with heavy-looking floral displays. I can almost smell them from here.

I remember the odor of carnations, mingled with the scent of incense, at the funerals of the old issei friends of my grandparents in the Buddhist church, when I was a child.

My father gets out of the car. Through the display window I see him enter the store. I follow his jet-black head, touched with white, as it weaves among the bulbous flowers, turning, stopping, hesitant, as if suddenly lost in the vision of a toddling child with flaming cheeks and bowl-shaped cap of hair.

"I was really crushed when I realized that your parents didn't want to hear what I had to say," Jeff wrote in a letter from Canada. "I wanted us to face the pain together, to tell them about this daughter of theirs, her thoughts and feelings that only I knew. But that has passed. I don't care anymore."

My father stops before a bucket of spring blossoms.

"I don't blame your father for being bitter. But I do condemn him for not admitting that she was a person different from the person he wanted her to be. He will die with bitterness, never having known her. . . ."

When my father comes out of the store, he carries a delicate branch of spring blossoms. He gives them to my mother, and we cross the road. We pull into a circular drive, stop on the dusty road. Everything is still. The engine dies. My father fumbles with the doors as we get out. My parents lead the way, heads bowed, and I want to run, to bolt away from the dusty and inevitable avenue.

But something catches my eye. On the ground at my feet is a single pink petal, flickering in the dust. Another falls, in my father's footsteps.

"You say you want to understand me. There's a book you might read, about the mountains. I'll send you a copy. Your sister loved it too. You might even learn something about her. Love, Jeff"

I start slowly down the avenue of tombstones where we hid as children; I come seeking her again. My father turns the corner and I turn the corner and there is her name, her name.

R. A. SASAKI *is a third-generation San Franciscan. Winner of the 1983 American Japanese National Literary Award,* The Loom and Other Stories *is her first published collection.*

VIJAY SESHADRI

Wild Kingdom

Made in the Tropics

Bobby Culture ("Full of Roots and Culture")
and Ranking Joe ("Man Make You Widdle
Pon Your Toe") shift down
in the gloaming, snap off
their helmets, kill their engines, park
one thousand cubic centimeters
of steeled precision Japanese art.
Their bands drive up
in fur-trimmed vans, unload and unwrap
the hundred-watt speakers, thousand-watt amps,
mikes and mike stands,
guitars, cymbals, steel cans,
at the Blue Room Lawn on Gun Hill Road
by the Bronx botanical gardens.
The sun over Jersey
kicks and drops
into the next of its ready-made slots,
and, like a dark lotion
from a pitcher poured, night fills

the concrete hollows, and the grass
cools in the projects,
the glowing lakes contract
around their artificial islands,
the gardens breathe
easier in the dwindling fever
of today's unbearable summer.
They say the tropics
are moving north,
the skullcap of ice melting
from both the pole now pointed
toward the sun
and the one pointing away.
But what they say is hardly heard here,
where the cooling brickwork
engine red Edwardian
railroad flats empty
their tenants, who gather
in twos and threes, float down
from the stations,
and congregate at the Blue Room Lawn
to celebrate Independence
Day in Jamaica.
The bass line fires up.
From Savanna-La-Mar to Gun Hill Road
the backwash of reggae spirals
to its perch, ripples
and flares its solar wings
along the upended moving limbs,
as if a chain were passed through every wrist,
as if a chain were tied from hip to hip.
The sun does what it does because the earth tilts.

This Fast-Paced, Brutal Thriller

There's always a killer with a name like Tony,
a tie-dyed shirt, and a certain
sad history of deprivation:
just so much evil to get the plot going

down the edge of a formula
nickel-and-dimed
by years of repetition.
There's always an ocean near Hawaii or California

where the detective ponders the copy of a psalm
he once gave in commemoration
to his friend, the victim
(they shared a tin hut in Vietnam),

over whose body the salt water swarms.
Something as strange and uncanny
as Taiwanese packing twine
has been wrapped around the legs and blue arms,

giving the detective, for his deduction, a sign
that the script changed tongues
in the middle of a scene,
and only he's left to render this line

to the bored, puzzled girl on whom the camera can't focus
because she stepped over for a look
from another channel.
She stares right past him as she says, "Jesus,

this show, it's the pits."
And the faces start blending
on the molten screen:
screen before which the defeated imagination sits.

A Werewolf in Brooklyn

Still almost blind in his thinking eye,
the last of the moon, as it zeros in
on the preordained spot, to modify
his downside structures and curry his skin

with its lucent brush, so the dog flares up,
he only can grasp as a metaphor.
A lozenge dissolves in a silver cup
out of which such emptinesses pour

to prove for him the Buddhists right
who say that wolfpacks of nothingness stalk
the signature stinks and blood trails of man,

but that to race with them and let them bite
will do for him much better than
Ping-Pong, kind visitors, electroshock.

from An Oral History of Migration

Back in 1935 the Lord
told me, Go buy a guitar.
You be that thing, He said.
It was 6:47, almost 7:00 A.M.
The nettles and blackberry
I'd cut back the last spring
were already rooting at the stile
and bothering the chicken fence.
I was shoeing the team in the shed.
My mother called from deep in the yard:
"Run bring me a pail," she said.
Well, you can't fetch light with a pail,

at least not our pail,
so I pretended not to hear
and kept on working.
I was good shoeing horses, I'd
rasp and trim every hoof first,
then go around and drive the half-flat nails
flat side out into shoe and hoof
with a double stroke a little like a banjo lick.
But not too deep
or you drive to the quick.
You be that thing, He said.

Some people think if you keep jumping
over a patch of ground, jump
like some bighorn sheep,
that patch of ground eventually go away.
It don't; it's always there.
Up in Harlem after the war I quit the shipyards,
got myself a Gibson and a little reputation.
I've been turning it over ever since.

VIJAY SESHADRI *was born in India and came to America at age 5. He lives in Brooklyn, works at the* New Yorker, *and teaches at Sarah Lawrence College.* Wild Kingdom *is his first book of poetry.*

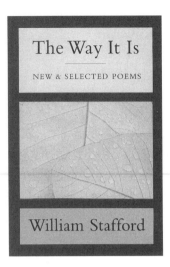

WILLIAM STAFFORD

The Way It Is

The Way It Is

There's a thread you follow. It goes among
things that change. But it doesn't change.
People wonder about what you are pursuing.
You have to explain about the thread.
But it is hard for others to see.
While you hold it you can't get lost.
Tragedies happen; people get hurt
or die; and you suffer and get old.
Nothing you do can stop time's unfolding.
You don't ever let go of the thread.

You Reading This, Be Ready

Starting here, what do you want to remember?
How sunlight creeps along a shining floor?
What scent of old wood hovers, what softened
sound from outside fills the air?

Will you ever bring a better gift for the world
than the breathing respect that you carry
wherever you go right now? Are you waiting
for time to show you some better thoughts?

When you turn around, starting here, lift this
new glimpse that you found; carry into evening
all that you want from this day. This interval you spent
reading or hearing this, keep it for life—

What can anyone give you greater than now,
starting here, right in this room, when you turn around?

Ask Me

Some time when the river is ice ask me
mistakes I have made. Ask me whether
what I have done is my life. Others
have come in their slow way into
my thought, and some have tried to help
or to hurt: ask me what difference
their strongest love or hate has made.

I will listen to what you say.
You and I can turn and look
at the silent river and wait. We know
the current is there, hidden; and there
are comings and goings from miles away
that hold the stillness exactly before us.
What the river says, that is what I say.

At the Bomb Testing Site

At noon in the desert a panting lizard
waited for history, its elbows tense,
watching the curve of a particular road
as if something might happen.

It was looking at something farther off
than people could see, an important scene
acted in stone for little selves
at the flute end of consequences.

There was just a continent without much on it
under a sky that never cared less.
Ready for a change, the elbows waited.
The hands gripped hard on the desert.

Bi-Focal

Sometimes up out of this land
a legend begins to move.
Is it a coming near
of something under love?

Love is of the earth only,
the surface, a map of roads
leading wherever go miles
or little bushes nod.

Not so the legend under,
fixed, inexorable,
deep as the darkest mine
the thick rocks won't tell.

As fire burns the leaf
and out of the green appears
the vein in the center line
and the legend veins under there,

So, the world happens twice—
once what we see it as;
second it legends itself
deep, the way it is.

A Ritual to Read to Each Other

If you don't know the kind of person I am
and I don't know the kind of person you are
a pattern that others made may prevail in the world
and following the wrong god home we may miss our star.

For there is many a small betrayal in the mind,
a shrug that lets the fragile sequence break
sending with shouts the horrible errors of childhood
storming out to play through the broken dyke.

And as elephants parade holding each elephant's tail,
but if one wanders the circus won't find the park,
I call it cruel and maybe the root of all cruelty
to know what occurs but not recognize the fact.

And so I appeal to a voice, to something shadowy,
a remote important region in all who talk:
though we could fool each other, we should consider—
lest the parade of our mutual life get lost in the dark.

For it is important that awake people be awake,
or a breaking line may discourage them back to sleep;
the signals we give—yes or no, or maybe—
should be clear: the darkness around us is deep.

Traveling through the Dark

Traveling through the dark I found a deer
dead on the edge of the Wilson River road.
It is usually best to roll them into the canyon:
that road is narrow; to swerve might make more dead.

By glow of the tail-light I stumbled back of the car
and stood by the heap, a doe, a recent killing;
she had stiffened already, almost cold.
I dragged her off; she was large in the belly.

My fingers touching her side brought me the reason—
her side was warm; her fawn lay there waiting,
alive, still, never to be born.
Beside that mountain road I hesitated.

The car aimed ahead its lowered parking lights;
under the hood purred the steady engine.
I stood in the glare of the warm exhaust turning red;
around our group I could hear the wilderness listen.

I thought hard for us all—my only swerving—,
then pushed her over the edge into the river.

Smoke

Smoke's way's a good way—find,
or be rebuffed and gone:
a day and a day, the whole world home.

Smoke? Into the mountains I guess
a long time ago. Once here, yes,
everywhere. Say anything? No.

I saw Smoke, slow traveler, reluctant
but sure. Hesitant sometimes, yes,
because that's the way things are.

Smoke never doubts though:
some new move will appear.
Wherever you are, there is another door.

WILLIAM STAFFORD *was born in Hutchinson, Kansas in 1914 and died in Oregon in 1993. Stafford authored 67 volumes of poetry in his lifetime, including the 1963 National Book Award winner* Traveling through the Dark, *and after serving as the Consultant in Poetry to the Library of Congress, Stafford was named the Oregon Poet Laureate in 1975. His work is collected in* The Way It Is: New & Selected Poems.

JACK & ROCHELLE SUTIN

Jack and Rochelle

A Holocaust Story of Love and Resistance

Edited by Lawrence Sutin

From the Bunker to the Atrad

JACK

It was a joy for me to see, as the weeks went on, that Rochelle began to seem more relaxed and happy. Before, when we had sung songs during the night, she would only sit and listen. But then she herself began to sing Polish songs, Russian songs, and also Yiddish songs like "Oifun Pripichok" and "Papirosun."

She got me to be more careful on the raids. As we fell more and more in love, I thought more and more about living.

ROCHELLE

It was in every sense a real love affair. But then you may wonder how a love affair is conducted when the two of you are living like wild animals in a hole in the ground with ten other people.

A normal mind—a mind that has always lived in a safe and comfortable civilized state—can never understand what it was like. I don't know myself how to explain. It was very cramped and crowded in the bunker. If you moved to the left or to the right, everyone else had to move from the left to the right. There was no privacy, no intimacy . . . none. What was happening around us I cannot say. It was pitch dark at night. You could hear people moving. But there was no verbal expression. It was like a silent movie. For us, those conditions meant that in the bunker itself we hugged each other, we petted, we kissed . . . and no more. It wasn't like having a normal sexual relationship and making love when you wanted to.

Once, I remember, we paid a return visit to the Kurluta family, to whom Jack had introduced me as his wife some two months before. I had been so shocked by his statement then. But this time, we did behave like newly-weds, and the family fed us and treated us beautifully. And on the way there, in the woods, we had stopped and made love.

But private moments like that were few and far between.

There was an activity, I remember, that took up a lot of our time that winter, in common with the other members of the group. It was removing the parasites from our bodies. On sunny days, we used to take turns slipping out of the bunker hole, taking off our clothes, and squeezing off the lice, which we were all full of. One of those, a breed that dug into our skin and fattened on our blood, we called *mandavoshkes*. They would get into your pubic hair, under your armpits, around your eyes. Only when you sat naked in the outdoor light could you see fully what was happening to your body. One day, I recall, I woke up and sensed that my eyelids were heavy. I put my fingers up to feel and there were little black bumps all along my eyelashes. I went outside, taking with me a straight pin and a tiny mirror that we all shared. I poked these out one by one, but had a hard time holding my hand steady because I was so revulsed by the fact that what I was poking at was my own filthy body. My fingers, my hands . . . everything was itching.

Once I tried hard to get rid of them from my clothing. My basic daily outfit was Jack's pajama top, a pair of men's pants, and some boots. There was no brassiere or underwear. The basic way to rid your clothes of lice was to hold them close to the fire until the little creatures overheated and jumped off. But one time I was determined to go further than that. I took the shirt and the pants and boiled up a pail full of melted snow and threw these clothes in the boiling water. Then I hung the clothes up outside on a nearby tree branch. They were quickly frozen stiff, like icicles. So then I took them back into the bunker, thinking that they would be free of vermin at least for a little while. But when they defrosted near the fire, I could see the trains of tiny white lice still crawling over the fabric! It was impossible, but it was happening before my eyes.

All of us, that winter, took turns killing the lice, the worms, and God knows whatever else we found on ourselves. Those who had somehow paired up would help each other out with backsides and hard-to-reach spots.

I helped not only Jack but Julius as well—I treated him as if he were my own father. I would wash him, scrape the lice from him. Julius was a very calm and patient man. He had the ability to be almost oblivious to the physical conditions in which he was forced to live. That was remarkable enough, given what those conditions were, and especially so for a man who was already in his late fifties. I remember that he often wore a hat with a little visor, and that the lice were parading around on that visor like cars on a highway. Big ones! I would watch him for a while and then ask, "Doesn't it bother you?" He would shrug and say, *"Beist mir nit"* ["They don't bite me"]. That would exasperate me, so I would grab his hat off his head and shake it, to show him how many lice would fly off from even one shake. Finally, seeing this, he would take a piece of wood and scrape the rest of the lice off this hat. That was the way he was. He didn't clean himself—he didn't feel the itching the way the rest of us did. One of the reasons I was willing to clean him was that I figured that, if I didn't, the lice would jump from him onto us after we had already cleaned ourselves.

But not everyone retained a sense of family. Most did, but there were terrible exceptions: Jack and I had personal knowledge of one of those. It involved a mother and a daughter who ran away from the Mir ghetto at the same time that Jack did. What happened to them shows how family bonds could break down terribly under the weight of hardship. The daughter was maybe seventeen, and her mother was somewhere in her forties—an age that seemed very old to the Jewish youth who were hiding out in the forest. Well, the daughter found a young group who was willing to accept her but not her mother. I should mention that this daughter also had a boyfriend who was a son of a bitch, as bad a character as she was. I say she was bad because what she told her mother at that point was that she, the daughter, had a chance to survive and that the mother was only a burden to her. One of the members of her group had a small bottle of poison, and as a solution to the difficult situation the daughter convinced the mother to drink the poison! The mother didn't want to, but her daughter basically forced it upon her as the only way out. It went from worse to worse—the poison didn't take right away, it wasn't strong enough. The mother suffered for a whole day before she went—gasping, suffocating, thrashing. They watched and waited a whole day for her to die.

Any attempt to hold onto traditional family bonds was difficult, given the conditions that were faced by the early small groups. Everyone was desperate, fearful of being found out, trapped, tortured, killed. There were cases we heard of, in a few of the bunkers, where mothers had escaped with young children—toddlers and a bit older—who would make noise or cry too persistently. The others would demand that something drastic be done, and when the mothers refused to suffocate their own offspring, the others would grab and kill the child!

Julius acted as a father both to Jack and to me and took care of us in his own ways. Because of his age, his most frequently assigned job in the partisan groups was to keep the fire fueled and going at night. Sometimes he would take a few raw potatoes from the food supply and stick them under the hot ashes to bake. He wasn't supposed to do that . . . it was like stealing. But he would do it so that he could wake Jack and me—his *kinderlach* [children]—in the middle of night and give us a little extra food. Julius was always very sweet and protective to me because he had seen how unhappy his *zunele* [affectionate term for son] was during the time I ran away.

That was how we lived in the first months together. But Jack and I did not have much time to get used to any sort of rhythm of life in the bunker. Because in March 1943, our location—as well as that of the other two Jewish bunkers in the Miranke region —was discovered by the Germans. Who knows how? Maybe one of the farmers in the vicinity saw the smoke from our cooking fire.

JACK

There had been pressure on the Germans to do something about the Jewish partisan activity. I won't say it was their first priority, but it mattered to them because they wanted to win the trust of the local Polish population and establish confidence in the stability of their rule.

Don't forget, we were basically living off the local Polish farmers. If we didn't raid their houses, we would go into their fields and dig up their beets, potatoes, or whatever else they were planting. Also, many of the farm families—as well as other members of the local Polish population—had husbands or sons who were now serving in the Polish police. None of those families wanted living Jewish witnesses who might someday testify as to how they had cooperated with the Germans. Even though the progress of the war at that time seemed to be favoring the Germans, the Russians might return and rule Poland again someday—as happened, in fact, in 1944. If the Soviet regime was reinstalled, those who had collaborated with the Germans could expect to pay dearly.

So all of those families were on the lookout for Jewish partisans. And even farmers who had no strong feelings about Jews one way or the other were intimidated by the Germans. They were afraid that if they helped us— or even if they seemed merely to be withholding information as to our whereabouts—they would be burned out and killed by the Germans and their Polish henchmen. So we were in danger of being spotted and in- formed upon from all sides. If we heard the sound of sawing nearby us in the woods, we were terrified, for it meant that a Pole stocking up on fire- wood might have seen us.

ROCHELLE

One day there was an ambush. We heard shooting all around us. One of the nearby bunkers was completely caught unaware—the Germans dropped a grenade down their entry hole and they were all killed at once. Exactly our own worst nightmare. Thank God we were spared that. But they advanced toward the two remaining bunkers—ours and Gittel's—lobbing hand grenades and firing steadily with their machine guns.

All of us in our bunker ran. There was nothing else we could do, taken by surprise like that. We took nothing with us but our weapons and the clothes on our back. We ran deeper into the wilderness, into the Nalibocka Forest, which despite its name contained large stretches of pure swamp- land. Into that swampland they did not follow us. We were afraid to go back to our hole or to any other dry portion of the Miranke woods. There might be other German sweeps. So in the swamp we stayed.

It was still winter, but from March through May we slept outside. It was freezing! Our beds—trees and branches to lift us off the snow and the muck—were all we had to keep us off the swampy ground. Food was a terrible problem. When the German and Polish police drove us out of the Miranke woods, they made sure to kill off any animals or livestock—horses, cows, rabbits—in the region that we might be able to steal and live on. A kind of scorched-earth policy. But they didn't reckon with our desperation and our hunger. At night we used to go out and find the dead carcasses in the woods or on the outskirts of the swamp. In most cases they had been lying there for days, maybe even a week or more. And we would cut slabs of rotting flesh off those carcasses and stuff our pockets with them. Then we would go back to our camp in the swamp and chew on this meat, getting ourselves to swallow as much as we could.

And no one got sick from the food—the mushrooms were not poisonous, and the germs and bacteria in the dead carcasses were not strong enough.

JACK

We must have been fated to live.

ROCHELLE

For the first few days of our hiding in the swamp, before we constructed pallets from trees and branches, we were often standing in water. There were leeches that would attach themselves in clusters to our legs, which were already swollen from the water.

During that time I developed a terrible pain in one of my legs . . . from the moisture and the cold. Maybe a nerve became inflamed. To move at all I had to hop on one leg. When, in May, we heard nothing more of German patrols, we left the deeper swamp area and returned to the more solid ground of the woods. But we were still outside, and cold, and miserable. Who would have thought that I would ever have missed the bunker?

JACK

What made our situation even more difficult was that we had no way of knowing what was happening with the war in a wider context. We had little idea of what was happening with the German offensive in Russia, for example. Later, when news reached us through some Polish farmers of the defeat of the German army at Stalingrad [in late 1942], we felt a little hope that maybe, maybe. . . .

But during that winter of 1943, as we hid in our swamp, we could only suppose that the Germans were marching in triumph toward Moscow and that the Nazis would be ruling Poland and Russia without any effective opposition. It was difficult to see any long-term possibilities other than death at German hands. Even if we made it back to dry land, how long could we expect to live by stealing food from mainly hostile farms?

On the other hand, there were terrible things that we did not know that would have made us feel even worse. We did not know at the time about the concentration camps. It was a secret that the Germans kept carefully hidden from the Jews, so as to keep as much hope in the minds of the remaining ghetto Jews as they could, and thereby reduce the likelihood of desperate resistance. What we thought at that time was that all the Jews were being killed the way our families had been killed . . . town by town, through shootings at mass graves. We also had no idea how many Jews had survived. For all we knew, the groups in the Nalibocka Forest were the only survivors. Not many parts of Poland had a wilderness equal in size to this— it could have been that we were uniquely fortunate. But we were Jews who were still alive, and that was something. It was enough, at least, to push us from one day to the next.

In May 1943, after a springtime with no major German activity in the area, we decided to risk leaving the swamp for a higher woodland site. At that point we had only nine in our group. We kept far away from our old bunker site. That time, instead of digging underground, we built little huts out of branches that were meant to be very temporary. Our plan was that we would change our location constantly, and in that way reduce the risk of being informed upon and ambushed. This was strictly a warm-weather tactic. For the coming winter, we figured that we would have to construct a new bunker due to the cold. Looking back, I can see that the plan was not a very good one. The part of the Miranke woods that we were in then was a relatively confined one—we could have been easily surrounded. As we were stealing food from the local farmers regularly, the danger of being spotted was especially high. Even if we had built a bunker, I doubt we could have survived the winter.

In our wanderings, we found a few other small Jewish groups, and that was a bit of an encouragement to us. But from those groups we also heard terrible news about the ongoing liquidations of the Polish ghettos.

ROCHELLE

Things didn't always go smoothly for us with the other Jewish groups. People were desperate, and that made some of them behave badly.

For example, Jack had been carrying with him all that time in the woods a small diamond necklace that had belonged to his mother. It had great emotional importance to him. And we also saw it as a means of buying food or ammunition if things reached a point of absolute emergency. During the spring we decided that it was too risky to be constantly carrying the necklace. So we put it in a little box and buried it under a tree, making a little mark on the tree that Jack and Julius and I alone would recognize.

But a Jew from another group, an older man named Moshe, spotted us while we were burying the box. Later he went back and dug the necklace up and kept it for himself. We found out, but when we confronted Moshe, he refused to give it back. He told us that he was an uncle to some young nephews whom he had to help support—and so he needed the necklace more than we did. That was his defense. Moshe hid it in a different place so that we could not grab it from him. Moshe wasn't afraid because he knew what kind of a person Jack was—Jack wouldn't kill him in cold blood for a necklace. So the necklace was gone, and we never got it back.

JACK

As the summer went on, it became obvious that we would have to come up with a better plan for survival through the winter and after. We were small in number, without a safe home base, without options in terms of any kind of military action aside from desperate food raids in the middle of the night.

Our problems were not only with the German troops and the Polish police. The Russian partisans who shared the woodlands with us could not bring themselves to let us alone. In the very large Russian partisan groups, the officers in command did try to maintain the official Soviet policy of non-discrimination toward Jews. But there were always individual Russians who would hate the Jews who had managed to survive in the woods. If our boys from the bunker went out for food at night, and they ran into a small band of Russian partisans, those partisans would take their food and kill them. While that was happening, the Russians would also complain that the Jewish partisans only stole food and never fought with the Germans. We were in tiny groups—and not military groups, but ones that included men and women, older and younger people, even sons and daughters taking care of their parents, as I was taking care of Julius. We were barely surviving, and the Germans, Poles, and Russians alike were our enemies. Where were our allies? Many of my friends were killed not by the Germans or by the Poles but by our supposed allies the Russian partisans. They killed fourteen boys from my hometown of Mir in a single day.

One day, in the woods, we ran into a young Russian Jew who gave us some news. He told us about a large Jewish partisan *atrad* that consisted of roughly 80 percent Jews from Minsk [a large western Russian city not far from the Polish border] and 20 percent Jews who had escaped from various Polish town ghettos. They were located deep in the Nalibocka Forest. There were no farmers or little towns in that vicinity—no one to observe your movements.

The Nalibocka Forest was a massive exception to the open farmland that was most common in eastern Poland. Its dense wilderness allowed for a more large-scale partisan organization such as the *atrad.* In fact, we learned that there were not only two Jewish *atrads* operating in this wilderness, but also a dozen or so Russian partisan *atrads.* Approximately 15,000 to 20,000 partisans all told. One of the Jewish *atrads* was led by the Bielski brothers—Jewish brothers from eastern Poland. But the *atrad* we were told about by the young Russian Jew was led by Simcha Zorin, a robust middle-aged man with a large reddish mustache. There were some 300 Jews in that *atrad*—a distinct and real Jewish fighting force. That was exciting news, both for what it meant in terms of our own possible survival, and for what it meant about the survival of at least a small remnant of the Jews in the region.

Zorin had been a Jewish officer in the Soviet army, and so he had actually received formal military training in organization and tactics. He had organized the decision making of the *atrad* to include a chief of staff and other military-type leaders. Those persons had considerable power. When they told you to go out on a food raid, you went, no matter how you felt about it. It was a very regimented form of life as compared to the small group structures we were used to. But on the other hand, there would be a chance to go on missions that could have a real impact—missions that would involve enough men so that you would have a real chance in battle if you ran into a force of Germans or Poles. A larger group would also mean that we could reduce the risk of being killed one by one by the Russians.

The young man we met was a member of Zorin's *atrad.* He invited eight or so of us to come along with him and see what it was like. If we wanted to join, we could. If not, we could remain on our own. We walked for miles and miles into the most dense part of the Nalibocka Forest until we reached the camp of Zorin's *atrad.* It took us two full days. It seemed to us that the Germans and Poles would never venture that far. They could be trapped and ambushed too easily.

Of course, if we were to live so far from the farms in our own little group, the logistics of carrying out food raids would have become impossible. But, as the young man who guided us there explained, with a large-scale *atrad,* you could carry out a variety of raids in larger numbers. Different men could take turns, rather than the same ones risking their lives every night—and you could still maintain a safe and stable camp. There was another difference that the young man explained to us. In the winter, the *atrad* members did not have to live completely underground. They built shelters that were dug halfway into the earth, and then were completed with branches and even boards. Each of these shelters housed twenty-five to thirty people.

ROCHELLE

It was a major change—you lived less like an animal and more like a human.

JACK

We decided to join. It helped that there were some six or seven survivors from the Stolpce ghetto living in that *atrad*—some people we knew from before the war. And it felt safer to be with a large group. Personally, I felt relieved not to be so much in charge as I had been in the smaller groups. Now that Rochelle and I were together, I had something to live for. We were never optimistic, but we couldn't help but begin to hope that we could have a life together after the war. The *atrad* made that hope seem more real.

The population of the *atrad* was very mixed—young and old people, even some children. It was like a big family. And with 300 some people, you had a range of skills that was incredible, considering that we were living in the midst of the wilderness. There was a woman doctor from Russia. Though she rarely had the medical supplies she needed, her being there to give diagnoses and suggestions felt reassuring. There were tailors who could mend clothing, shoemakers who could keep boots intact. If a cow was brought in from a food raid, there were butchers who could make sausages from it. There was a big camp kitchen area in which someone was always in charge, overseeing a group that had to cook for 300 every day. My father Julius worked here. The younger men were the fighters and the raiders for the *atrad*, but men and women and children of all ages had chores and responsibilities. Everyone took a hand in the survival of the group as a whole.

There was a strict day-and-night security routine. We kept constant guard by way of six outposts located in different directions within a mile or two from the camp. We had passwords that everyone coming and going had to know. The guards at the outposts would shout, "Halt!" and would shoot if the password wasn't given. It was essential to keep out police spies. I and the other men were assigned guard duty every two days or so—in four-to-six hour shifts, sometimes in the morning, sometimes afternoon, sometimes at night. When we relieved one another, we had to say the password.

ROCHELLE

In the woods, I don't know of any cases in which Jews betrayed each other. No Jew would walk back alone into a German-held town and inform on partisan locations. Not after all the butchering. There were no illusions left about making deals with the Germans. When Jack and Julius and I first arrived at the *atrad*, the introduction from our guide was enough to establish that we were Jews and could be trusted. The problems with spies came in the mixed-population partisan groups—with Poles and Russians and Jews together. In those cases, again, it was not a Jew doing the informing. But the rumors constantly circulated that the Germans had sent Jews into the woods to join up with Russian partisan groups and then inform on their location or even poison their food. There was also the rumor—one that Tanya and I had lived with during our time with the Russian partisans—that Jewish girls with venereal disease had been sent by the Germans to sleep with the Russians. That was the poison that spread amongst the Russian partisans, even when their leaders were trying to keep to a less anti-Semitic policy.

JACK

Another difference with the small groups—in them we fought and raided simply to survive. In the *atrad*, we not only went on missions for food, but we also, for example, placed mines under railroad lines that the Germans were using to transport their supplies to the Russian front. But the discipline of Zorin and his lower "officers"—for that is what they were, even if they did not all have formal commissions as did Zorin—was severe. They killed their own people who refused to obey. In exchange for greater security, we had placed our lives in the hands of Zorin and his officers.

ROCHELLE

Zorin was himself a loyal Communist, yet he managed to maintain the independence of that Jewish *atrad*, even though the Russian partisan groups would have preferred that Zorin be directly under their command. That was the official Soviet policy as issued by Comrade Stalin himself. Special officers were sent by the Soviets to join up with the Russian partisan groups in the Nalibocka Forest and to impose a disciplined unity on *all* partisan efforts. And there was Zorin with a group that was not at all organized on strict military lines. None of the Russian partisan groups allowed old people and children. Few of them allowed wives. A minority percentage of Zorin's *atrad* consisted of precisely these people. But Zorin was dedicated to saving lives. Because he was a charismatic man and a sincere Communist, he kept the Russians from controlling him. He deployed the fighting forces of the *atrad* in numerous joint missions with the Russians. But at the same time, he prevented the *atrad* from falling directly under Russian command—which would have meant constant and severe losses, as the Russians would have preferred to risk Jewish lives rather than their own. The *atrad* would have been decimated. So Zorin was no mean politician.

Zorin himself plainly enjoyed the power and privileges of being commander in chief of the *atrad*. He rode a beautiful palomino horse that had been taken during one of the raids. And, of course, though Zorin was in his late forties, he had taken a young girl as his "wife." She was from Minsk, maybe twenty years old at most.

You would be amazed how, even in that group of ragged Jews living in hiding, social classes and distinctions took on such life and power. There were the commanders, the fighters, the craftspeople, the washers, and the cleaners. But Zorin's woman was the queen. If fine clothes were brought back from a raid, they went to her. So even within our camp she was dressed in the height of fashion. She had her own horse that she rode alongside of Zorin and his palomino. They were the royal couple. They would ride by and we would wave and smile. We knew that our lives depended upon them. Zorin was a good commander and he took care to save the lives of as many Jews as he could. But *his* way was the way things went, and his woman had great power as well. If they wanted to get rid of you, they could send you on missions from which you would never come back.

The top echelon of officers in the camp was comprised exclusively of

Zorin's fellow Russian Jews. His chief of staff was named Pressman. This Pressman had also taken a "wife" and he had a secure position of power because Zorin liked him. But Pressman wasn't too smart and he really didn't have the experience to make the decisions he was called upon to handle.

That was the reason Pressman came to rely heavily on the judgment of one of his assistants, a Jew from western Poland named Wertheim. Wertheim was in his mid-thirties. He and some of his family had escaped to Stolpce when the Germans first invaded in 1939. During the two years of Russian rule, his brother Manik had been dating a girlfriend of mine. Because of that, I was already very friendly with him. Wertheim took to Jack as well once he met him in the *atrad*.

I would say that Jack is alive today because of Wertheim. There were times when I would learn that the top officers were planning to send Jack out on a highly dangerous mission. I would go to Wertheim and beg him . . . tell him that Jack was sick. Some of the times he *was* sick, and sometimes he wasn't. Wertheim knew that I was often faking. But he would agree to keep Jack back in camp.

JACK

All this is true. But it is also true that I did go out on a number of armed missions and food raids. Rochelle could not keep me out of everything, and I would not have let her try. I wanted to live and be with her. But I also wanted to serve the *atrad* and to fight.

The main military focus was on selecting areas where we could get the food and clothing that would allow the *atrad* to survive. Sometimes we would plan raids specially to obtain medical supplies. The usual raiding group numbered twenty to twenty-five people. The groups had been smaller—four or five people—early on. But there was a terrible incident in which one of the groups had been murdered on the way back from a raid by Russian partisans, who then stole the sleighs filled with supplies. They let the Jewish boys do the work and then took their lives.

By the time I arrived, procedures had been worked out for encounters with Russian partisans. On first sighting them, we would immediately fan out into smaller groups, protecting whatever food or supplies we had taken, and we would show, by readying our weapons, that we were ready to fight back. That ended the problems. It wasn't worth it to the Russians to get into a fight with us on that scale.

ROCHELLE

There was another factor at work as well. Don't forget that we are talking about the summer of 1943. The Germans weren't doing so well on any of their fronts. We had at last a flicker of hope that they might be defeated and that the Russians might be coming back. For the Russian soldiers in partisan groups, it meant that they had to start thinking about what might happen to them if the returning Russian authorities learned that they had been killing off Jewish partisan fighters. As soldiers of the Soviet Union, they would have been subject to severe punishment. They knew that, and so they disciplined themselves and behaved better—more like military comrades and less like Jew-haters.

JACK

And they had good reason to behave like military comrades, because we were making a contribution by repeatedly blowing up the rail lines and the main highways with our mines and dynamite. That was weakening the German advance into the home country of the Russian partisans. The mines were not only blowing up trains and trucks with supplies—they also cost the Germans hundreds of casualties when their troop carriers were the target. Our good friend Simon Kagan, who had escaped from the Mir ghetto at the same time I did, had joined up with a Russian partisan unit. Simon was especially good at planting dynamite in the track beds and detonating—from his hiding place a short distance away—at just the right moment. He demolished plenty of trains. It took great skill and nerve.

Zorin and his commanders realized, just as the Russian partisans did, that the war was showing signs of turning against the Nazis at that point. They wanted it clearly understood that they had been helping the Russian effort against the Germans. It would not have been enough for them to say only that they had been saving Jewish lives.

ROCHELLE

During that first summer in the *atrad*, Jack developed a terrible infection that covered nearly his entire body. As best we could tell, it was partly due to the filth in which we all lived, and partly from malnutrition—nearly two consecutive years of eating very badly by that point.

There were boils from his feet to his neck and face, and especially on his legs and in his pubic area. They looked like big bumps, red and raw, and if you so much as touched them, yellow pus as thick as honey would run out of them. His body was a bundle of bones and pus.

JACK

I checked with our doctor in the *atrad* but she told me there was nothing she could do. She had no medications for a case like that. She thought it might disappear on its own. But I didn't see how it could disappear—it was all over me! The doctor also happened to mention that, if the infection should spread to my bloodstream, that would be the end of me.

ROCHELLE

Things were so bad that Jack could no longer physically bear to wear shoes. Instead he wrapped his feet in rags. The rags stuck to his boils, and so when he would take them off, the scabs would tear off and the pain and infection would become even worse. It was terrible with those rags, but the problem existed with any clothes Jack would try to wear. They stuck to him like glue. I thought that maybe exposing his body to the air might help to dry up the boils. But when we tried keeping him naked, all kinds of worms and bugs would start to feed on him.

It went on for three months and more. Jack was so sick—and so depressed. He was sick of himself! He told me at one point to go away, to stop bothering with him and trying to heal him. He said that he knew he was just making my life miserable, making the lives of others in the *atrad* miserable. He felt he couldn't take it anymore . . . he wanted to kill himself. So I took on the task of watching over him and not only trying to reduce the infection but also making sure that he did not end his own life.

There were others in the camp who were sick during that time, but none that were in such prolonged bad shape as Jack. I went to the chief of staff—not Wertheim but Pressman himself—and asked if Jack could be given better food. By that time Jack couldn't even walk. I kept him in the underground portion of one of the shelters, covered only with a thin blanket to reduce the sticking. I would give him part of my own meat and vegetable portions to try to build up his strength. But his depression grew worse and worse. I think that was the lowest Jack ever felt.

Nearly everyone felt sorry for him. But then there were others who were mean and vicious—including even so-called friends of Jack's. They would say to me, "Why are you futzing around with this guy? You're not married. He's not your responsibility. Why not just leave him?"

What a question. Not that it would have been difficult to accomplish. All I would have had to do was to take my one extra pair of pants and move two bodies further away in the shelter.

But I would *never* have left him. By that time I loved him so deeply. I was just praying every night that he would survive!

JACK

I was thinking about suicide a lot of the time. My preference was to go out on a dangerous mission and get killed in action while killing some Germans in the process. But I couldn't even move around the camp very well, so a long march was out of the question. I would have to do it myself. There were two or three occasions when I felt 99 percent ready.

What stopped me from killing myself wasn't Rochelle—I thought she would have been better off without me. But I was worried about my father Julius—I couldn't expect Rochelle to stick with him after I was gone, and he might have suffered terribly without her to care for him. Even so, the thought of suicide did not leave my mind.

As for Rochelle, she was such a good and kind soul! She not only cared for me during that time, but another man in the *atrad* as well. He and his wife—their last name was Farfel, I remember. Well, he had a bad case of boils himself. Not as bad as mine, but terrible enough. And the boils needed to be squeezed out—they had black things in their centers—and cleaned. There was no fancy way to do this—no gloves, no antiseptic equipment. Someone had to do it by hand, with rags. That was how Rochelle worked with me as well.

ROCHELLE

Farfel's wife—she was a common-law wife, you would say, like I was to Jack—she couldn't bring herself to clean him. He was in great pain, so I went to him and helped him. I remember he was lying on his stomach . . . kind of an ugly guy. And I was squeezing, so that he could begin to heal. The man's father was alive and a member of the *atrad* as well. He worked in the kitchen like Julius did. He would watch what I was doing. Once he said to me, "Why couldn't my son have a wife like this?"

I thanked him for saying this. But I was not trying to make the other woman look bad. It was easier for me to help him than to watch him lie there in pain.

JACK

At last, we discovered the method to cure me. It was a case of trial and error. We tried every substance available to us in the woods. Finally, it proved to be very simple. Tar.

ROCHELLE

We would peel the bark from birch trees and then char it and cook it. That produced a thick black sap that we could apply to the open boils. I can't explain why, but the sap seemed to kill off the infection.

JACK

The birch tar was so thick that, after the infections started to clear up, it was a real problem to wash the tar off. And even after the tar came off, I had red circular spots on my legs for years. I still have some on my left leg . . . like old war wounds that have never really healed.

Looking back, I can see that this awful experience was, at the same time, a good test of our relationship. Another girl in Rochelle's place would have gone away. But she stuck with me and that proved that our love was very strong. I vowed to myself that if we survived I would protect and take care of her for all of our lives.

JACK & ROCHELLE SUTIN *have been married for over fifty years and have two children. They have lived in Minnesota since 1949.*

LAWRENCE SUTIN *is the author of the critically acclaimed* Divine Invasions: A Life of Philip K. Dick. *He lives in Minneapolis, and currently teaches at Hamline University. He worked with his parents on editing their wartime memoir* Jack and Rochelle: A Holocaust Story of Love and Resistance.

MORITZ THOMSEN

The Saddest Pleasure

A Journey on Two Rivers

Enroute to Bahia (excerpt)

An hour out of Rio and the houses start moving back from along the edges of the highway to hide themselves in scattered groups in small tropical gardens of bamboo, bananas, bougainvillea, mangos. The countryside, exploding, opens up in its immensity. Behind us a hundred motels, walled off and ominous, a hundred little barrios of mean huts built around factories, a thousand vacant lots, new factory sites, empty of everything but high grass and expensively fenced off with brick, barbed wire, or Cyclone fencing. It is strange to move through a land with so few people in it. Another hour and even the houses disappear or have begun to collect themselves into little towns in the middle distance, or on the edges of some large hacienda form into unlikely rows of identical shacks, squeezed together wall to wall as though the land were too valuable to waste on living space for human beings. Looking at these rows one thinks: Jesus, a healthy fart at midnight in cabin A will wake the whole town to hysterical laughter, A through Q, the simple pleasures of the poor. Forty or fifty houses without breathing space on the steep slope of a hill and around them miles of pasture or, further north, enormous and undulating miles of oranges or, still farther north, miles of sugar cane. The houses are adobe or wattle and where the thin mudlike skin has fallen away from the walls in patches, the inner wall of sticks against which the mud has been plastered can be seen. The houses are small. Imagining families of six or seven enduring the confusions of those two small rooms is distressing. That enormous twenty-room house of my father's was scarcely big enough to contain our rages even though our rooms were so far away one from the other that I could hardly hear the words when my father and his wife screamed out their ritual hatreds. These huts are all painted in bright colors, the roofs are tile or tin, the windows small and usually closed, houses under siege. What prowls the Brazilian countryside after the sun goes down that has turned the houses into fortresses? Don't the people know that the devils that will destroy them are locked inside with them, that they are sleeping in the next hammock?

For over a hundred miles the land is incredibly dramatic and unlike any other place on Earth that I have ever seen. The highway climbing and moving away from the coast enters narrowing valleys whose sides are formed by the same upthrusting black granite domes of Rio, their dark walls streaked with darker lines where small springs drip and stain. The domes are a thousand feet high, or higher, and on their tops or on the sides that more gently form these swellingly beautiful forms, heavy tropical forests grow. If I were only younger what challenges these soaring walls would offer; now I get scared just looking. It seems likely that some of these peaks have never been climbed and that their summits, heavy with great trees, are as empty of life as the day they came pushing up out of the earth's depths. Only birds, only the great birds can have explored these impregnable peaks—or those wild kids from the Sierra Club.

For a few hours I try to make sense of the landscape. I try to interpret the kind of life that country people might live here by studying their identical shacks or the grander but unimaginative houses of the *hacendados*, try to figure out who owns the rolling hills or the wide river bottoms by estimating the size of the farms, try to figure out by the dryness or greenness of the pastures what limitations the climate has laid over the land. Why are the shacks so small when the land is so rich? I am not smart enough to make sense of what I see; there is something else invisible laid over the land, and only hints of some sad truth can be seen in the general austere quality of the poverty and in the apparent hugeness of the individual land holdings.

The highway is superb and managed in an inhumanly precise way. Narrow steep dirt roads rutted by horse-drawn wagons connect the workers' huts to this elegant cement band. But the connection is merely symbolic and gratuitous. The highway is an intrusion of privacy as it curves and sweeps through another more tranquil, more feudal century. There is something shameful about its incongruity. Every hundred miles or so lounging police at checkpoints as spreading as the international border buildings between the United States and Canada stop and scrutinize the highway traffic (and collect a toll). Every two hours the bus arrives at other enormous installations where the passengers are allowed twenty minutes to pee and to drink coffee or eat something. Each of these places is built to one plan—a large shop full of incredibly boring tourist crap, a fancy restaurant with tablecloths and heavy-looking Spanish chairs (where no one ever ate); a fresh-juice store hung all around with sacks of oranges, papayas, avocados; and long counters manned by swift-moving youngsters. After stopping a few times to eat identical sandwiches from identical buildings, the trip begins to seem unreal. I don't know if I am hallucinating or if my cold has taken a turn for the worse.

Late in the afternoon we move away from the coast, or more precisely, since the coast has been invisible, away from the feeling of following a coastline. And to be even more precise or at least to indicate the limitations on my ability to be precise, I am not sure now that it was late or early in the afternoon. By this time I am running a fever and the view outside the bus window is turning into long stretches of blankness with here and there stopped-action scenes of meaningless but razor-sharp detail. To the west the wide river bottoms and the empty horizons of tide flats disappear and we skirt the edges of a hostile land as dry and forbidding as the most worthless parts of Texas or Mexico. Low blue mountains stand in the distance dimly seen through dusty air; arroyos cut across dry plains where nothing grows but cactus, spikey shrubs, and small frail trees with tiny dull green leaves. Very thinly scattered across this waste, low mean huts of wattle, some without walls, lean-tos of dry mud and straw, corrals of piled brush, a few goats, and a very few listless cattle, their lowered heads staring at the ground. Cow hides hang from sagging fences as raw and orange as flayed flesh, and whirlwinds, dust-devils of dirt, sticks and leaves move in the distance through the still air, whipping the earth.

We are crawling across the very edges of that awful land called the northeast, the *sertão* where years-long droughts have once again created a desert. Last year there were millions of people out there; they hung on and hung on until they were driven out by the realization that what they were contemplating in those dry clouds that passed over them month after month was the immediacy of their own deaths. The *sertão*, the very center of the world's poverty. The still seriously unpondered problems that it poses for Brazil and anyone else who thinks about such things are like great spreading, festering cancers. The land empties and fills with people as the rains either fall or fail to fall, but at its best it is a country of shamefully modest expectations. Is it love or desperation that drives the people back to the ruined farms after the first rains have started up the grass and the dead sticks of trees burst into life? Probably both. Man's deepest passions are centered on land and the water that brings it to life. And what suffering won't a man endure to live in his own hut on his own land, proud and half-mad with the delusion that to some extent he is in control of his own destiny.

Now the land is being emptied again; the cattle, covered with ticks and lice, are dying; the old people have died, the water holes are drying up; the springs no longer flow; the frogs no longer sing in the dry ponds behind the huts. The pretty young girls have wandered off to the cities to become whores; by the time they are fifteen they will be used up, their faces gray and lined. The men in orange jumpsuits sweep the parks or cut weeds along the highway with their machetes. There are supposed to be sixteen million homeless children in the country; most of them live in the big cities; you have seen pictures of them sleeping in doorways or curled up in little bunches like litters of wolf cubs, wrapped in old newspapers on the beach at Copacabana. In the poorer barrios they travel in packs like dogs, begging, stealing, whoring to stay alive. Some of them say they are going to be doctors when they grow up. Some of them are looking for a little length of rope that they can steal to hang themselves with. The northeast is a factory that mass produces these subhuman fucked-over creatures being driven to new lives of crime and squalor. Starved for protein, crippled by malnutrition, they have lost about twenty percent of their intelligence.

As the hours pass I become desperate and angry. In visualizing Bahia I had forgotten what had to be passed through to get there. I feel like a cheated tourist; like a traveler being taken to the temples of Nara, by way of Hiroshima, to Dresden with a tour of Auschwitz thrown in. For all the monotony of the land, it produces a choking intensity of emotion that cannot be discharged. It is only a little less distressing than driving past a rocky hill of no great splendor and learning that it is named Golgotha and that three crosses once stood upon its summit.

The *sertão*, while it has produced more morons than artists, boasts some of the great Brazilian writers. The rudeness of the life and the cruelty of the land, like the Israeli deserts, has been a breeding ground for men of intense, poetic, and fanatic emotions. A boyhood spent under that glare of sky, washed in the spaces of infinite distances, whipped to the bone by ruthless nature and by men made desperate and corrupt by hopelessness, and you can hardly ever write about anything else. Forty years later in Paris and the eyes still burn, and at night you groan. The desert has blasted open your soul. And if you have never learned to write, driven by luminous and inchoate feelings you turn into a religious prophet as cracked as some Spanish bishop in the Inquisition, or a Communist leader of people who smashes blindly at the corruptions of the ruling powers, or a bandit leader like Lampião whose head until very recently was exhibited in a medical museum in Salvador.

Lampião? That bad-ass Robin Hood of the northeast? Let me quote a few sentences from João Ubaldo's *Sergeant Getulio* about Lampião; it will give you a feel for the *ambiente*. "Often he would lose his temper over some little thing. He used to put a man's nuts in a drawer, lock it, throw the key out, and set fire to the house. Not without first leaving a knife within reach of the wretch. The way I see it, it's better to burn to death than to lose your nuts. Your voice gets thinner and thinner and so does your beard, you become pederastic, false to your body. But most people prefer to cut their balls off rather than turn into charcoal. Nowadays that kind of thing isn't done anymore. Would you put up with a thing like that? There was another time, when Lampião tied up a judge's wife, maybe it was in Divina Pastora or Rosario do Catete or Capela, he tied this wife of this judge to a tree and stripped her stark naked. Now whoever saw an old woman like that with so much hair on her parts? Have you ever seen such indecency? Not even the worst whores, how about that? And he peered over his glasses this way and that, and ended up pulling all the hairs off the woman's twat in front of everybody, everyone gathered there on Lampião's orders, because everything he did was always in front of everybody. There was great badness in him, he killed without ideas. So naturally he ended up with his head cut off in Bahia and put on exhibition like it was a wild bull's horns."

I have not read much of the Brazilian literature that has come out of the northeast. Very little of it has been translated into English, scarcely more than Graciliano Ramos, who grew upon a disintegrating cattle ranch with a family driven half-mad by defeat; Jose Americo de Almeida, who describes the endless lines of people staggering down the dusty roads away from a dead land to the slavery of the coastal *hacendados* with their empires of sugar cane; Jorge Amado, who writes about what happens to the girls who, having escaped the desert, end up in the coastal bordellos of Ilhéus or Salvador.

And João Ubaldo, the youngest and greatest of the regional writers and perhaps the strongest writer in Brazil today. His second novel, *Sergeant Getulio*, has been published in English. It is incredibly subtle, unbearably brutal, and while it has not made me want to see this land he writes about, it has made me want to see Ubaldo. I have made arrangements with his editor in Boston, and Ubaldo has sent back word that he will see me in Bahia. Meeting him will be the high point of my trip to Brazil.

The afternoon wears on, it is really quite endless. The mountains fade away in the distance behind us. Over on the left above the bushes something has died or is dying and where a moment before there was one black pair of circling wings, suddenly there are dozens of *gallinazos* settling lower, moving around and around like something dirty being slowly stirred in the sky. They look like the same vultures who always gathered on the farm when I was disking. They hopped behind the tractor with their ragged half-opened wings, snuffling in the sod for dead snakes. They are nature's garbage collecting squads, but I dislike them; they make me think of the many unpleasant ways that one may die. And speaking of *that*, it has been a long time since I have felt so clearly that some final struggle is about to take place in my lungs. As the day has passed I have felt a growing fever and that dry, naked tenderness in my nose and throat that means that all my defenses have been routed and that my poor membranes scraped clean are now being overwhelmed by bugs. Again. In the middle of one cold I am now coming down with another. Tomorrow, if I last that long, is going to be a bitch. Defiantly, as though I were committing suicide, I sit by the window staring out at the desert and smoking cigarettes. They are tasteless, hateful, painful, burning, my head aches and my throat is raw, but I sit there smoking two or three an hour, smoking them down to their nasty little filtered butts as though they are the only thing that can dull the tedium of this encircling desolation. My thoughts begin to tend toward incoherency.

From time to time we pass through little collections of buildings disguised as towns: a gas station, next to it an awful square closed-in building as dark as a grave that advertises food—roast or skewered chunks of beef, an adobe lean-to with a sign "Borracharia" that in Spanish has something to do with drunkenness but in Portuguese has something to do with flat tires. What is being suggested: that we get drunk while our tires are being repaired? A sign: "Tears of the Blessed Mary. Population, 32." The people in these places standing in shadow are dimly seen, diminished in the landscape to spots of dull color; they are swallowed up and transformed by the *sertão* into undifferentiated figures upon whose almost identical faces the land has stained a kind of vacant mediocrity. They frighten me. It is not the land but the people who frighten me. I look at the few passing faces with suspicion, lowering my eyes, menaced, thankful for the thick blue-tinted windows that separate us; for once I an unashamed to be a tourist, isolated in my privileged place, just passing through.

I have absorbed that little bit of Brazilian literature that defines these people and that has defined them as cruel, desperate, and casually murderous. The villains of the books I have read embrace all classes of the population: cops, priests, politicians, cowboys, storekeepers, the parents of small children with their knotted ropes, and grandparents with whips of leather, even the bored adolescents. It is the land itself, of course, that is the villain and that has brutalized the people. I see them as a threat to my sense of myself as a man. That guy over there with the curling mop of hair and the thick black moustache—he looks like someone who, for a snap of the fingers, would nail my nuts in a drawer for the sheer joy of lifting for a few minutes the heavy boredom that deadens his face. I don't want my nuts nailed in a drawer and the house on fire and the knife in my hand. Decisions like this I can do without; fuck these macho exercises. I don't even want to walk down one of these dusty streets to confront and test myself against the lazy insolence of the men's stares. I am no Norman Mailer who staggers around on the ledges of high buildings testing the authenticity of his vibes. These Brazilian tests are too macho, the failure to pass, too permanent. Let Mr. Mailer get his nuts nailed in a drawer, not this kid. Would his next book after that experience take on a kind of high-pitched whining? The way I see it is this: in 1943 I flew twenty-seven combat missions over goddam Europe in a B-17; I am a goddam hero and have the papers to prove it; I believe they are signed by Franklin D. Roosevelt. No more tests. I can be a self-respecting coward for the rest of my life. Drive on, driver; let's get the hell out of here.

MORITZ THOMSEN *was born in the Pacific Northwest in 1915, and at the age of 48, he enlisted in the Peace Corps and worked in Ecuador. He is the author of the memoir* The Saddest Pleasure, *which chronicles his Peace Corps years and his journey across Brazil. His other books are* Living Poor: A Peace Corps Chronicle; The Farm on the River of Emeralds; *and* My Two Wars. *Thomsen died in 1993.*

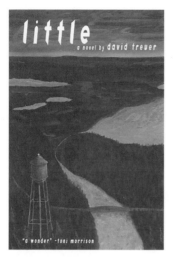

DAVID TREUER

Little

Wisconsin

NOVEMBER 1968

The winter of 1968 was the last winter it snowed deeper than three feet and the branches of birch, aspen, and jack pine snapped under the weight. The ditches leveled off at the top with blowing snow, connecting with the fields that stretched from central Minnesota all the way to the Rocky Mountains. The Rockies stared across the barren plains to Minnesota and judged the nakedness that lay out for all to see.

During the summer months the leaves and grass could hide what shouldn't be seen. When the heat came in those months the surface growth, whether pine or brush, grass or weeds, could cover the deficiencies of right, the diminishing borders, even the history. This could not be done when it snowed and the living growth had retreated or died. But just the same, in November the weather delivered so much that was unexpected, when everyone had assumed that they had seen it all before. The flakes and jumble of snow that fell so hard and so thick was out of place in November. The weather had been too cold for the snow and for the winds that came from the south, blowing off Lake Michigan and across Wisconsin. When it warmed to zero and the red alcohol thermometers began to work again, the winds swept over the lakes and rivers, blending them with the fields. The November winds blew the snow from the ground, shook it from its frozen place on the bare branches of trees, and broke it from the crested drifts along the sides of barns and ditches. It was swept from the fields that used to yield wheat second only to the Nile valley, but that had long before given up their last bit of topsoil to spring oats and winter wheat. The fields that used to yield corn, beets, soybean, and sunflower to farmers who came from Germany, Sweden, and Norway were choked with quack grass. The descendants of the Germans, Swedes, and Norwegians now worked as auto mechanics, store owners, policemen, telephone repairmen, truckers, pipeline supervisors, carpenters, plumbers, roofers, welders, sheet-metal workers, and as agents of history. As the snow lifted and swirled through the air they remembered for their fathers and mothers, and remembered to their children who sat at kitchen tables in Levis, their blond hair under greasy baseball caps. The gusts reached in and shook the window panes from where they sat in their sashes, as the sons and daughters of immigrants remembered the day the Iron Range had produced more iron ore and taconite than any other mining district in the United States. They remembered before iron was discovered, when the great pine logs were loaded on trains and shipped north to Winnipeg and south to Minneapolis. They remembered before the railroads, when the logs were hauled by steamship up the Red River and down the Mississippi, and before that when they were sledged out in the winter on sleds pulled by horses, and in the summer on carts pulled by oxen.

They put more wood in their stoves, and staggered a bit as their arthritis kicked in, or the continual pinch of a sciatic nerve jerked along the run of a back. Lowering themselves into squeaky aluminum chairs they remembered before the logging, when their ancestors first arrived by boat and quarreled with the French for the land of Minnesota. They remembered the French trappers who, escaping from a life of crime, played out their fantasies trading with the Indians.

Then they remembered their great-great-grandparents who left the famines of Europe. They remembered that their ancestors brought with them only a few plates that had been decorated with painted rose petals and laurels during the long Scandinavian winters in which the sun would never set, in which it would hover at the edge of the horizon taunting them with its simultaneous presence and distance. They remembered those plates standing next to the ones painted by their great-grandparents during the long, dark, and bone-cracking cold Minnesota winters. They even remembered why there were no others. Why, where there should have been similarly decorated plates painted by their parents, even themselves, there were only empty spaces. There were only empty spaces, gaping holes where there should have been some porcelain history because they and their parents had been too busy with the farm—with the construction of the silo, with fixing the far wall of the barn that had begun to lean—to spend time weaving paint onto something that was used to eat off. And now, now they did not know how to create the arc of vine and leaf along porcelain rims.

They remembered it all to their children in dirty jeans, clean blond hair, and greasy baseball caps who still lived at home. Their children lived at home and kept odd hours because they worked in town as grocery baggers, pizza-delivery boys, gas-pump attendants, and night janitors. They remembered to their daughters whose skin was clean and whose hair was done with large waves of bangs, supported by patience and hair spray. They worked as hairstylists, waitresses, and girlfriends who were too alone to say no to their overanxious boyfriends, and too Lutheran to say yes above a whisper in the back seat of a car.

They remembered their past and constructed the present with mortgages and loans to pay the property taxes on their fathers' land in whose fields and pastures stood rusted skeletons of farm machinery too broken down with age to be sold at the county auction. They told these stories in earnest at kitchen tables over potbellies and Pabst Blue Ribbon, sometimes coffee, to their children who had long ago quit listening.

They remembered to children who took loans they could never pay back on pickup trucks. These were children who grew up under the floodlights that attracted moths, june bugs, and fish-flies at the Dairy Queen just off the main streets of small towns with names like Dent, Durkel, Deadwood, Badger, Armistice, and Hope. And who in the winter went to the Thursday night hockey games played by their teams who were always hopelessly outmatched by their rivals from the rich suburbs of Minneapolis: Edina, Minnetonka, and St. Louis Park.

But there were places where their memory could not go. When this happened they smoothed over the gaps and jumps of what life was like before they got there. They couldn't remember what the land looked like before it was logged the very first time. They couldn't let themselves guess. These memories had no place next to the kitchen tables and they couldn't be spoken over bowls of peeled potatoes still steaming into the damp kitchen light. Conversations about before their arrival, about who had lived there before were never given audience when fathers and sons squinted together under the belly of the tractor tightening the crank shaft or securing a cowling with bailing wire so the dirt that was knifed up wouldn't cake in the gears.

When they padded the bottom of the pickup truck with hay and then placed the crated eggs on top so they wouldn't break down the rutted roads, the talk and remembering was always about last year's hay, or this batch of eggs. During the slow ride to town the talk shifted between the here and now and the not so here and now; about the hen that strutted the yard in front of the barn protecting what she thought were her eggs but were only a few pebbles or rocks that had been loosened from the packed dirt by boots or the hooves of the cows. It didn't go much further than before the crossing-over, because their memory wasn't made for that, couldn't contain who had lived and walked before, and who was beginning to emerge again, to speak again.

So they stitched and sewed, smoothing over the spaces that to them appeared as silences, though that was a sentiment far from the truth. What they could remember was how the boats pitched and sloughed through the waves and how it was dark down in the third-class compartments that were wet and smelled of urine and mildew. If it had been a freight then the memories were of whatever the boat had held before them. Sometimes it was coal, and the passengers scrubbed for weeks to get rid of the smudges that had worked under their skin from chaffing against the metal walls. Some of the dirt never went away. Other times the cargo had been potatoes or beets and the conversation was less rueful about the washing because the great-great-grandparents were never able to enjoy those foods again. The smell never washed out and there had been too many rats. The cattle freight spoke of rotting hay and the sloshing of urine and shit, because the crew knew that they would still have boarders even if it was rotten and dark.

These conversations could be accommodated because when the mother peeled potatoes, they were reminded because the potatoes were right there, safely being disassembled in the family's own kitchen. They were reminded of these modern stories when the father hosed out the cattle trailer because it was new and because there was a loan that would always be newer than the trailer. The father would remember only as far back as the crossing because if he remembered further back he would be forced to go back even before the tractor and its use. His son was there, hosing, wishing he wasn't. The father's conversation found no purchase with his son, and as soon as the last of the manure left the trailer the boy went to shoot mourning doves with his BB gun or to go with his friends to the bridge where they dared each other to jump off into the river.

There were memories longer and deeper than these that touched the land, especially when the snow got deep or the drought brought not only heat but also wind. The topsoil was lifted off and it looked so easy, it left so readily while the farmer just watched it go into the wind. When he looked windward he saw that the horizon was hazy and the sun was blood red because of all the dirt in the sky that had been stolen by the winds from everyone's fields. When this happened the farmer thought back and counted how many times this had happened to him, or his uncle, or his father. He kept searching for a time when the soil stayed neat and the rows were crusty and straight, glistening with just the right mixture of loam, sand, and clay so that there was neither too much water nor too little and it stayed topside neither too briefly nor too long. The farmer would have to think back behind the farms to the logging days, but then the barges broke or the band on the saw melted from the heat. While out logging in the bush there had been the times when the wind blew from the wrong side just when the last wedge had been cut from the trunk. As the tree fell the other men couldn't hear the sound of its fall, so the warnings didn't help, the frantic waves and yells that were shouted from a distance did little good. They fell on the unlucky ones, splitting bone and lopping off arms. The blood spilled onto the floor of pine needles thicker than any of their memories and seeped through.

On a Thursday night of rememberings, forgettings, and hand jobs under blankets on the plastic seats at local hockey games, a car was driving north and west from Wisconsin. The car had no story to tell of sex that had been gotten after conquering the high school's cutest cheerleader. It spoke of no nights out shining deer during the summer. It had never had children begging to ride on the hood, their sticky hands plastered with the remnants of Push-Ups or Mr. Freezees. It had never had teenagers spilling beer on the seats, worrying if their parents would smell it. It had never drag raced other cars down the many straight side streets in Sheboygan.

The brown Impala had been first purchased by an old woman named Myrtle Jacobsen who never used it to go to faraway places. She used it to drive from home to the grocery store and back, or to the hospital for her weekly checkups. She thought she was dying of cancer and she longed to go through the living agony of chemotherapy, but the doctors told her again and again that she didn't have cancer and that she was in good health.

The woman named Myrtle who first owned the brown car lived like that for eight years until one day she dropped dead while feeding her cat. The car was sold by her son who flew all the way from Oakland to tie up the loose ends of her meager estate. It was an estate that consisted of a small house in Sheboygan filled with pictures, a doll collection of no value, and a brown Chevy Impala. He really had to get back to Oakland so he sold the house to a Century 21 realtor and he sold the car to the first used-car dealer he saw on his drive back to the airport.

The used-car dealer, Bill Henderson, paid more than he should have for the car partly because the son from Oakland was greedy and partly because Mr. Henderson was thinking of the necklace this deal would buy for the nineteen-year-old with whom he was having an affair.

The nondescript car sat in Bill's lot for a year, until an Indian man and his shaggy-headed boy came looking for a car. Normally Bill Henderson would have waved them away, or showed them the most expensive car so they were cowed and wouldn't waste his time, or he would have feigned activity of great import. However, his mind was on other things, on secrets of his own, so he did not see the Indian until it was too late to assemble his defense, and then he saw that the Indian in fact had money in his pocket. The Indian had enough money because he sold Rubbermaid household products door-to-door. It was a job that usually didn't pay so well, but the Indian had the knack for finding women who really wanted nothing more than a spotlessly clean floor. They wanted a clean floor and brooms with straight straws because their husbands were having affairs and there was nothing they could do about it. They couldn't leave their husbands because they couldn't market their skills as housewives. Their once-proud breasts and firm thighs—Scandinavian through and through—sagged, and their blue eyes were clouded from advancing age. They wanted to spite their husbands with toilet bowls that sparkled a dewy white, like ivory. They wanted to caress the linoleum with firm sponge mops and smooth the counters with unfrayed dish towels, as they imagined their husbands caressing and touching younger women with firm breasts that their husbands oohed over and likened to chamois or silk, neither of which they had ever seen. The wives who hated their own wrinkles and stretch marks somehow loved their husbands. Their love was coupled with spite, so they wanted to scour frying pans thick with crusted grease, just as their husbands devoured the inner thighs of other women so white and smooth that they spent their money just to get to the tight, wet, forgiving sex, flesh that they had purchased with their treats of movies, rings, and flowers.

It was because of this that the Indian and his small boy had enough money to buy the brown Impala. They didn't have to pay as much as they might have, considering the age of the car and the race of the used-car dealer. But Bill Henderson's mind wasn't on the price of the car. He had found out that his wife was having an affair too, with the father of the nineteen-year-old girl he was fucking in the back seats of all the cars he owned. The brown Impala that had stood at the end of the lot was the sole exception. Surprisingly, given its obscure location under the branches of a leaning oak tree and its expansive back seat, they had never used its seats for anything. Bill used subcompacts and compacts, working his way across the lot, but he had never reached the Impala. Bill Henderson got a kick out of fucking in cars during the A.M. and test-driving them with prospective buyers during the P.M., but the Impala was a decidedly unappealing car. So the Indian with his three-year-old boy bought the car with very little interesting history, got in, inserted the key, turned the motor over, and pulled out and away.

Once out of the lot, they didn't go back to an apartment to gather belongings. They didn't stop at a Perkins or a Country Kitchen to have a nice waffle breakfast. They didn't drop by anyone's house to say good-bye over three or four cups of good coffee with lots of condensed milk and sugar. The Indian got behind the wheel and his little boy sat in the passenger seat and stared out the window as the low buildings and cement sidewalks ended and the fields began.

At first the car was cold, but the heater was good so the car became warm and the frost on the windows started to disappear. The little boy, impatient for his view, scraped off a patch of frost from his window and stuck his fingers and the ice shavings in his mouth. The fields rolled on and then stopped every few miles when the maple and oak forests closed in on the sides of the highway. These soon gave way to pine and rolling hills as the brown Impala passed Black River Falls and Tomah, where the old Indian boarding school had been. The man drove past it and he never knew of its history or even its existence, curtained as it was from the road by sloping ditches and windbreaks of large blue spruce.

The man and the boy stopped in Superior, Wisconsin, where they ate in a small diner. There were only a few people eating; it was after dinner hours and there was a single waitress serving. She carried a frown, her mind on how to avoid the glances of the short-order cook who had a missing tooth, half a growth of beard, and nice wrinkled eyes. Anyone else might have liked those eyes, but she couldn't appreciate them. They were too soft, perhaps they could see too much. She wanted a man with hard eyes. A man with steel blue eyes. Outside the temperature began to drop and snow started down in lazy circles, lightly covering the dirty gray sidewalks as the man sat with his boy and deliberated only a little. The man ordered for himself and his boy, while the child took no notice of what was going on around him. He never asked where they were going or even why. He preferred instead to play with the crayons left for him on the table. As the waitress took their order she was aware of her left hand, with its empty ring finger. She wondered as the man ordered the egg skillet and black coffee and as he ordered pancakes for his boy. She wondered why no one courted her. Why no one brought her home at four in the morning, begging her to let him come upstairs so she could smile demurely and swing her backside, just a little, as she ascended the stairs alone, in full confidence that they would make love in the future, and that it would be so good that she would cry. She wondered as the boy drew on his place mat why it was that no one got her flowers in the middle of the winter, the petals just a little brown from the frost. She would have liked that. Flowers in the winter. Flowers in the wintertime, even slightly browned ones would have spoken of devotion. Devotion from a steel blue-eyed man would have been priceless to her.

That was why after the Indians left she gave the short-order cook a smile that was only a little like defeat. It was like this that she went home with him and wondered at his softness and his hands that patched her and shored up her sides. No one would have thought that hands used to caressing frozen hamburger patties and hash browns could show her how low she hung and lift her up, just a little bit, enough to know that it was better than nothing. It made her cry, but just a little bit.

It was like this that the Indian and his boy crossed into Minnesota, leaving nothing behind. The apartment they had lived in was almost empty. There were no family heirlooms to put in storage, or to wrap in newspaper and pack into boxes, to carefully fit in a trunk. There was no furniture to sell at a rummage sale or to give to friends in a fit of charity. The apartment itself was situated above a Woolworth five-and-dime store. It used to be storage space for the Woolworth's but the heyday of five-and-dimes was long over and the owner needed the rent money just to float his store. The apartment wasn't decorated. The very idea of hanging pictures or putting up curtains seemed to defy what the apartment was about. It was about temporary things; a halfway place between jobs, wives, husbands, or the streets and jail. It was about peeling paint that no one wanted to fix and that some even liked that way. To the Indian it was about another home that wasn't really, and another job that was. So he left with his son, taking with him the only memory that he dared let pin him down. His son wasn't a link or an arrow that he'd fashioned. His son was a weight that would hold him under the water. His son would be the one who held his hand as the snow drifted into his mouth while he drowned. His son was the one who showed him exactly who he was, which served to remind him of what he was not.

In most men this would serve to instill a hatred of the boy. The violent aggressions that the boy's living generated would have been taken out on him. To this Indian, though, it was different. He didn't hate his son. This is not to say that he loved him either—the boy's mother had been a woman who worked in the Woolworth's below the apartment and they had fucked exactly five times before they both lost interest. Nine months later she dropped the baby boy off at the apartment and left without a word. The man could see her through the window as she got into a light blue pickup truck, a truck the color of leaving.

He couldn't hate the boy, just as he couldn't hate the apartment because it was just a temporary stage, between lives. The boy, too, was just a place devoid of pictures and curtains. He was merely a time between leavings and arrivals. The man had never met his own father, had never been told of the funny things his father had done when he was a young man. He had never been hit by his father or held on his lap. He couldn't hate his father either.

In this absence of feeling he drove west through the snow that now was driving down in gusts and blanketing the roads, the ditches, and the fields. He bent his head close to the windshield and tried to find the yellow lines in the middle of the road. The map said that the highway would go straight through the middle of the reservation. He had never been there, the reservation his father was from. His mother admitted she wasn't exactly sure who his father was, but she had narrowed it down to two men. They were identical twins, she had said. She had had sex with both of them the same night in the same car. What she didn't tell her son was that once she had passed out, the twins had stolen the car and she had never seen them again. She felt that it really didn't matter. She never exhibited any need or desire to go find them, those two opposites; one quiet, one full of stories and jokes. Regardless of their differences, she had said, they were both good in the sack. That had been the end of it for her. She also said that at the time they had been working in the steel mills in Sheboygan, Wisconsin, where she met them at a bar. As he drove, he kept hold of these absences of memory, held them at a distance, and pulled them close; it really didn't matter which, because he had nothing to know. But he wondered whether his father would have laughed and joked, whether he had enough confidence so that upon making a mistake he would simply laugh, or if he held his coffee cup in both hands or between a single finger and a thumb. Whether he whistled in the morning.

It was with rememberings like these that the Indian man and his boy drove west. The brown Impala split the snow and it swirled even thicker around the car and across the road. The boy was asleep on the seat, wrapped in an old quilt that the father had purchased at a rummage sale. No kind grandmother had sewn it for the boy out of love or loneliness. None of his aunts, sitting around smoking Benson & Hedges menthols, drinking coffee, had sewn it for his birthday. It was a discard thrown away at a rummage sale after all the children had grown and gone to college on the East Coast. It was a rag with all of the memories laundered out.

The car slowed to twenty miles an hour and crawled past the sign announcing the reservation boundary without even a pause or a sigh of recognition. The sign, like any state line, marked no change at all, marked changes that couldn't be seen with the eye. So the sign went unnoticed by the Indian and his boy just as they went unnoticed by the sign and the pines that grew close to the road. They didn't notice the snow getting deeper and deeper, trapping the car. The Impala carried a cache of nonmemories in a place where every tree, ditch, gully, river, lake, house, field, and person was remembered.

The car hit some ice the grader had missed and was swept smoothly into the ditch. It slid while the father wondered at the smoothness of the ride and his inability to steer. It hit a power box. The boy stayed on the seat but the man hit his head against the steering wheel. He slipped sideways and under the steering wheel and lay bunched down by the gas pedal and the brake, knocked out cold.

It went unnoticed like this: a brown Chevy Impala sat in the ditch with a sleeping boy and an unconscious father. The snow kept on getting deeper, piling around the car and the temperature dropped lower and lower. There was no sound but the sound of the wind prying at the windows and door handles, creeping under the hood and through the floor. Even that was muted by the glass and metal surrounding them. It was late and most people nursed cups of coffee or tea made with a generous amount of sugar in the comfort of their own homes. Most people sat in their kitchens and told stories about the last time it had snowed so much and so hard, which was close to twenty years ago this coming April.

The father managed to rouse himself. He crawled out from the nest on the floor and the first thing he noticed was that the window on the passenger's side had been smashed in, something he didn't remember from before.

The second thing he noticed was that the bundle of quilt and little boy that was his, was gone. The seat next to him was bare and the back seat, too, was empty. His eyes searched the ditch and along the road because he had heard of people being thrown from cars when they crashed. He found nothing but snow and ice. He looked for tracks leading away from the car, and they were there—muffled dents in the blowing snow.

He kicked around in the drifts, scraped with his booted foot under the front bumper and leaned on the grill, breathing in the wet snow.

The man knew that this was the end. It was the end of a long string of apartments where the little boy slept on the couch, or under the kitchen table. This was the end of more than four years of nonmemories and secondhand clothes.

This end was also the beginning of more than Donovan could ever have imagined. When the headlights of a westbound truck came into view, the man opened his door, pushed the snow out of the way, and staggered onto the highway. The truck slowed and the Indian man got in. The truck started up again and traveled west toward Grand Forks. In its turn it would travel through many small towns and larger cities whose names were too numerous and full of people alive and warm to be said out loud.

DAVID TREUER *is Ojibwe. He grew up at Leech Lake Reservation in northern Minnesota. His first novel is* Little *and he has another novel forthcoming.*

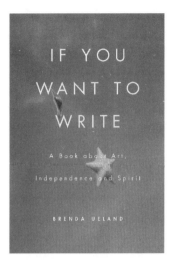

BRENDA UELAND

If You Want to Write

Know that There Is Often Hidden In Us a Dormant Poet, Always
Young and Alive   —DE MUSSET

I used to have to drive myself to work. You cannot imagine what an un-
comfortable, effortful thing it was to be supposed to be a writer. To work at
all I had to be a jump ahead of the spears—to need money very badly. After
three hours of work[1] I would be pithed and exhausted. I could not work in
the afternoon or evening at all, because I was absolutely certain I would not
be bright then. All fear and conceit.

It was my class who showed me that I was working in the wrong way.
For these humble and inexperienced amateurs suddenly—if only I could
lift fear off them—revealed all of them such wonderful gift.

I learned from them that inspiration does not come like a bolt, nor is it
kinetic, energetic striving, but it comes into us slowly and quietly and all
the time, though we must regularly and every day give it a little chance to
start flowing, prime it with a little solitude and idleness. I learned that you

---

1. Except when finishing a story or article. I could work all day then because it was
mostly just copying. But to work for an hour or two on the first draft, the first inven-
tion, that would nearly kill me. What flying from it! what boredom! what drinks of
water! telephoning and other evasion!

should feel when writing, not like Lord Byron on a mountain top, but like a child stringing beads in kindergarten,—happy, absorbed and quietly putting one bead on after another.

Once I posed for a lot of twelve-year-old girls who wanted to try some oil painting. I said that I would sit for them for three days and all day long, until their portraits of me were all entirely finished and the very best that they could do.

None of these children had painted with oil paints before. I sat in a chair against the sitting room wall with the light from several eastern windows on me, and this battery of four little girls and three adults faced me, peering at me athwart their canvases. I had nothing to do but to watch them for long hours.

Now a roomful of seven adults means always a good deal of noise and loud talking. With four children among them it is din, pandemonium. And children, as we all know, do not have (in school or church or at a lecture) much power of prolonged, silent, focused concentration, especially on something that takes intense mental struggle and effort. And everyone knows what a mysteriously difficult thing it is to draw something if you are not used to it: the weird difficulty of expressing the third dimension on flat paper! to draw a nose front view is just a frightful problem! Moreover, to paint with oil paints for the first time—I can only describe it by saying it is like trying to make something exquisitely accurate and microscopically clear out of mud pies with boxing gloves on.

Well, that is what these children were trying to do. Yet while they were painting me there was utter dead silence in the room. You could hear their breathing. Only those burning eyes were looking up at me and down again. Perhaps after twenty minutes or so there would be a groan or a yell of despair: "Oh, Brenda! I have made you look so HAG-GY!"

After long periods they would remember that I was merely human and let me rest for a few minutes, but only with reluctance because it was hard to be torn from their work. But the moment their brief rest time came, the deep religious, blissful silence, absorption and contemplation was supplanted by the uproar, shouting, interrupting, whacking and thumping that one normally gets from a roomful of children. Even the dogs who had been peacefully dozing began weaving in and out, barking and wrestling.

Now these children worked for five or six hours at a stretch (and this will be the way you are going to work at your writing) for two and a half days—working with the blissful, radiant power of a Michelangelo or Blake. Their paintings were all remarkable,[2]—all different, astonishing in their own way, because the creative impulse was working innocently, not egotistically or to please someone, an instructor, say, who threw in the anxious questions: is it art? has it balance? design? and so on. The creative power was working innocently, each child simply trying to show in paint what she saw and felt.

I tell you all this because it is the way you are to feel when you are writing—happy, truthful and free, with that wonderful contented absorption of a child stringing beads in kindergarten. With complete self-trust. Because you are a human being all you have to do is to get out truthfully what is in you and it will be interesting, it will be good. Salable? I don't know. But that is not the thing to think of—for a long time anyway.

And again I tell you this because I want to show you that the creative impulse is quiet, quiet. It sees, it feels, it quietly hears; and *now*, in the *present*. You see how these children painting my portrait were living in the present? It is when you are really living in the present that you are living spiritually, with the imagination.

I have noticed that two or three very rare, extraordinary, creative people I know, when they are truly magnetic, fascinating, oracular, seem to be living in the present. Francesca is one of them; a little Swedish mystic who sees visions as Blake did is another; and Carl Sandburg, the poet, is the third.

Francesca, for example, *always* seems to be living in the present: now! now![3] You can never get her to gossip chattily, to repeat long narratives or listen to them, not because she disapproves of gossip, far from it, but because to her, I think, mere narrative is not a thing to bother about because

---

2. The colors were very beautiful. A fine portrait painter who saw them cried out; groaned almost, with envy at the colors and the draftsmanship, at the genius that would lead a child to make the floor a pale turquoise instead of its own color, etc.

Each portrait was entirely different. But each was a portrait of me and my personality (infinitely more so than a photograph), and each was a portrait of the child who painted it and *her* personality. This always happens in writing or painting: what you are, you show.

3. Sometimes say softly to yourself: "*Now* . . . now. What is happening to me now? This is *now*. What is coming into me now? this moment?"

Then suddenly you begin to see the world as you had not seen it before, to hear

298 | BRENDA UELAND

it is only memory,[4] a recounting of the past in which nothing new can come in. It is not inspiration, the present.

No, she never says very much but sits looking at you with loving, shining eyes, gently swaying as though to unheard music, and listens to you and understands perfectly, and wisdom seems to descend into her gently from some place, from beyond some place, as though she heard and understood in that moment St. Joan's voices. And then she says something (without beginning[5]) that at once seems to me so remarkable, true and important and fills me with something that is wonderfully consoling and illuminating.

I have never heard her talk merely from memory (that is merely repeating something she heard or thought yesterday[6]) but always creatively. She has never uttered a perfunctory word, never anything that was not felt and felt at that very instant.

Carl Sandburg—the poet—I have seen him do this. He talks in his beautiful voice dreamily and inspiration seems to come out of him now . . . *now* as he goes along, as though whatever imagination entered into him, out it came freely and like music.

Once driving around the lake by our house we stopped and looked at the sunset, a December sky. He spoke of "the gunmetal sky" and looked for a long time. I felt some awe: "This is really the way a poet feels when he is moved." For I could feel what was going on in him while he looked at the

---

people's voices and not only what they are saying but what they are trying to say and you sense the whole truth about them. And you sense existence, not piecemeal—not this object and that—, but as a translucent whole.

4. She tells, of course, things she remembers, but they always throw some light on her present creative moment.

5. She always plunges right into the middle of a truth, never leading up to it with apologetic explanations, proofs and qualifying phrases. And that is what I want you to do when you write. And like Francesca, since she is always truthful, never care if you are believed or not.

6. She does not do this consciously at all. She does not plan or *will* to be a person who never repeats things (and God forbid that you should do that!). She is just one of those happy creative people who do not ever waste time accumulating facts and proofs from memory. She just accepts what her imagination shows her and lets out this new truth, without comparing anxiously this and that and testing all for its soundness. I have no doubt she tests truths inwardly. But she does not have to (egotistically) establish her soundness, before people.

sky,—some kind of an experience, incandescent and in motion. But *I* was living ten minutes hence in the future, feeling a little self-conscious and anxious to please and full of small compunctions, though I exclaimed: "Isn't it perfectly wonderful!" Well, Carl Sandburg was living in the present and having a poetic experience. But I was too full of other cerebrations, concern about being a polite hostess and getting home on time to dinner.

Now you and I and everybody often live in the present before a sunset. And we have felt things about it, just as Carl Sandburg has, or Dante or Shakespeare. Saint-Beuve said: "There exists in most men a poet who died young, whom the man survived." And de Musset said: "Know that there is often hidden in us a dormant poet, always young and alive."

You all know this is so. And since all are poets I suggest living in the present part of the time, as great poets and artists do. Incidentally, when you say perfunctorily about the sky just to talk: "What a beautiful evening!" that is not poetry. But if you say it and mean it very much, it is.

I do not know whether to keep these foregoing passages in this book or not. You might get to scowling and intellectualizing about this and making rules (which you must never, never do!) and saying to yourself: "Be careful. Am I doing this correctly? Is this Memory or Imagination I am using now?"

Heaven forbid that that should happen. Before the end of the book I will probably strike this out so there will be no danger of that. Of *course* we use memory all the time, and the clearer and more copious it is the better. If you are writing stories, of *course* you use your memory and put in all the details of your elopement and so on. But do not forget to keep re-charging yourself as children do, with new thinking called "Inspiration." I just describe this "living in the present" because you might like to try it: that is, be free and open to all things and don't pretend and don't fret.[7]

---

7. Yes, I am all against anxiety, worry. There are many people, you can see, who consider worry a kind of duty. Back of this I think it is the subconscious feeling that Fate or God is mean or resentful or tetchy and that if we do not worry enough we will certainly catch it from Him.

But they should remember that Christ said that we should cast off anxiety so that we could "seek first the Kingdom of Heaven and His righteousness" (i.e., live creatively, greatly, seekingly, in the present) "and all these things" (beauty, happiness, goodness, talent, food and clothing) "will be added unto you." Of course He is right.

See how the Mexicans and southwestern Indians live in the present, doing what they must do happily and quietly and taking no anxious thought for the morrow. They say a Mexican will sit on his haunches smoking a cigarette and happily looking at nothing for hours.

And see how all people in Mexico are such remarkable artists! The poorest Mexican cannot touch any work without making it lovely,—a two-cent tin pail or sandals made out of automobile tires. I think this is because they live in the present. There is more contemplation there: that is to say, they take time to love beauty.

But we northerners have become too much driven by the idea that in *twenty years* we will live, not now: because by that time our savings and the accrued interest will make it possible. To live *now* would be idleness. And because of our fear we have come to think of all idleness as hoggish, not as creative and radiant.

Perhaps I can describe "living in the present" in this way. In music, in playing the piano, sometimes you are playing *at* a thing and sometimes you are playing *in* it.[8] When you are playing *at* it you crescendo and diminish, following all the signs. "Now it is time to get louder," you read on the score. And so you make it louder and louder. "Look out! Here is a pianissimo!" So you dutifully do that. But this is intellectual and external.

Only when you are playing *in* a thing do people listen and hear you and are moved. It is because *you* are moved, because a queer and wonderful experience has taken place and the music—Mozart or Bach or whatever it is— suddenly is yourself, *your* voice and your eloquence. The passionate and wonderful questions in the music are *your* questions. And with all the nobility and violence and wonderful sweetness of Beethoven, say, it is *you* talking to those who listen.

One more example.

Look at those people who have a genius for being funny. When they are mimicking someone you can see that they are really in a kind of trance. They *are* the person they are mimicking. If instead they are self-conscious

8. I know a fine concert pianist who says sadly of a terribly hard-working but hopeless pupil: "She always practices and never plays."

(like me) and cannot get lost in this trance, this identification, if they are saying to themselves, "Now I do this and now I go cross-eyed and everybody will laugh," it is not funny at all and everybody looking on is pained and embarrassed and does not know where to look.[9]

Well, this same kind of identification, freedom, carelessness, should be there when you are writing. Then it will be good.

Now some will interpret this as meaning they should stop thinking. No, I don't mean that. When you are writing you will probably think harder than you ever have in your life and more clearly. But self-consciousness, anxiety, "intellectualizing" (i.e., primly frowning through your pince-nez and trying to do things according to prescribed rules as laid down by *others*)[10] will be untied from you, will be cast off.

Dean Inge says that the great mystic philosopher Plotinus described this "living in the present" like this:

"In our best and most effective moments, when we really 'enter into' our work, we leave it behind. . . . This is the experience of Pure Spirit when it is turned toward the One. When we reach this stage we often doubt that the experience is real because the 'senses protest that they have seen nothing.' Hence there is a kind of unconsciousness in the highest experiences of the Soul, though we cannot doubt them, not in the least."

In other words, it is when you are really living in the present—working, thinking, lost, absorbed in something you care about very much, that you are living spiritually.

And so once again I have driven home the point: it will be good for you if you will work at your writing.

One more thing about our feeling that unless we are in action we are either idle or stupid:

---

9. Self-consciousness comes from an anxiety that you will *not* impress people. The would-be clown cannot be funny because he is afraid that his audience will not think he is.

The really funny man doesn't think about the audience at all. If it doesn't laugh, he has had his own fun and doesn't care. If the audience laughs it just frees him even more and fills him (Inspiration) with further and more absurd, unpremeditated antics.

10. And bearing in mind a thousand things *not* to do.

You sit down to write, to think (vaguely conceiving of "thinking" as something that a college professor does). No logical thought comes in the first minute or two that you try it. A sort of paralysis follows, a conviction of your mental limitations, and you disconsolately go downstairs to do something menial and easy like washing the dishes, while doing so (though not knowing it) having some wonderful, fascinating, extraordinary, original, illuminating thoughts. Not knowing that they are thoughts at all, or "thinking," you have no respect for them and do not put them down on paper—*which you are to do from now on!* That is, you are always to *act* and express what goes through you.

And that is the tragedy of so-called worthless people. They perhaps have more thoughts than us rushers, but they never get them out on paper or canvas or in music or work because of many things that I have enumerated: self-doubt, fear of failure, and so on.

The tragedy of bold, forthright, industrious people is that they act so continuously without much thinking, that it becomes dry and empty.[11]

But we have to act. But often the idle man does not act, not because he is lazy but because he is afraid in some way. He does not know that action should follow thought simply and pleasurably with absorption (like the child stringing beads). He thinks action is painful and hopelessly hard[12] and almost certain to end in failure.

Listen to what the poor, great, impassioned Van Gogh said about this:

"Because there are two kinds of idleness," he wrote to his brother, "that form a great contrast. There is the man who is idle from laziness, and from

11. Very forceful, active men might say that acting makes them *think* better. But if they took more time for idling and thinking, perhaps, the Imagination would show them much greater actions than the ones they are engaged in.

12. Because of all the disciplinarians and Stoics and duty-people in the world. And I do not mean that we should do nothing that is hard and unpleasant. Columbus discovering America went through a hard and uncomfortable time. But it was love and Imagination that got him to do it. He would never have done it from duty alone. Duty would have made him stay sternly at home making money and rearing his children in the way they should go. No, he would never have attempted anything so rash, free and glorious from duty!

lack of character, from the baseness of his nature. You may if you like take me for such a one. . . .

"Then there is the other idle man, who is idle in spite of himself, who is inwardly consumed by a great longing for action, who does nothing because he seems to be imprisoned in some cage, because he does not possess what he needs to make him productive, because the fatality of circumstances brings him to that point, such a man does not always know what he could do, but he feels by instinct: yet I am good for something, my life has an aim after all, I know that I might be quite a different man! How can I then be useful, of what service can I be! There is something inside me, what can it be!

"This is quite a different kind of idle man; you may if you like take me for such a one. A caged bird in spring knows quite well that he might serve some end; he feels quite well that there is something for him to do, but he cannot do it. What is it? He does not remember quite well. Then he has some vague ideas and says to himself: 'The others make their nests and lay their eggs and bring up their little ones,' and then he knocks his head against the bars of the cage. But the cage stands there and the bird is maddened by anguish.

"'Look at the lazy animal,' says another bird that passes by, 'he seems to be living at his ease.' Yes, the prisoner lives, his health is good, he is more or less gay when the sun shines. But then comes the season of migration. Attacks of melancholia,—'but he has got everything he wants,' say the children that tend him in his cage. He looks at the overcast sky and he inwardly rebels against his fate. 'I am caged, I am caged, and you tell me I do not want anything, fools! You think I have everything I need. Oh, I beseech you, liberty, to be a bird like other birds!'

"A certain idle man resembles this bird. . . . A just or unjustly ruined reputation, poverty, fatal circumstances, adversity, that is what makes men prisoners. . . . Do you know what frees one from this captivity? It is very deep, serious affection. Being friends, being brothers, love, that is what opens the prison by supreme power, by some magic force. But without this one remains in prison.

"There is where sympathy is renewed, life is restored.

"And the prison is also called prejudice, misunderstanding, fatal igno-
rance of one thing or another, distrust, false shame. . . . But I should be very
glad if it were possible for you to see in me something else than an idle man
of the worst type."

BRENDA UELAND *was born in Minneapolis, Minnesota in 1891. She spent many years liv-
ing in New York, where she was part of the Greenwich Village bohemian crowd that in-
cluded John Reed, Louise Bryant, and Eugene O'Neill. After her return to Minnesota, she
earned her living as a writer, editor, and teacher of writing. Brenda's later years were
marked by her breaking an international swimming record for over-80-year-olds and being
knighted by the King of Norway. She died at the age of 93 in 1985. Her books include* If You
Want to Write, Me, *and* Strength to Your Sword Arm.

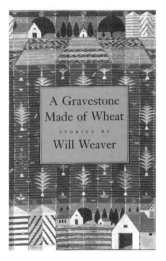

WILL WEAVER

A Gravestone
Made of Wheat

A Gravestone Made of Wheat

"You can't bury your wife here on the farm," the sheriff said. "That's the law."

Olaf Torvik looked up from his chair by the coffin; he did not understand what the sheriff was saying. And why was the sheriff still here, anyway? The funeral was over. They were ready for the burial—a family burial. There should be only Torviks in the living room.

"Do you understand what he's saying, Dad?" Einar said.

Olaf frowned. He looked to his son, to the rest of the family.

"He's saying we can't bury Mom here on the farm," Einar said slowly and deliberately. "He's saying she'll have to be buried in town at Greenacre Cemetery."

Olaf shook his head to clear the gray fuzz of loss, of grief, and Einar's words began to settle into sense. But suddenly a fly buzzed like a chainsaw—near the coffin—inside—there, walking the fine white hair on Inge's right temple. Olaf lurched forward, snatching at the fly in the air but missing. Then he bent over her and licked his thumb and smoothed the hair along her temple. Looking down at Inge, Olaf's mind drew itself together, cleared; he remembered the sheriff.

"Dad?" Einar said.

Olaf nodded. "I'm okay." He turned to the sheriff, John Carlsen, whom he had known for years and who had been at the funeral.

"A law?" Olaf said. "What do you mean, John?"

"It's a public health ordinance, Olaf," the sheriff said. "The state legislature passed it two years ago. It's statewide. I don't have it with me 'cause I had no idea . . . The law prohibits home burials."

"The boys and me got her grave already dug," Olaf said.

"I know," the sheriff said. "I saw it at the funeral. That's why I had to stay behind like this. I mean I hate like hell to be standing here. You should have told me that's the way you wanted to bury her, me or the county commissioners or the judge. Somebody, anyway. Maybe we could have gotten you a permit or something."

"Nothing to tell," Olaf said, looking across to Einar and Sarah, to their son Harald and his wife, to Harald's children. "This is a family affair."

The sheriff took off his wide-brimmed hat and mopped his forehead with the back of his sleeve. "The times are changing, Olaf. There's more and more people now, so there's more and more laws, laws like this one."

Olaf was silent.

"I mean," the sheriff continued, "I suppose I'd like to be buried in town right in my own backyard under that red maple we got. But what if everybody did that? First thing you know, people would move away, the graves would go untended and forgotten, and in a few years you wouldn't dare dig a basement or set a post for fear of turning up somebody's coffin."

"There's eighteen hundred acres to this farm," Olaf said softly. "That's plenty of room for Inge—and me, too. And nobody in this room is likely to forget where she's buried. None of us Torviks, anyway."

The sheriff shook his head side to side. "We're talking about a law here, Olaf. And I'm responsible for the law in this county. I don't make the laws, you understand, but still I got to enforce them. That's my job."

Olaf turned and slowly walked across the living room; he stood at the window with his back to the sheriff and the others. He looked out across the farm—the white granaries, the yellow wheat stubble rolling west, and far away, the grove of Norway pine where Inge liked to pick wildflowers in the spring.

"She belongs here on the farm," Olaf said softly.

"I know what you mean," the sheriff said, and began again to say how sorry . . .

Olaf listened but the room came loose, began to drift, compressing itself into one side of his mind, as memories, pictures of Inge pushed in from the past. Olaf remembered one summer evening when the boys were still small and the creek was high and they all went there at sundown after chores and sat on the warm rocks and dangled their white legs in the cold water.

"Dad?" Einar said

The sheriff was standing close now, as if to get Olaf's attention.

"You been farming here in Hubbard County how long, fifty years?"

Olaf blinked. "Fifty-three years."

"And I've been sheriff over half that time. I know you, I know the boys. None of you has ever broken a law that I can think of, not even the boys. The town folk respect that. . . ."

Olaf's vision cleared and something in him hardened at the mention of town folk. He had never spent much time in town, did not like it there very much. And he believed that, though farmers and townspeople did a lot of business together, it was business of necessity; that in the end they had very little in common. He also had never forgotten how the town folk treated Inge when she first came to Hubbard County.

"What I mean is," the sheriff continued, "you don't want to start break- ing the law now when you're seventy-five years old."

"Seventy-eight," Olaf said.

"Seventy-eight," the sheriff repeated.

They were all silent. The sheriff mopped his forehead again. The silence went on for a long time.

Einar spoke. "Say we went ahead with the burial. Here, like we planned."

The sheriff answered to Olaf. "Be just like any other law that was bro- ken. I'd have to arrest you, take you to town. You'd appear before Judge Kruft and plead guilty or not guilty. If you pled guilty, there would be a small fine and you could go home, most likely. Then your wife would be disinterred and brought into town to Greenacre."

"What if he was to plead not guilty?" Einar said.

The sheriff spoke again to Olaf. "The judge would hold a hearing and review the evidence and pass sentence. Or, you could have a trial by jury."

"What do you mean by evidence?" Olaf asked, looking up. That word again after all these years.

The sheriff nodded toward the coffin. "Your wife," he said. "She'd be the evidence."

Evidence . . . evidence; Olaf's mind began to loop back through time, to when Inge first came from Germany and that word meant everything to them. But by force of will Olaf halted his slide into memory, forced his attention to the present. He turned away from the window.

"She told me at the end she should be buried here on the farm," Olaf said softly.

They were all silent. The sheriff removed his hat and ran his fingers through his hair. "Olaf," he said. "I've been here long enough today. You do what you think is best. That's all I'll say today."

The sheriff's car receded south down the gravel road. His dust hung over the road like a tunnel and Olaf squinted after the car until the sharp July sunlight forced his gaze back into the living room, to his family.

"What are we going to do, Dad?" Einar said.

Olaf was silent. "I . . . need some more time to think," he said. He managed part of a smile. "Maybe alone here with Inge?"

The others quietly filed through the doorway, but Einar paused, his hand on the doorknob.

"We can't wait too long, Dad," he said quietly.

Olaf nodded. He knew what Einar meant. Inge had died on Wednesday. It was now Friday afternoon, and the scent of the wilting chrysanthemums had been joined by a heavier, sweeter smell.

"I've sent Harald down to Penske's for some ice," Einar said.

Olaf nodded gratefully. He managed part of a smile, and then Einar closed the door to the living room.

Olaf sat alone by Inge. He tried to order his thoughts, to think through the burial, to make a decision; instead, his mind turned back to the first time he set eyes upon Inge, the day she arrived in Fargo on the Northern Pacific. His mind lingered there and then traveled further back, to his parents in Norway, who had arranged the marriage of Olaf and Inge.

His parents, who had remained and died in Norway, wrote at the end of a letter in June of 1918 about a young German girl who worked for the family on the next farm. They wrote how she wished to come to America; that her family in Germany had been lost in the bombings; that she was dependable and could get up in the morning; that she would make someone a good wife. They did not say what she looked like.

Olaf carried his parents' letter with him for days, stopping now and again in the fields, in the barn, to unfold the damp and wrinkled pages and read the last part again—about the young German girl. He wondered what she looked like. But then again, he was not in a position to be too picky about that sort of thing. It was hard to meet young, unmarried women on the prairie because the farms were so far apart, several miles usually, and at day's end Olaf was too tired to go anywhere, least of all courting. He had heard there were lots of young women in Detroit Lakes and Fargo, but he was not sure how to go about finding one in such large cities. Olaf wrote back to his parents and asked more about the German girl. His parents replied that she would be glad to marry Olaf, if he would have her. He wrote back that he would. His parents never did say what she looked like.

Because of the war, it was nearly two years later, April of 1920, before Olaf hitched up the big gray Belgian to his best wheat wagon, which he had swept as clean as his bedroom floor, and set off to Fargo to meet Inge's train.

It was a long day's ride and there was lots to see—long strings of geese rode the warm winds north, and beyond Detroit Lakes the swells of wheat fields rose up from the snow into black crowns of bare earth. But Olaf kept his eyes to the west, waiting for the first glimpse of Fargo. There were more wagons and cars on the road now, and Olaf stopped nodding to every one as there were far too many. Soon his wagon clattered on paved streets past houses built no more than a fork's handle apart. The Belgian grew skittish and Olaf stopped and put on his blinders before asking the way to the Northern Pacific Railroad station.

Inge's train was to arrive at 3:55 P.M. at the main platform. Olaf checked his watch against the station clock—2:28 P.M.—and then reached under the wagon seat. He brought out the smooth cedar shingle with his name, Olaf Leif Torvik, printed on it in large black letters. He placed it back under the seat, then on second thought, after glancing around the station, slipped the shingle inside his wool shirt. Then he grained and watered the Belgian and sat down to wait.

At 3:58 her train rumbled into the station and slowly drew to a stop, its iron wheels crackling as they cooled. People streamed off the train. Olaf held up his shingle, exchanging a shy grin with another man—John William Olsen—who also held a name-sign.

But there seemed to be few young women on the train, none alone.

A short Dutch-looking woman, small-eyed and thick, came toward Olaf—but at the last second passed him by. Olaf did not know whether to give thanks or be disappointed. But if the Dutch-looking woman passed him by, so did all the others. Soon Olaf was nearly alone on the platform. No one else descended from the Pullman cars. Sadly, Olaf lowered his shingle. She had not come. He looked at his shingle again, then let it drop to the platform.

He turned back to his wagon. If he was honest with himself, he thought, it all seemed so unlikely anyway; after all, there were lots of men looking for wives, men with more land and money, men certainly better-looking than Olaf.

"Maybe my folks made the mistake of showing her my picture," Olaf said to the Belgian, managing a smile as the horse shook his head and showed his big yellow teeth. Olaf wondered if he would ever take a wife. It seemed unlikely.

Before he unhitched the Belgian, he turned back to the platform for one last look. There, beside the train, staring straight at him, stood a tall, slim girl of about twenty. Her red hair lit the sky. In one hand she clutched a canvas suitcase, and in the other, Olaf's cedar shingle.

Inge Altenburg sat straight in Olaf's wagon seat, her eyes scared and straight ahead; she nodded as Olaf explained, in Norwegian, that there was still time today to see about the marriage. She spoke Norwegian with a heavy German accent, said yes, that is what she had come for.

They tried to get married in Fargo, in the courthouse, but a clerk there said that since Olaf was from Minnesota, they should cross the river and try at the courthouse in Moorhead. Olaf explained this to Inge, who nodded. Olaf opened his watch.

"What time do they close in Minnesota?" he asked the clerk.

"Same as here, five o'clock."

It was 4:36; they could still make it today. Olaf kept the Belgian trotting all the way across the Red River Bridge to the Moorhead Courthouse.

Inside, with eight minutes to spare, Olaf found the office of the Justice of the Peace; he explained to the secretary their wish to be married, today, if possible.

The secretary, a white-haired woman with gold-rimmed glasses, frowned.

"It's a bit late today," she said, "but I'll see what I can do. You do have all your papers in order?" she asked of Inge.

"Papers?" Olaf said.

"Her birth certificate and citizenship papers."

Olaf's heart fell. He had not thought of all this. He turned to Inge, who already was reaching under her sweater for the papers. Olaf's hopes soared as quickly as they had fallen.

"All right," the secretary said, examining the birth certificate, "now the citizenship papers."

Inge frowned and looked questioningly at Olaf. Olaf explained the term. Inge held up her hands in despair.

"She just arrived here," Olaf said, "she doesn't have them yet."

"I'm so sorry," the secretary said, and began tidying up her desk.

Olaf and Inge walked out. Inge's eyes began to fill with tears.

"We'll go home to Park Rapids," Olaf told her, "where they know me. There won't be any problem, any waiting, when we get home."

Inge nodded, looking down as she wiped her eyes. Olaf reached out and brushed away a teardrop, the first time he had touched her. She flinched, then burst into real tears.

Olaf drew back his hand, halfway, but then held her at her shoulders with both his hands.

"*Ich verstehe,*" he said softly, "I understand."

They stayed that night in a hotel in Detroit Lakes. Olaf paid cash for two single rooms, and they got an early start in the morning. Their first stop was not Olaf's farm, but the Hubbard County Courthouse in Park Rapids.

At the same counter Olaf and Inge applied for both her citizenship and their marriage license. When Inge listed her nationality as German, however, the clerk raised an eyebrow in question. He took her papers back to another, larger office; the office had a cloudy, waved-glass door and Olaf could see inside, as if underwater, several dark-suited men passing Inge's papers among themselves and murmuring. After a long time—thirty-eight minutes—the clerk returned to the counter.

"I'm afraid we have some problems with this citizenship application," he said to Inge.

When Inge did not reply, the clerk turned to Olaf. "She speak English?"

"I don't believe so, not much anyway."

"Well, as I said, there are some problems here."

"I can't think of any," Olaf said, "we just want to get married."

"But your wife—er, companion—lists that she's a German national."

"That's right," Olaf answered, "but she's in America now and she wants to become an American."

The clerk frowned. "That's the problem—it might not be so easy. We've got orders to be careful about this sort of thing."

"What sort of thing?"

"German nationals."

"Germans? Like Inge? But why?"

"You do realize we've been at war with Germany recently?" the clerk said, pursing his lips. "You read the papers?"

Olaf did not bother to answer.

"I mean the war's over, of course," the clerk said, "but we haven't received any change orders regarding German nationals."

Olaf laughed. "You think she's a spy or something? This girl?"

The clerk folded his arms across his chest. Olaf saw that he should not have laughed, that there was nothing at all to laugh about.

"We've got our rules," the clerk said.

"What shall we do?" Olaf asked. "What would you recommend?"

The clerk consulted some papers. "For a successful citizenship application she'll need references in the form of letters, letters from people who knew her in Germany and Norway, people who can verify where she was born, where she has worked. We especially need to prove that she was never involved in any capacity in German military or German government work."

"But that might take weeks," Olaf said.

The clerk shrugged. Behind him one of the county commissioners, Sig Hansen, had stopped to listen.

"There's nothing else we can do?" Olaf asked, directing his question beyond the clerk to the commissioner. But Sig Hansen shook his head negatively.

"Sorry, Olaf, that's out of my control. That's one area I can't help you in." The commissioner continued down the hall.

"Sorry," the clerk said, turning to some other papers.

With drawn lips Olaf said, "Thanks for your time."

They waited for Inge's letters to arrive from Europe. They waited one week, two weeks, five weeks. During this time Olaf slept in the hayloft and Inge took Olaf's bed in the house. She was always up and dressed and had breakfast ready by the time Olaf came in from the barn. Olaf always stopped at the pumphouse, took off his shirt and washed up before breakfast. He usually stepped outside and toweled off his bare chest in the sunlight; once he noticed Inge watching him from the kitchen window.

At breakfast Olaf used his best table manners, making sure to sit straight and hold his spoon correctly. And though they usually ate in silence, the silence was not uncomfortable. He liked to watch her cooking. He liked it when she stood at the wood range with her back to him, flipping pancakes or shaking the skillet of potatoes; he liked the way her body moved, the way strands of hair came loose and curled down her neck. Once she caught him staring. They both looked quickly away, but not before Olaf saw the beginnings of a smile on Inge's face. And it was not long after that, in the evening when it was time for Olaf to retire to the hayloft, that they began to grin foolishly at each other and stay up later and later. Though Olaf was not a religious man, he began to pray for the letters' speedy return.

Then it was July. Olaf was in the field hilling up his corn plants when Inge came running, calling out to him as she came, holding up her skirts for speed, waving a package in her free hand. It was from Norway. They knelt in the hot dirt and tore open the wrapping. The letters! Three of them.

They had hoped for more, just to make sure, but certainly three would be enough.

Olaf and Inge did not even take time to hitch up the wagon, but rode together bareback on the Belgian to Park Rapids. They ran laughing up the courthouse steps, Olaf catching Inge's hand on the way. Once inside, however, they made themselves serious and formal, and carefully presented the letters to the clerk. The clerk examined them without comment.

"I'll have to have the Judge look at these," he said, "he's the last word on something like this." The clerk then retreated with their letters down the hall and out of sight.

The Judge took a long time with the letters. Twenty minutes. Thirty-nine minutes. Olaf and Inge waited at the clerk's window, holding hands below the cool granite counter. As they waited, Inge began to squeeze Olaf's hand with increasing strength until her fingers dug into his palm and hurt him; he did not tell her, however. Finally the clerk returned. He handed back the letters.

"I'm sorry," he said, "but the Judge feels these letters are not sufficient."

Olaf caught the clerk's wrist. The clerk's eyes jumped wide and round and scared; he tried to pull back his arm but Olaf had him.

"We want to get married, that's all," he said hoarsely.

"Wait—" the clerk stammered, his voice higher now, "maybe you should see the Judge yourselves."

"That's a damned good idea," Olaf said. He let go of the clerk's arm. The clerk rubbed his wrist and pointed down the hall.

Olaf and Inge entered the Judge's chambers, and Olaf's hopes plummeted. All the old books, the seals under glass on the walls, the papers; the white hair and expressionless face of the Judge himself: they all added up to power, to right-of-way. The Judge would have it his way.

Olaf explained their predicament. The Judge nodded impatiently and flipped through the letters again.

"Perhaps what we should do for you," the Judge said, "is to have you wait on this application for a period of say, one calendar year. If, during that time, it is determined that Inge Altenburg is loyal and patriotic, then we can consider her for citizenship. And, of course, marriage."

"One year!" Olaf exclaimed.

The Judge drew back and raised his eyebrows. Sig Hansen, the commissioner, had paused in the doorway. He shook his head at the Judge.

"Christ, Herb," he said, "you ought to run it through, let 'em get married. They're harmless. They're just farmers."

Inge rose up from her chair. There was iron in her face. "Come—" she commanded Olaf, in English, "it is time we go to home."

They rode home slowly, silently. The Belgian sensed their sorrow and kept turning his wide brown eyes back to Olaf. But Olaf had no words for the big animal. Inge held Olaf around his waist. As they came in sight of their buildings she leaned her head on his shoulder and he could feel her crying.

They ate their dinner in silence, and then Olaf returned to his cornfield. At supper they were silent again.

Come sundown, Olaf climbed the ladder to the hayloft and unrolled his bedroll in the hay. He wished he could have found some good thing to say at supper, but it was not in him. Not tonight. Olaf felt old, tired beyond his thirty-three years. He lay back on the loose prairie hay and watched the sun set in the knotholes of the west barn wall, red, then violet, then purple, then blue shrinking to gray. He hardly remembered going to sleep. But then he knew he must be dreaming. For standing above him, framed in the faint moonlight of the loft, stood Inge. She lay down beside him in the hay and when her hair fell across his face and neck he knew he could not be dreaming. He also knew that few dreams could ever be better than this. And in his long life with Inge, none were.

Olaf rose from his chair by her casket. That night when she came to him in the loft was forty-five years past. That night was Olaf's last in the hayloft, for they considered themselves married, come morning—married by body, by heart, and by common law.

And Inge never forgot her treatment at the Hubbard County Courthouse in Park Rapids; she rarely shopped in the town, preferring instead Detroit Lakes, which was twelve miles farther but contained no unpleasant memories.

Nor did she become a citizen; she remained instead without file or number, nonexistent to federal, state, or local records. She was real, Olaf thought, only to those who knew her, who loved her. And that, Olaf suddenly understood, was the way she should remain. As in her life, her death.

Before Olaf called the family back into the room, he thought he should try to pray. He got down on his knees on the wood floor by the coffin and folded his hands. He waited, but no words came. He wondered if he had forgotten how to pray. Olaf knew that he believed in a great God of some kind. He had trouble with Jesus, but with God there was no question. He ran into God many times during the year: felt of him in the warm field-dirt of May; saw his face in the shiny harvest grain; heard his voice among the tops of the Norway pines. But he was not used to searching him out, to calling for him.

Nor could he now. Olaf found he could only cry. Long, heaving sobs and salty tears that dripped down his wrists to the floor. He realized, with surprise, that this was the first time he had cried since Inge's death; that his tears in their free flowing were a kind of prayer. He realized, too, that God was with him these moments. Right here in this living room.

When the family reassembled, Olaf told them his decision. He spoke clearly, resolutely.

"We will bury Inge here on the farm as we planned," he said, "but in a little different fashion."

He outlined what they would do, asked if anyone disagreed, if there were any worries. There were none. "All right then, that's settled," Olaf said. He looked around the room at his family—Einar, Sarah, the children, the others.

"And do you know what else we should do?" Olaf said.

No one said anything.

"Eat!" Olaf said. "I'm mighty hungry."

The others laughed, and the women turned to the kitchen. Soon they all sat down to roast beef, boiled potatoes with butter, dill pickles, wheat bread, strong black coffee, and pie. During lunch Harald returned with the ice. Einar excused himself from the table and went to help Harald.

Once he returned and took from a cupboard some large black plastic garbage bags. Olaf could hear them working in the living room, and once Einar said, "Don't let it get down along her side, there."

Olaf did not go into the living room while they worked. He poured himself another cup of coffee, which, strangely, made him very tired. He tried to remember when he had slept last.

Sarah said to him, "Perhaps you should rest a little bit before we . . ."

Olaf nodded. "You're right," he said, "I'll go upstairs and lie down a few minutes. Just a few minutes."

Olaf started awake at the pumping thuds of the John Deere starting. He sat up quickly—too quickly, nearly pitching over, and pushed aside the curtain. It was late—nearly dark. How could he have slept so long? It was time.

He hurriedly laced his boots and pulled on a heavy wool jacket over his black suit-coat. Downstairs, the women and children were sitting in the kitchen, dressed and waiting for him.

"We would have wakened you," Sarah said.

Olaf grinned. "I thought for a minute there . . ." Then he buttoned his coat and put on a woolen cap. He paused at the door. "One of the boys will come for you when everything is ready," he said to Sarah.

"We know," she said.

Outside, the sky was bluish purple and Harald was running the little John Deere tractor in the cow lot. The tractor carried a front-end loader and Harald was filling the scoop with fresh manure. Beyond the tractor some of the Black Angus stretched stiffly and snorted at the disturbance. Harald drove out of the lot when the scoop was rounded up and dripping. He stopped by the machine shed, went inside, and returned with two bags of commercial nitrogen fertilizer.

"Just to make sure, Grandpa," he said. His smile glinted white in the growing dark.

"Won't hurt," Olaf said. Then he tried to think of other things they would need.

"Rope," Olaf said. "And a shovel." Then he saw both on the tractor.

"Everything's ready," Harald said, pointing to the little John Deere. "She's all yours. We'll follow."

Olaf climbed up to the tractor's seat and then backed away from the big machine-shed doors. Einar and Harald rolled open the mouth of the shed and went inside.

The noise of their two big tractors still startled Olaf, even in daylight, and he backed up farther as the huge, dual-tandem John Deeres rumbled out of their barn. A single tire on them, he realized, was far bigger than the old Belgian he used to have. And maybe that's why he never drove the big tractors. Actually, he'd never learned, hadn't wished to. He left them to the boys, who drove them as easily as Olaf drove the little tractor. Though they always frightened him a little, Olaf's long wheat fields called for them—especially tonight. Behind each of the big tractors, like an iron spine with twelve shining ribs, rode a plow.

Olaf led the caravan of tractors. They drove without lights into the eighty-acre field directly west from the yellow-lit living-room window of the house. At what he sensed was the middle of the field, Olaf halted. He lowered the manure and fertilizer onto the ground. Then, with the front-end digger, he began to unearth Inge's grave.

Einar and Harald finished the sides of the grave with shovels. Standing out of sight in the hole, their showers of dirt pumped rhythmically up and over the side. Finished, they climbed up and brushed themselves off, and then walked back to the house for the others.

Olaf waited alone by the black hole. He stared down into its darkness and realized that he probably would not live long after Inge, and yet felt no worry or fear. For he realized there was, after all, a certain order to the events and times of his life: all the things he had worked for and loved were now nearly present.

Behind, he heard the faint rattle of the pickup. He turned to watch it come across the field toward the grave. Its bumper glinted in the moonlight, and behind, slowly walking, came the dark shapes of his family. In the bed of the pickup was Inge's coffin.

The truck stopped alongside the grave. Einar turned off the engine and then he and Harald lifted the coffin out and onto the ground. The family gathered around. Sarah softly sang "Rock of Ages," and then they said together the Twenty-third Psalm. Olaf could not speak past "The Lord is my . . ."

Then it was over. Einar climbed onto the tractor and raised the loader over the coffin. Harald tied ropes to the loader's arms and looped them underneath and around the coffin. Einar raised the loader until the ropes tightened and lifted the long dark box off the ground. Harald steadied the coffin, kept it from swinging, as Einar drove forward until the coffin was over the dark hole. Olaf stepped forward toward it as if to—to what?

Einar turned questioningly toward Olaf. "Now, Dad?" he said.

Olaf nodded.

Swaying slightly in the moonlight, the coffin slowly sank into the grave. There was a scraping sound as it touched bottom. Harald untied the ropes and then Einar began to push forward the mound of earth; the sound of dirt thumping on the coffin seemed to fill the field. When the grave was half filled, Einar backed the tractor to the pile of manure and pushed it forward into the hole. Harald carried the two bags of nitrogen fertilizer to the grave, slit their tops, and poured them in after the manure. Then Einar filled in the earth and scattered what was left over until the grave was level with the surrounding field.

Olaf tried to turn away, but could not walk. For with each step he felt the earth rising up to meet his boots as if he were moving into some strange room, an enormous room, one that went on endlessly. He thought of his horses, his old team. He heard himself murmur some word that only they would understand.

"Come Dad," Sarah said, taking Olaf by the arm. "It's over."

Olaf let himself be led into the pickup. Sarah drove him and the children to the field's edge by the house where Einar had parked the little John Deere.

"You coming inside now?" Sarah asked as she started the children toward the house.

"No, I'll wait here until the boys are finished," Olaf said, "you go on ahead."

Even as he spoke the big tractors rumbled alive. Their running lights flared on and swung around as Einar and Harald drove to the field's end near Olaf. They paused there a moment, side by side, as their plows settled onto the ground. Then their engine RPMs came up and the tractors, as one, leaned into their work and headed straight downfield toward Inge's grave.

The furrows rolled up shining in the night light. Olaf knew this earth. It was heavy soil, had never failed him. He knew also that next year, and nearly forever after, there would be one spot in the middle of the field where the wheat grew greener, taller, and more golden than all the rest. It would be the gravestone made of wheat.

Olaf sat on the little tractor in the darkness until the boys had plowed the field black from side to side. Then they put away the tractors and fed the Angus. After that they ate breakfast, and went to bed at dawn.

WILL WEAVER's *books include* Striking Out; Red Earth, White Earth; A Gravestone Made of Wheat; Farm Team; *and* Hard Ball. *Weaver lives in Bemidji, Minnesota.*

PETER WELTNER

How the Body Prays

Andrew Willingham Odom (excerpt)

The second Sunday morning in November 1940, Drew sat between his mother and grandfather in the Odom pew. The Germans had occupied most of Europe. They had ceased their daylight raids over London and the other English cities and had begun to bomb and terrorize them in the night.

"Our country is still at peace," the Right Reverend Thornton Welles said toward the end of his long sermon, "and may it ever remain at peace. Americans have no desire to become entangled again in Europe's endless civil war. Yet in such a time as ours the soldier stands for all of us. We hear of terrible battles, of awful conquests, of conflicts that when retold a thousand years from now will still strike terror in all mankind. You have all heard the saying that there are no atheists in foxholes. Perhaps that's true. Perhaps death's imminence would terrify even the profoundest skeptic or most scoffing denier into faith. But woe to those who believe," he preached as his voice grew louder and more stately, "only because they are afraid. Such faith belongs to the devil, not to God, and is dreadful to contemplate. The true believer believes not because he is afraid but because he knows in his soul God's Love is present. Let all who seek Our Lord cast aside all fear. For there can be no fear anywhere there is love. Amen."

Back home, Drew studied his face in the bathroom mirror. What did he see there? "I'm a pacifist," he told himself as if he were speaking to a stranger. "I don't believe in killing anyone. I don't believe in war. I'm not a coward. I'm not afraid to die. I'm not afraid. I'm a pacifist," he repeated, staring himself in the eye. But the stranger to whom he'd been speaking looked unconvinced.

Shortly before his ninety-third birthday, Drew's grandfather had started to slow down. He went to bed earlier, he got up later, he took long naps every afternoon. Leaving most of the farm's daily business to his daughter-in-law, he spent hours alone in his study, picking up one book after another as if he were following some trail of facts that might actually lead him to his long-desired goal. What was he searching for? Drew didn't dare ask. Whenever he peeked into the den, his grandfather would be asleep in his big chair, his swollen legs resting on a hassock. Books were strewn everywhere. Several lay open on his lap.

Early one Monday morning, before he caught a ride to work on a delivery truck, he joined his mother in the kitchen for coffee. "Grandfather was making a lot of mistakes last night." He poured himself a cup from the pot and stirred in some sugar. "The 'Notturno' is an easy piece."

She was standing at the window, staring eastward, her body framed by light. "Yes. I suppose it is."

"His fingers won't do what he orders them to do anymore."

"No. They won't." She sounded distracted.

"I'm taking the train back to New York on Tuesday, Mother," Drew said, seizing the opportunity. "It's taken over a year for me to save enough again, but I've finally done it. Mrs. Talbot is giving me a week off."

"Is she? That's kind of her so close to Christmas."

He set his cup down on the counter. "Mother . . ."

"Not now, Drew. Look," she said, pointing out the window.

He stood directly behind her, easily a half foot taller. Overnight there had been an ice storm. Everything Drew could see from the tops of the trees down to the moss and grass was covered by a paper-thin sheet of glass that seemed to magnify slightly each object it encased. The whole world shimmered and glittered like rippling water beneath a dazzling sun still lying low in a platinum sky.

His mother reached behind her for his hand and clasped it firmly. "Isn't it glorious?" she said.

It was raining hard when Drew walked out of Pennsylvania Station onto Seventh Avenue. Although he'd packed lightly, his suitcase felt increasingly heavy the closer he got to the hotel where he had stayed during his last trip. By the time he reached Thirty-eighth Street and Ninth Avenue, he was sopping. His room stank of wet plaster and rust. But he pretended he didn't mind. After all, if he skimped on unimportant things like lodging and meals, he might be able to stay a few days longer.

But the rain wouldn't quit and each day the air grew colder. The newspapers promised icy sleet or snow by noon the next day. On his way to his third concert, he had to buy an umbrella so he wouldn't have to sit through Toscanini's performance of the Verdi *Requiem* drenched to the bone and steaming in the warmth of Carnegie Hall.

After the concert, it was storming harder. Although all the limousines and taxis had departed and everyone else had at least begun their trip back home, Drew and one other man continued to linger outside the entrance just a few steps off Fifty-seventh Street. Although they stood only a few feet apart, the other man's face was almost entirely hidden by the wide, turned-up collar of his black overcoat, his black scarf, and his broad-brimmed black hat. He might have been playing a gunsel in a movie starring Cagney or Robinson or Raft. His gloved fingers gripped the lapel of his overcoat as he studied the firmament. "It's never going to stop."

Had he been speaking to Drew? "How far do you have to go?" Drew asked.

"Only a few blocks." When he turned toward Drew, the streetlight illuminated his face. His features were sharply thin, but he was much younger than Drew would have guessed. "I hate to get wet," the boy said.

Drew held up his umbrella. "It's brand new, but it leaks." The rain splashed like hail in the flooding gutters. "Want to risk it anyway?"

"Why not?" The boy wiped his forehead with the back of his hand. "My uncle's waiting for me."

Drew slid his umbrella open and held it over their heads. "Which way?"

"Right. Then right again on Sixth Avenue."

Several minutes later they reached a bakery with two large windows facing the street on either side of the entrance. The boy tugged on Drew's coat. "This is my stop," he said and laughed.

The neon sign, the windows' lights, all the lights inside were dark, but behind one of the counters an open door glowed. The boy knocked on the door using a signal of taps and pauses that he repeated several times before a big, not quite heavyset man stepped through the light and into the front room to unlock the door. A gold watch chain fit tautly across the vest under his heavy tweed suit. His face was beaming. "How was the great man's concert? Perfection?"

"Not quite," the boy said. "Moscona entered too early a couple of times. Björling made some mistakes too. Milanov seemed scared to death of the high B-flat in the 'Libera Me.' She started gasping for breath bars before she finally hit it, more or less. But, Uncle Joe, it really was beautiful. Toscanini's a genius."

"That he is, Aaron my boy," he said, slapping him on his back. "And he believes in liberty, too." He held out a hand to Drew. "And you are?"

"Odom. Drew Odom."

"I'm sorry," the boy said. "You were good enough to walk with me all the way under the protection of your umbrella and I didn't even ask you your name. Or tell you mine. I'm Aaron Rose. And this is my . . ."

"His uncle Joe Rose. Come in, come in, both of you. Let's indulge in some poppy-seed cake and a cup of hot tea on a cold night, what do you say? Then Aaron and I should be on our way back to Jersey City. Oh, how I love that new tunnel. It makes our trips so fast now, doesn't it, Aaron?"

"I shouldn't stay," Drew said. "My hotel is still a long way away. It's late."

"You're a visitor to our town?" the uncle said. "May I guess? From the South, yes? I did detect a sweet magnolia scent in your voice, sir, did I not?"

The boy rolled his eyes. "The farthest south Uncle Joe has ever been is the boardwalk in Atlantic City."

"This is my third trip to Manhattan," Drew boasted.

"Then you're practically a native. Where are you staying?" Uncle Joe inquired. When Drew told him, he shook his head disapprovingly. "Not so good, son, not so good. Not very wise. A bad neighborhood. You mustn't walk. I'll drive you there. But, first, you must taste the best poppy-seed cake in the whole of greater New York. Rose's was voted the best, the very best. It says so right here," he said tapping a cutting from a newspaper that had been pinned to a cork board that hung on a wall in the huge back room where a half dozen bakers were stirring batter or opening and closing oven doors or decorating cakes. Had the kitchen back home while his mother was baking pies or cookies ever smelled half as sweet? "A family business," Uncle Joe informed Drew as he escorted him and Aaron into the office. "Mine, my brother Theodore's, my sister Ethel's, my sister Eva's. Aaron works here, too, when we can drag him out of his little basement room where he's all the time composing music that he never lets us hear. So does his sister Miriam and their cousins Judith and Samuel. My parents, God love them, started it right here on this very spot over forty-two years ago in 1898. David and Nettie Rosenbaum. Wonderful people. So kind. From Berlin originally. Came over on the same boat when neither of them had yet turned twenty. Out of nothing, they built this thriving business." He slapped his hands against his thighs in pride and admiration. "What don't we all owe to them and their generosity and hard work. They both died too young." His face lost all its glow for a moment, but then he winked at Drew. "Wait until you taste one of our sublime cheese Danishes. Sit down, both of you. I'll bring you some with the cake. We'll eat like gods, drink a little tea, and then I'll drive us all where we want to go, agreed?"

PETER WELTNER *was raised in piedmont, North Carolina. He currently teaches modern and contemporary American fiction and poetry at San Francisco State University. His books include* How the Body Prays, The Risk of His Music, In a Time of Combat for the Angel, Identity and Difference, *and* Beachside Entries/Specific Ghosts.

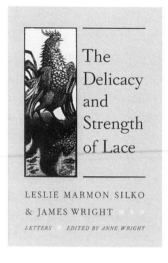

Letters between

LESLIE MARMON SILKO
& JAMES WRIGHT

The Delicacy and Strength of Lace

LESLIE MARMON SILKO
& JAMES WRIGHT

LETTERS   EDITED BY ANNE WRIGHT

New York, N.Y.
December 18, 1979

Dear Leslie,

I'm afraid this will be a short note for the moment—I'll write at great length later on. I have some bad news about myself which I nevertheless want to tell you.

I have learned that I have cancer. It is very serious, but it is not hopeless. My doctor is a good man and a highly skilled specialist, and he has assured me and Annie that the operation—radical surgery in the throat—will save my life. I will emerge from the surgery with a diminished capacity to speak, and this will create a problem, since I make a living by speaking. But there is a good chance that I will be able to continue teaching all right. The operation is supposed to take place early in the month of January. I will be recuperating here at home most of the time. Because the operation will be serious and debilitating, I have arranged to take off the spring semester from teaching.

It is a shock, of course, perhaps the most cruel shock that a middle-aged person can face. But I have found that I have a number of considerable powers to help me. I have always been happy with my marriage to Annie, for example, but I suddenly have a deeper and clearer understanding of how very strong this marriage is. Furthermore, in determining who to tell, I have considered that I want to share the worst of this news with a very few people whom I admire and value the most, and it is interesting to me that you stand very high in my mind among those—the people, I mean, who strike me as embodying in their own lives and work something—some value, some spirit—that I absolutely care about and believe in. Of course, my dear friend, over little more than a year we have become excellent friends, and I would hope always to send you happy news. But the tragic news belongs to you too. Please don't despair over my troubles. I will find my way through this difficulty somehow, and one of the best things I have is my knowledge that you exist and that you are going on living and working. I'll be in touch again soon (by the way, if you're in N.Y.C. on February 5th please *do* call us).

Love,
Jim

Tucson, Arizona
January 3, 1980

Dear Jim,

Your letter was waiting when I returned from Christmas in Gallup. I wanted to wait a few days to digest it in case my feelings changed, but they have not and I trust them. I feel a great deal of distress about your speaking voice because I imagine how you must be feeling about it; but myself, I have always felt that the words and the feeling they were spoken with matter most, and I sense that this is your deepest understanding too, otherwise your letter would not have been so calm. When I was a girl my grandpa on my mother's side had just the same operation. In those days they didn't have the electronic mechanisms they have now. But all my memories of him are of his expressiveness, which I did not perceive before, although I was younger before, and maybe this is the reason. He smiled and gestured a lot and like always, he would cry when he was very happy—he was often overcome with feelings, and my mother is the same, and I am too. We can be in an airport or train depot not even seeing anyone off and when they call the train or plane, we cry. I don't know what or who we cry for, but we do. Grandpa was always that way, but after the operation it always seemed to me much more a way of speaking than simply some overflow of feeling. I supposed it is because of this and because the operation was successful for him that I read your letter calmly. Perhaps I am seeing your crisis too much like a child, and perhaps this confidence that you will be here for quite some time is my way of protecting myself from pain, but I think not. I know such things immediately; the feeling hits me and I'm never able to think fast enough to create a rationalization. I feel you will be all right, that your health will be restored. You will manage the part about your voice because voice never was sound alone. Which doesn't mean that you won't feel angry sometimes—Grandpa did, but then he learned his own new language.

I know all the stories which are told at times like these—I suppose I hesitate because there is a sort of cultural context in which they exist and New York now must be even more distant from it. Or maybe not.

It seems strange how some people get far more than their fair share of illness or trouble. I suppose Spinoza would say that Existence never heard of "fair." Hugh Crooks came to Laguna in the 1920s from somewhere in the East or Midwest. He was in his early 20s and his doctors sent him to the Southwest with tuberculosis so bad they told him just to plan on spending his last months in New Mexico. He came and waited and then nothing happened so he got a job running the store for Abie Abraham there at Laguna (this was before my Grandpa Hank had the store). My dad remembers Hugh then, always in a short-sleeved shirt even when it was snowing, and always coughing, always real skinny. My dad was just a mean little kid then, and one time he set fire to the boxes of paper and trash by the back door of the store Hugh was managing for Abie. My dad hid on the big hill north of Laguna and looked down and watched Hugh carry buckets of water to put out the fire. It seemed like Hugh never got over the t.b., but the years went by, and the next thing that happened was a terrible car wreck. Hugh was driving down the old road to Los Lunas and collided with a truck. People from Laguna who happened to drive past reported that it was all over for Hugh—I remember the graphic description—they said his pelvic bones were shoved clear up to his armpits, though that sounds a lot like embroidery. But no, he recovered in time, and the years went by, and I think he liked to drink a lot. I don't remember hearing much about Hugh other than this litany which I am reciting to you, Jim, this litany of his physical disasters. I think now that there wasn't much that was remarkable about Hugh otherwise—he wasn't a mean man and he didn't cheat people, but I think he had a pretty ordinary life except for these terrible illnesses and accidents for which we have always known him. Anyway, I guess he did some drinking, though it was never the sort that led to broken screen doors or fights. He never married, and it wasn't until many many years later that my mother figured out why that might have been. Anyway, the next thing we knew, someone had been to the hospital to see Hugh, and this time it was his liver and they said Hugh won't make it this time, his liver is swollen up as big as a watermelon, and everyone went to visit him thinking that this was it. Aunt Florence went to see him, and Aunt Mary, and they both said that it was true that he had survived the t.b. and the car wreck but this time the cirrhosis had him. Well everybody said it was too bad, but after all it was lucky he had lived this long, and that it was funny too that one or two of the people who had seen him in the wreckage of his truck and pronounced him a goner—well, they were gone by this time, in one way or another. But this time . . . Hugh got out of the hospital and was back in his pickup truck driving around, still smoking, still coughing, in his short-sleeved shirts. Pretty soon he was running a bar at Swanee, which is where old U.S. 66 used to intersect the old highway to Los Lunas. Swanee is just off the Laguna reservation and near the Navajo reservation land at Cañoncito. Anyway, the bar was always busy with Lagunas and Navajos buying liquor and with passersby on U.S. 66 and the Los Lunas road. Hugh liked keeping the bar pretty well because he liked talking to people and he liked his regular customers, and I guess he liked being able to drink some himself too. I think he wasn't very ambitious and he never seemed like he had much money or cared whether he did. Anyway, one night some hold-up men passing through on 66 held up Hugh's bar (crooks traveling on Highway 66 from Chicago to L.A. or vice versa used to run out of money right around the Laguna area and then they'd break in or do a hold-up). Hugh took out a .38 he kept under the counter and shot one of the hold-up men (didn't kill him), but then the other shot Hugh in the chest with a .38. He was in critical condition for a long time, and then just when he was getting better he got pneumonia, and the doctors (doctors who knew Hugh also knew better than to say anything but these doctors didn't know and so they) said he wouldn't pull through. All Grandpa Hank would say was "I wonder if Hugh will make it this time," and he did; and it was right after this that my mom was driving to Albuquerque on Highway 66 and she saw Hugh picking up a young hitchhiker, and then coming home she saw him on the other side of the highway picking up another hitchhiker (he wasn't running the bar any more), and that was when we got some idea maybe about Hugh and his life and why he wasn't married and why he had friends like my mom and my aunts who were women, but no girl friends to speak of. Not long after this, my Grandpa Hank died and Hugh came to the funeral, and someone made the remark later that it was funny how Hugh was still going long after many of the people who had always expected Hugh to die before they did.

I don't think Grandpa Hank thought this, but a lot of others did. Aunt Florence was already gone by then too, now that I think of it, and she had been *so sure* that time Hugh had the liver trouble. By this time now it had become pretty clear to all of us, but when Hugh went into the hospital for cancer of the gums, Aunt Lorena and Aunt Mary saw him and reported that this *absolutely was it* for Hugh, and they stood their ground when Grandma Lillee and my dad reminded them of the people who said that before and who were gone. Somewhere during this time too there was some mention of Hugh's liver and cancer, so maybe that's why as Aunt Lorena was driving to Mass with her little granddaughter in Los Lunas she had a stroke and was gone. A year or so later, Aunt Mary got one of her asthma attacks and didn't recover. Hugh Crooks is almost eighty now. It's my dad's generation and mine (and a lot of my dad's generation are gone now too)—we who grew up in awe of Hugh because the adults around us were always talking about him being on his last legs—it's we now who are left, and of course time changes perspectives. We got to know something which the older people didn't because they didn't have the benefit of time. Yet beyond this simple parable level I'm not sure what this story means.

But I like the story because there's this humor in it right along and it intrigues me that there is this man who is known almost solely for the simple fact that he is alive. When I think I'm getting more than my fair share of trouble I always remember Hugh Crooks stories or Harry Marmon stories (Harry got out of the physical ones unscathed, but there were always jail and police and lawyers and fines, and still Harry is a free man). Maybe if a person can manage way more than his or her fair share of trouble, then another sort of perspective or dimension is involved, I don't know. At Laguna they say it just makes you tougher. In the old days even where there was plenty of food they'd all practice for famine—it wasn't puritanical or Calvinistic at all—it was simply practical to make yourself tough enough, because famine is inevitable.

Today, Jim, I am going to work on my garden plot. I hope to grow a few snow peas, some spinach, and some sweet peas. I will be happy just with sweet peas which do very well down here in the winter and early spring. I have chosen a place about 20 feet below the drain for the kitchen sink water and will grow these crops with dishwater. We've had no winter yet to speak of and having a garden will make me very happy.

You are a dear dear friend, Jim. In so many ways it was you who helped me through those difficult times last year. At times like these I often wish I had more to say, but somehow it comes out in a story. I hope all this does not strike you as too strange. I seem not to react like most people do at times like these. I think I sense your calm and your deep faith. I know it has to do with your wonderful writing and, more important, with the visions that emerge from it.

Love,
Leslie

James Wright was hospitalized in mid-January 1980 with cancer of the tongue, diagnosed upon hospital entry as terminal. He was able to read Leslie's letter of January 3rd before he was too ill to remain in his home.

Leslie came to speak at the Manhattan Theatre Club in New York on February 5th. On the following day I arrived at the hospital after work to find Leslie sitting by James's bedside. Although unable to speak, James did respond to Leslie's conversation by writing on a yellow-lined legal pad.

He wrote this about the people who cared for him: "People are lovely to me here. Mr. Edwards and Mrs. Holmes are amazing, understanding, companions. They are skilled and I trust them."

Later that evening, after Leslie had gone, James wrote me a note about her visit. "I have the sense of a very fine, great person—a true beautiful artist. And I'm glad we've all made friends."

In March James and I wrote a post card to Leslie together. It was the only thing he wrote while in the hospital.

This is the message we wrote together from the hospital.

Dear Leslie,

I can't write much of a message. Please write to me.

Love,
Jim

We loved seeing you last month. James is moving to a fine new hospital on Friday.*
We miss hearing from you. How is the roadrunner?

Love,
Annie

[Leslie's last letter to James, dated March 24th, arrived after his death.]

Tucson, Arizona
March 24, 1980

Dear Jim,

I have been trusting another sort of communication between you and me—a sort of message from the heart—sent by thinking of you and feeling great love for you and knowing strongly that you think of me, that you are sending thoughts and feelings to me; and you and I, Jim, we *trust* in these messages that move between us.

---

*Calvary Hospital in the Bronx.

I cannot account for this except that perhaps it is a gift of the poetry, or perhaps it should be called "grace"—a special sort of grace. I am never far from you, Jim, and this feeling I have knows that we will never be far from each other, you and I. Aunt Susie has taught me this much and my Grandpa Hank and Great-Grandma have too—that knowing and loving someone has no end, and that we are together always, over at the Cliff House or walking along the lake edge not far from the home Catullus keeps.

It is not easy to avoid confusion. What I wanted to do was stay in New York, move in with Annie, and sit with you and talk with you. But that would have been confusing one present time with another present time.

Anyway, I know you understand, Jim, and I know Annie does too.

In one present time, you and I can count the times we've met and the minutes we've actually spent together. I think I was very shy in Michigan when we were introduced, and think I just told you how much I liked your reading. You had been sick and you were careful to rest a lot then. And then in New York this February with you in the hospital, I sat and talked and could already feel that there is another present time where you and I have been together for a long long time and here we continue together. In this place, in a sense, there never has been a time when you and I were not together. I cannot explain this. Maybe it is the continuing or on-going of the telling, the telling in poetry and stories.

Since the rains have come, the roadrunner is busy in other places, although he still roosts on the northwest side of the house, up on the roof.

After sundown the other night I was sitting on the road with Denny, and a great owl with eight-foot wings landed on a tall saguaro close to us. Jim, this owl was so big that, after he folded his wings, his size matched the diameter of the saguaro and he became part of the cactus top. It was only with the most careful concentration that I could see the owl swivel his head and thus believe that there was an owl sitting there. I thought about you then, Jim, as I always will when I am visited by the owls. He is probably the owl who carries off the cats the coyotes don't bother to catch, and after that night I was ready to believe this owl carries off whatever he damn well pleases.

It is so overwhelming to see your writing on the post card and to feel how much I miss your letters. There is no getting around this present time and place even when I feel you and I share this other present time and place.

Anyway, I treasure the words you write—your name most of all. But no matter if written words are seldom because we know, Jim, we know.

My love to you always,
Leslie

New York, N.Y.
March 25, 1980

[To Leslie Silko:]

The best days are the first to go. The best of men has gone too.

Love,
Annie

LESLIE MARMON SILKO *is a Laguna Pueblo Indian, born in 1948. Her published work includes* Laguna Woman, Ceremony, Storyteller, Almanac of the Dead, *and* Garden in the Dunes. *Her correspondence with the poet James Wright is collected in* The Delicacy and Strength of Lace.

JAMES WRIGHT *was one of our most profoundly visionary poets. He was born in Martins Ferry, Ohio. He taught at the University of Minnesota, Macalester College, and Hunter College. He was well known for his translations of Vallejo, Trakl, and Neruda, as well as for his poems about the Midwest. His* Collected Poems *won the Pulitzer Prize in 1972. Wright died in 1980, at the age of 52. His wife, Anne Wright, edited his correspondence with Leslie Marmon Silko in* The Delicacy and Strength of Lace.

Graywolf Press Publications

As with many such enterprises, those involved in Graywolf's early days were so busy making books that they didn't realize they were also making history. Twenty-five years later, those of us currently responsible for keeping the wolf at bay have done our best to recreate a Graywolf publication history. We know our list has flaws, omissions, and inaccuracies. We hope you'll be tolerant of them, and, if possible, fill us in on how to correct them against the day, in another twenty-five or so years, when we set out on a similar mission.

1974

Twelve Poems, Volume I, Number one, Fall 1974

1975

Popham of the New Song and Other Poems by Norman Dubie (*Twelve Poems*, Volume I, Number two, Winter 1974–75)
Rain Five Days and I Love It by Richard Hugo
Twelve Poems, Volume I, Number three, Late Spring 1975

1975–1976

Graywolf Pamphlet Series I
Waiting to Be Fed by Ray A. Young Bear
The Stance by William Bronk
The Funeral Parlor by James Heynen
A Guide to Dungeness Spit by David Wagoner
New Season by Philip Levine
The Sun on Your Shoulder by John Haines

❧ 1976

Instructions to the Double by Tess Gallagher
Nearing Land by Anthony Piccione
Inner Weather by Denis Johnson
Travelling Light by David Wagoner
The Salt Lesson by Carol Frost
Catawba: Omens, Prayers, & Songs by A. Poulin, Jr.

❧ 1977

In a Dusty Light by John Haines
A Journey South by William Pitt Root
Tapwater by Laura Jensen [no date]
Nothing Lives Long by Terry Lawhead [no date]

❧ 1978

On Your Own by Tess Gallagher
Saltimbanques by Rainer Maria Rilke, trans. by A. Poulin, Jr.
Under Stars by Tess Gallagher
Dream of Dying by William Logan
The Lincoln Relics by Stanley Kunitz
Crossing the Phantom River by James Masao Mitsui
Smoke's Way by William Stafford

❧ 1979

The Roses & The Windows by Rainer Maria Rilke, trans. by A. Poulin, Jr.
The Man Who Kept Cigars in His Cap by Jim Heynen
Ashes by Philip Levine

❧ 1981

Cypresses by Jon Anderson
Too Bright to See by Linda Gregg
Journey from Essex: Poems for John Clare, edited by Sandra McPherson

৯ 1982

Other Days by John Haines
The Salt Ecstasies by James L. White
The Woe Shirt: Caribbean Folk Tales by Paulé Bartón, trans. by Howard
    Norman
Eight Poems by Linda Gregg
Monolithos: Poems, 1962 & 1982 by Jack Gilbert
Orchards by Rainer Maria Rilke, trans. by A. Poulin, Jr.
The Astonishment of Origins by Rainer Maria Rilke, trans. by A. Poulin, Jr.

৯ 1983

Smoke's Way: Poems from Limited Editions, 1968–1981 by William Stafford
Times Alone: Twelve Poems from Soledades *by Antonio Machado,* trans. by
    Robert Bly

৯ 1984

We Are Not in This Together by William Kittredge, foreword by Raymond
    Carver
Willingly by Tess Gallagher
Across the Mutual Landscape by Christopher Gilbert
Free and Compulsory for All, Tales by David Romtvedt
The Ceremony & Other Stories by Weldon Kees
The Migration of Powers by Rainer Maria Rilke, trans. by A. Poulin, Jr.
A Pagan Place by Edna O'Brien
The Pegnitz Junction by Mavis Gallant
Stringer by Ward Just
My Uncle Silas by H. E. Bates, drawings by Edward Ardizzone
My Christina & Other Stories by Mercè Rodoreda, trans. by David H.
    Rosenthal
The Graywolf Annual One: Short Stories, edited by Scott Walker

ᘒ 1985

In Shelley's Leg by Sara Vogan
Wild Onion by Robert L. Jones
Mrs. Munck by Ella Leffland
Last Courtesies & Other Stories by Ella Leffland
Buying Time: An Anthology Celebrating 20 years of the Literature Progam of the National Endowment for the Arts, edited by Scott Walker
The Delicacy and Strength of Lace: Letters between Leslie Marmon Silko and James Wright, edited by Anne Wright
The Time of the Doves by Mercè Rodoreda, trans. by David H. Rosenthal
The Lay of the Love and Death of Cornet Christoph Rilke by Rainer Maria Rilke, trans. by Stephen Mitchell

ᘒ 1986

The Graywolf Annual Two: Short Stories by Women, edited by Scott Walker
Daily Horoscope by Dana Gioia
As Long As You're Happy by Jack Myers
The Complete French Poems of Rainer Maria Rilke, trans. by A. Poulin, Jr.
Friday Night at Silver Star by Patricia Henley
The Honeymoon by Kathleen Spivack
The Boat of Quiet Hours by Jane Kenyon
The Graywolf Annual Three: Essays, Memoirs & Reflections, edited by Scott Walker
River of Light by Brenda Peterson
Fair Augusto & Other Stories by Laura Kalpakian

ᘒ 1987

Cardinals in the Ice Age by John Engels
A Momentary Order by A. Poulin, Jr.
If You Want to Write by Brenda Ueland
Family: Stories from the Interior, edited by Geri Giebel Chavis
Walking on Air by Pierre Delattre

Owning It All by William Kittredge
Pound As Wuz: Essays and Lectures on Ezra Pound by James Laughlin
Amplitude: New & Selected Poems by Tess Gallagher

❧ 1988

Blood Line: Stories of Fathers and Sons by David Quammen
A Book of Seeing with One's Own Eyes by Sharon Doubiago
The Graywolf Annual Four: Short Stories by Men, edited by Scott Walker
Becoming the Enemy by Brenda Peterson
Full Measure: Modern Short Stories on Aging, edited by Dorothy Sennett
Altazor by Vicente Huidobro, trans. by Eliot Weinberger
A Plan for Escape by Adolfo Bioy-Casares, trans. by Suzanne Jill Levine
A Guide to Forgetting by Jeffrey Skinner
Diminishing Fictions: Essays on the Modern American Novel and Its Critics
    by Bruce Bawer
Feeding the Eagles by Paulette Bates Alden
The Selected Poems of Rosario Castellanos, trans. by Magda Bogin
The Courtship of Joanna by Catherine Gourley
The Graywolf Annual Five: Multicultural Literacy, edited by Scott Walker
    and Rick Simonson
The Perfect Stranger: A Memoir by P. J. Kavanagh

❧ 1989

The Stars, the Snow, the Fire by John Haines
The Invisible Enemy: Alcoholism & The Modern Short Story, edited by
    Miriam Dow and Jennifer Regan
A Farm under a Lake by Martha Bergland
Green the Witch-Hazel Wood by Emily Hiestand
In the North by Nina Bogin
The Graywolf Annual Six: Stories from the Rest of the World, edited by Scott
    Walker
The Saddest Pleasure: A Journey on Two Rivers by Moritz Thomsen

ᚅ 1990

Mottetti: Poems of Love by Eugenio Montale, trans. by Dana Gioia
A Gravestone Made of Wheat by Will Weaver
Name and Tears & Other Stories: Forty Years of Italian Fiction, edited and
  trans. by Kathrine Jason
Skywater by Melinda Worth Popham
An Autobiography by Edwin Muir
The Cardboard House by Martín Adán, trans. by Katherine Silver
Through and Through: Toledo Stories by Joe Geha
The Graywolf Annual Seven: Stories from the American Mosaic, edited by
  Scott Walker
Licorice by Abby Frucht
A Mountainous Journey: A Poet's Autobiography by Fadwa Tuqan, trans. by
  Olive Kenny
Let Evening Come by Jane Kenyon
The Animals by Richard Grossman

ᚅ 1991

Nearsights: Selected Poems of Valerio Magrelli, edited & trans. by Anthony
  Molino
Cave Dwellers by A. Poulin, Jr.
Vital Signs: International Stories on Aging, edited by Dorothy Sennett
The House Tibet by Georgia Savage
Fruit of the Month by Abby Frucht
The Subversive Scribe: Translating Latin American Fiction by Suzanne Jill
  Levine
The Gods of Winter by Dana Gioia
Island Sojourn by Elizabeth Arthur
Ten Seconds by Louis Edwards
The Sacraments of Desire by Linda Gregg
The Graywolf Annual Eight: The New Family, edited by Scott Walker
Daddyboy : A Memoir by Carol Wolfe Konek
The Loom and Other Stories by R. A. Sasaki

❧ 1992

As If It Matters by Eamon Grennan
Moon Crossing Bridge by Tess Gallagher
Cloudstreet by Tim Winton
The Lover of Horses by Tess Gallagher
Sweet & Sour Milk by Nuruddin Farah
Sardines by Nuruddin Farah
Close Sesame by Nuruddin Farah
Beyond PC: Toward a Politics of Understanding, edited by Patricia
    Aufderheide
The Horse Has Six Legs: An Anthology of Serbian Poetry, edited & trans. by
    Charles Simic
Unravelling Words and the Weaving of Water by Celia Vicuña
The Last Studebaker by Robin Hemley
The Graywolf Annual Nine: Stories from the New Europe, edited by Scott
    Walker
The Secret of Cartwheels by Patricia Henley
Can Poetry Matter? Essays on Poetry and American Culture by Dana Gioia

❧ 1993

Beyond the Mountain by Elizabeth Arthur
The Estuary by Georgia Savage
Sister by Jim Lewis
The Body in Four Parts by Janet Kauffman
Episodes by Pierre Delattre
The True Subject: Writers on Life and Craft, edited by Kurt Brown
The Estate of Poetry by Edwin Muir
The Owl in the Mask of the Dreamer: Collected Poems by John Haines
Collaborators by Janet Kauffman
The Aspect of Eternity by Bruce Bawer
Voices over Water by D. Nurkse
Still Life with Insects by Brian Kiteley
Leah, New Hampshire by Thomas Williams

Camellia Street by Mercè Rodoreda
Shallows by Tim Winton
Constance by Jane Kenyon
Warrior for Gringostroika by Guillermo Gómez-Peña
The Graywolf Annual Ten: Changing Community, edited by Scott Walker
All the World's Mornings by Pascal Quignard, trans. by James Kirkup

⅔ 1994

The Misunderstanding of Nature by Sophie Cabot Black
Burning Patience by Antonio Skarméta
South Wind Changing by Jade Ngoc Quang Huynh
The Men in My Life by James Houston
Chosen by the Lion by Linda Gregg
Lighting Out: A Vision of California and the Mountains by Daniel Duane
The Painted Alphabet by Diana Darling
The Ancestor Game by Alex Miller
Rainy Lake by Mary François Rockcastle
Stonework of the Sky by Joseph A. Enzweiler

⅔ 1995

Apricots from Chernobyl: Narratives by Josip Novakovich
From the Island's Edge: A Sitka Reader, edited by Carolyn Servid
Jack and Rochelle: A Holocaust Story of Love and Resistance, edited by
    Lawrence Sutin
Dream House: A Memoir by Charlotte Nekola
English Papers: A Teaching Life by William Pritchard
Beachcombing for a Shipwrecked God by Joe Coomer
Yolk by Josip Novakovich
Cortège by Carl Phillips
Little by David Treuer
So It Goes by Eamon Grennan

❧ 1996

Fables and Distances: New and Selected Essays by John Haines

Places in the World a Woman Could Walk by Janet Kauffman

Wild Kingdom by Vijay Seshadri

Watershed by Percival Everett

Big Picture by Percival Everett

Take Three: 1 AGNI New Poets Series

Otherwise: New & Selected Poems by Jane Kenyon

A Song of Love & Death: The Meaning of Opera by Peter Conrad

Frenzy by Percival Everett

The Apprentice by Lewis Libby

Graywolf Forum One: Tolstoy's Dictaphone: Technology and the Muse, edited by Sven Birkerts

Kabloona: Among the Inuit by Gontran de Poncins

Diary of a Left-Handed Birdwatcher by Leonard Nathan

Wise Poison by David Rivard

❧ 1997

North Enough: AIDS and Other Clear-Cuts by Jan Zita Grover

Characters on the Loose by Janet Kauffman

The Risk of His Music by Peter Weltner

Take Three: 2 AGNI New Poets Series

Night Talk by Elizabeth Cox

Red Signature by Mary Leader

Burning Down the House: Essays on Fiction by Charles Baxter

Idle Curiosity by Martha Bergland

Beyond the Bedroom Wall by Larry Woiwode

One Crossed Out by Fanny Howe

Raised in Captivity: Why Does America Fail its Children? by Lucia Hodgson

The Outermost Dream: Literary Sketches by William Maxwell

❧ 1998

Graywolf Forum Two: Body Language: Writers on Sport, edited by Gerald Early
From the Devotions by Carl Phillips
A Four-Sided Bed by Elizabeth Searle
Donkey Gospel by Tony Hoagland
The Way It Is: New & Selected Poems by William Stafford
Salvation and Other Disasters by Josip Novakovich
New York Literary Lights by William Corbett
Except by Nature by Sandra Alcosser
Dead Languages by David Shields
Central Square by George Packer
Nola: A Memoir of Faith, Art, and Madness by Robin Hemley
Crossing the Expendable Landscape by Bettina Drew
Relations: New & Selected Poems by Eamon Grennan
How the Dead Live by Alvin Greenberg
Take Three: 3 AGNI New Poets Series

❧ 1999

Readings by Sven Birkerts
Tug by G. E. Patterson
Feeling as a Foreign Language: The Good Strangeness of Poetry by Alice Fulton
Graywolf Forum Three: The Business of Memory: The Art of Remembering in an Age of Forgetting, edited by Charles Baxter
How the Body Prays by Peter Weltner
The Graywolf Silver Anthology
The Wedding Jester by Steve Stern
A Hundred Daffodils by Jane Kenyon
My Lesbian Husband: Landscapes of a Marriage by Barrie Jean Borich
Northern Waters by Jan Zita Grover
Things and Flesh by Linda Gregg
The Delinquent Virgin: Wayward Pieces by Laura Kalpakian
Glyph by Percival Everett

Visit Us and Join Us

We invite you to visit our web site at www.graywolfpress.org that features a Graywolf *Poem of the Week* and selected titles. You can also find details about our new membership program. Graywolf Press is a nonprofit publisher. This allows us to take artistic risks that may not have an immediate financial return. Every year we rely on foundations and generous individuals to support our mission to promote excellence, intelligence, and creativity in contemporary literature. Join our literary pack and receive free copies of some of our recent books. If you are interested in joining, but do not have online access, please write to us at: Graywolf Press, 2402 University Avenue, #203, Saint Paul, MN 55114. Thank you for your support.

The text of this book has been set in Adobe Garamond, drawn by Robert Slimbach and based on type cut by Claude Garamond in the sixteenth century. This book was designed by Wendy Holdman, set by Stanton Publication Services, Inc., and manufactured by Bang Printing on acid-free paper.